PIPPA
and the PRINCE
of SECRETS

LADY
CHARLOTTE'S
SOCIETY *of*
ANGELS

GRACE CALLAWAY
USA Today Bestselling Author

Cover Design Credit: Erin Dameron-Hill/ EDH Graphics

Cover Image Credit: Period Images

PRAISE FOR PIPPA AND THE PRINCE OF SECRETS

"We all have our top ten list of favorite romances. It has been forever since I have read something that enthralled me enough to add to my list. The book must be unique, something that resonates with me on an elemental level; it must have a beautiful storyline, intense passion, and unforgettable characters. *Pippa and the Prince of Secrets* checks all those boxes." -*Reading Rebel Reviews*

"I LOVE a hero that is from the streets like Cull. Gives me Derek Craven vibes....There's a lot of chemistry and attraction between the couple, but Pippa is scared of trusting Cull. Eventually they begin to trust each other with lots of sexy times, too! The mystery is really good and surprised me. I love a book with adventure and mayhem, where the MCs work together side by side... Once again, Grace Callaway has written a quality, sexy, mysterious historical romance!" -Nancy, *Goodreads*

"This re-telling of a Beauty and the Beast love story focusing on tender acceptance and loving empowerment is heart-stopping. Mixed in are a dangerous mystery and charismatic secondary characters. The power of the love between the couple isn't something you read every day; this includes the exquisite physicality of the novel. The story stirred my emotions and delighted my imagination." -Jenna, *BookBub*

"There are so many things to love about this story. First, the mystery is a actually a mystery. Often times I can figure out the mystery well before the end of the story. Not this time. Grace Callaway has delivered a plot that keeps you engaged the entire time! Next, the MCs are both flawed, but likeable people that you can't help but cheer for from the beginning. Finally, I absolutely love the way Grace Callaway revisits characters from previous books. Her *Wanton Wager* is one of my all time favorite stories. To have the chance to see how Gavin Hunt behaves as a father of a grown daughter is priceless. If you are looking for a sexy romance and a really great read, I HIGHLY recommend this story!" -Michelle, *Goodreads*

REVIEWS FOR LADY CHARLOTTE'S SOCIETY OF ANGELS SERIES

"A very hot and perfectly paced page turner, all the way to happily ever after." -*NPR*

"An exciting rollercoaster of a love story! This book delivers on a variety of levels. A slow burn, friends to lovers story. The plot is intricate, intimate, and all consuming. The couple's passion burns through the pages." -*Jenna's Historical Romance Blog*

"Get out the high velocity fan because you will need it while reading this story. It is hotter than hot, I am not kidding. I love a tortured hero and if you do also, then grab this story right away...I love how Grace can pull you into the story of these characters and make you feel as if you are there with them. I was totally enthralled with reading, and I swear I felt as if I was in their dilemma. Astounding storytelling."-Angela, *Goodreads*

"Olivia and Ben are so wonderful together. It is rare to find a match where the H & h share such a deep bond.... This book has it all—lead characters you truly love, fabulous side characters, murder, mystery, action, and a generous helping of steam and romance!" -Nazmin, *Goodreads*

"Despite the age gap, Ben and Livy's friendship is so natural. Their friendship never feels awkward and the transition from friends to lovers is done tastefully (and steamily). Grace Callaway is always reliable when it comes to writing romances that are both romantic and steamy." -*Romance Library*

PRAISE FOR OTHER BOOKS BY GRACE

"Readers looking for a good historical mystery/romance or a historical with a little more kink will enjoy *The Duke Who Knew Too Much*." -*Smart Bitches, Trashy Books*

"Grace Callaway writes the way Loretta Chase would if she got kind of dark and VERY naughty." -Nicole, *Goodreads*

"Fairy tale meets Eliza Doolittle. Grace Callaway saves the best Duke book for the end of the series. It was hot, steamy, and warm-hearted." -Stacy, *Goodreads*

"Can a fairytale be sweet, funny, touching, action packed and super hot all at the same time? Yes. This series ender is all that and more. This book is like the fireworks display to end a spectacular series." -Joanne, *Goodreads*

"I have read hundreds and hundreds of different authors over the past five years but actually only have a handful of all time favorites. I have to say Grace Callaway is by far one of those favorites.... Her characters have so much depth and you just feel like you are a part of their story...You can never go wrong by picking up any of her books but be prepared...you will love them so much you will buy every book she has." -Pam, *Goodreads*

"I've now read each of Grace Callaway's books and loved them— which is exceptional. Gabriel and Thea from this book were two of the best characters I read this year. Both had their difficulties and it was charming to see how they overcame them together, even though it wasn't always easy for them. [*M is for Marquess*] is my favorite book of 2015." -*Romantic Historical Reviews*

"Has everything that makes a tale excellent; a headstrong lovely heroine, a damaged too serious hero, a rowdy bunch of loving family members that are living and close and then the amazing adventure to peel back like an onion to find the many layers of the plot. This writer to me is in the leagues of Johanna Lindsey, Lisa Kleypas, Julia Quinn and Amanda Quick." -Kathie, *Amazon*

"Callaway is a talented writer and as skilled at creating a vivid sense of the Regency period as she is at writing some of the best, most sensual love scenes I've read in a long while." -*Night Owl Reviews*

"Grace Callaway is becoming one of my all-time favorite authors. The Kents remind me so much of the Mallory-Anderson saga from Johanna Lindsay or the Spy series from Julie Garwood. I've read those books so many times and now I find myself rereading Grace's books." -Vivian, *Amazon*

Her Protector's Pleasure

Her Prodigal Passion

CHRONICLES OF ABIGAIL

Abigail Jones

For the lovers and dreamers

In the golden lightning
Of the sunken sun,
O'er which clouds are bright'ning,
Thou dost float and run;
Like an unbodied joy whose race is just
    begun.

-from *To a Skylark* by Percy Bysshe Shelley

PROLOGUE

T imothy Cullen surged awake on a wave of agony.

Each breath jostled cracked bones and torn flesh, and when he bit his lip against a moan, he tasted blood. Feral gratitude flashed through him because pain meant that he was alive. The bastards hadn't killed him, hadn't...he scanned his body, hot relief pushing against the back of his eyes. While Crooke and his gang had beaten the stuffing out of him, they hadn't violated him in a worse fashion.

Cull's last moments in the flash house returned. Crooke's brutes had strung him up to a post and flogged him until he'd blacked out. They had wanted to make an example of him; at fifteen, he was one of the oldest mudlarks, the urchins who made their living scavenging the Thames. Since the death of their leader, the Prince of Larks, men like Crooke had tried to take over the gang, wanting to profit from the children in despicable ways.

Cull welcomed the searing throb of his injuries because it was the pain of resistance. Of not standing down or giving in, even when your enemy thought you were too powerless and weak to matter. Even when you doubted yourself.

"A mudlark's strength lays in his loyalty." The Prince of Larks had drilled this message into his charges. *"Alone, we are easy to defeat. Together, we are invincible."*

Other than his eleven-year-old sister Maisie, the mudlarks were the only family Cull had. No bastard was going to take over and force them into working for a bloody bawd—not if Cull still had breath to fight.

He took stock of his present situation. Patting himself down gingerly, he discovered that someone had dressed his wounds and wrapped him up in enough bandages to rival an Egyptian mummy. His eyes were nearly swollen shut—the brutes had given him twin shiners—so he carefully pried one open with his fingers, huffing out a pained breath...and then one of surprise as he got a good look at his surroundings.

"Bleeding 'ell," he said hoarsely. "'Ow'd I end up in a castle?"

Afternoon light seeped through a crack in the velvet drapes, casting everything in a golden glow. He was in a huge tester bed with a feather mattress. The room was fit for a king, with walls covered in blue silk and a soaring white ceiling where plaster cherubs gamboled in the corners. The place even smelled nice... like the flower market in Covent Garden mixed with a lady's expensive perfume.

Maybe I've cocked up me toes and gone to 'eaven after all, Cull thought, bemused.

His gaze landed on a small table next to the bed. When he saw the gleaming silver pitcher of water and spotless glass, his parched throat clenched. He wondered if whoever had fixed him up would mind if he helped himself. As he was reaching for the pitcher, the door opened. He jerked his hand back like a thief, wincing when his injuries protested.

"Oh. You're awake."

The voice was the prettiest Cull had heard. It reminded him

of an exotic bird he'd once seen at a fair, which had sung a tender song from its cage. A girl came into view, and even through the puffy slits of his eyes, he saw that she was a Diamond of the First Water.

Curls the color of sunshine framed her oval face. He guessed she was near his own age, her slender figure in the first bloom of womanhood. Beneath her white beribboned frock, which probably cost more than he'd earned in his entire life, she had small, high breasts and a waist that made his hands itch to span it.

She came closer, bringing with her that clean, flowery scent. When she peered at him, he saw that her eyes were an angelic blue. He felt a stirring beneath the blankets...Jesus wept, was he getting hard? He was no stranger to lust, having lost his virginity to an experienced milkmaid two summers ago, but getting randy while beaten to a pulp was a first.

"Maisie will be so relieved," the girl said in her musical voice.

"Maisie?" His voice was sandpaper against his throat. "You know me sister?"

The girl's gilded curls swung against her cheek as she nodded.

"Maisie is a student at the academy run by my parents," she explained. "She's been by your side for the last two days. I offered to watch over you so that she could have a lie-down in one of the guest bedchambers. Perhaps she has mentioned me? My name is Pippa Hunt."

Since Cull's younger sister chattered like a magpie, he couldn't keep track of all her ramblings. He spent time with Maisie when he could...which hadn't been too often, given the pressing troubles of the mudlarks. Although he made his living in the underbelly of London, he didn't want the same for his sister. She deserved better.

After their mam died a year ago, he'd debated taking Maisie to live with him at the Nest, the flash house and headquarters of the mudlarks. Instead, he'd brought her to the Hunt Academy, a school for orphans that was known to treat its students well and train them in respectable trades. He'd interviewed the founders, Gavin and Persephone Hunt, to make sure they weren't a pair of dodgy bamboozlers. The pair had earned Cull's trust, which was saying a lot. He hadn't survived fifteen years by being a gull.

The Hunts had tried to get Cull to stay on at the academy, but he wasn't a domesticable sort. Maisie, however, had blossomed in her year at the school, learning her letters and improving herself. Cull was relieved and proud of her progress. During his visits, she'd prattled on happily about the other pupils, and now that he thought of it, she had mentioned this Pippa, claiming that the Hunts' daughter was sweet-natured and kind, never putting on airs.

What Maisie hadn't mentioned was that Miss Hunt was also every lad's bedtime fantasy.

Realizing that he was staring at his hostess like a booby, Cull opened his mouth to reply but was seized by a coughing fit. Pain punched him in the ribs.

"Here, try some of this," Miss Hunt exclaimed.

She held a glass to his lips, tipping it slowly. The cool liquid soothed his dry throat, and he sucked it down in greedy gulps.

"You mustn't drink so fast, you poor dear," she said. "You might choke again."

Cull couldn't remember anyone calling him a "poor dear." Among friends, he went by the shortened version of his surname that was as rough-and-ready as he was. Among enemies, he was referred to as one of the three B's: *bastard*, *bugger*, or *blaggard*. An alley rat born and bred, he was used to respectable folk looking down at him from their high horses, yet Miss Hunt seemed oblivious to their differences in station. Setting down the emptied glass, she dabbed stray droplets from his lips with a soft scrap of linen.

The handkerchief smelled like her. Flowers warmed by sunshine.

She handed him a paper packet filled with white powder.

"This is willow bark. It tastes dreadful, I'm afraid, but the doctor said it would ease the pain."

Cull downed the contents, which did indeed taste like shit.

She gave him more water and smiled at him. "Feeling better?"

He was, but he didn't think it was on account of the medicine. Her eyes...up close, they were mesmerizing. Rare and unique. Golden suns surrounded her pupils, illuminating her blue irises, and though he was no poet—hell, he could barely write his own name—her eyes were the exact shade he imagined heaven would be.

Time halted as he lost himself in her gaze. He saw only her; her eyes held only him. The rest of the world vanished as he leaned closer, drawing her scent into his lungs. Breathing her in. Her mink-colored lashes swept up, but she didn't move away. Her lips, which were the shiny pink of a boiled sweet, parted ever so slightly...

"Tim, oh Tim!" Maisie's voice shattered the spell. "You're awake!"

Cull jerked his gaze to his sister, who came running toward the bed, her brown plaits bouncing against her thin shoulders. She looked scared, her freckles pronounced against her pale cheeks. Knowing she needed reassurance, he braced himself and held his arms open. With a sob, she ran into his embrace.

The hug hurt like the devil, but he managed not to grimace.

She took a step back, studying him with anxious eyes. "Are you badly hurt, Tim?"

"Nah, been clobbered worse." He chucked her beneath the chin. "Nothing to worry your pretty li'l noggin o'er."

"Patrick brung...brought me to you," Maisie whispered. "He said Crooke had his men beat the stuffing out of you after you refused to let the mudlarks be sold to a bawd."

Cull hated that his sister knew about such things. Although their departed mam had made her living on her back and drowned her sorrows in blue ruin, he had tried to protect Maisie against the harsher realities of life. It was why he'd taken her to the Hunts—to get her away from the filth of the streets. Even though he knew Patrick, a fellow mudlark and his best friend, had only wanted to help, he wished the other hadn't involved Maisie.

"Patrick should've left you out o' it," he muttered.

"If it weren't for Patrick, you might be dead," Maisie said, her voice hitching. "We were trying to get you free when Mr. Hunt and the Earl of Revelstoke arrived. They took care of that nasty old Crooke and brung...brought you here."

Cull added Hunt and Revelstoke to his mental tally. A mudlark never forgot a favor or a wrong. He would be paying his debt when he could.

"You'll stay, won't you? You won't leave me again?" Maisie's pleading look twisted his insides with guilt. "There's plenty of room at the academy."

As much as Cull wanted to reassure his sister, he wouldn't lie to her. It was just a matter of time before another bastard like Crooke made a move. The mudlarks needed Cull—needed someone older and stronger, in truth. But he was all they had; he couldn't let them down.

His temples throbbed. "I'll stay for as long as I can," he said.

"How long?" Maisie persisted.

"Your brother looks like he could use some refreshment," Miss Hunt cut in gently. "Perhaps you could fetch some of Cook's beef tea, Maisie?"

Maisie hesitated, then said, "All right. I'll get some beef tea for you, Tim. You'll like it."

His sister scampered off, leaving him with Miss Hunt.

"Thank you," he muttered. "For looking after Maisie."

"She is a dear." Miss Hunt studied him. "I think, however, that she would prefer that you be the one watching out for her, Mr. Cullen."

He knew that. And Miss Hunt's well-intentioned words plunged the blade of guilt deeper.

"I do wot I can," he said gruffly. "And it's Cull."

"Pardon?"

"Cull. That's wot me friends call me."

"Oh." Her silky lashes fanned upward. "Well, my friends call me Pippa."

"Pippa." He liked the feel of her rolling off his tongue. "That's a right pretty name."

Although her cheeks turned pink, her gaze was amused. "Sir, are you flirting with me while sporting a pair of shiners?"

He flushed. Jesus wept, what was he about, trying to dally with this goddess when he looked like something the cat dragged in?

"I didn't mean no offense," he said.

"None taken." A smile edged her lips. "I had best inform Mama and Papa that you are awake; they'll want Dr. Abernathy to take another look at you."

She turned to go.

"Wait," he called.

She pivoted slightly, looking over her shoulder. "Yes?"

Don't go. Stay wif me. Let me rest me sore eyes on you, 'ear your sweet birdsong voice...

"I...I'll be seeing you later, then?"

She smiled. "If you wish, Cull. Now get some rest."

He watched her leave the room. Surrounded by soft linens and her lingering scent, he drifted off. And when he dreamed, his dreams were of her.

❧ I ❧

1849

Pippa Hunt Lumley tracked her target, Viscount Hastings, through the dusk-filled streets of Limehouse. The close of the week drew out the rowdiness of the neighborhood, home to those involved in the seafaring trades. She avoided the sailors stumbling in and out of the dockside taverns and bawdy houses, situated conveniently side by side. Some men opted for the cheaper prostitutes flitting beneath the streetlamps like gaudy butterflies.

As Pippa passed a dark vein between two buildings, animal sounds spilled out. The glow of a fire pit limned two figures, a man leaning against a brick wall, a woman on her knees in front of him, her head bobbing. A shiver chased up Pippa's spine; she ignored it and continued on.

At eight-and-twenty, she was no innocent miss. She was a widow whose husband had died because of his involvement in a disreputable business. The last year had made her immune to shock.

The past is done, she told herself. *Concentrate on the mission.*

Pippa continued her discreet surveillance of Hastings. She'd followed him from a dockside gaming house, where he'd lost a sizeable sum in less than an hour. When he turned onto a narrow lane, she counted to ten before following him. This was an infamous street, the glow of opium dens forming a red constellation, the sweet scent of oblivion perfuming the air. Despite Limehouse's shady reputation, opium lured men from all strata of society to its crooked streets.

Pain pierced Pippa's chest like a swift dagger. Her dead husband, Edwin, the Earl of Longmere, had been a victim of a terrible drug...and she had failed to help him. Failed to see through his excuses and lies until it was too late.

Hastings paused in the street, pivoting suddenly, his gaze landing on her.

Months of training kept her composure in place. As she and Hastings traveled in the same circles, she knew him to be an immoral rake. On several occasions, with their spouses within earshot, he'd suggested that they "get to know one another better" beyond the ballroom. The advances, and the predatory flash in his eyes when she'd refused him, had made her skin crawl.

Despite his prior lewd interest, she doubted that he would see through her present disguise. She looked nothing like the Countess of Longmere, paragon and grieving widow. She'd tucked her blonde tresses beneath a short brown wig, a battered cap shadowing her eyes and a mustache obscuring the shape of her face. The drab, loose uniform of a dock worker concealed her figure as she adopted the stumbling gait of a fellow three sheets to the wind.

Losing interest in her, Hastings started down the lane again.

Pippa felt a spark of triumph. The months of training under the guidance of Lady Charlotte Fayne, founder of the Society of Angels, a covert female investigative agency, were paying off.

Pippa had joined the agency after Edwin's death. Tonight, she and the other agents, known as Angels, were working on behalf of

Lady Julianna Hastings, who'd hired them to monitor her husband's activities. Armed with information, Lady Hastings could make better decisions about her future. She would not have to stumble in the dark of ignorance, filled with uncertainty and fear...

Tamping down her emotions, Pippa continued after the viscount. She conceded with a pang that Jeremy Hastings reminded her of Edwin. He was tall and handsome, with a similar refined build. Clad in exquisite tailoring, he moved with arrogant assurance, a peacock ripe for the plucking to the denizens watching him from the shadows. When he took another turn, this time down an alleyway into a courtyard bordered by decrepit tenements, Pippa hesitated.

Lady Charlie's instructions rang in her head. *Observe Jeremy Hastings, but do not leave the dockside until reinforcement arrives. Angels work best as a team, and you must not take any unnecessary risks. I mean it, Pippa.*

Pippa was on thin ice because of the last mission, when she'd tracked down a jewel thief. With insufficient time to alert her fellow Angels, she had made the decision to apprehend the target on her own. Despite Pippa's successful handling of the case, and the reward paid by the grateful client, Charlie had deemed Pippa's behavior "reckless."

For most of her life, Pippa had been the opposite of rash. She was the conventional and easy-going member of her family. Mama was a famous novelist who wrote dashing sensation novels, and Papa had risen from the underbelly of London to become a successful industrialist and philanthropist. Pippa's younger brothers, Garrett and Hugh, were lovable rogues prone to mayhem.

Pippa, however, was a lover of ordinary things. She liked domesticity and managing the household. Her favorite activities included spending time with family and friends, painting in sunlit solitude, and working with the children at her parents' academy for foundlings. Yet after Edwin's death, everything had changed.

Edwin's cousin had inherited the townhouse where Pippa had lived. Her parents had wanted her to return to their home, but she'd declined, preferring to be alone. As much as she loved her family, her marriage had strained her relationships with them—with her papa, especially—and their time together was a stilted and painful reminder of the mistakes she'd made.

Thus, she had used her small stipend to rent a cottage in Bloomsbury. She had her independence, yet she still felt...lost. Her relationship with Edwin had slowly eroded her identity; without knowing how or when it happened, she'd lost parts of herself.

Now she no longer knew who she was. Her beloved routines failed to hold her interest. Painting, which had once been a source of joy, roused terrible guilt. Edwin, a rising painter, had died because of his art...and Pippa had unwittingly hastened his demise.

When she picked up a brush, she saw it dripping with his blood.

She hadn't painted in months and might never again.

Trapped by the unrelenting weight of bombazine, grief, and other festering emotions, Pippa had felt herself unraveling. Needing distraction, she had jumped at Charlie's offer to train her to be an agent. Even now, her memories lurked, ready to pounce and shred her equilibrium to pieces. Luckily, danger had a way of absorbing her senses, helping her to evade the claws of the past.

Once upon a time, she'd striven to be a proper countess, a good wife who would make her husband proud. Now she had only herself to please.

The other Angels will catch up soon, Pippa reasoned. *I must discover what nefarious business Hastings is up to.*

She entered the mouth of the alley, her footsteps stealthy on the packed dirt. The shadows sucked her in like a tar pit, the air heavy with overripe smells. When something squished beneath her boot, she shuddered. She made it into the courtyard, where the light from the surrounding tenements illuminated rows of clotheslines. The garments swayed like a field of frayed ghosts.

Is Hastings hiding here? Pippa drew back her shoulders. *There's one way to find out.*

Pushing aside a patched sheet, she ducked beneath the clothesline and looked down the row: the only movement was the flutter of fabric. Indistinct shouting and laughter came from the nearby buildings as she advanced another row, then another. Soon she was halfway through the field of clothes, her nose itchy from the fumes of lye and starch.

Did Hastings go into one of the tenements? Or did he pass through here?

She swept aside a sheet...and a hand closed around her arm. She was yanked backward into a man's chest. Cold metal pressed into her temple.

A pistol. Cocked and loaded.

"Why are you following me?" The tremor in Hastings's voice betrayed his fear.

He pressed his forearm against her throat, a hold she could escape. Her next moves flashed through her head. *Stomp on his insole and drop down before he pulls the trigger. Kick out low, knock him off his feet. Grab his pistol and gain the upper hand.*

That would be a last resort, however. Her goal was to gather information about Hastings, not give him a beating. As satisfying as the latter option might be.

"Gor, guv, you've got the wrong fellow." She used a Cockney accent and pitched her voice low. "I ain't following ye. I'm 'ere to visit me kin."

"Don't lie to me," Hastings hissed. "I saw you earlier. You followed me from the docks, and you'll tell me why—or I'll put a goddamned bullet through your brain."

Dash it. His arm was shaking.

If I don't calm him down, he might shoot me out of nerves.

"Easy there, guv," she soothed. "I ain't lying. Me sister lives 'ere, and I've come for a visit—"

"Uncle Peter, you're 'ere!"

Hastings jerked at the sound of the child's voice, and Pippa tensed, ready to carry out her escape plan if necessary. But three children burst through the sheets. The tallest one, a brown-haired boy around twelve years old, held a lantern that lit up the trio's cherubic faces and shabby but clean clothes.

"Mama made 'er special hotchpotch, and we've been waitin' on ye..." The boy was addressing...Pippa? He trailed off, his gaze landing on Hastings and the pistol aimed at her head. "Crikey, what are ye doin' to me Uncle Peter?"

"Nothing." Hastings released Pippa with a shove. "It was a misunderstanding."

"Me ma will 'ave your 'ead if ye 'urt 'er favorite brother," the second tallest child, a pretty girl with blonde ringlets and a fierce scowl, declared. "A word from us, and she'll be down 'ere in a blink wif 'er frying pan."

"Ma's pan packs a wallop." The warning came from the youngest child, a tow-headed boy whose huge spectacles magnified his wide-set eyes.

"Bloody hell, I said it was a mix-up," Hastings muttered. "I don't have time for this."

He stalked off, shoving his way through the field of laundry, leaving fallen fabric in his wake. As Pippa watched him exit the courtyard, she debated following. Sighing, she acknowledged that she couldn't risk further action. She was lucky that Hastings hadn't seen through her cover.

Actually, it wasn't luck. Why had the children intervened on her behalf?

She turned to thank her diminutive rescuers...only to see them scampering off.

"Wait," she called. "Why did you help me?"

They didn't look back and kept running, disappearing down

the alleyway from which she'd entered. Her curiosity hooked, she took off after them.

Despite their short legs, the tots ran like the wind. They dodged people and vehicles with seasoned ease. She tried to catch up, but they were too quick. They ran down a pier, leaping onto a docked barge. By the time she reached the dock, the barge had glided off on the black water of the Limehouse Cut, a canal bordered by tenements and manufactories.

Catching her breath, Pippa braced her hands on her hips and stared after the vessel. A lamp at the stern limned a large, cloaked figure. She squinted...it was a man, tall and broad-shouldered, his face obscured by a hood. He lifted his hands, and the mournful notes of a flute stirred the hairs on her nape.

The flute was the signature instrument of the Prince of Larks, a mysterious and powerful figure in the London underworld. The prince ruled the mudlarks, children who scavenged the Thames for second-hand goods, but whose real trade was that of information. It was said that little happened in London without the prince's knowledge; if one wanted answers, he could provide it... for a price.

The price could be money or something dearer. Part of the prince's mystique lay in his ruthless and mercurial nature. Rumors swirled about how his enemies disappeared, never to be seen again. Even his face was a mystery, for he ruled from the shadows and behind a mask. Charlie, on occasion, employed his group to discover information. Yet even she, formidable lady that she was, urged caution when using his services.

"The mudlarks are driven by forces beyond the understanding of outsiders," Charlie had said. *"Never underestimate them or take any favors unless you know what is expected in return."*

Pippa's chest tightened. From personal experience, she knew better than to accept anything from the prince. For swathed in that cloak of mystique was none other than Timothy Cullen, the lad who'd spent a month recovering in her home fourteen years ago. An image flashed in her head of the handsome boy who'd befriended her and given her a kiss...then left.

Without so much as an adieu.

Just another male who has exited my life under mysterious circumstances, Pippa thought darkly. *Why did Cullen interfere in my plans tonight? What is his purpose?*

She curled her hands. She was no longer a naïve chit, a pawn in any man's game. After burying Edwin, she'd vowed that she would learn from her mistakes. She, and no one else, would decide her fate.

Scanning the canal, she saw that the barge had come to a stop. The boat ahead of it had gotten stuck beneath the low railway bridge that crossed the canal about a hundred yards ahead. She gauged the distance from the bridge to the deck of the barge and judged it to be less than ten feet.

In a split second, she made her decision. She ran from the dock to the street parallel to the canal, sprinting toward the railway bridge. With a glance to make sure no train was approaching, she dashed onto the bridge and peered over the railing. The previously stuck boat was now sailing under, the mudlarks' barge approaching.

From here, the drop looked a wee bit farther than she'd calculated. Her blood rushing through her veins, she climbed over the railing and prepared to jump. To discover what, after all these years, Timothy Cullen wanted from her.

"What is holding up that bloody lighter ahead of us?" Cull demanded.

"The mast got caught on the bridge, by the looks o' it," Long Mikey replied from where he navigated the barge. "Sodding amateurs."

At eighteen, Long Mikey was one of Cull's trusted captains, having worked his way up the ranks since joining the mudlarks at the age of six. He'd sprouted in the last year, his moniker no longer ironic now that he was over six feet, nearly seeing eye to eye with Cull. Mikey was an experienced sailor and the man to have at your back during trouble; despite his boyish looks and mop of brown hair, he was an expert with the daggers tucked in his boots.

Of course, Cull's policy was to avoid violence where possible. He taught this tenet to every mudlark from the day he or she enlisted. As their leader, it was his job to keep them all safe, and he'd found more creative ways of solving problems than bloodshed.

"I'm seein' movement, Cull," Fair Molly called from the bow. "They're off and away!"

At fourteen, the curly-haired girl was another captain and a rising star in the gang. The three other mudlarks who'd participated in the mission tonight—Honest Harvey, Plain Jane, and Keen-Eyed Ollie—were part of the team she headed. The small trio stood around her, snacking on a sack of pork pies.

"About bleeding time," Cull said. "Let's get a move on, Mikey."

"Right-o, Captain."

Cull felt on edge, and he didn't fool himself as to the cause. He'd allowed himself to get too close to Pippa tonight. It was one thing to watch over her from the shadows—something he'd done for years—and another to step into the light. Light did no favors for a cove like him. He should have kept out of her sight.

But her reckless behavior had worried him. He'd tracked her down; from the alleyway, he'd seen her struggle with Hastings. Not wanting to foil her mission, he'd sent the larks in to help. It was supposed to be an in-and-out job; once Pippa was safe, he and his charges had raced back to the barge. Instead of going into the cabin, however, he had made the mistake of looking back...and had been arrested by all that was Pippa.

Even dressed like a lad, she'd taken his breath away. With her long, slender legs showcased in trousers, her hands fisted upon her hips, her pose had been defiantly graceful. His memories had stripped away her disguise, and he saw the girl he'd kissed in the bell tower fourteen years ago and who'd haunted his dreams since. While he could never talk to her face-to-face, not with him looking the way he did, he'd craved any kind of connection to her.

So he'd taken out his flute and played her a song.

Sardonic humor pulled at the damaged side of his face, the sensation of movement still there beneath the deadened layers. He'd spent years perfecting the mysterious and all-powerful image of the Prince of Larks, yet here he was, serenading a lady like some lovestruck mooncalf. Truth be told, he'd never wanted power or enigma, but the more people feared him, the less they

dared to cross him or his larks. The image of power was as important as power itself.

People feared what they did not understand. It was a tradition
for the Prince of Larks to wear a mask—a way to keep the legend
alive, no matter what happened to the flesh-and-blood man
beneath. Cull had adopted the practice, even before his injury.
Now he never left the Nest, the mudlarks' headquarters, without
the black leather covering that started beneath his eyebrows and
ended at the line of his jaw, leaving only his eyes and mouth
exposed.

He also leveraged gossip in the stews to his advantage. When
two of his rivals disappeared, he planted rumors that he'd
dispatched them in cold blood, the stories of his ruthlessness
proliferating like weeds. By last count, he'd "executed" some
hundred foes. When someone described his flute playing as "chill-
ing," he made sure to play eerie melodies as his barge floated past
London's darkest neighborhoods. Now people ran when they
heard his tunes.

It amused him, the dread his name invoked. He wondered
how people would react if they knew that the vast shadow of the
Prince of Larks was cast from a regular man with regular longings.
The most potent of which involved a golden-haired beauty who
could never be his.

Yet he would always look out for Pippa. The same way he
looked out for his sister Maisie, despite their estrangement.
While Cull could not be a lover worthy of a lady like Pippa—or
the brother that Maisie deserved—there was one thing he was
good at being: the Prince of Larks.

And the prince protected his own.

Cull was relieved to see the lighter ahead clearing the low arch
of the bridge. He was eager to be off—away from Pippa and the
dangerous yearning she stirred in him. Yet she'd left him no
choice but to come to her aid tonight. Since her husband's death,
she'd been acting unlike herself. A product of the rookery, Cull

was no stranger to death and knew the myriad effects grief could
have on people. Some got buried by it; others pushed on.

In Pippa's case, it had made her a trifle...batty.

She was, by nature, a sweet and gentle creature. A ray of
sunshine that lit up any room she entered. Because of her, those
weeks he'd spent recuperating at her parents' home were the
finest of his life. He'd loved talking with Pippa and hearing her
melodious voice as she read to him. During his supposed naps, he
had secretly watched her sketch and paint by his bedside.

She'd grown from a peerless girl into a woman who sparkled in
Mayfair ballrooms, who strolled along Bond Street or beneath the
leafy bowers of Hyde Park, twirling a parasol in her delicate
hands. Predictably, she'd married Edwin John Gaston Lumley, the
Earl of Longmere, a blueblood with an ancient title...and empty
coffers, but one couldn't have it all. Not that Pippa needed money,
with her papa's vast wealth.

Since Longmere's passing, however, Pippa had lost her mind.
She'd joined a secret investigative society headed by the
indomitable Lady Charlotte Fayne. Instead of spending her time
at home in proper mourning, she was prancing through the
darkest alleys of London. Having observed Pippa's skills, Cull had
to admit they were impressive, and he wouldn't have interfered if
it weren't for her damned recklessness.

Last week, she'd chased down a thief on her own. Tonight, she
hadn't waited for her partners, instead tracking a suspect into the
perilous reaches of Limehouse. Cull's jaw tightened. It was as if
Pippa was purposefully courting disaster...which meant he had to
take an active role in ensuring her safety.

If the ploy with Honest Harvey, Plain Jane, and Keen-Eyed
Ollie hadn't worked, Cull would have had to intervene with that
bastard Hastings personally. He still might, given how that
blighter had manhandled Pippa. But that didn't solve the larger
problem. Day by day, Pippa grew bolder and more self-destruc-
tive, making it bloody difficult to protect her from a distance.

"Crikey." Ollie stopped mid-bite, his bespectacled eyes blinking as he pointed at the bridge. "Wot's that cove doing?"

Cull swung his gaze to the bridge. A dark silhouette stood on the span, dangerously close to the edge.

"If 'e's a jumper, 'e ain't going far." Fair Molly snorted. "That bridge ain't 'igh enough to do damage. Except to 'is pride for being a fool."

Their barge reached the bridge, their lanterns limning the figure above. Cull's heart slammed into his ribs. An instant later, he sprinted toward Pippa as she leapt.

Pippa planned to break the impact of her fall with a roll, the way Mrs. Peabody, one of her instructors at the society, had taught her.

Do not fight momentum. Mrs. Peabody's crisp voice rang in her head. *Use it to your advantage.*

Having maneuvered many drops, Pippa did not anticipate any problems. The deck where she intended to land was clear. She timed her jump perfectly. As she sailed through the air, she readied herself to land and roll.

"Oof." The sound whooshed from her lungs as she collided with a wall of muscle. Her momentum took them both down, and she braced herself for the fall, but arms closed around her, keeping her tucked against a muscular body that bore the brunt of their combined fall.

She ended up sprawled atop the man, the wind knocked out of her. Panting, she raised her head; her wig had fallen off, and she had to push her own heavy blonde locks out of her eyes. She stared at the male beneath her. His hood had fallen back to reveal a thick mane of chestnut-brown hair. His black leather mask covered his face from beneath his eyebrows to the edge of his jaw, exposing only his eyes and mouth. Through the mask's holes, familiar brown eyes glinted at her.

When he reached a hand to her face, she froze. But he didn't touch her, merely plucked off the moustache dangling from her upper lip.

"That's better," he murmured.

His voice was deeper, rougher, but still had that teasing quality she remembered. Now she had no doubt: the man she was lying on top of was Timothy Cullen...the Prince of Larks.

She became aware of Cullen's large, hard body beneath her. In her current outfit, sans feminine layers, there was little to separate them. Through his thin linen shirt and trousers, his heat seemed to penetrate every fiber of her being. Her breasts felt hot and achy smooshed against his sinewy chest. Ridges of steel pressed into her belly. When she squirmed, she felt a large protrusion prodding her thigh.

Her eyes widened. *Heavens...is that what I think it is?*

Recovering her senses, Pippa struggled to get free. Cullen grunted and loosened his hold. She scrambled to her feet, retreating a step when he rose as well. At five-foot-seven, she wasn't used to men towering over her, but Cullen did. Not just physically. With his dark cloak swirling around his brawny form, his expression hidden behind his mask, the man had a larger-than-life presence.

She stifled a shiver, tilting her chin up. She was not about to be intimidated by any male...especially not this one.

"Mr. Cullen," she said in crisp tones. "It has been some time, has it not?"

If he was taken aback by her use of his name, he did not show it. Instead, a corner of his mouth edged upward. Her artist's eye couldn't help but notice how his mask framed the sensual shape of his lips: the bottom one was slightly fuller, its curve juxtaposed against the unyielding line of his jaw.

"Fourteen years, my lady," he said with a bow.

She squelched the teensy spurt of pleasure that he'd remembered her. Instead, she took note of the changes: his polished accent and gentlemanly manners, which were at odds with his casual and rather well-worn attire.

"After all this time, why are our paths crossing?" she asked coolly.

Pippa cast a pointed look at the trio who'd interrupted her encounter with Hastings. The children looked as innocent as ever, munching on meat pies and watching the exchange between her and their leader like they might a performance of Punch and Judy. When the littlest one, the bespectacled scamp, came over and wordlessly offered her a pie from a greasy sack, Pippa had to fight a smile and shake her head.

She reminded herself that mudlarks—no matter how adorable they appeared—could be dangerous. Two other members of the gang, a tall lad and curly-haired girl, trained watchful stares upon her. She had to understand what the mudlarks wanted...why they'd put themselves at cross purposes with her.

"This is a discussion better had in private," Cullen said. "Shall we withdraw to the cabin?"

Pippa didn't take the arm he offered. While her instincts told her he posed no threat, she would not lower her guard, nor let him treat this like a social call.

In businesslike tones, she said, "Lead the way."

He studied her, and his mouth gave an odd twitch.

"As you wish," he said gravely.

She followed him, aware of the gazes that tracked them.

C ull led the way into the cabin. As the barge had been fashioned with speed in mind, the space was small and Spartan, furnished with a table and cushioned benches against the walls. Narrow windows gave views of the passing river. Pulling the curtains closed, he faced the woman who'd haunted his dreams since he was a lad...and realized that she'd changed.

Pippa was no longer the young miss of his fantasies. Her cheeks had lost some of their youthful roundness, her bones elegantly pronounced in her sculpted face. While the color of her eyes hadn't altered, the way they looked upon the world had. Her gaze was no longer guileless and sparkling with spirited innocence; instead, it was shadowed by suspicion. She studied him, taking his measure, the same way he took hers.

She was still tall and slender, maturity adding to her curves. When she'd been draped over him, he would've had to be a saint not to notice the soft bounty of her tits pressed against his chest. She had bound them to go along with her disguise, but he would have wagered money that he'd felt the enchanting poke of her budded nipples. Or maybe that was wishful thinking. Still, he hadn't imagined the lushness of the hips he'd grabbed onto when trying to break her fall...or the sleekness of her thigh when it had rubbed against his burgeoning erection.

God, she made him hard.

Age had deepened her power over him, for now she was no longer a pretty, well-bred virgin on a pedestal beyond his reach. She was a stunning, sensual, experienced widow...

And even more out of your reach, his inner voice pointed out. *She's a bleeding countess now. And you...have you forgotten what is beneath your mask?*

Cull hadn't, of course. He saw himself every morning in the looking glass when he shaved...the side of his face that still sprouted whiskers, that was. He'd never been a man who avoided reality. In the rookery, doing so would get a man killed, and there was a reason he'd reached the ripe old age of nine-and-twenty.

He focused instead on the opportunity before him. To spend a few stolen moments with Pippa. To hear her voice, which still had the sweet lilt of birdsong that her newfound willfulness couldn't hide. Not that he blamed her for being prickly. She'd been through a lot, waiting years for that sod Longmere to marry her, only for him to get himself killed and in such a bloody *stupid* fashion.

Any man blessed with a wife like Pippa ought to do everything in his power to keep breathing and, more importantly, to make her happy. Longmere, the asinine fop, had done neither. Instead, he'd left Pippa with a broken heart, burdening her with grief and regret. A volatile mix for anyone to contend with, let alone a sweet and gentle creature like Pippa.

Was it any wonder that she'd sought out distraction? That she'd used adventure and, aye, danger, as a shield against pain? Cull didn't account himself an expert in much, but having observed Pippa for years, he had an inkling of her inner workings. At present, she reminded him of the wounded birds in his sanctuary. In the glass aviary he'd built for them atop the Nest, they flapped in crazed trajectories until they found their wings again.

He could help Pippa. Be her friend in this moment if she let him. Although he longed for more, he would take what he could get.

"Well, Mr. Cullen?" Pippa arched her curving brows, which were a shade darker than her hair. "We have privacy. Would you care to explain why you have been meddling in my affairs?"

Even dressed like a dockworker, she had a countess's poise. She'd put the table between them, her chin angled up and arms crossed. Her hair was a golden cascade that reached her hips. She kept her balance like a ballerina, her slender body swaying gracefully with the river's currents.

"It's Cull," he reminded her. "We were friends once."

"I am not interested in the past." She narrowed her glorious eyes at him. "What I want to know is why you got in my way this eve."

There was no point beating around the bush. From the information Cull had gathered, she'd been avoiding the Hunts, her loving family. She'd told her parents that she needed privacy to mourn, and they'd given her what she asked for...enough rope to hang herself.

No, what Pippa needed wasn't solitude; it was the company of truth.

"You were out of your depth," Cull said bluntly. "You needed help, and I provided it."

Her cheeks reddened, the ring of gold blazing in her heaven-blue eyes. "How *dare* you presume to know me or what I need."

Instead of arguing, he gave her the facts.

"After your husband died, you joined Lady Fayne's operation. You've been working as a covert agent. You're talented...but also reckless and impulsive. You have a habit of charging ahead on your own, of endangering yourself and the mission," he summarized. "Tonight, you should have waited for the other Angels. Instead, you went after Hastings and nearly destroyed your cover. If the mudlarks hadn't intervened, you would have tipped Hastings off to the fact that you were tailing him. That his own wife was having him investigated. In short, you could have ruined your case."

Breathe. Stay calm and in control.

As a debutante, Pippa had been known for her sunny and amicable nature. She'd never liked conflict and found it natural to see the best of people and situations. In fact, sniggering wags had dubbed her "Patient Pippa" due to her drawn-out courtship with Edwin. She'd believed in his promises and waited years for him to come up to scratch. All she'd wanted was to spend the rest of her life with her true love.

What she got was a year of marriage, along with doubts about whether love was all the poets made it out to be. Well, that wasn't true. She'd grown up with parents who adored each other, their passionate devotion a shining example of what she'd yearned for. Which meant that the problem wasn't with love but with her.

Maybe she wasn't the kind of woman who inspired unconditional love in men. Maybe that was why Edwin had kept her waiting for years, unwilling to make that final commitment. Why he'd kept secrets from her throughout their short union. And maybe that was why Timothy Cullen had kissed her once, left without saying goodbye, and now had the gall to lecture her like she was some ninny.

Although she strove to keep her surprise hidden, she was astonished by Cullen's depth of knowledge about her. Knowing that the Prince of Larks had eyes and ears everywhere was one thing; having that attention placed on *her* was another. She didn't like feeling exposed.

Her training allowed her to keep her voice even. "My life is no concern of yours. You are not my husband, my family, not even a friend. You have no right to interfere."

"There you are wrong, my lady," Cullen said steadily. "I am your friend."

"Some friend," she scoffed. "As I recall, your last words to me were, *I'll see you later.* That was fourteen years ago."

He cocked his head like a predator sensing prey. "You remember what I said to you?"

Dratted man. No way was she going to let him know that she'd spent months secretly pining after him. Dreaming of her first kiss with the rough-edged lad whose soulful eyes had seemed to see to the heart of her.

"That's hardly the point," she retorted.

"Then what is?"

"The fact that you're an unreliable bastard who has no right to tell me what to do."

"Aye, I am a bastard. No arguing that, is there?"

At his bland reply, Pippa felt a stab of shame. She'd used "bastard" as a reference to his character, not his origins. She knew that Cullen and Maisie were born out of wedlock and raised by their mama. Cullen had taken care of his sister while their mother walked the streets to keep a roof over their heads, eventually drowning her miseries in drink.

As Pippa's own papa had been born on the wrong side of the blanket, she believed that a person's worth lay not in the circumstances of their birth, but what they made of themselves. Timothy Cullen, for all his high-handed ways, had looked after his sister and found her a safe place to land. And rumors of his ruthlessness aside, he'd carved out success as an elite purveyor of information and a leader who had the fierce loyalty of his group.

"I didn't mean it literally," Pippa muttered. "I was referring to your character, not your parentage."

"Is that better or worse?" he said wryly.

"Since one has no control over the circumstances of one's birth, one can do nothing about it. On the other hand, one has perfect control over one's behavior," she said pointedly. "One can, for example, strive to be less of a nosy and interfering jackanapes."

His eyes glinted at her...then he barked out a laugh. The sound was as rich and warm as a drink of chocolate, and her tummy fluttered. She quelled the reflexive quiver of her lips.

"This jackanapes has your best interests in mind," he replied.

"As I've said, you have no right to care about me or my interests." She narrowed her eyes at him. "What is it that you're really after, Cullen?"

"I'm looking out for you, sunshine. Your husband is dead, and you've pushed away your family. If you won't take proper care of your pretty self, then I'll have to step in."

Her reaction was a jumble of emotions. Anger at his arrogance, shock at his acuity...and a teensy, mortifying spike of pleasure that he'd remembered the endearment he'd once used with her. An unbidden memory floated to the surface...

"Why do you call me 'sunshine'? Is it because of my hair?" she'd once asked.

"Partly." Despite his fading bruises and rough-hewn looks, his slow, crooked smile had made him the most handsome lad she'd ever met. *"But mostly on account o' the fact that you light up any room you enter."*

The next day, he was gone. And she, like a ninny, had wondered if she'd done something wrong...if she'd somehow lost the supposed sparkle that he'd seen in her. It was the sort of stupid thing an adolescent girl *would* think, she thought darkly.

Luckily, she was no longer that silly miss; she was a woman who wasn't fooled by a man's careless compliments. By the kind of trifling flirtation that Timothy Cullen probably employed with every female he met.

She clenched her jaw. "I can take care of myself."

"If that's the case, why don't you?" His mild tone didn't mask the challenge in his question. "Why *aren't* you taking better care of yourself, Pippa?"

Her breath caught as his question pierced her armor, the answer plunging into her with unerring accuracy. *Because I killed the man I married, and I deserve whatever happens to me.*

Edwin's final masterpiece flashed in her head: the woman with the red-gold tresses, beautiful face, and desperate longing in her eyes. *Portrait of a Lady Dreaming* had won Edwin his heart's true desire—recognition. If only the price had not been his life.

As Pippa tried to shove the memories back into their locked box, the barge lurched, knocking her off her feet. Childish laughter rang outside as she went flying. Cullen dove, his arms encircling her, his brawny body twisting to take the impact of the fall. They landed on a cushioned bench; winded, she found herself sprawled atop him once more.

His eyes, the rich brown of buried earth, drew her in. Her hair fell in a curtain around them, blocking out the world, and she couldn't look away, couldn't move as he reached up. The brush of his knuckles sent feathers of heat over her skin. His scent of sea, soap, and male wafted into her nostrils, and her senses brimmed with awareness.

Of his uncompromising masculinity and strength. Of her own sudden desire to melt into it...

"You all right, sunshine?" he asked.

Reality returned in a blink. She couldn't let this stranger unravel her. Wouldn't be weak and exposed and pathetic once more.

"I don't need your help," she stated.

She scrambled to her feet; he followed suit.

"Everyone needs help sometime," he countered.

"The way your sister tells it, you're not exactly a fellow one can count on, are you?"

His mouth tightened, telling her that her barb had hit home.

Although Pippa didn't know the entirety of what had gone on between the siblings, she'd heard Maisie's bitter complaints that Cullen hadn't been there when she needed him. After kissing

Pippa, Cullen had left the Hunt Academy and never returned, missing his sister's milestones. After Maisie graduated, she and Pippa had mostly lost touch, save for the occasional catch-up letter. In her missives, Maisie wrote about her life as a house-keeper in Bristol and omitted any mention of her brother.

Being intimately acquainted with regret, however, Pippa saw it in Cullen's gaze. She didn't like hurting him—hurting anyone—but she wanted him to stop pestering her.

"Would my friendship be such a terrible thing?" he asked quietly.

Perhaps not...if she trusted him. Which she did not. While his intentions seemed harmless, she didn't understand why he'd bothered to look out for her. She wished she could trust her intuition to guide her; when it came to males, however, her instincts had led her down the wrong path one too many times.

She leveled a look at him. "Does a *friend* hide behind a mask?"

"There's a reason for my mask," he said in a curt tone.

"I know the reason. You're the *mysterious* Prince of Larks."

Lines bracketed his mouth. A knock cut off whatever he would have said next.

"Cull, Long Mikey says to come on deck quick!" A girl's voice came through the door. "A lighter pulled up, wif a giant fellow and group o' ladies who look like they mean business."

Reinforcements had arrived; Pippa welcomed the excuse to end this encounter.

"Those are my friends," she said. "As they do not like to be kept waiting, I'll bid you adieu."

She marched to the door, but Cullen beat her to it.

Opening it, he inclined his head.

"Good evening, my lady," he said. "We'll finish our discussion another time."

"We have nothing left to say."

"When you're ready to talk about Longmere, about what happened with him, come to me." His penetrating gaze seemed to see far too deeply. "Whatever you may believe, I *am* your friend. You have my word that you and your secrets are safe with me."

"I have no secrets." *None that I would share with you.* "And you should continue doing what you've done for the past fourteen years: stay out of my way."

She brushed past him without another word.

❦ 4 ❦

1835

"Quickly, follow me!" Pippa said, her voice hushed. "No one will find us in the bell tower."

"It's just a game." Cull gave her one of those slow, crooked grins that made her heart knock against her ribs. "Not life or death."

In the weeks Cull had been staying with her family, his injuries had healed. His chocolate-brown eyes were free of bruising. Although the housekeeper had given him a trim, his chestnut hair remained shaggy. Pippa suspected that no scissors could tame that unruly mane, but she thought the rough-edged style suited him.

During his recuperation, she'd kept him company at his bedside, reading to him and chatting. She'd concluded that she'd never met a boy like him. The ones she knew were interested in boxing, horses, poetry, and the latest gentlemen's fashions. Cull, on the other hand, had told her he'd never had time for sports; the only fighting he'd done was in the streets. He wasn't a connoisseur of horseflesh and could hardly read and write. And he clearly didn't give a whit about his clothes.

Currently, he was wearing cast-offs from the academy. His wide shoulders stretched the worn linen shirt, the plain brown waistcoat hugging his lean torso. Due to his height, the trousers ended several inches higher than they should have above his large, scuffed boots. He wasn't refined, well-groomed, or anything like Pippa's other male acquaintances.

Yet what made Cull truly different from other boys was the way he focused on *her*. Unlike most fellows, he was more apt to listen than talk. He asked her questions and seemed fascinated by what she had to say. She'd always thought of herself as ordinary, especially compared to her remarkable parents. Cull, however, made her feel worthy of attention, his presence setting off a strange, tingling awareness inside her...

"Come out, come out, wherever you are!" Maisie's sing-song voice broke Pippa's reverie.

Pippa had supervised a writing class at her parents' school today. She'd promised the children a game of hide-and-seek for completing their lesson, which had led to the alphabet being copied in record time. Making good on her promise, she'd let the class draw straws; Maisie had selected the shortest, which made her the seeker. When Cull had shown up, Maisie had roped him into playing.

Hearing Maisie's voice grow nearer, Pippa whispered, "It may be just a game, but I am *not* losing. Come with me or find your own way...it is your choice."

She reached for the door to the tower; Cull beat her to it.

He opened the door for her, saying easily, "I'll go wif you."

Pippa's blue skirts rustled as she led the way up the winding stairwell. When she and her brothers were younger, they had loved racing up these wooden steps to see who could get up to the top first. The prize was the view: when she stepped into the belfry, her pulse raced with exhilaration. The cupola sat five stories above the ground, a stone balustrade the only barrier between her and the grey sky and migrating clouds. A reflexive thought struck her: what would it be like to plunge over that railing and fall into the vast void? She shuddered, the fear heightening her excitement, making her heart pound faster.

Gripping the waist-high railing, she gazed down at the sprawling campus of the academy. Its long buildings formed a quadrangle, which contained a tree-filled garden. From this height, the students appeared tiny as they ambled along the graveled paths.

"Jesus wept, this is a view," Cull said from beside her.

She smiled at the wonder in his voice. "It is my favorite spot."

Cull peered at the empty vault above them. "What 'appened to the bell?"

"No one knows for certain. It was already missing when Papa purchased the property." Pippa slid him a mischievous look. "There *are* rumors, however."

Cull raised his brows. "What sort o' rumors?"

"The place used to be a spice warehouse, and the bell was used to summon the workers at the end of the day. Apparently, one night was so foggy and dark, with not a star in the sky, that the fellow who rang the bell misjudged where he was and fell to his death. The next day, when the warehouse opened, the bell was gone." Pippa lowered her voice, the way her mama did when getting to the good part of the story. "They say the man's ghost took it, and if you listen closely on the darkest nights, you can hear him ringing the bell."

Cull's rugged features paled. "You're pulling me leg."

"I have heard the bell ringing myself."

"There ain't no such thing as ghosts." He didn't sound entirely convinced.

She widened her eyes and pointed. "Then what is that standing behind you?"

When he jerked around, she let out a peal of laughter.

"Very amusing." He rolled his eyes, rubbing the back of his neck.

"You fell for it." Lips twitching, she said, "Don't feel too badly. Garrett and Hugh jumped higher than you did when I told them that story."

He shook his shaggy head. "You're a mystery, ain't you?"

"Hardly." Wrinkling her nose, Pippa returned her gaze to the view below, checking for Maisie and the others. "I'm the least interesting person in my family."

Cull leaned his forearms on the balustrade. "You're not boring to me."

"That is kind of you to say."

"I ain't being kind. I find you...interesting."

She glanced at him beneath her lashes, only to find him staring back. His brown eyes had a molten intensity that set off those strange tingles again. No male had ever regarded her with such blatant admiration. Even though her parents allowed her more freedom than most, she knew she shouldn't be alone with Cull—with any member of the opposite sex—yet she wasn't quite ready to end their time together.

Cull was exciting and different. In some ways, he was so much wiser and experienced than she was. He'd survived a life in the slums that she couldn't even fathom. She respected his strength and the way he cared for his sister. Papa, himself a product of the stews, had even remarked upon Cull's fine qualities.

At the same time, Cull lacked social polish. When it came to manners, he was ragged around the edges and didn't flirt the way some boys were beginning to do with her. He was forthright, sometimes unnervingly so. Although his earnestness could make for awkward moments, she found it an appealing change from flowery compliments and witty innuendoes.

She couldn't resist teasing him. "What do you find interesting about me, sir?"

"I like the way you talk. It doesn't even matter what you say... your voice, it's soothing. I like the way you are wif the children— you don't talk down to 'em like most misses o' your station would.

I like that you read and paint and act like a lady. But that you also 'ave a streak o' mischief and boldness." He came closer, and she turned, her back to the balustrade. He settled his palms on the railing on either side of her. "Last, but far from least, I like the way you look, sunshine."

Her pulse fluttered wildly. No one had ever spoken to her in so blunt a manner. Or described her in such a fashion.

"Why do you call me 'sunshine'?" she blurted. "Is it because of my hair?"

"Partly." His lazy smile sent butterflies swarming through her belly. "But mostly on account o' the fact that you light up any room you enter."

Her lips formed a soundless "oh" of surprise. The heat in his eyes mesmerized her, making her feel light-headed. She swayed backward, feeling a moment's panic when her shoulders met with air.

He caught her by the arms, pulling her away from the edge.

"Easy there. You all right, sunshine?"

"I...I felt dizzy," she said breathlessly. "For an instant, I thought I might fall."

"I would never let you fall."

He tipped her head back, and she saw that his eyes had gone as dark as midnight. His mask of politeness had been ripped off, revealing something feral. Hungry. Something she didn't quite understand. Yet she knew that he was going to kiss her...and she didn't want to stop him. When he lowered his head, she squeezed her eyes shut in anticipation of her first kiss.

It was gentle and lovely. Cull courted her mouth, his firm yet velvety lips moving against hers with drugging sweetness. She didn't know that a kiss would have a flavor, but it did. Cull tasted of peppermint and salt and himself. The combination made her heart thump, a wave of warmth rushing through her. When he licked the seam of her lips, she gave a start of surprise, clutching onto his lapels for balance.

He broke the kiss, tightening his arms around her.

Resting his forehead against hers, he said hoarsely, "I'm sorry, sunshine. Was that too much?"

It was as if some invisible hand had tight-laced her corset strings. She couldn't breathe. Her skin felt hot and flushed, her insides itchy with a strange heat.

"Is anyone up here?"

Pippa jumped at the sound of Maisie's voice floating up the steps. Panic besieged her. She couldn't be caught up here alone with a boy—and one she'd just kissed, no less.

She pushed at Cull, but he pulled her closer, whispering in her ear, "Stay here and let me take care o' Maisie. I'll see you later?"

She managed a shaky nod. He let her go, pausing to tuck a fallen curl behind her ear. His callused fingertips brushed the curve of her cheek, and she quivered.

His mouth curved slowly. Then he strode away, disappearing down the tower steps, calling, "Maisie, you clever girl. Found me, didn't you?"

Alone, Pippa waited to regain her equilibrium before going to the balustrade and peering over the edge. She watched as Cull exited the tower with his sister. He looked up; even though she couldn't see his expression, she *felt* his smile. She tingled from head to toe, and this time it wasn't because she was afraid of falling.

PRESENT

The following afternoon, Pippa arrived at the appointed time at Lady Charlotte Fayne's gracious Mayfair residence. She looked the part of the grieving widow in her black bombazine dress with a fitted bodice and narrow sleeves, the plain skirts draped over layers of petticoats. An autumn breeze stirred her black veil as she climbed the steps, an echo of her inner tempest.

How is Charlie going to react to my actions last evening? she thought with gnawing worry. *How am I going to explain Timothy Cullen's reappearance in my life?*

Pippa set aside her fretting to return the greeting of Hawker, Charlie's butler and one of the Angels' instructors. He was a big man with an even bigger heart, hidden beneath a gruff and rather piratical exterior. He directed her to the private chamber adjacent to Charlie's study, where Pippa's fellow Angels were waiting.

Lady Olivia Wodehouse, Miss Fiona Garrity, and Lady Glory Cavendish greeted her with cheery hellos. Pippa joined the ladies on the divan in the sitting area, where they were taking refreshment. Chairs were lined up along the wall that separated this chamber from Charlie's study; through discreet viewing holes, the Angels would be able to observe Charlie at work when she brought in the next client, Lady Hastings.

A wealthy widow, Charlie maintained a spotless reputation. The world believed that her Society of Angels was a genteel charity. Only a select few knew the truth: Charlie ran an investigative agency to help women whose interests had not been served by the male establishment. For these clients, the Angels were their last hope; Pippa knew this because that was how *she* had felt when she'd hired Charlie to uncover Edwin's secret.

At the time, Pippa hadn't known that Livy, Glory, and Fi were the inaugural members of Charlie's covert team. Charlie simply told her clients that she had "contacts" who could find information; no one suspected that those contacts were three well-bred young ladies, which was the beauty of Charlie's plan. Her detectives were hiding in plain sight and had access to society's highest echelons.

Pippa had only discovered the truth when Livy found Edwin's body. Having known Livy, Glory, and Fi for ages—the girls' parents and Pippa's were close friends—Pippa had been astounded by the younger women's audacity. Her shock had gradually turned into curiosity.

Could ladies become investigators? What skills were necessary to carry out clandestine surveillance? How did one keep up the subterfuge of being a lady by day and an agent by night?

Those questions had led Pippa back to Lady Charlotte. Charlie had revealed her own story: she, herself, had once sought help from male investigators who either did not take her seriously or tried to take advantage of her. Thus, she had taken it upon herself to learn the trade of detection, and the Society of Angels represented her desire to empower future generations of ladies with her hard-won knowledge. To teach these members of the "weaker sex" to hone their physical and mental strengths...and to enable them to determine their own destinies.

Having lost her own husband at a young age, Charlie had come straight to the point with Pippa.

"Loss can either destroy one or make one stronger," she'd said. *"Which will it be for you?"*

The choice had been easy. The work had given Pippa purpose and the company of friends who understood her situation in ways her other genteel acquaintances could not. Knowing what they did of the dark business that had killed Edwin—which Pippa kept under wraps to preserve his honor—Livy, Glory, and Fi had offered Pippa their unconditional support. They'd even made her an honorary member of the club they'd started back in finishing school: the "Willflowers" aptly described the ladies' unconventional and spirited approach to life. One that Pippa now embraced.

She and the Angels helped themselves from a cart of refreshments, chatting as they awaited Charlie and Lady Hastings's arrival.

"I cannot believe you jumped off a bridge and onto the Prince of Larks's barge," Livy said as she poured out the tea.

A petite brunette whose jade-green frock matched her eyes, Livy possessed an inquisitive and determined nature. Last year, she had wed her longtime crush, the Duke of Hadleigh, and two months ago, had given birth to a baby girl named Esmerelda (Esme for short). Being a new mama didn't seem to hamper Livy's natural exuberance; if anything, she was even *more* energetic. Pippa fretted about her friend overdoing things.

Luckily, Livy's husband was as protective as he was doting. The duke supported Livy's independent spirit, including her work with the Angels; at the same time, he kept a close eye on her. The loving acceptance between Livy and her husband filled Pippa with admiration...and regret. If her own marriage had been as intimate and free of secrets, then perhaps Edwin might be alive today.

"As I said last night, the Prince of Larks left me no choice."

Accepting the tea from Livy, Pippa took a sip of the fortifying brew. "He intruded upon my surveillance of Hastings."

"But *why* did he do so?" Livy pressed.

Pippa chose her words with care. "I met him briefly fourteen years ago when he recuperated from an injury at my parents' home. His real name is Timothy Cullen, and his sister Maisie was a pupil at the Hunt Academy. After Cullen recovered, he left." She made her shrug nonchalant. "I haven't the faintest idea why he showed up last night and chose to make an inconvenience of himself."

"Perhaps Mr. Cullen feels he owes your family for helping him," Glory suggested as she helped herself to an egg and watercress sandwich.

Glory was a sporty girl with russet-brown hair, hazel eyes, and a dusting of freckles on her nose. There was a hint of her paternal Chinese heritage in her pretty features. Curled upon Glory's shell-pink skirts was her pet ferret, Ferdinand II. Ferdinand II raised his furry white head expectantly, his dark eyes bright and pink nose twitching. When Glory gave him a bit of her sandwich, he gobbled it down.

"But why show up now?" Fiona narrowed her blue eyes. "After fourteen years?"

The morning light set Fi's red curls aflame. She wore an *à la mode* white carriage dress and matching pelisse, a gold ceinture circling her tiny waist. At nineteen, she'd already been declared an Incomparable, with suitors lining up outside her door, but she enjoyed adventure more than ballroom flirtation. Or, rather, she saw no reason not to engage in both.

"That is a good question, Fi." Livy furrowed her brow. "And how would Mr. Cullen know you were in need of assistance, unless...has he been watching you?"

Pippa's nape tingled at the notion. She wasn't used to garnering male attention. Truth be told, she'd worried about keeping Edwin's interest. In the early stages of their courtship, he'd lavished her with praise and trinkets, his attention making her feel special and loved. Once they were engaged, however, his compliments had taken on the flavor of criticism. The change had been so subtle that it had taken her months to notice.

"A fine effort, my dear," he would say of a portrait she'd painted. *"Next time, you might consider flowers or fruit as your subject. Something more suited to your feminine sensibilities."*

When it came to his own painting, he liked to use sultry redheads and brunettes for his models. He'd claimed that his work captured the "decadent drama of humanity"; as a homebody who liked domesticity, Pippa had feared she didn't supply her husband with the excitement he seemed to crave. When she'd mustered up the courage to ask, his reply had been dismissive.

"There is nothing more tedious than insecurity, my dear," he'd said.

She'd shut up after that. The irony of it was that she'd only discovered her own capacity for adventure after his death. When it was too late. When it no longer mattered how intriguing she became.

The fact that Timothy Cullen—who was not her husband, her family, her *anything*—would take an interest in her was baffling to say the least. Why would he look out for her and claim to be her friend? At any rate, Pippa needed a man ruling her life like she needed tighter lacing on her corset. She was learning to breathe freely once more, and no overbearing male was going to stop her.

Pippa set her cup down. "I told Cullen in no uncertain terms to stay away from me."

"Having males constantly underfoot can be tiresome," Fi drawled.

"You would know." Glory gave the redhead a teasing look. "I nearly got trampled by your horde of admirers at the ball last week."

Fi sighed, giving her pristine skirts an expert flick. "There was not an interesting fellow in the bunch. Lemmings, all of them...no offense, Ferdinand."

"Ferdinand isn't offended," Glory replied as the ferret bobbed its head in agreement. "Lemmings are rodents, a different family from ferrets entirely."

"Is it too much to ask for a suitor who is clever, rich, and attractive?" Fi mused. Then she turned to Pippa. "By the by, you haven't told us what the fabled prince looks like."

Big. Muscular. Overwhelmingly masculine.

"I wouldn't know," Pippa said casually. "He was wearing a mask."

Yet her artist's imagination had filled in the spaces hidden by black leather. She'd pictured the lad she'd known as a full-grown man with blunt cheekbones and rough-hewn features. Raw and powerful lines that defied conventions of beauty.

"Was he tall?" Fi inquired.

Pippa gave a reluctant nod.

"Young?"

"He is a year older than I am."

"Broad-shouldered? Full head of hair? In possession of all his teeth?"

Pippa dipped her chin grudgingly in response to Fi's rapid-fire questions.

Fi arched her brows. "And he left *no* impression upon you?"

The sensation of being pressed up against Cullen's sinewy ridges flooded Pippa with warmth. Her insides fluttered as she recalled one ridge in particular. His male member had felt shockingly...substantial. Much larger than anything she'd encountered in her marital bed.

Good heavens. I cannot seriously be comparing Cullen's manhood to Edwin's.

Fighting back a blush, she answered firmly, "None whatsoever."

"Then you are a more sensible woman than I am," Fi said. "If some virile masked stranger came to *my* rescue, I would be hopelessly intrigued."

"If you didn't need to be rescued," Glory argued, "wouldn't you find his interference annoying?"

"It depends."

"On what?"

Fi's eyes sparkled. "On what lies behind the mask, of course."

Livy and Glory chuckled, and even Pippa had to smile at Fi's irreverence.

"Whatever the case," Livy said thoughtfully, "what if he obstructs Pippa's work again? We cannot have him getting in the way."

"Charlie will have a plan for dealing with him," Glory said.

Pippa fought a surge of anxiety. "Charlie probably blames me for going after Hastings on my own. What if she holds me responsible for Mr. Cullen's interference—and thinks I'm more trouble than I'm worth?"

"She would never think that." Reaching over, Livy patted Pippa's hand. "Don't forget our vow. We Angels stick together."

Upon joining the society, the Angels had taken an oath of secrecy and sisterhood:

> *No matter what danger may await*
> *An Angel is loyal, brave, and true.*
> *We will not betray our society's aim:*
> *"Sisters first" will see us through.*

"Following one's instincts can land one in hot water." Glory shrugged. "You'll get used to it."

"Following my instincts or getting into trouble?" Pippa asked.

"Both," her friends chorused as one.

Their laughter was cut short by approaching voices. They quieted instantly, moving to the chairs in front of the viewing holes. Peering through, Pippa saw Charlie lead Lady Julianna Hastings into the study.

A thin, plain brunette, Lady Hastings was around Pippa's age.

At social gatherings, Pippa had found the lady timid, always defer-ring to her charismatic spouse. The viscountess's violet silk dress and matching bonnet emphasized the pallor of her cheeks, her gloved hands clutching her reticule as she took the seat facing Charlie's desk.

In contrast, Charlie radiated vitality, and it wasn't just because of her lustrous honey-gold hair and flawless figure, shown to exquisite advantage in a flounced butter-yellow gown. Charlie had an innate, magnetic confidence: one couldn't help but be drawn to this woman in her prime, who lived life as it suited her.

Not long ago, Pippa had occupied the same chair as Julianna Hastings. She remembered her own desperation and hope as she'd divulged her troubles to Charlie. As she'd shared things she hadn't shared with anyone else.

"Do you have information on my husband?" Lady Hastings asked in a timorous voice.

"He was in Limehouse last night." Charlie handed the client a cup of tea; she'd perfected the art of being comforting yet direct. Seating herself across the rosewood desk fancifully carved with birds and flowers, she said, "He visited a gaming house, where he lost five hundred pounds on dice."

Lady Hastings's hand flittered to her bosom. "F-five hundred? In one night?"

"He has gambled three out of the seven nights since you hired us to watch him, wagering similar sums. He has also indulged in..."—Charlie paused, no doubt to prepare the lady—"other vices."

"Such as?" Lady Hastings said faintly.

"Whores and opium."

"Father was right." Lady Hastings spoke as if to herself. "He married me for my money."

The only child of wealthy mill owner Jonas Turner, Julianna had married the impoverished Hastings against her father's wishes three years ago. Hastings had apparently wooed her with promises of love. After her father's death, Hastings had shown his true colors, promptly taking control of Julianna's inheritance and squandering it on depravity.

Charlie's expression was sympathetic. "At our last meeting, you mentioned seeking legal counsel?"

"I spoke to a solicitor." Lady Hastings's chin quivered. "Even if I were willing to brave the scandal, I haven't sufficient grounds for divorce. Hastings is too well connected; his cronies in Parliament would kill any petition I submitted for a divorce. And the truth is...I am afraid."

Even through the peephole, Pippa saw the fear etched on the lady's face.

Charlie grew still. "Has your husband hurt you?"

"He...he hasn't laid a hand on me, if that is what you mean." Lady Hastings exhaled. "But he constantly criticizes me, and nothing I do is ever good enough. As hard as I try, I can never please him. I know that he has been keeping secrets from me since the start of our marriage."

Anguished empathy squeezed Pippa's chest. *God help me, I have more in common with Julianna Hastings than I realized.*

"I have no say in anything, and sometimes..." The lady's voice hitched. "Sometimes I fear he wants to be rid of me altogether."

Pippa's blood ran cold. Looking at her fellow Angels, she saw their brooding expressions. Was Lady Hastings implying that her husband wanted to kill her?

"Are you in danger?" Charlie demanded. "Life-threatening cruelty *is* grounds for divorce—"

"I am being dramatic." Lady Hastings's smile had a forced quality. "Hastings wouldn't hurt me."

"That's hardly convincing," Pippa said under her breath.

"You have been of great help, Lady Fayne. Now that I know the extent of my husband's vices, I will plan for my future accordingly." Depositing an envelope on the desk, Lady Hastings rose. "The remainder of your fee, with my thanks."

Charlie got to her feet. "Please wait. Are you certain there is nothing else—"

"When our mutual friend, the dowager duchess, told me that you'd assisted her and were a champion of women, I did not believe her. But now I do." Lady Hastings gave a graceful nod. "You have listened and taken my concerns seriously, and for that I am most grateful. Now I must ask that you respect my wishes and terminate the case. I shall see myself out. Good day."

After hearing the front door close, Pippa and the Angels rushed into Charlie's study. Their mentor was sitting at her desk, tapping a pen against the blotter. Lady Hastings's distinctive violet, musk, and ambergris fragrance lingered as heavily as the concerns she'd shared.

"What do you think?" Charlie asked pensively.

"I think it is dashed unfair that Lady Hastings is bound to such a cad." Glory's pink skirts swished as she paced in front of the hearth, her ferret trotting at her heels.

"Is she safe?" Pippa nibbled on her lip. "Perhaps we should continue surveilling Hastings."

"Lady Hastings terminated our services. She is an adult, and we must respect her decision...even if we disagree." Sighing, Charlie tossed the pen into a filigree tray. "Knowing our role and honoring our client's wishes can be the hardest part of the job."

"I suppose we did help," Livy said. "Now she knows what she is dealing with."

"A pyrrhic victory," Fi muttered. "To find out that one will forever be haunted by one bad decision."

Pippa's throat clenched. *I know how that feels.*

"On that cheery note, I'd best be on my way," Livy said. "I am spending the afternoon with Esme since Hadleigh and I have an event this eve."

"The Westerfield ball?" Fi asked.

"The British Museum. They have a new exhibit of spiders"—

Livy lovingly rubbed her thumb over her spider-shaped engagement ring—"and Hadleigh has arranged for a private viewing."

"I'll never understand your interest in museums," Fi said. "Visiting them is such a bore."

"Not with Hadleigh." Eyes twinkling, Livy asked, "Shall I drop anyone off on my way?"

Before the Angels could reply, Charlie said, "Pippa, I'd like a word with you in private."

Unease prickled Pippa. The others gave her sympathetic looks as they left.

Pippa drew a breath. "If this is about last night, I had everything under control—"

"You broke the most sacrosanct rule of the Angels. *Sisters first*," Charlie said with emphasis. "You are part of a team, Pippa, not some rogue agent."

"I know. But Hastings was moving quickly, and I was so close—"

"By putting yourself at risk, you also endanger others. The rest of the team will go after you, no matter the peril. You are fortunate the prince meant no harm last night."

Guilt swelled. She opened her mouth...and closed it. Because she had no valid excuse for her recklessness.

"Now you will tell me what he wanted from you." Charlie's grey eyes were as sharp as a steel blade. "All the details, if you please."

Faced with her mentor's scrutiny, Pippa had no choice but to relate her history with Timothy Cullen. She did, however, leave out her inexplicable physical reactions to him, which were as mortifying as they were irrelevant.

At the conclusion of the report, Charlie gave Pippa an assessing look. "When you told Mr. Cullen to steer clear of you, how did he respond?"

I am your friend, sunshine. You have my word that you and your secrets are safe with me.

"He seemed to understand that I was serious," Pippa hedged.

Charlie leaned back in her chair. "Do I need to have a parley with him? While the Prince of Larks may be a ruthless and powerful man, I will not countenance him interfering with our work."

"He won't," Pippa said in a rush. "I promise." *If he does, he will answer to me.*

"Very well. I will let this go for now. But I wish to be apprised of any further contact by the prince, Pippa. Do I make myself clear?"

Nodding, Pippa said, "If there's nothing else, I thought I would get some sparring practice in with Mrs. Peabody—"

"About that." Charlie's expression was grave. "I think you should take a break."

Pippa's pulse skittered with fear. "I do not need a break. I have naught better to do."

"And that is the trouble. My dear, I brought you on because I thought the work would be a good distraction—"

"It has been. The very best diversion." *The only thing keeping me afloat.*

"But your entire life cannot revolve around a diversion." Rising, Charlie crossed over to Pippa, taking her hands in a gentle yet firm grip. "I have been where you are, my dear, and I won't lie that investigation gave me purpose and the will to carry on. At the same time, I see signs that the work may be affecting you in less desirable ways."

Pippa pulled away. "The work is doing me good."

"It is also feeding a latent recklessness in you. It worries me, my dear. No matter how important a lead may seem, nothing is more important than your well-being. You *must* take better care. If the mudlarks hadn't intervened, you might have found yourself in quite the predicament."

"I was perfectly capable of handling the situation," Pippa protested.

Charlie lifted her brows. "By handling, do you mean engaging in combat with the target who wasn't supposed to know that you were there? Or perhaps you meant to do nothing and let him shoot you in the head?"

Pippa's cheeks flamed.

"In this instance, we owe the Prince of Larks," Charlie said sternly. "And I do not like to be indebted to anyone, least of all a man with murky motivations."

"It is not as if I invited him to meddle in my affairs!"

"Be that as it may, if he approaches you again, you will tell me." Charlie headed to the door, her yellow skirts rustling. "In the interim, get some rest. It will do you good."

Heart pounding at the thought of the long hours alone in her cottage, Pippa choked out, "How long am I to be barred from participating in the society?"

"This isn't a punishment, my dear." Turning, Charlie pursed her lips. "I genuinely believe that a respite would be healthful. Perhaps you could take up a hobby; was painting not a passion of yours?"

Pippa saw the blood dripping from her brush, and a cold droplet slid down her spine.

"How long until I may return?" she repeated.

Sighing, Charlie opened the door. "Take a week, my dear. Then we'll revisit the matter."

When Pippa returned to her cottage that afternoon, she was greeted by Whitby, her butler. She had hired her small and loyal staff based on Charlie's referrals. To Pippa, her servants were a dream: they didn't gossip or question her comings and goings, nor did they bat an eye when she went out at night in one of her myriad disguises. Balding and built like a teapot, Whitby, especially, was the soul of discretion.

"Good afternoon, my lady," he said with a bow. "How was the visit with Lady Fayne?"

Pushing back her despair, Pippa managed a smile. "It was fine."

"A letter arrived. I left it on your desk." The butler cleared his throat. "It was delivered in person by Mrs. Hunt."

A vise clamped around Pippa's temples. She wasn't ready to deal with her family. During supper three months ago, Papa had gone on a rant about Edwin's character. She couldn't argue with Papa's points; Edwin *had* been condescending toward her relations. Yet what point was there in speaking ill of the dead? Moreover, Pippa bore responsibility as well, for she'd made the choice to wed Edwin contrary to parental advice.

She'd sat tight-lipped through course after course, frustration and despair decimating her appetite. Since then, she'd been avoiding her family. She loved them but didn't know how to mend the rift caused by her marriage. Taking the coward's way out, she'd kept her distance.

Entering the parlor, Pippa went to her escritoire and picked up the letter. A spasm hit her chest at the sight of her mama's untidy script. She traced the seal with her index finger but didn't break it. She knew her mother was worried about her and was likely asking her to visit...or to move home. Despite Pippa's yearning to return to the vibrant, loving household of her youth, something in her balked.

Because you cannot go back. You have made your bed and now you must lie in it.

Plagued by restless melancholy, she went to look out the window...and froze.

Stationed across the street was a child in a scruffy cap. By all appearances, he was a crossing sweep, cheerfully wielding his broom and accepting a coin from a passing couple. Pippa, however, *knew* that adorable bespectacled face. It was one of the mudlarks from last night...and there could only be one reason for his presence outside her cottage.

"Devil take you, Cullen." She balled her hands. "Haven't you interfered with my life enough?"

Because of him, she'd lost Hastings. Because of him, Charlie had discharged her from duty. Anger charged through Pippa in a cleansing, powerful rush.

I am no longer the naïve chit you once knew, Timothy Cullen. You wish to play with me? she thought with grim anticipation. *Then let the games begin.*

✣ 6 ✣

"Here is the information you requested, Fanny," Cull said.

He placed the packet of documents on the desk before settling into the velvet armchair that faced it. As usual, his favorite drink was waiting for him on the mother-of-pearl inlaid side table. He picked up the glass and took a sip, enjoying the mellow burn. In line with everything else at Corbett's, the most exclusive bawdy house in London, the whisky was first-rate.

Fanny Grier, the proprietress of the club, insisted upon quality. She and her husband Horace owned the pleasure house and several others. Their strategy of offering the best, along with a reputation for discretion, had proved an unbeatable combination. The pair could have retired years ago, but Fanny enjoyed the challenge of her work.

A former prostitute, Fanny had fought for her success every inch of the way, and she deserved to be proud of her achievements. Seated across the mahogany desk in the luxurious office, she looked like any other wealthy matron. Her grey silk gown and jewelry were tasteful and expensive, and her silver-streaked dark hair was styled in an elegant twist.

Putting on her spectacles, Fanny reviewed the documents Cull had brought. Truth be told, he could have sent a mudlark to deliver the information, the way he did with other clients. But he'd known Fanny for over a decade, and she'd done him a personal favor years ago that he would never forget. He would be forever indebted to her for helping his sister through a dark crisis. He was honored to call Fanny and Horace his friends.

Besides, it was good for Cull to get out of the Nest. Since his accident, he'd spent too much time holed up in the mudlarks' compound. The Griers' office was one of the few places outside of his own home where he felt comfortable without his mask. Where he knew he would not draw undue stares or looks of revulsion.

Fanny set down the papers. "A thorough job, as usual."

Her accent was polished by elocution lessons. She was a great believer in advancement; in fact, she'd been the one to introduce Cull to the tutor who'd taught him his letters and how to speak like a gentleman. That had been before Cull's scarring, when he'd still had a secret dream of courting Pippa. When he had still believed that he could one day be worthy of her.

"Based on your reports of their financial situations, I'll be denying three of last month's applicants," she went on. "You've saved me a good deal of trouble, Timothy."

Fanny was one of the few who called Cull by his Christian name, and he didn't mind when she did. It was what his mam had called him; if the blue ruin hadn't killed her, she would be about Fanny's age. Cull felt the familiar pang, thinking about the sacrifices his mother had made.

If only he'd been able to support their family, then she wouldn't have had to resort to whoring. Maybe she wouldn't have turned to the bottle for comfort. Maybe she would still be alive; maybe she would have prevented Maisie from falling prey to disgrace...

Cull pushed aside the old guilt. While his mam and Fanny had a lot in common, Fanny had been wiser in her choice of a mate.

Horace Grier was a stand-up fellow, whereas Cull's sire had been a
heartless cad who'd deserted his woman and children.

"It's what you pay me to do," Cull said.

He focused on the whisky and plush surroundings. While he
wouldn't trade the Nest for the finest mansion in Mayfair, he
appreciated the finer things in life. And Corbett's was all about
the finer things.

As if reading his mind, Fanny said, "Supper will be brought in
shortly. I've asked Monsieur Georges to prepare your favorite
dishes."

Cull's stomach gave a happy growl at the mention of the
French chef's delectable creations. There was a reason why he
scheduled his meetings with Fanny around mealtimes.

Fanny shook her head. "I'll never understand why you don't
get rid of your dreadful excuse for a cook."

"One doesn't get rid of Mrs. Halberd," Cull said, suppressing a
shudder.

The cook had been with the mudlarks since before Cull's
time. The old battle axe had a mean temper; as a boy, he'd had his
ears boxed by her more than once. He would rather face down an
army of cutthroats than her and her wooden spoon, and the idea
of ousting her was laughable. Besides, there probably wasn't
another cook alive who would be willing to put up with a house
packed with mischief-loving urchins.

"You're lucky her food hasn't killed you." Fanny snorted. "You
should be living better."

"As the old prince used to say, we mudlarks got a roof over our
heads, food in our bellies, and each other." Cull shrugged. "A
fellow doesn't need more than that to survive."

Fanny went to pour herself a whisky from the sideboard and
returned with a fresh one for Cull, who'd risen when she had. He
minded his manners around Fanny, who deserved respect. She
leaned against the edge of the desk and waved him back into his

chair; the meditative sip she took conveyed that she had something on her mind.

"At some point, a man ought to do more than survive," she said. "You're a wealthy cove, Timothy. With the sums your customers are paying, your coffers must rival that of Croesus. Yet I don't see you spending any blunt on yourself. You could use new clothes and a haircut."

Fanny liked to harp on his appearance. But what was the point of dandying himself up when half his face was a mangled, burned mess? Besides, mudlarks valued function over fashion, and Cull liked the comfort of his well-worn clothes. He would toss his shirt when it developed holes...maybe.

"I have everything I need," he said.

As he spoke the words, Pippa filled his mind's eye...and all of his senses. He recalled the silken fall of her hair, her soft yet sleek curves draped atop him, her lily-and-sunshine scent making his mouth pool. Her charms were far more than physical. He was drawn to her feistiness—her fire and the vulnerability he sensed beneath. She'd invaded his dreams last night, and he'd woken up, hard and aching. He'd had to take matters into his own hands...twice.

She was an itch under his skin. One he could never assuage and maybe didn't want to. By nature, he was a realist. Harboring a fantasy about Pippa was about the only impractical thing he'd done, and he felt possessive over it. Over having something just for himself, even if it was futile.

"Needs and wants are two different things." Fanny downed the rest of her Scotch, placing her glass down with a precise click. "It is high time you got yourself a woman."

Cull choked on a mouthful of whisky. He coughed before answering.

"You've laid eyes on this mug o' mine, haven't you?" He angled the damaged side of his face toward Fanny, not that she could miss the swirling ridges of melted skin. "I ain't exactly bait for a treacle tart."

"First of all, there's more to you than your face. Many a female would consider you a man in your prime...and don't you roll your eyes at me, Timothy Cullen. I am not deaf; I hear what my wenches say about your stamina."

Cull's face heated. Jesus wept. The last thing he wished to discuss with Fanny was what her whores said about his sexual prowess. He didn't make use of the club's services often; when he did, he mostly watched in the public rooms. Observing from the shadows had become a habit for him. Only when his craving for physical contact grew too great did he participate. During the deed, he kept his mask on. Call him vain, but he found bed sport more pleasant when his partner wasn't staring at him in horror.

"We're not talking about this," he muttered.

"We can leave the wenches' praises out of this," Fanny said. "But onto my second point: it's not just a sweetheart you ought to be after, but a wife."

At that, Cull barked out a laugh. "Now I *know* you're pulling my leg. There ain't ever been a Princess of Larks, and you know it. The curse of solitude comes with the job."

It was a tradition that the Prince of Larks ruled alone. Whether it was because his demanding duties made it impossible to look for a bride or because no woman with good sense wanted to take on a man who was responsible for hundreds of street urchins, Cull didn't know. All he knew was that a century of history backed up this fact. And he, with his wrecked mug, wasn't about to be the one to end the curse.

For folk like us, there'll be no lucky stars lightin' our way. He could hear his mam's voice, drenched in sorrow and gin. *To last in this world, Timothy, you 'ave to learn to survive in the dark.*

"You could be the first to wed," Fanny argued.

"Aye. And pigs could fly."

Fanny's gaze slitted. "Don't be smart with me. You aren't

getting any younger. And there's more to life than looking after mudlarks and those injured birds of yours."

Soon after Cull's injury in the fire, a mudlark had brought in an injured sparrow. Figuring it was an omen of some sort, Cull had nursed the bird back to health. Somehow fixing up hurt birds had become a hobby, and he'd built an enclosure atop the Nest, where his feathered charges recovered until they were strong enough to fly away.

"You need someone to look after you for a change," Fanny insisted.

Luckily, the opening door relieved Cull of the necessity of a reply. Fanny's husband entered. Horace Grier was a large Scot with a grizzled beard and gruff manner. Cull rose to shake hands with him before the latter ambled over to Fanny.

"Supper ain't ready yet, love?" Grier asked.

Fanny huffed, her arms akimbo. "Is food all you men can think about?"

Grier transferred his gaze to Cull. "What bee got into her bonnet?"

"Marriage," Cull said succinctly.

"Ah." Bravely but unwisely, Grier said, "We talked about this, lass. I thought we agreed you weren't going to pester our friend 'ere about 'is marital plans."

"You said to leave off the subject," Fanny retorted. "*I* did not agree to anything."

Grier lifted his bushy grey brows. "Now you ken why the lad ain't keen on getting leg-shackled?"

Cull had to swallow a laugh at Fanny's annoyed expression. Arguing was the pair's way of showing affection. Sure enough, when Fanny slapped her husband's arm, Grier snatched her hand and kissed it.

"Surrounded by nodcocks, I am. The pair of you keep this up, and neither of you are getting any supper," Fanny muttered.

"Ain't a chance I'm missing out on Monsieur Georges's fancy

cooking," Horace returned. "It's the least I deserve for putting up with that temperamental Frenchman."

"He's an artist." Fanny waved a hand. "All artists are dramatic."

"Tell that to the scullery maids who come crying to me," Horace said.

"They come to you on account of your giant soft heart. And you had better not be offering them that brawny shoulder of yours to cry on, Horace Grier."

A smile slashed through Horace's beard. "Jealous, lass?"

That earned him a glare from Fanny that would have felled a lesser man.

Supper was carted in, interrupting the Griers' banter. The delicious meal of chicken stew, herbed potatoes, and side dishes was accompanied by wine and easy conversation. As Cull was tucking into dessert, a creamy blancmange and assortment of buttery cookies, Grier brought up a more serious topic.

"'Ave you given any thought to my suggestion o' 'iring on guards, lad?" the Scot asked.

Cull finished a cookie. "I appreciate the concern, but I don't need guards."

"Those larks o' yours are excellent scouts. But they ain't fighters," Grier insisted. "I've said it once and I'll say it again: a man who deals in secrets can't be too careful. Should think it obvious, after what 'appened."

Grier was referring to the incident two weeks ago when a carriage had nearly hit Cull as he was leaving the club. The vehicle hadn't slowed after Cull had dived out of harm's way. Cull knew it was no accident, yet he balked at hiring guards. Mudlarks managed their own business. He'd informed Long Mikey and the other team leaders, who were instructed to keep a sharp lookout.

He'd also started gathering information on possible suspects. He'd narrowed the list down to five bastards who'd long wanted to get their greedy paws on the larks: Melville, Crane, Hannity, Igden, and Squibb. The cutthroats were known to use violence to keep their gangs in line. They wanted to expand their power by absorbing the mudlarks' territory and reaping the profits from the information trade.

Cull despised the blackguards. He refused, however, to start a battle that would turn into a massacre. As far as he was concerned, there were no winners in war; when he retaliated, it would be clean and efficient, as bloodless as he could make it.

"I've everything in hand." Cull shrugged. "Danger is the price of doing business."

Being products of the underworld, the Griers understood that as well as he did.

"Even so," Grier began.

"Save your breath, luv," Fanny said. "The lad has more pride than sense. Thinks he can handle cutthroats without shedding blood."

"Killing begets more killing." The inked tally on Cull's back was a reminder of that fact, and he would do everything in his power not to add to it.

A mudlark never forgets.

The door was flung open, and Ollie scampered in, his spectacles askew.

Cull frowned. "What are you doing here? You should be keeping watch on—"

He cut himself off. The last thing he needed was for Fanny to find out about Pippa. Christ Almighty, he would never hear the end of it.

"Why aren't you with the target?" he finished.

Ollie didn't reply, mesmerized by the plate of cookies on the table. Sighing, Cull offered it to him. Ollie stuffed two buttery rounds into his mouth, pocketing the rest.

"I tried to tail 'er," the boy said through a mouthful of crumbs. "But she pulled a fast one and disappeared."

Bloody hell, that wasn't a good sign. Where could Pippa have gone?

"Thank you for the hospitality." Pushing his chair back, Cull got to his feet and bowed to the Griers. "If you'll excuse me, I must attend to some business."

Ollie showed Cull where he'd lost Pippa, at a busy corner of the Strand. As it was clear that there would be no picking up her scent, they headed back to the Nest.

The carriage wound through the narrow streets toward the mudlarks' headquarters in the Devil's Acre, located in the heart of Westminster. Here in the shadows of the grand old Abbey and Houses of Parliament lived real London. Reformers had taken to these low-lying streets near the Thames, documenting their outrage over the population of beggars, thieves, and prostitutes who eked out a squalid living, in the same neighborhood where bluebloods decided the fate of the nation (always and unsurprisingly to their own advantage). The do-gooders tried to start schools to educate the "heathen children" in the ways of Christianity.

Some campaigners even knocked on Cull's door. Demanded that he release the children in his care...as if he kept them behind bars. The doors of the Nest were open for mudlarks to come and go as they pleased. The children Cull took in were like him: products of the stews, who'd survived poverty and loss and worse. They were outsiders who valued freedom and lived by their own rules.

One time, a crusader had kidnapped an adolescent mudlark named Matches from the Nest, forcing him to join one of the "ragged schools" designed to reform poor children. Knowing Matches could take care of himself, Cull hadn't been too worried. Sure enough, the boy returned two days later, smirking, his spiky dark hair singed from the hobby that had earned him his moniker.

The do-gooders never did rebuild the burned-down school...nor did they come back for Matches.

The reformers couldn't understand that, for some folk, liberty was more important than respectability. Choice more alluring than security. And those who chose the way of the mudlarks knew that their soul was worth more than new clothes and bowls of gruel.

Since Cull had become the leader, he'd done his best to steer his group away from the darker trades. The prince before him had begun to shift the work of the mudlarks from scavenging and theft to dealing in information, and Cull had pushed that agenda. The decision had proved a profitable one. Fanny hadn't been wrong when she said the gang's coffers were overflowing. Cull had instituted a system whereby each of the larks had a share of the profits, based on their years of service and contributions. The funds were kept tucked away at Gruenwald's Bank until they were ready to fly the coop.

Increasingly, mudlarks were choosing to stay on into their adult years. Cull had been working on a program to train the older larks in a profession that would provide them with a sustainable future. He hoped, in time, to create a legitimate enterprise, one that would permanently lift his brethren out of the dangerous streets while providing them with the autonomy they craved.

The carriage drove by sagging flash houses and gin shops, alleyways teeming with vice and danger. The swirling fog carried the stink of the streets and the Thames and might have offended some nostrils, but to Cull, it was the smell of home. They arrived at the Nest, a riverfront property that had once been a tenement. Cull descended first, turning to see a hackney pull up behind him.

The door opened, and a slender trouser-clad figure hopped down.

Bloody hell...Pippa? What is she doing here?

He stared at her, wondering if she was a figment of his feverish imagination. As she came up to him, the scowl on her face confirmed that he wasn't fantasizing. She was no less gorgeous when she was angry, however; from beneath her cap, her eyes blazed with heavenly fire.

Those eyes suddenly widened. "Cull, behind you!"

Her panic made Cull spin around. A brute had emerged from the shadows; face hidden by a kerchief, he aimed a pistol straight at Cull. As Cull tensed to spring away from the danger, a shot tore through the night. A moment later, a force rammed into him and sent him to the ground.

7

Once again, Pippa found herself on top of Timothy Cullen, the breath knocked out of her. Since she'd done the knocking down this time, she supposed she couldn't complain. She twisted her head in the direction of the shooter; the villain was gone. Absorbed back into the shadows of the alleyway from which he'd emerged.

A wise move on his part. The driver of the carriage was now on the ground, a pair of pistols in hand. The little bespectacled mudlark who had exited the carriage after Cull was blowing frantically on a whistle. The shrill call summoned his brethren, who were spilling out of their flash house, armed to the teeth.

Pippa peered down at Cull. "Are you all right?"

Framed by his mask, his eyes were dazed.

"Pippa?" he said hoarsely. "What are you doing here?"

"Saving your hide, apparently," she muttered.

Judging that he wasn't harmed, she rose and dusted off her trousers. Before she could offer him a hand, he was on his feet. When he pushed her behind him, putting himself between her and where the shooter had been, she rolled her eyes at his belated gallantry.

"The assailant took off down that alleyway," she said. "Did you recognize him?"

Cull shook his head. "A cutthroat for hire, by the looks of him."

"Who hired him?"

He continued scanning the environs for danger. "The list is too long to get into now."

A pair of mudlarks came running up. Pippa recognized the curly-haired girl with the striking amber eyes and the gangly brown-haired lad, both of whom had been on the boat last evening.

"We're ready to go after the bastard, Cull." The girl's words were as fierce as the way she slapped a cudgel against her palm. "We'll show 'im what 'appens when 'e attacks one o' us."

"No, Fair Molly," Cull said firmly. "You're not to pursue."

The lad scowled. "Fair Molly 'as the right o' it. We should make whoe'er is behind this pay...*in blood.*"

"Violence isn't the only way to exact retribution, Long Mikey." Cull's tone brooked no refusal. "I want the two of you to set up a perimeter: six larks out front, six in the rear, rotating every two hours. No outsiders in or out. Get the others back inside."

As Cull gestured to the milling larks, Pippa noticed his slight grimace. Then she saw the tear in the right arm of his coat. A stain darkened the fabric.

"You're hurt," she said with concern. "Why didn't you say anything? Did the bullet hit you?"

"It's a scratch," he said dismissively.

"A physician should look at it. Wounds can fester—"

"I don't need a quack. The bullet barely grazed me."

For heaven's sake, she thought in exasperation. *The man is acting as if he gets shot every day.*

Then she realized that perhaps this *wasn't* unusual for him. This tough, brawny fellow who seemed inclined to protect all those around him...except himself.

"At the very least, the injury should be examined," she insisted. "Then we can decide whether a physician is required."

He gave her a brooding look. "We?"

"Since you clearly cannot be trusted to take care of the wound," she said tartly, "I had better look at it."

His stony countenance awakened her inner butterflies. She didn't know how to interpret it...or the dark energy coming off him in waves.

"Come inside, then," he said.

Pippa took in Cull's residence with a mixture of fascination and curiosity. The "Nest," he'd explained, housed upward of two hundred mudlarks. At present, many of them seemed to be hanging from the rafters of the high-ceilinged great room. Others congregated around the scarred trestle tables, where they alternated between digging into the heaping platters of food and throwing morsels at one another. Still others lounged on the room's battered furnishings, playing cards, palavering, or napping.

The place was absolute mayhem. It looked like it hadn't had a proper cleaning in weeks. Maybe ever.

"What did I say about swinging from the lights?" Cull's voice boomed. *"Off."*

Three children dropped from the heavy metal ring of the chandelier onto a table, chortling as they ran off to engage in some other mischief. Seeing those tots play warmed Pippa as much as the fire crackling in the massive stone hearth. For shining through the dirt and disorder was that rare, sought-after vein of happiness. She was reminded of the loving chaos of her own childhood home. Of witnessing the foundlings at the Hunt Academy flourish under caring attention.

An unexpected wave of longing washed over her. As Longmere hadn't gotten on with her family nor approved of her being so "hands-on" with the foundlings, she'd spent less and less time at the academy. Since Longmere's death, she hadn't returned. Not out of a lack of interest but because she was...ashamed.

Of how easily she'd given up the people and work she loved. Of how readily she'd traded her independence—*herself*—to gain her husband's approval.

"I've been looking for a housekeeper," Cull said. "They are surprisingly hard to come by."

The brusque words made her realize that he had been studying her. That he'd misinterpreted her silent anguish as a reaction to his home.

"What makes a home isn't the housekeeping but the welfare of those inside. Your larks look happy and healthy," she said quietly.

He grunted. "They're a pack of bleeding savages."

His gruff affection did that funny thing to her insides again. When she'd first met Longmere, he'd given her butterflies too. The thought chilled her.

Timothy Cullen and his mudlarks are no concern of yours, she reminded herself. *You came to tell him to leave you alone, remember? See to his wound, deliver your message, and get out.*

"Where do you want me to look at your arm?" she asked abruptly.

"We'll use the infirmary."

She knitted her brows. "You have an infirmary?"

Cull suddenly looked behind her, barking, "What did I just say, Teddy?"

Pippa's heart seized when she saw that a ginger-haired boy had snuck back onto the chandelier and was swinging upside down by his knees. Suddenly, he lost his hold, plummeting head-first to the ground.

Swearing, Cull raced over.

Thankfully, the boy got to his feet and appeared generally undamaged.

"I ain't feeling so good," he said woozily.

"Maybe next time you'll listen, Teddy." Sighing, Cull hauled the tot under his good arm, carrying him like an untrained puppy. "Come with us."

From the great room, Pippa followed Cull through a warren of passageways. Anyone unfamiliar with the Nest would get lost in the winding maze, and she kept her steps brisk to keep up with her host. As they passed various chambers, she noted with some surprise the resemblance with the Hunt Academy. There were dormitories for the boys and girls, and what appeared to be...classrooms?

Adult larks were giving lessons to the younger ones. Pippa passed a room covered in mats, where a female lark demonstrated defensive maneuvers and ways to evade an attacker. In the next room, a male lark was blowing on a whistle as his smaller comrades scaled ropes suspended from the ceiling and practiced balancing upon narrow wood beams. The room after that had a group of adults clustered around a chalkboard, writing down...the prices of crops and coal? One of the larks spotted Pippa and closed the door.

"You train your charges rigorously," Pippa mused.

Cull cast a glance back at her. "I don't send them out unprepared."

Hearing his disgruntled tone, she realized she'd unintentionally offended him. Before she could apologize, the boy tucked beneath Cull's arm spoke.

"Cull don't let us go on missions unless we're ready." The tot twisted his head to look at her. "I 'aven't gone on one yet on account o' failing the reading test."

"You're taught to read?" Pippa said in surprise.

The mudlarks' curriculum had more similarities to the Hunt Academy than she'd first supposed.

"Curb your tongue, lad," Cull said curtly. "That is mudlark business."

Teddy fell silent until they reached the infirmary, which contained neatly made cots and a wall lined with cupboards. A woman with salt-and-pepper hair was folding linens on a table. When Cull set Teddy down, the boy ran over to her.

"Mrs. Needles!" Teddy cried.

The lady crouched, meeting him eye to eye. "Oh, dear. Back again, Teddy?"

"I banged me 'ead," the child said solemnly. "It 'urts."

"Let's go take a look at that lump, shall we?" Mrs. Needles stood up, her gaze landing on Pippa. "Beg your pardon, ma'am. I didn't see you there."

"This is Mrs. Needles, our matron." Cull paused, raising his brows in silent question.

Appreciating his discretion, Pippa introduced herself. "I am Pippa Lumley. It is a pleasure to make your acquaintance, Mrs. Needles."

"She pushed Cull out o' 'arm's way," Teddy exclaimed. "Brave one, ain't she?"

"Indeed. I am doubly pleased to meet you, ma'am." Mrs. Needles shifted her gaze to Cull. "Why, Cull, your arm is bleeding. I'll need to bandage that up."

"You take care of Teddy." Cull glanced at Pippa, his gaze unfathomable. "Mrs. Lumley has volunteered to look after me."

Cull was playing with fire, and he knew it.

Having Pippa this close was a mistake, but he couldn't make himself put a stop to it. They were in one of the private rooms, which Mrs. Needles used to treat more serious injuries. Cull's wound wasn't serious by any means, but he wasn't about to turn down an opportunity to be naked on a bed with Pippa. Even if the bed was a cot, and he was sitting on it while Pippa stood. And all right, he was the only one naked and hardly that: he was down to his shirtsleeves, his sleeve rolled up so that she could fix his arm.

But Christ Almighty, it felt good to be near her.

She didn't seem as taken with the situation. She kept her gaze studiously on his nicked forearm, cleaning the gash with hot water, an adorable furrow between her brows. Call him depraved, but he fancied her in men's garb, which accentuated her femininity. Her trousers outlined her long, slender legs. She'd removed her cap and coat, the rounded mounds of her breasts straining her waistcoat in eye-popping ways. Her hair was simply coiled at her nape, stray swirls of sunshine escaping and framing her face.

"You'll live," she announced.

I'd die a happy man where I am. "Thank you," he said.

"I didn't do much." She wound a bandage around his arm, her head bent over the task. "Just cleaned you up a bit."

"You risked your neck to save mine. You could have been hurt." Dark energy pumped through his veins; if anything had happened to her because of him, he would lose his bloody mind. "Don't do anything that stupid again."

Her head snapped up. "You are calling me stupid?"

Bleeding hell. He'd never been good with words.

"Not you. Your actions," he began.

She braced her hands on her slim hips. "So you are saying I *acted* stupidly."

Aye, bad with words he was. And even worse at explaining himself.

"You're right," she went on before he could dig himself a deeper grave. "I *am* foolish for bothering to help you, Timothy Cullen. When my *actual* purpose was to tell you to stay the blazes away from me!"

He blinked. A rumble started in his chest and escaped from his mouth.

Ire flashed in Pippa's eyes. "Are you *laughing* at me?"

He was trying to stop. He really was. But he'd never met a

woman as full of endearing contradictions as Pippa. Who was so
intent on protecting herself with a prickly shell that she'd
forgotten her own tender heart.

"I should have let you get shot," she said through pearly
gritted teeth. "But since you are regrettably alive, I will deliver my
message: call off your mudlarks. I neither want, nor need, your
interference in my life. In fact, I'll be happy if I never see your
blasted face again!"

She whirled to leave, and he couldn't let her go. He caught her
by the waist, pulling her between his legs. With her standing and
him sitting, they were eye to eye. She shoved at his shoulders, but
he held on tight.

"I'm sorry," he said.

At his apology, she stilled.

He pushed his luck further.

"I wasn't laughing at you but the situation. It's amusing," he
admitted. "That you'd save a fellow who you were going to tell to
sod off."

She stared at him, her thick lashes fanning. They were sable,
like her fine curving brows, and an alluring contrast to her golden
locks.

"That *was* silly of me," she said. "The shooter could have put
an end to my problems."

Since her lips had a wry curve, he decided that she didn't
really want him dead. Which was an improvement.

"By the by." She eyed him. "Why is there a list of people who
want you dead?"

"My charming personality?" When she didn't smile at his jest,
Cull sighed. "The mudlarks have enemies. Cutthroats who want
to take us over for power and profit."

"Like that blackguard Crooke who beat you when you were
just a lad?"

"Aye," he said in surprise. "I didn't think you would
remember."

"My memory is not lacking."

"Not a single thing about you is lacking."

She narrowed her gaze. "Are you flirting with me while sporting a bullet wound?"

The words echoed what she'd said to him all those years ago. Because of her, those had been the happiest weeks of his life. Yearning, hot and unrequited, incinerated his control.

"I would flirt with you even if I were at death's door. I've missed you, Pippa." The truth left him, stark and unstoppable. "I have never stopped thinking about you."

"You left," she said stiffly. "Without bothering to say goodbye."

"I'm sorry. I...I didn't want to leave, but the mudlarks needed me."

Uncertainty clouded her brow before she drew herself up. "It matters not. It is all in the past."

"Not for me." He pulled her against him, gazing into her wide eyes. "I'll always dream of you, sunshine. Dream of this."

Swooping down, he gave her the kiss of his fantasies.

What in heaven's name are you doing? Pippa's inner voice protested. *Push him away. Push him...ooh...*

The voice faded. There was only Cull and the hot possession of his mouth.

She'd wondered if time had romanticized her memory of their kiss in the bell tower. Of that toe-curling feeling she'd had of being worshipped. But, no, she hadn't imagined it: the tender drag of Cull's lips, the way he courted her mouth with gentle pressure, made her feel special. Wanted.

Yet she was no longer the innocent girl she'd once been. She was a woman who'd been through too much. Who'd gambled on love and lost. While she'd lost faith in that fickle emotion, however, a different kind of desire remained. A desire that her marriage had never assuaged, even though she'd tried to find pleasure with her husband.

"Pippa, whatever is the matter with you?" Edwin's appalled tones pierced her to the quick. *"Lie still; such forward behavior is unbecoming of a lady. You really ought to watch your wine at supper."*

She remembered her stammering apology. As she unearthed that buried trove of shame, what she felt wasn't embarrassment: it was a wave of strange and uncontrollable *anger.* She was tired of denying her needs. Of denying herself.

If Cull doesn't like me the way I am, she thought darkly, *then he can take himself off.*

Spearing her fingers into Cull's thick hair, she jerked him closer. She felt his start of surprise...and was ready to bolt the moment he rejected her. His response was a low growl that sent a tremor through her. The next instant, she was arcing through the air, and when she caught her breath, she was flat on her back.

On the cot. Pinned beneath Cull. His tongue was *inside* her mouth.

When he delved deeper, a bold and aggressive thrust, she answered with a moan. No one had ever kissed her this way before, and in case no one would again, she was determined to make the most of it. She let her instincts take the lead, licking him back, and his groan told her he liked that. She liked it too; the slick rub of their tongues released a cascade of sensations. The tips of her unbound breasts stiffened against her shirt, and damp warmth bloomed between her legs.

Cull plundered her mouth. She kissed him back, letting him sweep his tongue into her tender cove and doing the same to him. Abandoning herself to the dizzying discovery that a kiss could be so much more than a pressing together of lips. Tenderness gave way to hunger, and they ate at each other's mouths. She buzzed with energy as if she'd suddenly come awake after a lifetime of sleeping.

This is passion, she thought dazedly. *What I have always dreamed of.*

"Jesus wept, you're even sweeter than I remembered," Cull said in a guttural voice.

He trailed kisses over her cheek and nuzzled the curve of her ear. She shivered as he tongued the sensitive lobe before sucking it deep. Need pulsed from her ear to her breasts to her woman's place until she was throbbing everywhere. Needing everywhere. She ran her palms over Cull's shoulders, marveling at the thick ridges of muscle beneath the rough linen, the strength of this man whose lips were now fastened upon her throat.

Sucking, licking. Nipping.

She was light-headed, floating in his scent of soap and sea. He unbuttoned her waistcoat and cupped her breast. When he thumbed her nipple through the fabric of her shirt, she moaned. He licked a path from her collarbone to her ear while strumming her sensitive nub. When he pinched lightly, she felt that sweet throbbing between her legs. Poised on the precipice of pleasure, she was ready to leap.

He raised his head, and her heart stuttered at the ravenous desire in his eyes.

"You are so bloody beautiful," he rasped. "I've waited so long for this."

Mesmerized by his yearning, she felt an answering recognition. A sense of rightness. When he reached for the buttons of her shirt, she put her hand on his.

"Wait," she said.

He was motionless, his gaze questioning. "Do you want me to stop?"

"No, but please take off your mask." Feeling oddly shy, she said, "I want to see you."

His large body tensed above hers. "Pippa, I...I don't think that is a good idea."

She blinked. "Why?"

He sat up on the edge of the cot. Away from her.

Raking a hand through his hair, he said, "I don't take my mask off in front of outsiders."

A chill pervaded her. All of a sudden, she was thrown back to a year ago when Livy had informed her of Longmere's death and his heinous and clandestine activities.

Secrets and lies. Longmere had specialized in them. If Pippa had learned anything from her marriage, it was to avoid a man like her dead husband. A man she could not trust. Who would shower her with compliments, make her feel special, then pull the rug from under her feet. Yet here she was with the dashed *Prince* of Secrets...

Who already left me hanging once. Why am I such a fool?

Furious at herself, she surged to her feet. "I have to go."

"Pippa—"

"Don't, Cull." She cut him off with a glare. "This was a mistake. If you come near me again, I vow you will regret it."

Propelled by the threatening heat behind her eyes, she fled.

8

"My dear Pippa, how tired you look." The Dowager Countess of Longmere took a tiny sip of the Darjeeling and, with a slight grimace, set it aside. "Are you not sleeping well?"

Pippa kept her polite smile fixed in place. She'd had plenty of practice when it came to her mama-in-law. Five minutes into the monthly visit, the dowager had already found fault with the temperature of Pippa's parlor, firmness of the divan cushions, and texture of the biscuits.

"Thank you for your concern, Mama," Pippa replied. "My sleep has been undisturbed."

Unless one counted the dreams she'd been having about Cull. The ones where she woke up, dazed and damp with perspiration, the sheets twisted around her legs. The taste and smell of him filled her senses as she lay there, heart pounding and unmentionable parts aching. On several nights, matters had gotten so desperate that she'd had to resort to an improper relief.

The brief remedy she found for her bodily tension did not assuage her mental turmoil. Thoughts of Cull consumed her. How good he'd made her feel...and how wretched.

She was reminded all too keenly of the early stages with

Edwin. The giddiness and passion. While not as flowery and effu-sive as her dead spouse, Cull's seemingly honest professions had made her thrum with a familiar longing. And his touch...she'd never experienced such pleasure with Edwin. Cull had weakened her defenses, even though she knew full well the dangers of getting involved with him.

He was a fellow who could not be trusted. Who specialized in secrets. She was still licking the wounds inflicted by her marriage; the last thing she needed was another man in her life.

Even if that man looked after urchins who clearly adored him. Even if he had come to her aid. Even if he looked at her with soulful yearning and his touch made her come alive with desire.

Gah.

"You needn't hide your feelings." The dowager shook her head, which was covered in a severe black turban. Her rail-thin figure was draped in a matching shade that seemed to suck the light from the room. "We are family, after all. I know how hard it must be for you with dear Edwin gone. You must wonder what the point is in continuing."

Of all the things Pippa had been contemplating, not contin-uing hadn't been one of them. Not wanting to disappoint her mama-in-law, she said, "He has been greatly missed."

"He was the light of our lives, not to mention a luminary in the world of art." The dowager dabbed at her eyes with a black silk handkerchief. "To lose him and his genius in one fell swoop... how could Fate be so cruel?"

Pippa didn't have an answer for that. But seeing as the dowager asked the same question at every visit, she knew one wasn't expected.

"The Lord works in mysterious ways," she murmured.

Her mama-in-law's snort could have been construed as blas-phemous. "True grief—that of a mother for her only child—cannot be consoled by platitudes. Now, speaking of Edwin's art, I do not see his crowning achievement. Why has his *pièce de resistance* been moved from its place of honor?"

The dowager *would* notice. A few days ago, Pippa had moved *Portrait of a Lady Dreaming* from above the parlor mantel, replacing it with another of Edwin's paintings. Having the portrait of the woman with the red-gold hair and sad turquoise eyes on public display had felt too painful. It symbolized Pippa's mistakes, including the secret she'd kept that had led to Edwin's death.

"You did not sell the piece, did you, Pippa?"

"Of course not, Mama," she said hastily. "It is in my sitting room."

She didn't mention that she had left it on the ground, the canvas facing the wall.

"Where no one will see it?" Outrage amplified the shrillness of the dowager's voice. "Why would you dishonor my son's genius in such a fashion?"

"I thought it might be nice to rotate his paintings. The study of the fruit bowl looks quite charming above the mantel, don't you think?" Pippa said lamely.

If the fruits had been real, they would have spoiled beneath the heat of the dowager's glare.

"Need I remind you that *Portrait of a Lady Dreaming* was chosen to be exhibited by the Royal Society? That painting was Edwin's grandest achievement. I cannot think of a single reason why it should not be showcased in a place of honor, can you?"

Because that painting is a fraud. Because every time I see it, I want to cry. Or scream.

Pippa held her tongue; it wasn't for nothing that she'd earned the moniker of Patient Pippa. What people didn't realize was that she wasn't necessarily more patient than the next person. She was just better at curbing her words. Her thoughts, however, were a different matter.

As trying as she found these visits, Pippa would never hurt her husband's mother. The lady had lost her only child, and even though she thought Pippa wasn't good enough for her son—and Pippa knew this because she'd overheard the dowager say repeatedly to Edwin, *"That gel is not good enough for you, my darling boy"*—the lady had few close relatives. Even fewer friends.

Thus, it was Pippa's duty to look after the dowager.

"I shall have the portrait reinstalled above the mantel, if you wish," she said.

"See that you do." Looking somewhat mollified, the dowager said, "While we are on the subject of honoring my son, have you been keeping up your visits to Kensal Green?"

The dowager had insisted on burying Edwin in the exclusive General Cemetery for All Souls in Kensal Green. She'd wanted a mausoleum and a plot as close as possible to that of Prince Augustus Frederick, the Duke of Sussex. To afford that royal proximity, Pippa had sold off some of her jewelry.

She stifled a sigh. "Yes, Mama."

The dowager shifted her discontent to another target. "Have you done something different with your hair? It is distractingly bright."

Pippa's maid had arranged her hair into its usual style, parted in the middle, with ringlets falling to her shoulders. For her mama-in-law's visit, she'd worn a black lace-edged mourning cap that covered most of her coiffure.

"I've done nothing different," she said.

"Perhaps it is your gown then. Are you certain it is quite dark enough?"

Pippa looked down at her somber skirts. "My dress is black."

"A smoky shade closer to charcoal, I should say." The dowager pressed her lips into a line so thin her mouth nearly vanished. "And the luster of the fabric is suggestive of levity, most inappropriate given the occasion."

"It is bombazine." *Also known as the mourning cloth.*

"There is bombazine, and there is bombazine." The dowager

sniffed. "Where you come from, my dear, the difference may go unnoticed, but not so in your current position. Must I remind you of your duty? While my son may be dead, you still bear his name. Mourning him properly is the least you can do considering you bore nothing else of his."

Chewing the inside of her cheek, Pippa said nothing.

"I will give you the name of my modiste." Her mama-in-law gave her a once-over. "She can fix any problem."

It's always nice to be referred to as a problem, isn't it?

Pippa took a calming breath and asked, "More tea?"

The dowager stayed longer than usual. As a result, Pippa felt frayed by the time she headed over to Charlie's. The visit with her mama-in-law brought to bear the errors of her past, the ones she was determined not to repeat.

Ergo, she was done with men. What she needed was a different purpose.

A week had passed; hopefully, Charlie would deem her ready to start investigating again. Hawker, Charlie's butler and the Angels' teacher, ushered Pippa in. He looked his usual piratical self with his shaved head, dark beard, and eye patch.

He peered at her. "You ain't been sleeping well. Something troubling you, lass?"

Was the state of her emotions so dashed obvious?

"I just missed being here," she managed to say lightly.

"Your presence was missed." Hawker led the way to Charlie's study. "But a respite can be good for the body and mind. *The end of labor is to gain leisure.*"

"Aristotle?" she guessed.

While teaching practical skills such as lockpicking and developing "sticky fingers," Hawker also liked to infuse his lessons with the teachings of philosophers.

"Always were a sharp one, lass." A smile flashed in his beard as he opened the door to the study. "Go on in. Lady Fayne's expecting you."

Charlie was standing by the study's tall windows, the sun burnishing her honey-blonde hair, her full merlot skirts rustling as she turned. Relieved to see her welcoming smile, Pippa went over to exchange air kisses.

"It is good to see you, my dear." Charlie studied her with astute grey eyes. "How was your week?"

"Fine." Deciding to head off any comments on her appearance, Pippa said, "The reason I look peaked is because my mama-in-law paid me a visit."

"Ah." Charlie's mouth curved wryly. "How bad was it?"

"I feel like I was put through one of those new-fangled washing machines."

"Your forbearance is worthy of a saint. Especially since you have protected the dowager from the truth of her son's sins."

Not wanting to discuss her husband, Pippa said, "I am ready to work again, Charlie. If I don't find something to occupy my time, I fear I shall go mad."

"If you are certain you are ready—"

"I'm certain."

"Then I must first ask you a question."

Pippa tilted her head.

"What transpired during your visit to the Nest?"

Taken off-guard, Pippa stammered, "You...you had me followed?"

"I am concerned about your welfare. And about the Prince of Larks's interest in you," Charlie said bluntly. "If he is harassing one of my agents, I will deal with him."

Seeing Charlie's steely expression, Pippa knew that her mentor meant every word. While she planned to steer clear of Cull, she couldn't let Charlie think that he was an enemy of the Angels.

She took a breath. "He isn't harassing me. On the contrary, his intention has been to protect me—even though I neither need nor asked for his help. On the night in question, however, I went to him."

"Why?"

"At first, it was because I saw that one of Cull's larks had followed me home. It made me angry," she admitted. "I was determined to turn the tables on him, so I trailed him back to the Nest. I was going to tell him to back off...but when a ruffian came out of nowhere and tried to shoot him, I intervened."

Charlie's gaze narrowed. "Cull, is it?"

"That was what he went by. When I knew him all those years ago," she said falteringly.

"I need you to be honest, Pippa. What are your feelings toward him?"

The question battered at her dam of self-control. To her horror, heat swelled behind her eyes.

She fought back the tears, blurting, "I'm so confused."

"As men are perplexing creatures, that is no surprise. Do you wish to talk about it?"

Charlie's will was formidable, her compassion even more so.

"Even though Longmere has been gone for a year, I still haven't regained my equilibrium," Pippa said in halting tones. "There are times I feel fine, almost like myself. Then at others, I feel sad and confused and..."

"Angry?" Charlie said matter-of-factly.

Pippa swallowed. "It isn't fair of me to be angry. Longmere is dead. And he...he suffered for his mistakes."

"Grief isn't about fairness. It can take many forms, none of them right or wrong." Charlie's beautiful face hardened. "As widows, we are expected to mourn for our husbands, no matter what went on in our marriages. Sadness is the only public face we are allowed to show. It is only in private that we grapple with the complexities of what they left behind. I speak from personal experience. When Fayne passed, I grieved...but I also felt disappointment and rage."

The words resonated like a church bell.

"I have felt disappointment...and anger as well," Pippa confessed.

"That is a natural part of healing. You needn't feel guilty, my dear."

Pippa wished it were as simple as that. She hadn't told Charlie —or anyone—about the role she'd played in Edwin's demise. She couldn't undo her mistake, but she could preserve the one thing of value she'd given her husband.

"Now tell me how Timothy Cullen fits into the picture," Charlie went on.

"He kissed me. And I...I kissed him back."

"Ah." Charlie's jaw tightened. "How far did things go?"

"Not far...beyond the kissing. But they could have," Pippa said in a low voice. "If he hadn't refused to remove his mask. That brought me back to my senses. Made me realize that I was dealing with yet another man who would hide things from me. And I left."

"A wise choice," Charlie said with a brisk nod. "The Prince of Larks has made his fortune from secrets. I have never seen him without his mask; it's part of his enigmatic persona."

Pippa recalled the way Cull had been with the children at the Nest. In those moments, he hadn't seemed enigmatic. He'd been gruff, kind, and exasperated...as any big brother dealing with a houseful of unruly siblings would be.

"And yet, I felt things with him," Pippa divulged. "Things I've never felt before. Not even with..."

It was too shameful to say aloud. To admit that she'd experienced pleasure with a virtual stranger that she hadn't with the man she'd fallen in love with and married. Over the course of her marriage, she'd begun to fear that she might be...broken in some way. That there might be something wrong with her physically that prevented her from enjoying marital pleasures.

"Although Society tries to convince us otherwise, women have desires just like men do. And these desires are not always—and *rarely*, I daresay—satisfied in marriage," Charlie said.

With thrumming relief, Pippa said, "What I felt with Cull was rather powerful. And I don't want to repeat my mistakes because I am swept up in those feelings. I don't want to fall for a man and end up hurt in the end."

"Are you falling for Mr. Cullen or simply experiencing desire for him?"

Pippa furrowed her brow; she hadn't considered the difference. "I...I don't know."

"We ladies are taught that love and desire must go hand in hand; I call this the Great Lie, one that has been used since the beginning of time to control feminine passion," Charlie said crisply. "Desire is simply a need...like an appetite for food or drink. Love has naught to do with it; indeed, it can muddy the waters. After all, you see men indulging in lust without emotional attachments. Why should the same not hold true for women?"

Faced with that logic, Pippa could only think, *Why not indeed?*

With a flash of insight, she realized that she'd been afraid of the strong reaction Cull evoked in her. Afraid that it meant she was headed down the same painful path as her marriage. But lust —and yes, that had to be what she'd experienced with Cull, whom she hardly knew—was *not* the same as love. She wasn't falling for Cull the way she had for Edwin. Conversely, she hadn't felt half as much pleasure with her husband as she had with Cull.

Desire and love *were* different. If Charlie was correct, then desire was common—a mere appetite. Maybe what Pippa felt with Cull she could have felt with another man. With a dozen other men.

"Moreover, needs can be met outside the marital bower," her

mentor said. "In safe and discreet ways that are far more enjoy-able than sacrificing oneself on the altar of matrimony."

Intrigued, Pippa asked, "What ways?"

"You are a widow. As such, you have independence denied unmarried ladies. You are free to pursue your passions...as long as you don't get caught." Charlie gave her a considering look. "I know of an exclusive club where women of a liberated mindset go to explore their desires. Perhaps it is just the place to help put Timothy Cullen behind you."

9

"There's no need to be nervous, dearie." The proprietress of The Enchanted Rose, who'd introduced herself as Mrs. Loverly, gave Pippa's arm a maternal pat. "Lady Fayne told me to take special care of you, and any friend of the good lady is a friend of mine."

A *frisson* of excitement passed through Pippa. At the same time, her heart lurched at her scandalous undertaking. She couldn't believe that she'd worked up the nerve to visit a male bawdy house. Her talk with Charlie, however, had convinced her that she needed to expand her horizons. She was tired of being caged by grief, sorrow, and regret. Of feeling lost and confused.

Tonight, she wanted to be free.

As Mrs. Loverly led her down a sumptuous scarlet corridor, Pippa noticed the paintings. Framed in gilt, the pieces were close-up studies of flowers...that bore an uncanny resemblance to a woman's private part. Pippa stared at a rendering of a pink rose: the tiny bud was surrounded by lush petals dripping with pearly dew.

"The paintings are for sale." The bawd's wink was jovial, a

crimson plume bobbing in her improbably raven hair. "That one is called *The Peak of Pleasure*, and it's a bargain at fifty pounds. The frame is extra, of course."

"Oh." Cheeks flaming beneath her golden mask, Pippa cast about for another topic. "You, um, know Lady Fayne well?"

"She helped me out of a bind, she did. Took on my case when no one else would. Thanks to her, I was able to stop a blackmailer from bleeding me dry. From then on, I said to myself, we women must stick together."

"Indeed," Pippa murmured.

"Now, when we arrive in the drawing room, you go ahead and mingle as you would at any high-kick affair. In truth, many of the ladies will be your acquaintances but, like you, they will be masked and disguised. There's no need to feel uncomfortable, dearie. You're all here for the same purpose."

To find a lover for the night, Pippa thought with a tingle.

"I keep the finest studs in my stables. Anyone you pick will give you a splendid ride—and as many rides as you wish for the evening," Mrs. Loverly said with a throaty chuckle. "My mounts are known for their stamina."

Pippa's knees wobbled. *Am I really going through with this?*

It was too late for second thoughts, for they'd arrived at the drawing room. A pair of handsome footmen bowed and opened the double doors, releasing a swell of voices and perfume. The elegantly appointed chamber was packed with people. Ladies in elaborate costumes conversed with males whose physical assets were on shocking display. Although the men wore black demi-masks, they'd left off their shirts, their muscular torsos inviting the female gaze. Their lower halves were clad in tight leather breeches that left little to the imagination.

Swallowing, Pippa felt as if her feet were bolted to the ground. Her courage dissolved as she watched a lady run beringed fingers over the taut ridges of a man's abdomen and over his bulging groin.

This is a mistake, she thought in panic. *I cannot do this...*

"Come along, dearie." The proprietress took Pippa's arm and dragged her over the threshold. "Let me introduce you to the *crème de la crème* that The Enchanted Rose has to offer."

A glass of champagne eased Pippa's nerves. At least enough for her to observe her surroundings with curiosity rather than alarm. As Mrs. Loverly guided her around the chamber, she noted the mix of the clientele. Although the women were disguised, Pippa guessed that they spanned a range of ages. They were short, tall, plump, thin, and every shape in between. What they had in common was the boldness to pursue what they wanted. What society told them they should not want and could not have.

Pippa, whatever is the matter with you? Edwin's voice rose like a specter. *Such forward behavior is unbecoming of a lady.*

Back then, all she'd done was try to participate in their couplings—to do something other than lie still beneath him, close her eyes, and think of England. Edwin, however, had accused her of being unladylike.

If only he could see me now, Pippa thought wryly.

Remembering her anticipation on her wedding night and how it had fizzled into disappointment, she felt a smoldering beneath her breastbone.

Mrs. Loverly's voice cut through her thoughts. "Dearie, allow me to introduce you to Baldur."

Pippa eyed the golden-haired man. Mrs. Loverly's "studs" used the names of Norse gods, and this one lived up to his namesake. He was beautiful and refined, the smooth muscles of his torso gleaming in the candlelight. Below his half-mask, his chiseled lips formed a seductive curve.

He took Pippa's hand and kissed it. "The pleasure is all mine."

His touch wasn't unpleasant. Nor was his conversation. Mrs.

Loverly drifted off, leaving Pippa in a quiet corner of the room
with her potential lover for the eve. She and Baldur chatted about
light topics, and he shared an amusing anecdote. As the minutes
passed, however, she realized something was missing.

As handsome as Baldur was, she didn't feel any pull toward
him. Their conversation revealed they had little in common. Or,
perhaps, neither of them felt comfortable revealing anything of
substance. The superficiality of their exchange, the empty compliments and sultry innuendoes, wore on her nerves. She fished for
an excuse to leave.

"Pardon, I need to get a breath of air," Pippa said. "Alone."

Baldur's jaw took on a determined angle. Likely he didn't want
the time he'd invested in her to be wasted.

"Before you depart, sweeting." He planted his hands on the
wall behind her and leaned his body into hers. "May I give you a
sample of my talents?"

She could have refused. But he was close, and she was curious.
Might as well find out if kissing one man was any different from
kissing another. When his lips touched hers, she waited with
bated breath. For the spark. The sizzle. The fire of hunger that
Cull's kiss had lit in her.

And what she felt was...nothing.

Her heartbeat was calm, her breathing unaffected.

Strangely relieved, she broke the kiss. "Thank you. Now I
must go."

Baldur's charming smile did not reach his eyes. "Come find me
when you return."

Pippa took the back exit from the room. She found herself in
another sumptuous corridor, this one lined with closed doors. Her
insides quivered at the muffled sounds of passion. Memories of
being entangled with Cull on the cot swamped her. The scorching
need she'd felt in his arms. The mind-melting desire.

Why is he the only one who makes me feel that way? she mused.

A door opened at the end of the corridor, interrupting her thoughts. A couple slipped out...a brunette and a man with shoulder-length mahogany hair. When they glanced at Pippa, she froze. The man was singularly handsome, his eyes a striking shade of silver in his black mask. But it was the brunette who held Pippa's attention: although the woman wore a lacy white demi-mask, she looked a lot like Lady Julianna Hastings. Same thin build, same plain features albeit lacquered with paint. What was the lady doing in a place like this?

What are you *doing here?* Pippa's inner voice pointed out dryly. *Pot, meet kettle.*

Given what she knew of the lady's union, Pippa didn't judge the other for searching out extramarital pleasure. Lady Hastings turned back to her escort, showing no signs of recognizing Pippa. Of course, the viscountess only knew Pippa socially and had no idea that Pippa was part of the investigative society working on her behalf. Or, rather, the society that *had* been doing so. Pippa wished the lady hadn't terminated the Angels' services. She didn't trust Viscount Hastings and thought he might be capable of hurting his wife.

When Lady Hastings and her partner walked off, disappearing around a corner, Pippa considered following. She knew it wasn't her place, that she had to respect the client's decision, but she felt unsettled. She remembered all the times she'd ignored her intuition when it came to Edwin. When she'd stood by and done nothing while he'd dug himself a grave.

What can you do to help Lady Hastings? her inner voice reasoned. *It is not as if you can speak with her, try to convince her to let the Angels help.*

Nonetheless, Pippa's feet led her in the direction that Lady Hastings had gone. When she reached the end of the hallway, she peered around the corner: another corridor and no sign of the couple. Only a masked gentleman striding toward her. Unlike the other males, he was fully dressed, his stark evening wear fitted like a glove to his brawny form.

Awareness sizzled through her. Her heart came alive, a wild, thrashing thing in her chest.

"Dash it," she exclaimed as he came to a stop in front of her. "What are *you* doing here?"

10

"I could ask you the same thing," Cull gritted out. "Seeing as the answer is obvious, however, I'll spare my breath."

Pippa's eyes narrowed in the holes of her mask. Even with her brunette wig, those glorious blue orbs suited her. What didn't suit her was being in a godforsaken brothel teeming with male prostitutes. And *kissing* one of those undeserving bastards, to make matters worse.

Molten jealousy sizzled through Cull's veins. Logically, he knew that he had no claim on her, but he didn't give a bloody damn about rationality. A week ago, *he* had been the one kissing Pippa. *His* lips had been on hers; her sweet moans had belonged to *him*. Things might have progressed a great deal further, if not for his ugliness. When confronted with all her glowing beauty, how could he have revealed himself for the beast that he was?

He hadn't had an answer then, and he didn't have one now.

But he did know this: hell would freeze over before he let some Casanova-for-hire service Pippa. It was one thing when Cull couldn't offer her what she deserved: a respectable, high-class marriage. He'd stayed in the shadows, knowing that Longmere's world was the one she belonged in. But now Pippa wasn't after propriety, was she?

She wanted a night of pleasure.

And Cull *could* give her that. He burned to show her all the ways a man could satisfy a woman; hell, he'd been fantasizing about her for *fourteen bloody years*. If Pippa was willing to take on a masked stranger as a lover—one who hid behind the name of a Norse god, for Christ's sake—what did it matter if Cull kept on his mask? There had to be a way to make this work. For them to be together...if only for tonight.

He'd spent the week mulling over the matter like a namby-pamby fool. Vacillating between his desire for Pippa and what was best for her. Now clarity struck him: from the moment they'd met, he had wanted her...and always would. Why couldn't he, for once, go after what he wanted? If she wanted a taste of carnal bliss, why shouldn't he be the one to give it to her?

Of course, Pippa might need convincing of his plan.

"What I do is none of your dashed business." She crossed her arms. "How did you find me here?"

"Ain't a thing that happens in London without my knowledge, if I take an interest." Having made his decision, he saw no point in beating around the bush. "When it comes to you, sunshine, I'm definitely interested."

"Of all the arrogant, high-handed, *conceited*..." She balled her hands at her sides, apparently running out of synonyms.

In truth, Pippa was adorable spitting mad. He was wise enough not to share that observation. Her eyes had an alluring glitter, and in the low-cut vee of her violet gown, the creamy tops of her breasts heaved in a way that gave his eye muscles pleasant exercise. She was also sputtering as if she wasn't used to being angry. Or expressing it, anyway. He thought it was a positive sign that he could evoke strong feelings in her.

If those feelings could be something other than animosity, I'd be onto something.

Hearing voices approach, he took her arm.

"Let's discuss our business in private," he said under his breath. "Unless you want to air our laundry in public?"

She yanked her arm away and marched toward a door.

He got there first, opening it for her. The room was empty, thank Christ.

As he locked the door behind them, he saw that the chamber was designed with pleasure in mind. The black damask walls framed a large bed fitted with red silk sheets. To the right of it, a wide scarlet divan and rug sat before a blazing fire. Cull felt his eyebrows rise at the other feature of the room: a reclined seat made of leather straps was suspended from the ceiling by four ropes.

It swayed suggestively.

Pippa furrowed her brow. "Why would they have a swing in here?"

Cull cleared his throat, trying to think of a civilized reply while trying not to picture her lying naked in that swing. The things he could do to her...

Get your thoughts out of the gutter, you bastard. This is Pippa. She is a lady.

Just because he was about to propose a night of uninhibited passion didn't mean that he would act in an uncouth manner. Besides, he knew the kind of gents Pippa preferred: sensitive, lordly types like Longmere. Bloody Baldur was cast from a similar mold; slender and refined, he was Cull's polar opposite.

Cull couldn't change his physical attributes, but he did have manners.

"A diverting way to get off one's feet, no doubt," he said blandly. "Perhaps the divan is more to your liking?"

She narrowed her eyes at him. "We don't need to sit for this discussion. Answer my question: how did you know I would be here?"

Deciding he had nothing to lose, he told her. "After you left

Lady Fayne's yesterday, she sent a note to this establishment. Out of concern, I kept an eye on you. Sure enough, you headed here tonight."

"In other words, you were spying on me," Pippa said grimly.

"I am looking out for you."

"Spare me the semantics." Tossing him a contemptuous look, she stalked to the blazing hearth.

He tried not to notice how her movements caused the swing to rock subtly back and forth.

"You're ruining everything, and I want you to stop," she fumed.

Had she wanted to be bedded by that blond bastard then? The notion forced a growl from Cull. "What am I ruining? A cozy little romp with *Baldur*? Was he the one you were looking for just now?"

"For your information, I was on my way out when I saw a cl —" She cut herself off. "Someone I know."

Relief eased the knots in his chest. Running through his mental list of her clients, he deduced who was most likely to be in attendance.

"Lady Hastings?" he surmised. "I thought she terminated your services a week ago."

"How did you..." She planted her hands on her hips. "My business is none of yours."

"Was she why you were peering around the corner?"

"I was not *peering*. I was simply looking for her because I was worried."

"Because you think her husband has dastardly intentions toward her?"

She heaved out a breath. "Do you ever tire of being such a know-it-all?"

He laughed; he couldn't help it. He'd been called many things, but a know-it-all? Never.

"You're delightful," he said, earning another huff from her.

"And, yes, I do get tired of it. Of knowing things I'd rather not. Such as the fact that the woman I recently kissed planned to spend the evening with another man."

"You have no claim on me," she said. "I am my own woman. I can do what I want."

"Aye, you are, and you can." He strode toward her, and she froze like a cornered doe. He brushed his knuckles lightly along her jaw before dropping his hand. "And if you are in the market for a lover tonight, I'm applying for the position."

What is happening? Pippa thought dazedly.

One moment, she was annoyed; the next, she was...captivated. Unable to look or pull away.

The sincerity smoldering in Cull's dark-brown eyes was magnetic. Or maybe it was his humility, the way he cut to the truth of his desires without pretense or prevarication. It was the opposite of the nuanced flirtation that she was used to. Cull was telling her point-blank that he wanted to be her lover...and that it was up to her whether she wished to take him up on his offer.

If she wanted to have this man, she could. The choice was hers. The notion made her feel heady, as did his nearness. Baldur, for all his perfection, had affected her senses like a mild breeze. Cull, however?

He hit her like a thunderstorm, every part of her crackling with awareness.

Why should she deny herself what she wanted? It was why she'd come here, wasn't it? To exercise her freedom and experience desire free of emotional entanglements. And to do so on her own terms.

"What do you have to recommend you?" she asked. "As a lover, I mean."

A startled look came into his eyes, followed by an appreciative gleam.

"I know how to pleasure a lady," he murmured. "To my knowledge, I have never left one unsatisfied."

From another man, the reply could have come off like a boast. Yet Cull was clearly in earnest—clearly cared about his partner's pleasure. The fluttering in Pippa's belly increased.

She lifted her brows. "Would you know if you had?"

Edwin hadn't known. Or maybe he hadn't cared. After he'd found his satisfaction, he'd fallen asleep or gone back to his own chamber.

"I bloody well hope so," Cull said.

Again sincere. And flutter-worthy.

"You could be a contender," she allowed. "But I have terms."

"As do I."

Interesting. Cocking her head, she said, "First, this is a one-night-only affair."

"No strings attached," he agreed. "If both parties are amenable, however, we should not discount the possibility of future nights."

"I will not be amenable."

That would be far too dangerous. She could not let herself form an attachment; the whole purpose of this was to satisfy her physical needs without the risk of heartbreak.

He didn't look overly concerned. "Your other terms?"

"Precautions will be necessary."

Pippa was grateful that her mask hid her flaming cheeks. Charlie had coached her to institute this non-negotiable condition. It was one thing to indulge in a night of ardor, another to do so in a reckless manner. Truth be told, Pippa didn't know if she was even able to bear consequences, so to speak. She hadn't conceived in a year of marriage. Another failure that had been laid at her door.

"I have a contraption that will prevent unwanted eventualities," she said briskly.

"One could not accuse you of being unprepared." Humor in his eyes, he went on, "There are many ways to approach lovemaking, sunshine, some of which would render your contraption unnecessary."

She frowned. "I don't understand."

"It will be my pleasure to clarify matters." His mouth twitched. "For now, you have my word of honor that I would never put you at risk. Being acquainted with unwanted consequences—I, myself, being one of them—I have never acted carelessly in this regard."

"Oh." She didn't know what else to say. How to respond to the fact that he'd referred to himself as an "unwanted consequence."

It was getting harder to think in general. She felt a trifle warm, possibly because of the fire and most certainly because of this chat. It struck her as being the most intimate conversation she'd had with any man. Cull didn't seem at all bothered by her demands. In fact, he was studying her with an intensity and, yes, *hunger* that made her blood rush through her veins. Her nipples throbbed beneath her bodice, a matching pulse between her thighs.

"If you have stated all your terms...?"

Had she? "Um, yes."

"Then it's my turn. I have only one: my mask stays on." His shoulders braced, he said, "Last time, I didn't express myself well. It is not because of you that I can't take it off. It is because of me, because of who I am—"

"It doesn't matter," she interrupted.

Strange how this was true. Whereas last time his refusal had ignited her anger, now she found it a relief to have that small barrier between them. To set limits during her exploration of uncharted territory. Not seeing his face made everything less personal...and less potentially painful if this proved to be yet another bad decision on her part.

He drew his brows together. "It doesn't?"

"This is a one-night liaison, not a relationship," she said firmly. "And you're not the only one wearing a mask this eve. I'll keep mine on as well."

His shoulders eased; he released a breath that she hadn't realized he was holding. He brought his hand to her face again, his long fingers trailing along her jawbone and down her throat, the careful, callused touch tightening and loosening everything inside her simultaneously. She swallowed as he cupped the back of her neck, bringing her closer. Close enough to feel the heat radiating between them.

"Pity to keep something so beautiful hidden," he murmured. "Then again, you have countless other attractions to unwrap."

Anticipation made her light-headed as he bent his head. Yet he stopped, a sliver of space between them...and she realized that he was waiting. For her to affirm her choice. She tipped her mouth up, searching out his. The velvety warm contact elicited a sound from her, between a sigh and a moan. This was what she'd been longing for since the last time.

Heavens, the man could kiss.

During her marriage, kissing had become a perfunctory gesture. A peck of greeting or a routine prelude to bedding. But Cull...he kissed her as if he wanted to do it forever. As if there was no other end, nothing he wanted more than just to have his mouth on hers.

Her fervor matched his. When he licked at the seam of her mouth, she invited him in. The hot, bold thrust of his entry mimicked another act that would soon follow, and she shivered from head to toe. If kissing felt this good...

He took his time exploring her mouth. His male taste had an unexpected burst of peppermint. Dentifrice, she realized. She found it oddly endearing that he'd taken the effort to make himself agreeable to her. Not that he'd needed to: kissing him was addictive, his masculine flavor tinder to her fire. She wanted more of him, everything...

"Turn around," he murmured against her lips.

She did, bracing her hands against the wall. The black flock of the paper teased her palms as he unfastened her dress. There was reverence in the way he freed her from the constriction of buttons and laces, as he revealed her layer by layer. When she was down to her chemise and stockings, he kissed her nape, and her silk-covered toes curled with desperate wanting.

He moved closer, sandwiching her between the wall and his brawny frame. The sensation of being surrounded by hardness was delicious. The weight of his manhood pressed into the small of her back, the heft of his virility causing her to dampen with anticipation.

When he suckled her earlobe, her head fell back against his shoulder.

"Arms up, love," he murmured. "Time to show me what I've been waiting on all these years."

She raised her shaking limbs, and he pulled the chemise over her head. Now she was naked, save for her stockings, and bashfulness crept over her. She was no virgin, but she'd only been with her husband, and he'd never made her feel this...exposed.

"Turn for me, sunshine."

Inhaling, she did. Cull's hot, appreciative glance burned away her inhibitions.

"I didn't think it possible, but you're even lovelier than I imagined." His voice was both rough and soft, like the flock of the wallpaper against her spine.

He dropped a kiss on her shoulder, and an odd noise left her.

He gave a husky laugh. "That sound is almost as pretty as you are. Shall we see what else makes you purr?"

He took her hands, pressing them to the wall above her head. His kiss was slow and intoxicating. His brawny, fully clothed chest rubbed against her nipples, setting off sparks of bliss. Wanting more of that exquisite abrasion, she pressed herself against him.

"Impatient minx," he breathed against her ear. "I'll get to those pretty tits of yours. Be warned, however: I plan to suckle them thoroughly."

Heavens.

He took his sweet time getting there...not that she was complaining. He lavished attention on her ears and neck, dragging his tongue along her throat. She let out a surprised gasp when he spun her around again. Her palms flattened against the wall as he winnowed out sensation from parts of her she didn't know were designed for pleasure: the slopes of her shoulder blades, the length of her spine. He explored each vertebra with his tongue until she was trembling like an autumn leaf clinging to a branch.

He didn't stop there. Going down on one knee, he turned his attention to her garters. He undid them one by one, kissing the marks they left before unrolling the silk down her calves.

Rising, he murmured, "Now spread these long, beautiful legs for me."

Pressed against the wall, her cheek burned, but she did as he asked. When his fingers delved into her intimate folds, she whimpered.

"Jesus wept, you're drenched." A growl entered his voice. "I wager you could come for me right now, couldn't you?"

He probed deeper, finding her secret bud of sensation, rubbing it with demanding strokes that arched her back. Goodness, the way he caressed her...it was far better than her own furtive fumbling. Far better than anything she'd experienced. Pleasure gathered inside her, building and building.

"That's right. Ride my hand, love," he urged. "Work that sweet pussy until you spend for me."

His wicked words and skillful touch unraveled her control. She soared to a pinnacle then went over the edge, floating on gusts of ecstasy. Then she suddenly...plummeted. Shivering, disoriented, undone, she felt too good...too much. The release broke a dam inside her.

Cull nipped her earlobe. "Now that we have that out of the way, time for me to sample your delectable nipples..."

He turned her around just as emotions began pouring from her. A powerful flood she couldn't stop. Before she knew what was happening, a sob escaped.

"Pippa?" Cull's eyes blazed with concern. "What's amiss, love? Was I...was I too rough?"

She shook her head but couldn't stop the sounds crowding up her throat. Couldn't stop what she was feeling or explain it. Couldn't do anything but weep. He removed her mask, and too overwhelmed to stop him, she looked away. She didn't want him to see her exposed and pathetic and hurting. Her tears would probably send him running.

Better to be the one to leave.

"I...I have to go..." She reached blindly for her clothes.

And was pulled against Cull's chest, his burly arms holding her securely.

"You're not going anywhere," he said gruffly. "It's all right, sunshine. Let it out."

It wasn't all right. But the fact that he said that it was—that he was here—tore down her remaining defenses. Knowing she had a safe harbor, she surrendered to the torrent.

11

C ull stood at the prow of the barge as it glided over the fog-shrouded Thames, his gut churning like the dark water. Earlier on that day, he'd assigned Fair Molly, Plain Jane, and Keen-Eyed Ollie to surveil Lady Julianna Hastings. He'd given the trio strict orders to observe only and rendezvous at the Nest by nightfall.

The girls had returned without Ollie. Apparently, the three had separated to cover the entrances of the Hungerford Market where they'd seen Lady Hastings enter, agreeing to reconvene at the stairs below the market at eight o'clock. The girls had waited a half-hour; when Ollie hadn't shown, they'd assumed he had forgotten and made his way back on his own.

But Ollie hadn't returned to the Nest. Cull had assembled a search team, and they were on the way back to Hungerford Stairs, Jane and Molly peering anxiously into the fog.

"Ollie's all right, ain't 'e?" Plain Jane asked, a quiver in her voice.

"Course 'e is." Fair Molly put an arm around the smaller girl's shoulders. "'E probably lost track o' the time. 'E'll be waiting for us at 'Ungerford, you wait and see."

Despite the brave words, Cull saw the way Molly chewed on her lip. It was a tell-tale sign of anxiety. Jane's thumb crept toward her mouth...a habit she'd learned in the orphanage where she'd spent her first five years and one she'd worked hard to break. But stress brought back old habits; for mudlarks, danger to one of their own was the worst kind of stress.

For Cull, their leader, to be the cause of that strain made him the worst kind of failure.

Damn my own eyes, he thought savagely. *I shouldn't have sent them on this sodding mission. I shouldn't have compromised their safety...just to impress a woman.*

When Pippa had broken down weeping last night, his first alarming thought had been that he'd hurt her. That he'd been too rough in his lovemaking. But then he had looked at her beautiful, tear-stained face and recognized what she was feeling: heart-breaking loss.

He'd held her until she calmed. Then he'd dressed her and drove her home. They hadn't spoken during the ride: her outpouring had left her as wrung out as a dishrag. He remembered his mam's weeping bouts, how she'd stayed in bed for days. No matter how hard he'd tried, he couldn't ease her pain. His helplessness felt crushingly familiar.

Christ, it killed him to know that Pippa was still suffering over the loss of Longmere. Cull had thought she was done with griev-ing, yet she'd wept as if her heart was breaking, as if her husband had died only yesterday. Apparently, she still loved Longmere...so much that she couldn't let him go.

Did I push her into something she wasn't ready for?

The thought had brought about pounding remorse...and panic. Cull's fantasy and reality had finally merged, and he wasn't ready for them to part ways again. There had to be something he could do to make things right. To dry Pippa's tears, make her forget her undeserving husband. Make her look at *Cull* again with ardor shining in her eyes.

The solution had struck him. While he couldn't compete with Longmere when it came to proper courtship, he possessed one skill that the toff hadn't: the ability to find facts. Recalling Pippa's interest in Lady Hastings's activities, Cull had sent his larks off to gather information on the woman. He'd planned to call upon Pippa with an apology...and a dossier on the viscountess. He'd thought his offering would be more unique and practical than a bouquet or poem. And it would show Pippa that, while he was no elegant lord, he had other things to recommend him as a lover.

Which led to the present chaos.

Ollie is paying the price for my selfishness. Cull clenched his jaw. *How many people must I fail?*

The tally burned upon his back, and he remembered the sting of each one being etched on his skin. A reminder of the lives he'd failed to protect. He would be damned if he added one more to the count.

The Hungerford Stairs came into sight, and Long Mikey navigated the barge to a small wharf. The sprawling colonnaded market above the stairs stood dark and abandoned against the clouded night sky; in a few hours, the lighters would arrive with goods to fill the stalls of the bazaar. Molly passed around lanterns, and Cull led the way down the pier.

"Comb the shore before making your way up to the market," he said. "Molly and Jane are with me; Mikey, you take the others. The instant you find anything"—he pulled on the whistle that was identical to the ones all the larks wore around their necks—"raise the alarm."

Mikey barked out orders to his troop, their line of lanterns moving east while Cull led his team in the opposite direction, toward the footbridge that connected the market to the South Bank of the Thames. Along the muddy shore, the stink of the river was amplified by the market's unsold offal oozing its way into the water. As a child, Cull had scavenged here, competing with the big grey rats for scraps.

They reached a section of the shore littered with boats, which resembled beached seals in the darkness.

"Pair o' coves," Fair Molly said in a low voice. "Fifteen feet ahead."

Cull was already heading toward the flickering light. "Perhaps they've seen something."

He approached the two men slumped in the shelter of a propped-up boat. Their fire illuminated their drink-slackened expressions as they passed a bottle between them.

"Good evening," Cull said to get their attention.

One of the men raised a bleary gaze. "Gor, look at 'is fancy mask. What're you...a highwayman?"

His comrade snickered.

"I'm looking for a boy. Blond, wearing spectacles, this tall." Cull placed his hand at Ollie's approximate height. "Have you seen him?"

"No one's come by," the man replied.

Fair Molly planted her fists on her trousered hips. "So you 'aven't seen a boy?"

"'E didn't say that, did 'e, missy?" The second man's burp reeked of onions.

Cull bridled his impatience. "Did you see the boy or not?"

"Might 'ave," the first drunk said. "When I went to piss in me water closet, saw someone sleeping there, didn't I."

His pulse quickening, Cull asked, "Where is your water closet?"

"'E likes to do 'is business 'neath the bridge," the second man said.

Cull took off, Molly and Jane behind him. They reached the footbridge moments later. Holding up his lamp, Cull scanned the rocky shore beneath the bridge's span...and his heart slammed into his ribs when the light fell on the small body: a boy lying on his side, the tide tugging at his boots.

Please, God, let him be alive.

Cull sprinted over. Kneeling, he carefully turned the boy over.

Ollie's right temple was crusted with blood, his face bone-white in the darkness.

"Is Ollie...is 'e..." Jane said in a muffled voice.

Cull felt for a pulse on the boy's neck.

"He's alive." Relief pushed the air from Cull's lungs. "We'll get him back to—"

"Wot are those coves looking at?"

Molly's question diverted Cull's attention. She was staring at a dock on the other side of the bridge. Nothing was anchored there, but a few people had gathered around a dark form lying upon the wooden planks. The river breathed, stirring the shape, rustling what appeared to be layers of fashionably full skirts.

A cold premonition seized Cull's gut.

12

The next evening, Pippa ascended the front steps of the Nest and rang the bell. After a few moments, she rang it again. And again. Finally, the door opened to reveal the curly-haired girl she'd met before.

"Hello, Fair Molly," Pippa said. "I'm here to see Cull."

"'E ain't expecting visitors." The girl eyed her up and down. "And 'e's otherwise occupied."

"He will see me," Pippa stated. "Inform him that I won't leave until he does."

The girl studied her, then grumbled, "'Ave it your way. But this is the Devil's Acre, not Mayfair. You'd best wait inside if you don't want to be plucked like a bleedin' pigeon."

Although Pippa wanted to reply that the pistol in the pocket of her skirts was designed to forestall any plucking, she let the girl usher her through the door. She was one step closer to seeing Timothy Cullen. One step closer to obtaining crucial information.

The blasted man affected her emotions like a hurricane, spinning her out of control. Two nights ago, he'd not only made exquisite love to her, but he had also taken tender care of her afterward. He hadn't run from her tears or tried to stop them.

Instead, he'd held her, letting her purge the toxins from her soul. His strong, silent support had melted her defenses and her heart. She'd fantasized about having an affair with him...

Then Julianna Hastings had been found murdered early this morning.

Remorse and powerlessness furled Pippa's hands. The Angels had failed their client. They had let her walk away...straight into the lion's den.

"We will see justice done for Julianna Hastings," Charlie had said with steely resolve.

Charlie had gone to Whitehall Place, where the headquarters of the Metropolitan Police were located. As she had to conceal the true nature of her society, she'd claimed to be a close friend of Julianna Hastings. The rest of what she'd told the inspector was true: that Lady Hastings was unhappy in her marriage and had feared that her husband might do her harm. The inspector had agreed to pay Viscount Hastings a visit and question him.

That had been the first step. Pippa was here to take care of the second.

For it had been none other than Cull who'd informed Charlie of Lady Hastings's death. His missive had been perfunctory and dismissive; Pippa was on a mission to find out more. Why had Cull been the one to find the body? Had he discovered any clues at the scene of the crime? Hastings had summoned an undertaker to prepare his wife's body for the funeral, the process sure to erase the clues to her death. Cull, however, had seen Lady Hastings's remains, and Pippa was going to find out what he knew.

And I won't let my personal feelings get in the way, she silently vowed.

"Now wait 'ere and don't wander off," Molly admonished before heading down one of the corridors that branched from the great room.

Unlike Pippa's last visit, the chamber was quiet and devoid of merry mayhem. A few mudlarks flocked together, but they seemed listless and somber. Sitting at a nearby table was a young girl with a face as round as a clock and shiny dark braids. She pushed food around on her plate, looking so close to tears that Pippa couldn't help but go over.

"Hello, there," she said softly. "What's your name?"

The girl spoke to her plate. "Ain't supposed to tell it to strangers."

Fair enough. Having worked with foundlings, Pippa saw the wisdom in children being taught to guard their privacy.

"My name is Pippa," she said. "I was wondering why you aren't eating your supper."

Her heart clutched when the girl's bottom lip wobbled.

"I'm sad," the girl whispered.

"Why, dear?"

"Sally, are you still dawdling o'er supper?" Fair Molly's voice cut in. "It's time to wash up."

"Yes, Fair Molly." Sally jumped up and scampered off.

Glowering, Fair Molly said, "Wot did I say to you about staying put?"

Pippa raised her brows. "I didn't go anywhere."

"Well, keep your nose out o' mudlark business. And follow me; our prince ain't got all day."

As Pippa followed her hostess down one of the hallways, she wondered at the girl's bristly attitude. It went hand-in-hand with the Nest's current atmosphere; where was the cheerful warren of her prior visit? All the doors along the corridor were sealed shut, no sign of playful mudlarks anywhere.

Pippa felt a pang of disquiet. *Did something happen?*

Fair Molly stopped at a door that was cracked open, light spilling into the corridor.

"Don't you pester 'im none," the girl warned in an undertone. "'As 'is 'ands full, don't 'e, without 'aving to deal with the likes o' you."

Pippa was nudged inside before she could ask what the other

meant. The parlor was cozy, packed with mismatched furniture. But it was Cull who snagged her attention: standing by the fire, he turned to face her, and for an instant, she lost track of her thoughts. Of anything but him.

Even though he wore his mask, her artist's eye sketched in the blanks: straight brows and nose, smooth golden skin stretched over strong bones. He was dressed in his usual well-worn attire: a striped waistcoat hugged his wide shoulders and lean torso, his sleeves rolled up to reveal corded forearms dusted with hair. His trousers clung to the bulging contours of his legs.

The memory of bliss shivered through her. Of being pressed up against that hard, virile form as he pleasured her. She forced herself to take a calming breath. Then another as their eyes met and held. Cull's gaze was shuttered and passionless...a far cry from two nights ago.

Mortification welled. *What did you expect? You behaved like a lunatic.*

Never in her life had she come apart that way. She could only surmise that her first real taste of pleasure had unlocked a trove of emotions she'd buried deep. Later, back in her own bed, her thoughts had whirled.

The passion I've dreamed of does exist. And I am fully capable of feeling it; there's nothing wrong with me. I wasn't the problem in my marital bed...

Of course, Cull didn't know her past and probably thought she was a candidate for Bedlam. Remembering his devastating gentleness, even when she'd failed to give *him* any pleasure, swamped her with embarrassment. It reminded her of the night she'd gone to her husband's bedchamber, the one and only time she'd worked up the nerve to initiate their marital activities.

"This is your fault," Longmere had raged. *"This has never happened to me before. You don't have what it takes to satisfy a man..."*

Pain and confusion bled through Pippa. She didn't know if she wanted to apologize to Cull or run away and never see him again.

But she would do neither because she had a more important goal this eve: to find Julianna Hastings's killer.

Pippa squared her shoulders. "Thank you for seeing me."

"You should not have come," Cull said.

She flinched at his curt reply, but it was to be expected.

He may have wanted you once, her inner voice whispered. *But now he knows what a mess you truly are.*

She took refuge in her purpose. "I am here on behalf of the Society of Angels. I've come to discuss the message you sent to Lady Fayne."

Cull folded his arms over his wide chest. "I thought the message was clear."

Pulling the missive from the pocket of her skirts, she read, "Lady Hastings was shot and killed. Steer clear of this dangerous business. I will inform you when I've brought the villain to justice. Prince of Larks."

He cocked his head. "I fail to see the lack of clarity."

"Lady Hastings was *our* client," Pippa said fiercely. "What gives you the right to tell us to leave off our investigation? If anyone should get out of the way, it is *you*."

"This matter has become mudlark business."

The lethal edge to Cull's tone gave her pause. Reminded her that, for all the gentleness he'd shown her, he was a ruler of London's underworld.

"A woman was shot dead. This is a dangerous business," he said unflinchingly, "and your little ladies' society will only get in the way."

Little. Ladies'. Society?

Vermillion splattered across Pippa's vision. Marching up to him, she stabbed a finger in his chest. Bit back a wince when her digit jammed into an unyielding slab of muscle.

"We are trained investigators," she hissed. "We can handle ourselves. Moreover, we are going to bring our client's murderer to justice, and you had better stay out of *our* way."

Cull grabbed her wrist. "Don't be a damned fool. You're out of your depth, and I won't let you get hurt."

"You have no right to tell me what to do!"

"Don't I?" The possessive glitter in his eyes stalled her breath. "I've tasted you, made you wet. You came so hard you shook in my arms."

Cheeks blazing, she retorted, "It is ungentlemanly of you to mention that night."

His mouth twisted. "I'm no gentleman, sunshine."

"Anyway, it was just a meaningless liaison." She was proud of how nonchalant she sounded, as if she'd had dozens of lovers. As if she'd experienced sexual satisfaction on a regular basis instead of just that one, earth-shattering time. "It doesn't signify anything."

"It meant something to me."

Was that longing that flashed in his eyes?

"I'd give my bloody soul to make love to you again, but I can't." He released her and took a step back, his hands curling. "I am no good for you, Pippa. But what I can do is keep you safe. Upon my honor, I will bring your client's killer to justice. Trust me to take care of this for you."

Heart thumping, Pippa stared at him in befuddlement. He *did* want her then...despite how their encounter had ended? Yet if he wanted her, why couldn't he make love to her again? And why did the blasted man think that she needed him to "take care" of anything when she and the Angels were perfectly capable of solving their own cases?

Before she could utter a response, the door opened.

"Cull, you'd better come quick!" It was Fair Molly again, her expression agitated.

Cursing, Cull pointed a blunt finger at Pippa. "Stay here. I'll deal with you when I get back."

He strode from the room.

The nerve of the man. Does he think I'm going to take orders like a dashed spaniel?

Pippa waited a heartbeat before following.

Cull and Molly moved at a purposeful pace through the twisting corridors. They disappeared into a room that Pippa recognized as the infirmary. She followed the voices past empty cots to a private room. Cull stood at the foot of a bed, arguing with a silver-haired man in a dark suit while Mrs. Needles and Fair Molly watched on. Behind them on the bed...

Pippa's heart lurched as she recognized the young mudlark who'd surveilled her house...Ollie, his name was. He was scarcely recognizable as the adorable tow-headed boy who'd offered her a pork pie. His face was as white as the sheets tucked around him. A bandage was wound around his head, blood staining his tufts of fair hair. His chest moved in shallow waves, and one of his bare arms lay exposed atop the sheets. On the bed next to his frail limb lay an array of deadly-sharp blades.

"I am a respected physician with patrons in the highest circles." The silver-haired man looked down his long nose at Cull, his manner patronizing. "You persuaded me to look at this patient, and I am telling you that he needs to be bled."

"He's lost enough blood as it is," Mrs. Needles protested.

"Who are you going to listen to, this unqualified female"—the doctor gave the matron a contemptuous look—"or me?"

Cull raked a hand through his hair. "It took Mrs. Needles all night to stop the bleeding. And you want to start it up again? How will that help?"

"The theory is too complicated to explain to uneducated persons." The doctor sniffed. "Suffice it to say, bloodletting will purge the boy's fever. And whatever toxic miasma he is harboring from living in these filthy streets. If I am not allowed to do my job as I see fit, I will take my leave. This patient's death will be on your hands."

Cull's frame vibrated with tension. His shoulders were taut, his hands fisted at his sides. He looked large and dangerous...and utterly at sea.

The Prince of Larks knew everything except, evidently, how to deal with a snob.

Pippa crossed the threshold. "You are not going to bleed this boy."

The physician turned to her. He took obvious note of her expensive mourning gown and well-bred manner, and she could almost see the calculations running through his arrogant brain. Obsequiousness smoothed the sneer from his face; she couldn't say it was an improvement.

"Were you addressing me, madam?" he asked with a fawning smile.

"Yes, and I think you had better go. Now," Pippa clarified.

The physician turned florid. He shot an outraged look at her and then at Cull. "Sir?"

"Get out," Cull said flatly.

The physician collected his instruments of torture. As Molly led him out, he issued a parting shot. "Good luck finding another learned man of medicine who will treat this street rat."

"What a vile fellow," Mrs. Needles declared when the door closed. "Thank goodness for your intervention, Mrs. Lumley."

Pippa nodded but saw the strain that bracketed Cull's mouth.

"He was the most qualified quack who would come to Devil's Acre," Cull muttered. "No one else wanted to dirty their hands with a mudlark."

Mrs. Needles clutched her apron. "There must be someone better—"

"Send for Dr. Abernathy at 18 Harley Street," Pippa said.

"Abernathy?" Mrs. Needles's forehead pleated. "I have heard of him. He caters to the aristocracy—"

"He knows my family," Pippa assured her. "As he provides care for the foundlings at my parents' school, I can vouch that he is excellent with children. Tell him that Pippa, the Countess of

Longmere, is requesting his presence on an urgent case; he will come."

"Yes, Mrs.—I mean, my lady," Mrs. Needles said hastily. "I'll see to it straight away."

The matron hurried off. Pippa went to Ollie's bedside, tucking his arm back under the blanket. His skin was alarmingly cold to her touch.

"What happened to him?" she asked quietly.

Cull remained at the foot of the bed, his gaze on the boy's pale face. "Someone knocked him on the head and dumped him in the river. Probably thought he was dead when they threw him in, but he must have regained his wits long enough to swim to shore."

The tonelessly uttered words squeezed Pippa's heart. Who would do something so vile...and to a *child*? The realization rammed into her.

"Is Ollie's injury related to Lady Hastings's murder?" she exclaimed.

Cull gave a rough nod. "He was following her."

"Why?"

Cull said something under his breath. It sounded like, "Because I'm an idiot."

Pippa knitted her brows. "Pardon?"

He rubbed the back of his neck, his gaze not quite meeting hers. "At The Enchanted Rose, you seemed curious about Lady Hastings's activities. I thought if I provided you with information about her, you might be...pleased."

Pippa's jaw slackened. Although Cull's mask concealed his expression, his hunched shoulders conveyed his discomfiture. She had the wild thought that his face might be ruddy beneath the black leather. Something in her melted as she realized that this big, mysterious underworld prince had tracked Lady Hastings... for her. To please her.

"It was stupid and selfish." Cull's jaw was taut. "I should not have put my personal desires before the well-being of my larks. What happened to Ollie is my fault."

Hearing his self-recrimination, she said haltingly, "You didn't know what would happen. And Ollie is strong. He will recover."

"He will. And when he does, he'll tell us who did this to him and the Hastings woman. And that bastard is going to pay," Cull vowed.

Suddenly, Pippa understood why the mudlarks were so loyal to their prince. She'd seen it in every interaction between Cull and his charges. He cared for them and took responsibility for their welfare...perhaps putting them before his own wants.

"Now do you understand why I am no good for you?" His eyes smoldered with emotion. "If I fail in my duty as a leader, people around me get hurt. When I left you fourteen years ago, I did the right thing. My mistake was not staying away. You and I belong to different worlds. You deserve a toff who can offer you a carefree life of luxury and ease."

"That is not what I want," she whispered.

His chest gave a mighty surge. "I know losing your husband the way you did...it's affected you. But these risks you've been taking won't heal your broken heart. Nor will spending a night in bed with a cove like me. I shouldn't have approached you, shouldn't have taken advantage of your delicate state. You've a loyal heart, and if your reaction to our night together proved anything, it's that you need more time to grieve your husband."

She stared at him, utterly flummoxed. No man had expressed such earnest interest in her happiness before. Nor had one been so completely and utterly *wrong*.

She didn't know if she was touched or exasperated.

"You seem to know a lot about me," she said.

His smile didn't reach his eyes. "I'm the bleeding Prince of Larks."

"For the sake of your reputation, I hope the information you provide your clients proves more accurate."

He drew his brows together. "What does that mean?"

"It means that most of what you just said about me is *incorrect.*"

"How so?" He didn't sound convinced.

"First of all, being with a 'toff' won't make me happy. I have had that, and it's not an experience I care to repeat," she said candidly. "Second, how *dare* you assume that I am some delicate flower so overwhelmed by grief that I cannot handle a night of passion?"

He shoved his hands into his pockets. "You wept for your husband, Pippa. Like your heart was breaking."

Irked by his gentle tone, she said, "I wasn't crying *for* Longmere, you nodcock. I was crying for myself."

"I don't understand the difference," he said, angling his head.

"Maybe you would if you *asked* me how I was feeling instead of making assumptions." Annoyance took the edge off her nervousness. Allowed her to speak the truth that their encounter had unlocked. That she'd never given voice to. "Being with you made me realize what I've been missing all along. What I never felt in my marriage. I was crying because I finally understood that maybe...maybe there's nothing wrong with me after all."

"What could be wrong with you? You're bloody perfect."

Cull's incredulity warmed her, even if he was wrong.

Portrait of a Lady Dreaming blazed in her mind's eye. The woman's beautiful face and the desperate longing beneath. Symbols of Pippa's failure. Yet she was starting to see that she was not to blame for all the problems in her marriage. That she wasn't quite as...as broken as she'd believed.

"I'm far from perfect," she said tautly. "But one thing that I thought was wrong with me, that wasn't functioning the way I'd imagined it should..." She struggled to find the right phrasing. "With you, it, um, did. Everything appears to be in working order."

His eyes widened, his surprise evident despite his mask. "You mean you never..."

She couldn't admit aloud that she'd never found satisfaction with her husband.

"Pippa, I—"

Whatever Cull was about to say was cut off by a moan from the bed.

Pippa's gaze flew to Ollie. The boy's lashes were fluttering.

"Ollie?" With pounding hope, she leaned over the bed. "Wake up, dear. You can do it."

Cull was already on the other side. "Open your eyes. There's a lad."

The boy lifted his lashes; his hazel eyes gradually focused.

"Thank Christ." Cull's voice was thick with emotion. "You had us worried there, Ollie."

The boy blinked at him, then at Pippa.

"Who's Ollie?" the boy croaked. "Where am I?"

13

Pippa surfaced groggily from sleep. It took her a moment to realize that she was in her bedchamber. A gentle rapping at the door had awakened her.

"Come in," she said, yawning.

Suzette, her lady's maid, entered. "You asked that I wake you at eight o'clock, my lady."

"It's eight already?" Pippa said in surprise.

Her sleep must have been deeper than usual...no doubt because she'd stayed past midnight at the Nest, keeping Ollie company. The poor dear couldn't recall anything, not even his name; he'd been so frightened and lost. Luckily, Dr. Abernathy had come, and after a thorough examination, concluded that no permanent damage had been done. He didn't know when Ollie's memory would return and prescribed rest and calm as the best medicine.

Pippa recalled her relief—and that of Cull, who'd been standing there, shoulders taut, clearly braced for the worst. His throat had bobbed. Then he'd blinked and shoved his hands in his pockets, uttering a gruff thanks to the doctor. At that moment, Pippa had glimpsed the boy inside the powerful man's body. The lad she'd kissed in the tower. And she'd felt that same, inexorable pull toward him that fourteen years hadn't lessened.

"Shall I help you dress, my lady?" Suzette inquired.

Pushing aside the coverlet, Pippa got out of bed. "Yes. And please tell the driver to ready the carriage. I am headed over to the Duchess of Hadleigh's."

After she'd told Charlie about seeing Julianna Hastings at The Enchanted Rose the night before her death, Charlie had agreed that that could be an important clue. She'd arranged for Pippa to meet with Mrs. Loverly this morning, and Livy had offered to come along.

Arriving at the Hadleighs' Palladian mansion in Mayfair, Pippa was ushered into the drawing room, where a pacing Livy placed a finger over her lips, whispering, *"Shh."*

The greeting was understandable as Livy's infant daughter Esmerelda was sleeping on her shoulder. Pippa went over, taking in the tiny miracle with rosebud lips and wispy dark hair. She felt a thrum of longing for another piece of her old dream that had failed to come true.

"Esme was up all night, and I just got her to sleep," Livy said in a hush. "Once I put her down, we can leave."

Unlike most ladies of her station, Livy did not relegate Esme's care to staff. While Esme had a nursemaid, Livy liked to be hands-on with her child, a tradition passed onto her by her mother. Pippa's own mama had also taken an active role in raising the Hunt brood; if Pippa were ever blessed with a child, she would be the same way.

An unbidden image flashed of Cull tucking Teddy beneath his arm. His affection toward the larks was unmistakable. *What kind of a father would he be...?*

She shoved aside the thought, murmuring, "Esme is so beautiful. She has your looks, Livy."

As if sensing the compliment, Esme made a cooing sound. Pippa held her breath, praying the babe wouldn't wake. Esme's lashes fanned up, unfocused green eyes blinking. Her lips puckered, and she let out a demanding wail.

A deep male voice said, "She has her mama's temperament as well."

Pippa turned to see the Duke of Hadleigh approaching in his long-limbed stride. He was a handsome fellow in his thirties with thick, dark hair and blue eyes. His navy frock coat and dove-grey trousers fit his virile form like a glove, his cravat a work of art beneath his chin.

"Good morning, my lady," he said, bowing.

Pippa smiled and curtsied. "Your Grace."

When she'd first met the duke years ago, he'd been a hardened rake, known for his excesses and volatile first marriage. A friend of Livy's family, he'd attended many of the same functions Pippa had, and she'd noticed that, despite his black reputation, there'd been a special connection between him and Livy. A true and steadfast friendship despite their age difference. Last year, that friendship had blossomed into love...although Livy had confided that she'd had to work to convince Hadleigh to see her as a woman. As he had led a notorious life with his former duchess, Hadleigh had apparently believed Livy deserved a better man.

Seeing him now, the glowing contentment in his eyes as he kissed Livy before taking his daughter and tucking her in the crook of his arm, Pippa saw the evidence that love—true love— could change people. Heal them. Even if they had made bad choices in their past.

"You have the magic touch with Esme," Livy told her husband. "She was determined to kick up a fuss with me. But look at her now, quiet as a mouse."

The babe batted her eyelashes at Hadleigh, letting out a soft gurgle before falling asleep again. The duke looked at his daughter as if he couldn't quite believe that she was real.

"I have experience handling headstrong ladies." He winked at his wife. Then, he seemed to take note of the fact that Livy was dressed to go out in her rose-colored carriage dress and fur-lined cloak. "Where are you headed off to, my love?"

"Pippa and I are just running an errand," Livy said breezily.

A bit *too* breezily, for Hadleigh narrowed his eyes. "What kind of errand?"

"Oh, nothing of import."

"If it is not important, why are you avoiding my question?"

"Because you don't want to know the answer," Livy muttered.

"Regardless, I must know."

"Fine, but give Esme to Pippa, and we'll talk in the study. Your shouting will wake the babe."

Hadleigh looked offended. "I do not shout."

"There's a first time for everything," Livy said under her breath.

Pippa carefully took Esme as the Hadleighs excused themselves. In the doorway, Livy turned back to give Pippa a wide-eyed look, drawing a finger across her neck. The universal sign for *I'm in trouble now.*

Knowing Livy rather enjoyed courting trouble with Hadleigh, Pippa smothered a smile. She cuddled Esme closer, breathing in the babe's sweet, milky scent. In the distance, she heard the muffled sounds of a conversation.

Suddenly, Hadleigh's voice rose to a roar. "What the devil? That place is a male brothel!"

More muffled words. Then everything went quiet.

Pippa guessed that Livy had found a more persuasive way than words to win the argument. Sure enough, when the pair returned a few minutes later, Livy was rosy and breathless, and Hadleigh's cravat was rumpled.

"I'm ready to go," Livy said cheerfully.

Taking Esme, Hadleigh gave his wife a warning look. "Send word when you are done with your errand, little queen. The *moment* you are done."

"Yes, Your Grace," Livy replied with a saucy curtsy.

As the carriage headed to The Enchanted Rose, Livy folded her hands atop her rose-colored skirts and said, "Tell me what happened with the Prince of Larks last night."

Pippa filled Livy in on Ollie's attack and the likely connection with Lady Hastings's murder.

"The poor boy," Livy exclaimed. "I'm so relieved he will be all right. And what about Mr. Cullen?"

There went that annoying stutter in Pippa's heart. "What about him?"

Livy's brows arched over her knowing green eyes. "I can tell something is going on between the two of you."

"How, pray tell?"

"I can't explain it, exactly. But you have some of your old sparkle back."

"I wasn't aware I had any to begin with," Pippa said wryly.

"You've always lit up any room you entered," Livy said.

Years ago, Cull had said something similar, Pippa recalled with a pang. She could hardly remember being that happy, carefree girl; it seemed like a lifetime ago.

"If I may be frank..."

Amused, Pippa asked, "Do you know how to be otherwise, dear?"

"Hadleigh says I'm as subtle as a brick through a window," Livy said ruefully.

Pippa chuckled. "Your husband adores you."

"I know." A dreamy look flitted through Livy's eyes. "And you deserve the same."

Pippa tensed. "I have no intention of marrying again—"

"Oh, I don't mean marriage, necessarily. Just that you deserve to be happy. Since Longmere died, you haven't been yourself."

"Grieving has that effect."

Livy drew a breath as if she was about to say something difficult. "You were changing even before he died."

Frowning, Pippa said, "How do you mean?"

"Your light, Pippa. When you were with Longmere, he
dimmed it." Livy bit her lip. "I didn't see you as often after you
married, but when I did, you always seemed distracted. Or
worried. And when I saw the two of you together, the attention
was always on him. On his art. When anyone could see that you
were the better painter—"

"Don't." The clamp of guilt made it difficult for Pippa to
breathe. "There is no comparison. Longmere's art was everything
to him. He hadn't reached his full potential. If he had lived, who
knows what he could have accomplished—"

"Well, it's true that his last piece showed considerable
improvement over the rest."

Palms sweaty inside her gloves, Pippa held herself still beneath
Livy's keen gaze. She'd vowed to herself that she would not betray
Longmere's legacy. The one thing she'd given him that he valued.

"He never had a chance." She forced the words through her
constricted throat. "To show the world who he could have been."

"I don't mean to cause you distress, dear." Livy's delicate
features creased with concern. "I care about you and want to see
you happy."

Pippa shaped her lips into a smile. "I'm getting better."

"I have seen glimpses of your light returning." The teasing
note in Livy's voice alleviated some of the tension. "Whenever
we're talking about Mr. Cullen."

"That light you see is the glow of irritation."

"I'm married. Trust me, I'm aware of what irritation looks
like." Livy's grin was impish. "I see it all the time in Hadleigh's
eyes."

Pippa shook her head fondly. "You could *try* to be less of a
brat, dear."

"What fun would that be? Besides, Hadleigh likes me as I am."

Livy's confidence sparked a flame of yearning in Pippa. To have such unconditional love—

"And it's obvious that you have an ardent admirer as well. Why else would Mr. Cullen be trying to protect you?"

"Because he's a domineering ass?" Yet Pippa's words lacked heat.

"So is Hadleigh, from time to time. That doesn't stop me from adoring him." Livy's look was shrewd. "You are attracted to Mr. Cullen, aren't you?"

Pippa didn't have the wherewithal to lie. "I might be somewhat drawn to him."

"Has he kissed you yet?"

Pippa's cheeks flamed, betraying her.

"Oh my goodness, he *has*," Livy breathed. "Is he a good kisser?"

Pippa straightened a pleat in her skirts. "I'm not discussing it—"

"It's just you and me, and I'm a married woman now. You can speak freely about you-know-what."

"You-know-what?" With bubbling mirth, Pippa said, "If we're calling it that, then we're definitely not ready for this conversation."

"Fine. Let's call it what it is. Relations of a biblical nature."

"And Hadleigh says you're not tactful."

"You're evading the issue, Pippa."

Faced with the determined slant of Livy's chin, Pippa knew her friend wasn't going to let go of the issue. And the truth was she wanted to talk about Cull. With someone she trusted... someone other than Charlie, who had a bias against males in general.

"He is a good kisser," she admitted. *The best.* "That is the problem."

Livy frowned. "How is that a problem?"

Let me count the ways. She chose the simplest answer. "I am still in mourning. It doesn't feel right that I should be attracted to another man."

"You're widowed, not dead. And it's been a year since Longmere's passing—longer than that since he made you happy," Livy said acutely. "He deceived you, kept you in the dark, made you worry so much that you hired investigators to look into his activities. I know one shouldn't speak ill of the dead, but in this instance, I must do so to encourage the living. To encourage you, Pippa, to find the happiness you deserve."

Her friend's words were a balm to the chapped patches of Pippa's heart.

"Sometimes I think I've forgotten how to be happy," she said, her throat scratchy.

"It is like riding a horse. After a fall, it can be scary to get in the saddle again, but one must."

Pippa pinched her brows together. "Is the saddle a metaphor for a relationship?"

"Or for something else," Livy said in a suggestive tone.

"Olivia McLeod Wodehouse." Pippa burst out laughing. "You are incorrigible."

"Would it be so bad to enjoy the pleasures of the moment? You are a widow, after all. You have freedoms that you could exercise with Mr. Cullen. If you wish to."

"I think I do." It was a relief to say it aloud. "With all that was going on with Ollie and Lady Hastings's murder, however, Cull and I left things unsettled between us. He told me he's no good for me, but he also admitted that he does...that he is interested in me. It's all so confusing. And, heavens, I haven't even seen him without his mask."

Livy drew her brows together. "He's never removed it?"

Pippa shook her head. "I asked him to once, and he said he couldn't. According to Charlie, he's always worn the mask in her presence as well. To uphold his aura of enigma."

"It's one thing to remain masked in public as the Prince of Larks, but another when he is in private with you."

"It's strange, I know." Pippa sighed. "On top of that, Cull and I are locking horns on the matter of Lady Hastings's murder. He insists that I should stay out of it, and I told him to stop getting in my way."

"When a man tells a woman to stay out of it, does he actually expect her to obey?" Livy mused. "I have always wondered."

Pippa chewed on her lip. "So do you think I should see him again?"

"If the Prince of Larks is the kind of man I think he is, then you will undoubtedly see him again," Livy said sagely. "The question is how you wish to proceed when you do."

Mrs. Loverly received them in her office and was barely recognizable from the last time Pippa had seen her. She wore no wig, her mousy brown hair tied in curling papers. Her cheeks and lips were pale without cosmetics, and her tattered chintz wrapper covered her from neck to toes. All in all, she looked more like a frowsy matron than a notorious madam.

Pippa's surprise must have shown, for as the bawd waved them to the chairs by her desk, she said, "I only get dressed up for work, dearie. Speaking o' which, right now is my bedtime. I don't mind doing Lady Fayne a favor, but I need my beauty rest, eh?"

"Of course," Pippa said hastily. "We would like to see your guest list for the night when I was here."

Mrs. Loverly leaned back in her chair. "Afraid I can't do that, luvie. Even for Lady Fayne. She understands as I do that discretion is the bedrock o' our enterprises."

"Will you at least confirm if Lady Julianna Hastings was on the list?" Livy asked.

The bawd's gaze thinned. "You mean the lady wot got

murdered? It was splashed all o'er the papers yesterday and today."

Pippa nodded. "To bring her killer to justice, we need your help."

After a pause, Mrs. Loverly replied, "She weren't on the list. Never met the woman."

Undeterred, Pippa opened her black silk reticule and took out a small sketch book. Opening it to the two portraits she'd sketched—one of Julianna Hastings, the other of the mahogany-haired man with the silver eyes—she placed it on the desk.

"Do you recognize either of these people?" she asked.

The bawd studied the drawings. "They were at my club that night."

Pippa's pulse quickened. "Who are they?"

Mrs. Loverly tapped a finger on the sketch of the woman. "Gave her name as Mary Brown. Said she were a widow looking for some company. First-time patron and paid in gold." She turned to the drawing of the man. "Now him, I've had in my club a handful o' times. Uses the name Thor on account of his mighty, ahem, thunderbolt."

A snort escaped Livy. "What is his real name?"

"He didn't say, and I didn't ask. It ain't easy finding prime male specimens, so I take them as they come. Can't say for certain, but I'd pin him as an actor."

"Why do you say that?" Pippa asked.

"Call it a gut feeling." The bawd shrugged. "Quite a few actors work for me to make extra blunt when they're between jobs. And Thor struck me as the kind of fellow who landed mostly thinking parts."

In other words, non-speaking roles that didn't pay well.

"That's all I know. If there's nothing else..." Mrs. Loverly elevated her brows.

Seeing Livy shake her head, Pippa rose. "We appreciate your time, ma'am."

Pippa and Livy made their next stop at Charlie's.

"Not that we have much to share," Livy groused as they headed toward the study. "Trying to find this Thor will be no easy task. Unemployed actors in London are as plentiful as eels in the Thames. And are you certain the woman you saw that night was Julianna Hastings?"

"Not absolutely certain," Pippa admitted. "But I have a good memory for faces."

"Lady Hastings was rather unremarkable in her looks. A lot of women could resemble her."

"Perhaps. Yet 'Mary Brown' could have been an alias that Lady Hastings was using. Such a common name would be nearly impossible to track down..."

Pippa trailed off as Charlie came down the corridor toward them. She had never seen the other lady look so agitated.

With a rush of concern, she asked, "What is the matter?"

"I just received word." Charlie's eyes were icy with rage. "The police have concluded that Lady Hastings was the victim of a random crime. Jeremy Hastings has been cleared of any wrongdoing and won't be held responsible for the murder of his wife."

14

"Methinks the husband doth protest too much," Livy said in hushed tones as she and Pippa entered the Hastings's drawing room the following afternoon.

Taking in the lavish decorations, Pippa had to agree. Viscount Hastings took better care of his wife in death than he had in life. He'd spent a small fortune on the funeral, with huge white bouquets blooming throughout the room, their cloying scent unable to mask the faint smell of decay. Fine black crepe had been draped over the mirrors, and rows of chairs with black velvet cushions faced Lady Hastings's casket. Fashioned of gleaming wood, her coffin had an ornate breastplate, scrolled grips, and at least a half-dozen escutcheons. Afterward, the lady would be laid to rest in the exclusive Kensal Green cemetery.

With private disgust, Pippa noted the thread of titillation that wove through the crowd. Splashed on the front pages of all the newspapers, the gruesome murder had drawn curious onlookers in droves. Those who'd snubbed Julianna Hastings in life had no qualms salivating over her in death. Pippa's chest tightened: from personal experience, she knew that marrying above one's station, even for love, didn't erase one's middling class roots. Although she was not ashamed of her origins, she'd nonetheless worked hard to be a countess worthy of her husband's name.

Edwin hadn't paid much notice to her efforts...except to note her shortcomings.

Are you certain that frock is comme il faut, *my dear?*

There will be many true artists at the soiree, so do refrain from discussing your dabbling with paints, hmm?

As Mama says, a lady should be seen and not heard.

Wanting to please him, Pippa had redoubled her efforts, not realizing how, with each comment and underhanded criticism, he'd whittled down her self-confidence.

She yanked off the tentacles of the past and focused on Viscount Hastings, who was posed by the casket. For a bereaved widower, he looked rather dapper and well-rested. His black armband glinted against his dark coat, his hair bright as a guinea as he received condolences from a long line of well-wishers.

What a repugnant fraud, Pippa seethed.

"While Hastings is occupied, let's see what we can learn from the servants," Livy whispered. "I'll talk to the lady's maid over there. She looks like one of the few genuinely mourning her mistress. Perhaps she knows something useful."

Pippa nodded. "I'll find the butler."

They were on a reconnaissance mission to find evidence of Hastings's guilt. If anyone knew the state of affairs between master and mistress, it would be the servants.

Pippa found the butler in the antechamber. She'd taken stock of him when he let her and Livy in earlier. A tall, strapping man with greying hair at the temples, he had a distinguished bearing that suited his role as the male head of the staff. His face was carved with deep lines; shadows hung beneath his dark, rather piercing eyes.

Taking advantage of the lull, Pippa approached him. "Pardon me, sir..."

"It is Wood, my lady." His deep voice had a soothing quality. "May I be of assistance?"

Calling upon her training, she summoned creditable tears. "I seem to have forgotten my handkerchief. How silly of me, given the occasion..."

"Here you are, my lady." Wood slipped her a spare handkerchief with a circumspection that attested to his professional skill.

"Thank you, sir." She dabbed at her eyes. "I...I'm not usually a watering pot. But Lady Hastings and I were friends, and seeing her that way..."

Was that grief flashing through the butler's eyes? A moment later, his gaze shuttered.

"The situation would distress anyone, let alone a lady with delicate sensibilities," he said gravely. "Beg pardon, I had not realized that you and Lady Hastings were close."

"It was a recent friendship. We met at a ladies' function," Pippa improvised. "She and I had much in common, given our backgrounds."

The butler's expression softened a fraction. "I see."

Sniffling, Pippa asked, "Have you served the household long?"

"Not long, my lady. But I have known Lady Hastings since she was a girl, having been in her father's employ for nearly two decades. After Mr. Turner passed, Lady Hastings offered me this position."

Which meant Wood was a longtime retainer of the Turner family and likely loyal to Julianna rather than her husband.

Taking a gamble, Pippa said, "Lady Hastings and I confided in one another about our disappointments. Knowing her as well as you did, perhaps you were aware of her concerns?"

Wood's posture tensed. "Her concerns, madam?"

"She told me that things were not...as they should be between her and Lord Hastings. And she seemed rather fearful of him. Have you, by any chance, noticed anything amiss between them?"

The crevices deepened around Wood's mouth. He seemed to

be fighting himself. Torn, perhaps, between his butler's code of discretion and his loyalty to the Turners.

"Why do you ask, my lady?" he asked.

"Because I want to see justice served," Pippa said truthfully.

Wood's gaze flickered. After a pause, he said in a low voice, "As you said, my lady was not content in her marriage."

"Did you ever see Lord Hastings threaten her or hurt her in anyway?"

"Not physically. But my lord had a way of cutting her down."

Pippa's throat cinched. She knew that words could wound as well as a blade.

"More than once, I found Lady Hastings in tears," Wood said somberly. "Her lady's maid observed her distress as well."

"On the night she was killed, do you know where Lord Hastings was?"

"He was out all night," Wood said flatly. "He did not return until dawn."

"Do you know if anyone else might have wished Lady Hastings harm?"

The doorbell rang, and the butler straightened as if remembering his duty.

"I cannot think of anyone. I have said too much as it is." His bow was rigid. "If you'll excuse me, my lady."

"Yes, of course. And Wood...thank you."

He inclined his head and went to direct the newcomers.

Pippa headed back to the drawing room and reconvened with Livy.

"The lady's maid said that her master and mistress fought constantly," Livy whispered. "Lady Hastings was often reduced to tears by her husband's cruel words."

"The butler said much the same." Pippa chewed on her bottom lip. "We need to search the house. Look for evidence to link Hastings to his wife's murder."

"But how..."

Just then, Pippa's gaze collided with Hastings's. Under ordinary circumstances, the predacious interest in his eyes would have made her skin crawl. Right now, it fueled her resolve.

Pippa drew her shoulders back and donned a come-hither smile.

To Livy, she said softly, "Leave it to me."

The next evening, Cull met with the physician in a private room of the infirmary. "How is Ollie faring?"

"Better each day," Dr. Abernathy said. "Four days after the trauma, the lad is beginning to recall snippets of his past. He cannot remember the events surrounding his injury, but this is not unusual. I expect to see improvements day by day."

Cull nodded. For a quack, Abernathy seemed like a competent and honest fellow. In truth, Cull had only one complaint about the man. Years ago, while recuperating at the Hunts, Cull had been treated by Dr. Abernathy, who he remembered as being a crusty Scot with beetled brows.

This Abernathy was the son of the other one, now happily retired. In his twenties, Douglas Abernathy had the sort of clean-cut handsomeness that was a magnet for female attention. During his initial visit, he and Pippa had been full of smiles, chatting like the best of friends.

A dazzled Mrs. Needles had privately said to Cull that she couldn't believe such a celebrated physician had come to see their Ollie. Apparently, Abernathy was a favorite among the ladies of the Queen's Court...big surprise there. Cull would bet Abernathy had "attended to" plenty of high-kick ladies. He couldn't help but wonder if the doctor had ever treated Pippa. The thought of another man seeing her in a state of undress or putting his hands on her, for any reason, shot up the pressure in Cull's veins.

He'd been ruminating about Pippa and her stunning confessions:

First of all, being with a "toff" won't make me happy.

Did she truly mean that? She had trusted her body to Cull, but the agreement had only been for one night. When it came to an actual relationship, could she overlook their differences in class?

Being with you made me realize what I've been missing all along. What I never felt in my marriage.

Cull noted with frothing fury that Longmere had not only been a lying bastard, but a ham-handed one. Pippa was so sensual and sensitive, and the fact that she'd been deprived of such basic pleasure—and worse yet, had blamed it on *herself*—made Cull want to punch a wall. It had required all his self-discipline not to go to her, to show her what she'd been missing, what he *burned* to share with her.

But he couldn't. His priority had to be finding the villain who'd attacked Ollie and killed Lady Hastings. In doing so, he would also be protecting Pippa. He knew that the chances of her and the Angels standing down were practically nil. Case in point: she and the Duchess of Hadleigh had attended the funeral yesterday, and he'd wager his life's earnings it wasn't just to pay their last respects. He had to put an end to the dark business before the Angels got hurt.

On top of that, he had to address the attack on him outside his own headquarters. The larks had tracked down the shooter; yesterday, Cull had gone to have a chat with the bastard. After some "convincing" on Cull's part that involved exercising his knuckles, the assailant had sung like a bird: Chester Squibb had ordered the attack.

Squibb headed a group of sweeps that cleaned more than chimneys; they were known to steal anything that wasn't nailed down. The conniving bastard had been looking to expand his gang and no doubt coveted the larks, who were small enough to work

as climbing boys and smart enough to collect information and
goods.

As much as Cull despised the sweep, an out-and-out war was
his last resort. He didn't want to expose the larks to Squibb's
bloodthirsty band. Which meant Cull had to go about things with
care. He had scheduled a meeting with a formidable underworld
ally and planned to call in a favor she owed him. When Cull
struck, he didn't want Squibb to get back up.

After Cull took care of Ollie's attacker and the sweep, then
maybe he could see Pippa again. He would have to show her what
was behind his mask. If things were to progress between them, he
had to be honest with her. Had to ensure that she was making an
informed choice to be with him...with his scars and all. And that,
he thought bleakly, could stop their affair before it even began.

"I will be back in a few days," Abernathy said. "If anything
changes, send word."

Cull extended his hand. "Thank you for tending to Ollie."

"It is my pleasure." Abernathy's handshake was firm. "By the
by, I saw the basket of treats in the lad's room. A gift from Miss
Pippa—Lady Longmere, I mean to say?"

Cull stiffened at the familiar use of Pippa's name.

"I have not seen her since my first visit," Abernathy added.

Nor had Cull. Apparently, she'd paid a visit to Ollie while Cull
had been out hunting for information about Squibb.

"Does she visit at a regular time?" Abernathy inquired.

Cull clenched his jaw. "Why do you want to know?"

"Er, no particular reason." Ruddiness crept over the physician's chiseled cheekbones. "I used to see her frequently at the
Hunt Academy. Before she married. And I wished to inquire how
she was doing...health-wise, I mean. Widowhood can take its toll
on a lady's constitution."

"I will convey your concern," Cull said evenly.

Speculation entered Abernathy's eyes. "How did you say you
and Lady Longmere met?"

"I didn't."

"Ah." After a pause, the doctor muttered, "I must be on my way. Good evening, sir."

Bag in hand, Abernathy exited.

Long Mikey showed up a few minutes later.

Cull frowned at the mudlark. "Why aren't you tailing Lady Longmere like I told you to?"

"Calm your 'orses, I got eyes on 'er. But I thought you'd want to know what she's up to."

"What?" Cull asked with foreboding.

Mikey held up his hands. "First, promise you won't shoot the messenger."

15

"Would you care for some wine, my dear?" Hastings asked. Pippa bent her lips into an inviting smile. "That would be lovely."

As the viscount sauntered to the cabinet of spirits, Pippa took a quick survey of his suite. Gaining access to his home had been surprisingly simple. Yesterday, she'd approached him at the funeral. Feigning empathy, she'd told him how terribly lonely she felt after her own spouse's death. She'd added a few touches on his arm here and there. Like a lion sensing prey, Hastings had pounced. Before she knew it, he'd invited her over for a private *tête-à-tête* tonight so that they could "console" one another.

As Hastings prowled back toward her, she thought he suited the room's jungle-like ambiance with its tall potted plants and heavy wood furniture. He had a sleek, predatory air in his wine-colored smoking jacket, his blond hair slicked back from his widow's peak. Once again, Pippa was struck by his resemblance to her dead husband. The feline elegance and lordly manner...the trail of dark secrets he oozed in his wake.

He sat next to her on the damask settee, his thigh brushing her skirts. Since the night's theme was seduction, she had worn an evening gown of deep-plum taffeta that left her shoulders bare, the overskirt parting to reveal a flounced black underskirt. Her hair was arranged in ringlets, and she'd accessorized with a necklace and pair of earbobs made of jet.

Hastings handed her a goblet, purring, "To new friends."

"New friends." She touched her glass to his and took a drink of the ruby liquid.

Setting his glass down on the low table, he stretched his arm across the back of the settee, the hairs on her skin rising at his closeness. "I am surprised you came tonight."

Faced with his probing gaze, she said innocently, "Did you think I would not?"

"To be frank, I have been interested in your friendship for some time. I was under the impression that you did not prefer my company."

I would prefer walking over hot coals. Luckily, she'd prepared a story.

"After a year of mourning, I have been feeling rather lonely. I thought perhaps...perhaps we might find some comfort in each other's company." She bit her lip and willed herself to blush. "Am I being too forward, my lord?"

"Not at all. And please, call me Jeremy."

"Jeremy." Even his name felt oily on her tongue. "Both of us have lost someone dear. It gives us something in common, don't you think?"

A flash of anger—at his wife?—passed through his eyes; it was quickly smothered.

"It does lend a certain depth to our acquaintance." He smirked at her. "You'll find I am a man who enjoys *deep* connections."

What a disgusting pig.

She drained her glass, holding it out to him. "Would you mind, Jeremy?"

"It would be my pleasure," he said smoothly.

As he headed for the spirits cabinet, Pippa removed the tiny vial from the hidden pocket of her skirts. Leaning forward, she dumped the contents into his glass, the crystals fizzing as they dissolved into the wine. She shoved the vial back into her pocket just as he returned.

"Thank you." She took the glass he held out and said confidingly, "I think I have a bit of nerves. It has been quite some time since I've had, um, company."

Lust glittered in his gaze. "How long?"

"I have only ever kept company with my husband."

At his predacious smile, she knew she'd pinned him correctly as a man who enjoyed defiling innocence. He ran a finger along her bare shoulder, and she hoped her shiver would pass for one of interest.

She held up her glass. "Cheers to new adventures."

"Bottoms up," he drawled.

This time, she sipped while he drained his beverage. He took both their glasses and deposited them on the coffee table. Catching her jaw in his hand, he pressed his mouth to hers. She managed not to recoil as his tongue probed her lips. As his hands roamed.

"No need to be shy," he murmured.

Buy a few more minutes until the drug kicks in.

She pushed at his shoulders. "I...I think I heard something. Downstairs."

"There is no one here but you and me. As you requested, I dismissed the servants for the eve." His gaze slitted, showing the thinness of the charming veneer that hid the reptile beneath. "I went to rather a lot of trouble for you, Pippa."

And you had better give me what I want. His unspoken threat billowed Pippa's anger.

Was this how Julianna had felt? Cornered and helpless, no way of escaping except through capitulation? In the end, she'd paid the ultimate cost for trusting her heart to the wrong man. The image of Julianna lying in the casket flared in Pippa's mind. The lady had not looked peaceful in death. The undertaker's art couldn't hide the beginnings of putrefaction, greenish-black vines creeping into her face and hands. Her violet, musk, and ambergris scent had held notes of rot.

We'll bring your killer to justice, Julianna, Pippa thought fiercely. *So that you may rest in peace.*

Aloud, Pippa said, "I appreciate your efforts. Might we go to the bedchamber?"

Hastings's laugh skittered down her spine. "That is an excellent suggestion. Come, my sweet."

As she took the smooth, manicured hand he offered, she was reminded of Cull's touch. The honest strength of his callused hands, which had shown her such pleasure. She hadn't seen or heard from him since their last encounter at the Nest. She wondered what he would do if he knew what she was up to...and shivered.

What you do is none of his business, she chided herself. *Concentrate on your mission.*

In a practiced move, Hastings maneuvered her upon the bed. His weight pressed her into the mattress, his mouth wet and heavy on hers. She moaned in pretended delight, waiting for the drug to take effect. Was it her imagination or did he feel heavier, as if his muscles were relaxing?

She took advantage, rolling atop him. He looked up at her with glazed eyes.

"Allow me," she said in a sultry voice and began to unbutton his jacket.

"Eager wench, aren't you?" His words were slurred, his pupils dilated. "Well, prepare for the biggest, hardest..."

His eyelids closed before she got to the final button.

About dashed time.

She continued undressing him, huffing a little as she turned him over to tug off his clothes, tossing them on the ground as if they'd been removed in a passionate frenzy. Pulling down his smalls, she had to roll her eyes; Hastings's opinion of himself *and* his manhood were obviously inflated. Throwing a blanket over his naked form, she raced out of the chamber. She descended to the main floor, taking the servants' stairs down to the kitchens, where she opened the back door.

Her fellow Angels were waiting, dressed to blend in with the cover of night.

"How did things go?" Livy asked as Glory and Fi trooped in behind her.

"The sleeping draught worked like a charm," Pippa replied. "When he awakes, he'll think he fell asleep after a tumble. The draught only lasts an hour, so we had better hurry."

Livy stuck her hand out, the other Angels doing the same.

"Sisters first." They whispered their motto before splitting up.

Pippa and Glory went to search the upstairs floor while the other two made a beeline for Hastings's study.

"Lady Hastings's suite is on the left," Pippa whispered.

With a nod, Glory turned toward the lady's chamber and Pippa returned to Hastings's.

The suspect remained snoring on the bed. Pippa worked stealthily, methodically going through his bedchamber and dressing room. Despite Hastings's dire financial straits, he spared no expense when it came to himself. His fashions were of the highest quality, and he had more cravats than a dog had fleas. Her eyebrows rose at what she found beneath his stockings in a bottom drawer: a stash of opium and a volume titled *Miss Fanny and the House of Flagellation*.

Hearing a moan from the bed, Pippa hurried back to check on him. Luckily, Hastings had merely turned on his side, snoring again. She tiptoed to his desk, scribbling a note to thank him for the "unforgettable night" before meeting Glory at the stairs.

"I didn't find anything," she said in a low voice. "You?"

Glory's russet ringlets swung as she shook her head. "Someone must have gone through Lady Hastings's room. All her personal effects are gone. I hope the others had better luck."

They found their friends in the study. Livy and Fi were at Hastings's desk, studying documents laid out on the blotter.

Seeing their pleated brows, Pippa asked, "What are you reading?"

Livy looked up, her eyes troubled. "It appears to be a codicil to Jonas Turner's will."

"And it explains how Viscount Hastings convinced the inspectors that he did not have motive to kill his wife," Fiona said starkly.

Pippa followed her friends out the back door into the gated garden.

"Hawker's meeting us around the corner," Glory began.

She broke off as a shadow separated from a tree and blocked their path. Pippa's training kicked in, her hands coming up in a fighting stance. Her fellow Angels adopted similar postures. Pippa's heart knocked against her ribs when she recognized Cull.

"Dash it, what are you doing here?" she said in a fierce whisper.

"I could ask you the same." His voice was calm, but his eyes glowed like molten ore in his mask. "That is a conversation better had in private. Come, my carriage is waiting."

"She is not going anywhere with you," Glory said, her fists still up.

"You will have to take on all of us," Fiona warned.

"Heaven forbid." Although Cull's mouth curved faintly, there was a challenge in his eyes as he looked at Pippa. "I suppose the lady will have to come with me of her own volition, won't she?"

It was so like him to make it her choice. To know that she couldn't resist.

Pippa blew out a breath and tried to sound annoyed. "Very well."

"Are you certain it's safe?" Livy said in an undertone.

"She will always be safe with me," Cull stated.

Aiming her gaze heavenward at his proprietary tone, Pippa said to her friends, "I know what I'm doing. Report back to Charlie, and I'll see you tomorrow."

16

As the carriage rolled off, Pippa was torn between excitement and a healthy dose of wariness. Seated across from her in a shadowed corner, Cull was brooding and watchful. Neither of them spoke, as if daring the other to go first. Their unsettled business electrified the air.

Each breath Pippa took seemed to crackle with energy. She felt more alive than she had in months. Years, maybe. While some of that had to do with the night's adventures, most of it had to do with the man across from her. She couldn't help but think how different he was from Hastings...and Longmere.

Cull eschewed superficial elegance. His masculinity was as raw and untamed as the streets that had birthed him. Despite his overprotective nature, he was no predator. He used his strength to shield rather than take advantage. Thus, even though she could tell he was angry, she wasn't afraid.

Of him...or her own desire.

When Livy had asked what Pippa would do when Cull showed up again, Pippa hadn't known the answer. But the truth hit her now. Thrummed in her pulse and rushed hotly beneath her skin as she inhaled his scent of salt, male, and sea. She wanted to touch him, be touched by him. Wanted to explore the pleasures of being alive with this vital and enigmatic man.

First, however, she guessed he had other matters on his mind.

"What were you up to with Hastings this eve?" he ground out.

She had guessed right.

Stifling a sigh, she replied, "It is none of your business what I was doing."

"Did you seduce him while your fellow agents searched the place? Did you let him touch you, Pippa?" Cull's hands clenched and unclenched at his sides. "Did you enjoy it, his lordly attentions?"

Here we go again. She didn't know how he managed to stir such volatile emotions in her. With him, she wasn't Patient Pippa. She was Peeved and Provoked Pippa.

She scowled. "I don't have to answer to you."

"I've decided that you do."

"I beg your pardon?" she said in affronted tones.

"Given your lack of judgment, someone needs to look after you." He leaned forward, grooves deepening around his mouth. "Why in *blazes* did you go to Hastings's house?"

"Since you refused to provide any details," she said pointedly, "I was looking for clues to pinpoint him as a murderer, you dolt. I arranged the private *tête-à-tête* so that I could drug him and search his house."

Cull dragged a breath through his nose. "You drugged him. Searched his house."

She waved nonchalantly. "When he wakes, he will think he fell asleep after we engaged in a night of pleasure. The best of my life, according to the note I left him."

"Why the devil did you take such a risk when I told you I would take care of the matter?"

"Because I don't need you—or anyone—to take care of me," she rejoined. "I am an independent woman, and *I* will decide the direction of my life."

"You are steering yourself toward an early damned grave."

"If so, it will be *my* choice." She lifted her chin. "And it won't happen, because I am good at what I do, Cull. The Angels and I discovered things tonight—important things that alter our theory of Lady Hastings's murder."

"Such as the fact that Hastings had a financial motivation to keep his wife alive?"

She blinked. "How...how did you know?"

"The late Jonas Turner's solicitor, Fanshawe, had a copy of his last will. While Hastings gained control of Julianna's considerable dowry when he married her, her father was smarter when it came to the rest of his wealth. Before Turner died, he added a codicil." Cull sounded as pedantic as a schoolmaster as he listed off the facts. "His personal fortune would go into a trust for his future grandchildren, with Julianna and Hastings as the trustees. If no children were to come of the union, then the bulk of his personal assets—some four hundred thousand pounds—would be split between two beneficiaries: Howard Morton, the son of a distant cousin and Louis Wood, his manservant of many years. In other words, you have two new suspects."

Despite herself, Pippa was impressed. "You do have a knack for finding information."

"And I manage to do it without risking my neck."

"We have different approaches, each with their own merits," she said judiciously.

"Indeed?"

Encouraged by his civility, she said, "The mudlarks cast a broad net; you have eyes and ears everywhere, catching information in the outside world. The Angels, on the other hand, work from the inside. We are less broad, but more specific, if you see what I mean." She risked a smile. "The truth is, Cull, we should be joining forces. Working together to find whoever killed Lady Hastings and hurt Ollie."

"You want to work with me," Cull said neutrally.

The more she thought about it, the more she liked the idea. "It is the logical thing to do."

"I agree."

Delight bubbled through her. "I am glad. Of course, Charlie will need to be convinced—"

"I don't give a damn what Lady Fayne thinks. I am done keeping my distance from you, Pippa."

She swallowed at his blazing intensity. "Are we talking about the investigation or, um, personal matters?"

"Both." He rose, steady despite the swaying carriage. He crossed over and planted his palms next to her shoulders, caging her. "I thought I was doing what was best for you by staying away. But if the only way to keep you safe is to stake my claim, then so be it."

The truth hit Cull like a bolt of lightning. His strategy with Pippa —it had been all wrong.

She wasn't going to stop investigating, no matter what he said. And he knew he had no right to dictate her actions. The only thing he could do was protect her as she went about her business. Staying away from her wasn't helping her...and it sure as hell wasn't helping him.

"Staking your *claim?*" The golden suns flared around her pupils, firing up her blue eyes. Her ringlets bristled with indignation. "Of all the troglodytic—"

"I am an uncouth bastard. A man born and raised in the rookery. A man who makes his living dealing in dark secrets, and I am *still* a better man than that blighter you were with tonight."

"Of course you are." She frowned. "I never said you weren't."

A life on the water had taught Cull how to keep his balance, his body rocking with the carriage as he gazed at the woman he wanted more than his next breath. Her eyes were sparkling with defiance; they were not lost, lifeless, and grieving. Not cowed and afraid. Pippa had regained her spirit. Was she truly ready to move on from her marriage...to take him on as a lover?

"I want you," he said. "I haven't been able to stop thinking about that night at The Enchanted Rose."

"Neither have I."

Her breathy admission flooded his groin with heat.

"But we...we should talk first. And I can't do it with you towering over me."

She patted the cushion beside her, and he accepted the invitation. It had been a while since he'd seen her in something other than men's clothing or somber mourning garb. She looked sensual and sophisticated in her purple gown, her exposed shoulders glowing like a pearl. The brush of her skirts against his thigh felt like foreplay. Her lily-and-Pippa scent teased his nostrils and made him instantly hard. A common state for him when she was near. Elation spilled through his veins because now he knew he wasn't alone in his yearning.

He took her hand. It was the hand of a countess: delicate, slim, smooth. Although his grip attested to the roughness of his life, their fingers twined with natural ease on the cushion between them.

"You wanted to talk," he prompted.

She looked up from their joined hands, her expression bemused. "This feels easier than it ought to. Being here with you, I mean. After all...the complications."

"Maybe we're making things complicated. Maybe things are simple." He was speaking to himself as much as to her. "I want you, Pippa, and I think you want me too."

Her nod sent a surge of triumph through him. Bleeding hell, at long last...

"I want to explore whatever this is between us," she said slowly. "Without expectation. Or pressure. I have lived too long with both, and what I want, what I deserve, is freedom. I will not give up my independence again—for anyone."

"I understand." And he did.

I wasn't crying for Longmere, you nodcock. I was crying for myself, Pippa had told him. But while she might be done mourning her undeserving husband—*Halle-bloody-lujah*—Cull could understand why she wouldn't be eager to dive head-first into another relationship. With quiet rage, he recalled her poignant confession. *I was crying because I finally understood that maybe there's nothing wrong with me after all.* That Pippa should doubt, for even a second, that she was anything but perfect...it made him feel fit to kill.

Since Cull's fury wasn't going to help Pippa, he locked it away. Focused on the opportunity at hand. With a sense of irony, he recognized that her desire to keep her freedom might very well make her the perfect match for what he had to offer.

"I will not make demands beyond what you are ready to give. And the truth is..." He tightened his clasp on her, even as he said the words. "I have nothing to offer you beyond the moment."

Not when he had the mudlarks to look after. A target on his back.

Not to mention a face full of scars.

And while Pippa might be able to overlook their differences in station, he knew her place was ultimately in the lavish upper bowers of society. Not in the gutter with him. No lady in her right mind would relinquish the title of a countess to be with a man who didn't even bear his father's name.

"A thing of beauty is a joy forever," she said softly. "Its loveliness increases; it will never pass into nothingness."

He blinked. "Did you come up with that just now?"

"No, silly. That is from a poem by John Keats."

Her breathtaking smile caused his chest to ache along with his cock.

"You made me think of it. Of how beauty, no matter if it is fleeting, brings us enduring joy and changes us for the better.

While I have no need of promises from you, there is one thing I would ask."

Dazzled by her, he murmured, "What is it?"

"I want to see you without your mask."

Reality was colder than a plunge in the Thames. He'd been so caught up in the beauty of being with Pippa that he'd forgotten his own ugliness. Releasing her hand, he pulled away.

"If we are to be lovers," she carried on softly, "then you don't have to keep up appearances with me. It is you I want to get to know, Timothy Cullen, not the enigmatic Prince of Larks."

You must tell her. Do it and be done with it. Her reaction will be... what it will be.

No matter how he'd prepared himself for this moment, he still had to drag out the truth.

"It's never been about keeping an aura of mystery. Not with you." He inhaled. "Five years ago, the old mudlarks' headquarters caught on fire. It was the middle of the night, and the little ones were fast asleep. We managed to get most of them out, but two of the girls were missing. I went back for them.

"I found them, but as we were exiting, one of the beams collapsed on top of me, knocked me out. Luckily, the girls weren't hurt and went for help. Mikey and several others hauled me out, and I'm lucky to be breathing today." He thought of his best friend Patrick, who hadn't been as lucky; how could he feel sorry for himself when Patrick had sacrificed so much more? "I didn't escape entirely unscathed, however."

Pippa's eyes widened, and he wondered if she was imagining what lay behind his leather shield. Whether what she pictured was better or worse than what he saw in the looking glass every day.

"I'm lucky the job requires a mask." He tried to make light of the subject but realized he couldn't. "What's underneath here...it is ugly, Pippa."

Maybe she'll leave it at that. Tell me she's no longer interested and end things now.

A part of him almost wanted her to.

She gazed at him solemnly. "I want to see."

Christ. He hated the pounding anxiety he felt. It angered him, his wounded vanity. The fire had taken Patrick's *life*; what right did Cull have to mope over his damaged looks? Yet he flashed to the memory of Nan packing up her bags, her gaze avoiding his freshly disfigured face as she did so.

It was never going to work, Cull. You always put those mudlarks first. What 'appened to you...it's just more o' the same. I've 'ad enough o' peril, poverty, and ugliness. I ain't signing up for a lifetime o' that wif you.

He didn't blame Nan, but he resented his own weakness. Resented the way his hands hesitated before reaching up to untie the strings. The way he took courage from the dimness of the carriage—from the fact that the shadows hid, to some degree, the full extent of the damage.

He removed his mask and met Pippa's gaze squarely. Dared her to look away—to not look away. Dared her to pretend that he was anything but what he was.

Her gaze was steady, her voice a bit husky. "Does it hurt?"

"No."

"May I touch you?"

He gave a curt nod, and she reached up. He held miserably still as her touch feathered over the undamaged side of his face first, her thumb sweeping over his eyebrow, cheekbone, her fingers trailing along his jaw. She repeated the motion on the other side, his throat tightening as the same light caress now traveled over gnarled ridges and patches of unnatural smoothness. Despite his dulled sensation, he felt as if she were stroking the very heart of him, the place where hope refused to die. Where his dreams waged an agonizing battle with reality.

"I pictured what you looked like, you know." Her voice was as gentle as her exploration. "How the lad I met fourteen years ago had matured into a man."

"Not what you expected, am I?" he said humorlessly.

"No." Her gaze was direct and, thank Christ, devoid of pity. "You are far more. And you are not ugly, Cull."

It was so bloody stupid that he should care. That he should feel a burning at the back of his throat and an even more embarrassing surge of gratitude. Those feelings grew when Pippa leaned up and kissed him, right on his wrecked cheek.

"What you are is noble and brave." Even though he couldn't feel her whisper against his skin, it fed his deep, hungering hope. "And that is real beauty."

Her sweetness undid him. He yanked her onto his lap and crushed his mouth to hers.

P ippa wound her arms around Cull's neck, opening herself to his kiss. To him. This man who wore a mask not because he enjoyed being a mythic, mysterious figure...but because he thought he needed to. To hide himself when his injury, the cause of it, made his true beauty shine as brightly as a star.

Removing the mask stripped away a barrier that had stood between them. She felt their new intimacy in his kiss, in his plundering hunger. No one had ever kissed her like this, with such animal need. With such raw and honest passion. It made her feel wanted and wanton; she wanted to kiss and kiss him. To give him anything he asked of her and take everything in return.

Cull stroked her mouth with his tongue, his taste filling her senses. Curling her fingers in the rough silk of his hair, she tugged him closer. Until there was no space left between them.

His sensual chuckle heated her lips. "What a demanding chit you are."

She stilled, Longmere's words mocking her. *Such forward behavior is unbecoming of a lady.*

"Is that a problem?" she managed.

"Hell, no. I want you greedy for me." Cull's scorching honesty vaporized her doubt. "I want you panting, moaning, begging me for more."

If his words didn't convince her, then his actions did. He pulled her back against his front, his lips finding her ear. At the first hot lick against the sensitive curve, her spine bowed.

"I love how responsive you are," he murmured. "How you don't hide your reactions from me."

Would it be possible to contain what she was feeling? She didn't think so. When he dragged his lips down her neck and back up again, she *knew* she couldn't hold back. Didn't want to. She moaned as he flicked her earlobe before taking it into his mouth. The warm suction pulled her nipples into hard, throbbing points. An accompanying pulse started between her thighs, where she was already slick with need.

Arching against him, she clutched his rock-hard thigh. "Oh, Cull, I need..."

"You're so sweet when you beg."

At that, she turned to give him a narrowed-eye stare. His mouth took on a lopsided curve. It was a teasing and oh-so-sensual smile, and she wondered how he could ever think himself ugly. How he could believe that his scars could be the sum of his attractions.

"I never beg," she said primly.

"Then you haven't been properly made love to before." Wicked challenge smoldered in his earth-brown eyes. "Never fear. There is a first time for everything."

Her retort was lost in his playful devouring. His mouth was everywhere: on her mouth, her ear, her neck. He cupped her breasts, squeezing the aching mounds, rubbing her nipples against her bodice until they throbbed like twin heartbeats. Her breath pushed against the cage of her corset, her skin itching with need. She was restrained when what she wanted—what she craved—was to feel Cull, skin to skin.

He seemed to read her mind. He fisted her skirts, raising the voluminous mass, swearing as some of the layers eluded his grasp.

"You ladies wear too many damned clothes," he muttered.

Pippa wasn't only a lady; she was an Angel. And being an Angel had its advantages.

Feeling rather smug, she reached for the hidden fasteners that Mrs. Quinton, the Angels' genius modiste, had placed beneath the ruffle at her waist. A few deft tugs were all it took to detach the skirts and petticoats from her bodice. They pooled on the floor, leaving her in her drawers and black silk stockings.

"Designed for the physical demands of investigating...and practical for lovemaking as well," she said impishly.

"Now *that* is a dress," Cull rasped.

Then he got onto his knees in front of her. He ran his palms up her stockinged calves, his touch reverent and possessive. And the look on his face...

Pure, raw hunger.

He shoved her thighs apart with arousing roughness. The heat of his palms burned through the thin linen of her drawers. Her back slid into the cushioned corner of the carriage as he pulled her closer, spread her wider. So wide that the slit in her undergarment gaped, revealing her sex to his burning gaze.

"There's that pretty pussy," he murmured. "Sunshine down here as well as on top."

She squirmed, embarrassed and unbearably stimulated. The gleam in his eyes told her that he knew exactly how she felt. That he enjoyed her discomfiture.

"Are you going to just talk"—her attempt at haughtiness was foiled by her breathlessness—"or are you going to do something?"

"What would you like me to do?"

She refused to be embarrassed by her desires any longer. Not with Cull, who'd exposed his own vulnerability to her. Who made her feel beautiful and wanted...just as she was.

"Touch me," she said.

His eyes glinting with approval, he ran a thumb lightly down her intimate seam. "Like this?"

She had to bite back a moan. "More."

He stroked her again, up and down, his nostrils flaring. "I love how wet you get, Pippa. How these lips are as pretty, pink, and pouting as the ones you use to argue with me."

"I don't argue...*oh.*"

Her words dissolved into a whimper as he found the peak of her pleasure. As he rubbed and circled that throbbing bud, his gaze never left her face. The slick sounds of him fingering her filled the cabin, and she gasped as he slid a long, thick finger inside.

"Wet *and* tight," he growled. "Keep moving, Pippa. Fuck that sweet quim on my hand until you come for me."

His filthy words unleashed her primal instincts. Panting, she did as he instructed, moving, taking that fullness. He stretched her with another finger, stirring those thick digits, and her rhythm became desperate. When he curled his fingers, dragging the callused tips against a place high inside, a quickening started at her core. She cried out as bliss exploded, aftershocks cascading through her.

He murmured sweet nothings, still stroking her, gently easing her back to reality. Meeting his gaze, she saw banked flames that set off more tremors.

And that was before he withdrew his fingers, saying with male pride, "Everything appears to be in working order."

She didn't know whether to laugh or cry that he had remembered what she said. That he'd filed away that piece of information to use at an opportune time. Her witty rejoinder went up in smoke when he brought his fingers to his lips...and licked them.

Her quim quivered.

"Delectable," he said. "The perfect appetizer before the main course."

"M-main course?" she breathed.

His smile was wicked. "I'm a man who likes to feast."

The taste of Pippa...it was indescribable. The best damned thing he'd ever sampled.

And she seemed to be enjoying his feast as much as he was. Although she hadn't said it, he guessed from her shocked expression that she'd never had her pussy licked before. Yet another failing to lay at her cursed husband's door. At the same time, Cull couldn't deny that he liked being the first to give her this pleasure. The first to experience her delicious response.

Her fingers clenched in his hair, and he would have chuckled at her feminine demand if he wasn't otherwise occupied. She'd come again for him, her honey coating his lips as he'd licked and suckled her little pearl. He could tell she was on the verge once more...in working order indeed.

The woman had so much passion in her that it was a wonder she didn't burn him alive. And he'd be happy—no, bloody ecstatic —to go up in her flames. His cock felt like a throbbing iron bar, his bollocks pulled up taut. He'd never been this hard, this full of want.

When she'd kissed his cheek, the warmth of her lips had seeped through his numb layers, touching the part of him that had hungered for her light from the moment he'd clapped eyes on her fourteen years ago. To experience the sweetness of the girl rolled up with the passion of the woman was...he didn't have words for what he felt.

Lust and desire and something more. Something he'd never had. Something that was his for the moment, and he wasn't bloody going to waste it.

He parted her sunny thatch, swiping his tongue along her slit.

"Cull," she moaned.

His erection twitched. God, the sound of his name on her lips.

"I think," he said thickly, "that I've found my favorite meal."

Feeling her shiver, he delved deeper, licking into her tight passage. When she clenched around his tongue, he groaned. He diddled her love-knot while he ate her, her moans driving him on.

"Spend in my mouth now," he growled. "I want the taste of you sliding down my throat."

"Heavens, *Cull*."

She shrieked, coming in a honeyed gush, and he showed his approval by lapping up every drop.

When she sagged against the cushions, a sated glow upon her face, he sat on the bench next to her, pulling her close. Burying his nose in her fragrant hair, he strove to master himself. He was so aroused that he feared he might spill in his pants like an untried greenling. He concentrated on not unmanning himself... and jerked when her fingers feathered over his pulsing length.

"I want to see you," she whispered. "May I?"

Bloody hell, yes.

"If you're certain you want to," he managed.

Her eyes sparkled as she nodded.

He needed no further urging. He undid the fasteners, grimacing a little as he brushed his granite-hard prick. As he lowered the flap and shoved down his smalls, his erection fell out, the head glossy and engorged. When she delicately fisted him, a groan raked up his throat.

"You're very large," she said. "I can barely get my fingers around you."

He got even bigger at her words, at her light, too-careful touch. "You make me this way."

"Truly?"

He would have laughed at her pleased expression if her stroking wasn't driving him mad. He couldn't tear his eyes off her slim fingers wrapped around the thick pole of his flesh, the mesmerizing contrast of that ladylike hand and his rude length popping with veins. Her gentle caresses kept him on the razor's edge. Yet he enjoyed the sweet torture, that look of curiosity and lust on her cameo-worthy face.

"Am I doing this right?" she murmured. "Do you like me touching you this way?"

"You must know that I do," he said huskily.

Uncertainty flickered in her eyes.

Christ, what kind of an idiot *had Longmere been?* was starting to be a refrain in Cull's head.

She asked, "Will you, um, find satisfaction if I keep touching you this way?"

Cull saw no reason to hide how she affected him. "I almost did just watching you come. Having your hands on me is bliss." As if to prove his point, a drop of seed leaked from him, and he grunted when she smeared it around his sensitive head.

"You liked that," she purred.

"Yes." His balls pulsed as she circled his tip again, drawing forth more silky moisture. "You can frig me harder, sunshine."

She caught her bottom lip beneath her teeth. "How much harder?"

He surrounded her hand with his own, tightening her grip and moving it faster. "Like this."

"Oh," she said in a breathy voice. "That isn't too hard?"

"Hell, no." The words hissed through his teeth.

Pleasure blazed along his spine as she caught onto the general idea. Her firm stroking seemed to pull all the blood into his groin. When she slapped his hand aside, saying, "I can handle this on my own," he made a ragged sound. Christ, her touch...

As she frigged him like a goddamned expert, she asked, "Do you like being touched here too?"

She cupped his balls, squeezing gently.

"Bloody *fuck*," he gasped.

His blood roared, his seed pulsing up his shaft. His neck arched as he erupted in a hot blast. She continued milking him with her lady-soft hands, pulling his spend from him in long, blissful bursts.

When it was over, he dragged her close. Looking into her eyes, he said hoarsely, "Being with you is even better than I imagined it would be."

Her smile was so lovely that, unbelievably, his cock stirred.

"I'm glad. Because you're everything I imagined you would be..." She brushed her lips against his cheek, whispering, "And more."

18

"Concentrate, Pippa," Mrs. Peabody instructed. "You should have anticipated my strike."

Panting, Pippa rose from the mats. "I'm sorry, Mrs. Peabody."

They were in the training room, housed in the building behind Charlie's courtyard. Pippa was a bundle of nerves, for Cull had scheduled a meeting with her mentor later today. Before parting last night, they had deliberated over the best way to broach the idea of combining forces with Charlie. Pippa had warned him that it wouldn't be easy.

Cull had said, *"Leave it to me, sunshine. I will convince Lady Fayne."*

In retrospect, she ought to have at least asked about his plan. Spent and lazy after their lovemaking, she had merely agreed with a dreamy nod. Her blissful state hadn't worn off by the time he dropped her off at her doorstep, giving her one last toe-curling kiss. She'd fallen into the deepest, most restful sleep she'd had in ages.

Now, however, Pippa was beginning to worry. What would she do if Charlie refused a partnership with the mudlarks? Her loyalty lay with the Angels...but she also believed in Cull—

"You're distracted," Mrs. Peabody said, frowning.

The housekeeper was a petite half-Chinese, half-English lady with golden eyes and dark hair worn in a bun. She'd suggested that Pippa work off the excess energy with a few rounds in the sparring ring. An expert combatant, the housekeeper had trained the Angels in a unique fighting style that emphasized speed, accuracy, and creative maneuvers.

Pippa inhaled and refocused. "Ready for another round when you are."

Mrs. Peabody curled her fingers in a come-hither motion, and Pippa faced her teacher. Their tunics and trousers fluttered as they circled one another, arms raised. Mrs. Peabody's steady gaze revealed nothing. The longer the circling continued, the more Pippa felt the impulse to attack. Her muscles tensed; her eye twitched. Giving in, she went on the offensive.

She attacked with a series of rapid kicks and punches. Mrs. Peabody effortlessly parried each one. Pippa kept on going, determined to find the weak spot in her opponent's defense. Perspiration misted her brow as she landed blows, none of them enough to take the other down. Her limbs began to tire from her aggressive onslaught.

Finally, she saw her opening: Mrs. Peabody's right side was unguarded. Pippa feinted, then went in with a left hook...and found her arm caught in the other's grip. *A trap.* Mrs. Peabody spun around and flipped Pippa over her shoulder. Pippa's back smacked against the mat, the breath whooshing from her lungs.

When the stars cleared, she saw Mrs. Peabody's face hovering over her.

"Act first and think later is a losing strategy," Mrs. Peabody chided. "Patience is your friend. Let your foe wear herself out. Let her win the battle while you win the war."

Pippa took her teacher's hand and was pulled smoothly to her feet.

"Thank you for the lesson, Mrs. Peabody," she said with a bow.

The other Angels burst into the training room.

"Mr. Cullen has arrived," Livy announced.

"He's early!" Pippa clapped her hands to her cheeks. "And I look a fright."

"Don't worry. He just went into the study with Charlie," Fiona said. "We'll help you freshen up."

Within a quarter hour, Pippa and her friends rushed into the main house. Hawker informed them that Cull and Charlie were still in the study.

"Lady Fayne said to wait in the drawing room." Hawker pinned them with a one-eyed look. "And she said specifically not to eavesdrop."

Sighing, Pippa and the others went to the drawing room, where refreshments awaited on the coffee table.

"I'm sure everything will be fine," Livy said as she poured out the tea.

Fiona used silver tongs to select sliced fruits from a tray. "Or it will be a disaster."

"You're not helping matters," Glory said under her breath.

"I'm merely being honest." Fi arched her auburn brows. "Remember when Livy wanted to tell Hadleigh she was an Angel? Charlie does not like outsiders knowing about our society—especially male outsiders."

Worry gnawed at Pippa. Fiona was right. Charlie did not trust men in general, and she'd voiced her concern about Cull *in particular.*

"That was a different scenario," Livy said reassuringly. "Hadleigh didn't know about the Angels, and given his overprotective nature, was unlikely to support my participation. Mr. Cullen, on the other hand, is fully aware of what we do. And he doesn't have a problem with Pippa being an Angel, does he?"

A cool droplet trickled down Pippa's spine. Her inner voice whispered that she didn't need Cull's permission, or any man's, to do as she wished. She'd promised herself that she wouldn't go down the same path as she had with Longmere. She wouldn't give up her independence—*herself*—for anyone again.

She pulled her shoulders back. "Cull can be overprotective as well. But I've been clear that I am my own woman and don't have to answer to him or anyone."

She had made her conditions clear. That she wouldn't countenance any restriction of her freedom during their affair. And Cull had agreed to her terms.

Head angled, Glory asked, "How serious are things between you and Mr. Cullen?"

Pippa chewed on her lip. It was one thing to discuss what went on between a man and woman with Livy, but Glory and Fiona were both unmarried debutantes. Pippa felt protective of their youth and innocence.

"You are having an affair with him, are you not?" Fiona inquired.

Pippa's cheeks burned. "Fiona Garrity, what do you know of such things?"

"Rather more than people give me credit for," the redhead replied. "Being a debutante does not make me dim-witted. One cannot do the work we do and remain blind to the realities of life. It has been obvious from the start that Mr. Cullen has taken a special interest in you. Now it seems that you return it. Trust me, it would take far more than an affair to scandalize anyone in this room."

Fi had a point. The Angels' cases had taken them to London's darkest corners, exposing them to every kind of sin and vice. Charlie's philosophy was that empowerment came from education, not ignorance. To take charge of their destinies, women needed to know the facts. Pippa acknowledged with a twinge that innocence hadn't done her any favors.

"We only wish for you to be happy," Glory said earnestly.

As the cat was out of the bag, Pippa saw no reason to dissemble.

"Cull and I are enjoying each other's company for now." She succeeded in saying the words without blushing. "I'm still in mourning, after all, and not ready for anything permanent."

"Wise choice," Fiona concurred. "It's always good to shop around a bit."

"So says the perpetual browser," Livy teased.

"Are you ever going to settle on a suitor, Fi?" Glory's hazel eyes had a playful light. "Heaven knows you have your pick."

Fiona gave her ivory skirts a complacent flick. "I do not believe in settling. When the right gentleman comes along, I will know. I have excellent instincts when it comes to men."

Pippa wished she had Fi's confidence. She hated that her marriage had made her doubt her instincts when it came to relationships. She'd believed Longmere was her one true love...and now she had to confront the truth that he wasn't. At least the dagger of guilt didn't twist as strongly as before.

Maybe it was because Cull had opened her eyes to things that had been missing in her marriage. Not just physical pleasure. She enjoyed spending time in Cull's company, their banter and getting to know one another. For all his rough edges, he was a complex man. When he'd taken off his mask last night, he'd revealed another layer, and his vulnerability had touched her.

He never hid his admiration for her. His unconditional respect. With Cull, she felt worthy and special. It was the opposite of what she'd felt with her husband: the desperate fear that she wasn't good enough, that she needed to be more, something other than who she was.

The insight allowed her to say quietly, "There is no need to rush into anything, Fi. Discover who you are first. Then find the man who values you exactly as you are."

"Hear, hear." Fi raised her teacup in a toast.

They all leaned in to clink their cups together. A moment later, the door opened, and Charlie and Cull entered. His mask and threadbare blue frock coat did not detract from his brawny appeal. His gaze searched her out, and her heart thudded at the proprietary flare in his rich chocolate eyes.

"Mr. Cullen and I have agreed to a partnership for our present case," Charlie announced.

Pippa exhaled a thankful breath.

Cull raised his brows at her. As if to say, *Did you doubt me?*

When he took the chair next to hers, Pippa said in an undertone, "How did you convince her?"

"I'll tell you later," he murmured. "Tonight?"

Although her first impulse was eager agreement, she paused. *This is an affair. Don't get too attached. Put your independence first.*

"I have plans," she said cautiously.

Edwin had expected her to be at his disposal. She had made herself available to him, rearranging her schedule at his whim. Back then, she'd thought of it as doing her duty as a good wife but thinking of it now made resentment flare. Would Cull also expect her to jump at his bidding?

"Tomorrow, then?" Cull seemed unperturbed.

With burgeoning relief, she nodded because she did want to see him.

He rewarded her with his crooked smile.

"Mr. Cullen and I have discussed a plan for tracking down Lady Hastings's killer," Charlie said. "As it turns out, all roads lead to Rome; his reconnaissance and ours have led to the same conclusions. While Lady Hastings feared her husband, the codicil to her father's will suggests that Viscount Hastings had no motive to kill her...in fact, he had four hundred thousand reasons to keep her alive."

"Did Lady Hastings know about the codicil?" Pippa asked with a frown. "She never mentioned it."

Cull responded. "According to Turner's solicitor Fanshawe, Turner specifically instructed that the codicil was to be kept a secret from his daughter. He remained angry at her for choosing Hastings, whom he believed to be a fortune hunter, but he also believed that one should lie in the bed of one's own making, so to speak. Although he knew Julianna was unhappy, he wanted grandchildren and used the codicil as a means of leverage with Hastings. Fanshawe claims the only people who knew about the codicil's existence were Hastings and the two beneficiaries, Howard Morton and Louis Wood."

"It makes sense that Hastings would keep the codicil a secret from his wife," Charlie said in a hard tone. "Since she was already suspicious of him, knowing that he was bedding her to get his hands on the rest of her fortune would have increased her resistance."

"Does this mean we cross Hastings off our suspect list?" Glory furrowed her brow. "Let us not forget that Lady Hastings was afraid of him."

"I agree that Hastings cannot be summarily discounted as a suspect." Charlie took a meditative sip of tea. "But we must focus on the two new suspects as well."

"The wheels are in motion," Cull said. "I've started compiling the basics on Morton and Wood, including their financials, relationships, any gossip circulating about them, etcetera. Morton is taking more time as he lives in Hertfordshire. The dossiers should be ready within a few days and will help us decide where to focus our energies."

"When I spoke with Wood at Lady Hastings's funeral, he presented himself as a loyal retainer to the Turners," Pippa said. "He made no mention of the codicil. In fact, he pointed me toward Hastings as the killer...but now I wonder if that was a ruse. I hope my conversation with him didn't tip him off to our investigation."

"Your plan was logical, given the facts at the time. From here on in, we'll have eyes on Wood. The good news is the legal rigamarole required to disburse Turner's funds apparently takes time. Neither Wood nor Morton will be going anywhere until they have their money," Cull said. "And, as of this morning, I have another lead. A possible murder weapon."

Pippa's eyes rounded. "You found the weapon used to kill Lady Hastings?"

Cull casually removed an object bundled in green baize from a pocket of his frock coat. He set it upon the coffee table, parting the fabric to reveal a pistol. The piece was compact and elegant, designed to fit in a gentleman's pocket. The blued steel of the twin barrels flowed like water into the smooth walnut handle. Stylish double gold bands encircled the wooden grip.

"I've been on the lookout for firearms recovered in the Thames," Cull said. "This one was caught in a trawling net this morning. Not far from where Lady Hastings's body was found."

"May I?" With thudding excitement, Pippa gestured to the gun.

Cull nodded, and she picked up the weapon with care, feeling the balanced weight and examining the precise percussion mechanism. The gunmaker's mark was engraved in elegant letters on the lock plate: J PURDEY No 314 ½ OXFORD STREET LONDON.

"Obviously, we don't know if this was the weapon that was used to kill Julianna Hastings," Charlie said. "But Mr. Cullen makes a good case for it."

"Given the growing crowd and the arrival of the police, I could only do a precursory inspection of Lady Hastings's body. She had two wounds that I saw," Cull said. "One in the shoulder, one through the heart. The size and state of the wounds were similar, most likely made by a double-barreled weapon and at close range. Lady Hastings's hands were also free of any damage, her nails clean and unbroken. She didn't attempt to defend herself, which suggests the attack took her by surprise. Either she didn't see her killer coming...or she saw the killer but didn't expect him or her to attack."

Now Pippa understood why her mentor was amenable to a

joint effort. The Prince of Larks's information was extraordinary. Cull had won over Charlie with his skill and expertise.

Livy pursed her lips. "You mean to say Lady Hastings knew her murderer?"

"It is a possibility," Cull replied.

"The papers are claiming that her death is the result of criminal behavior among the lower classes," Glory said, wrinkling her nose. "Then again, they tend to blame the less fortunate for a variety of social ills."

"The papers profit from selling fear to the masses," Cull said. "This pistol is far too expensive to belong to a common thug. Its state indicates that it hasn't been in the river long—less than a week, I'd say. Which coincides with the time of the murder."

Pippa glanced at the ormolu clock on the mantel; it was nearing four o'clock. "I could go to Purdey's to see if anyone can identify the pistol's owner. If I leave soon, I'll get there before the shop closes."

"If you don't mind the company, I will escort you," Cull said.

Pippa beamed at him. "I would like that."

"Be discreet," Charlie advised. "In the meantime, we still have the mysterious Thor to track down and Hastings to monitor."

"I'll put larks on Hastings." Cull lifted his brows. "Who is Thor?"

Pippa shared what she and Livy had learned from Mrs. Loverly about the silver-eyed fellow, and the other Angels volunteered to start canvassing for him. In the meantime, Charlie would comb the drawing rooms for gossip related to the case.

Charlie set down her cup with a satisfied click. "It seems we have a plan."

19

Before the carriage door was fully closed, Cull hauled Pippa into his arms. A giggle left her as she tipped her head back for his kiss, looping her arms around his neck. It felt delightfully reckless carrying on in this fashion in a carriage in the middle of the day. Those thoughts melted away as Cull ran his tongue along the roof of her mouth, and the kiss caught fire.

By the time they broke apart, they were both panting.

"I was thinking about doing this the entire meeting," Cull murmured.

Catching her breath, Pippa said, "That is not very professional of you."

He smiled lazily. "I'm capable of concentrating on more than one thing at once."

"Really?" For some reason, his words ignited a spark of challenge. She'd never felt this carefree and playful with any man.

She trailed a gloved hand down his chest, feeling the powerful rise and fall of the man beneath the unassuming clothes. It made *her* feel powerful to know she had this effect on him...to hear the mysterious and all-knowing Prince of Larks groan when she found him hard as steel. She stroked his turgid length through the fabric, leaning up to nip his earlobe as she did so.

"Jesus wept." He leaned his head against the wall, his eyes shutting in pleasure. "You don't know what you do to me."

Emboldened, she caressed him the way he'd shown her the night before. His pulsing vitality strained the worn wool of his trousers, his burgeoned heat pushing into the curve of her palm. She imagined his flesh filling another part of her, and her intimate muscles clenched.

"Does frigging my cock make you wet, Pippa?" His simmering gaze read all her secrets. "Does that tight little cunny of yours want what's in your hand?"

Heavens. Here she was thinking that she was the one in control. Her body reacted instantly to Cull's wicked sensuality, even though he wasn't even touching her.

"When I woke up this morning, I could still taste you," he said in a gravelly tone. "It made me so hard that I had to do what you're doing now."

The image caused liquid heat to pool between her legs. Cull, his big fist wrapped around himself, jerking himself to her taste…

"I pictured you next to me, doing the same thing." His dark-as-a-river voice inundated her senses. "Touching yourself while I watched. Rubbing your needy little love-knot until you were so hot you begged for my prick."

She was about to beg him now.

"I spent so hard, imagining I was inside you."

Her breath puffing from her lips, she gripped him convulsively.

The carriage rolled to a stop. Cull bit out a groan, and she almost did too.

He dropped his forehead against hers. "Next time, minx, don't start your little games when we can't finish them."

"Isn't the playing of the game more important than the ultimate conclusion?" she asked coquettishly.

"I don't disagree. Just remember that two can play at that game."

At his carnal warning, her pussy quivered.

The voice of Cull's driver filtered through the door, breaking the sensual spell. "Looks like they're closing up shop. Best 'urry."

Pippa put herself to rights. When Cull sighed, she looked over...and laughed at the sight of his slow-to-subside desire.

"You gentlemen are at a rather sizeable disadvantage," she teased. "You had better wait here, or you'll scandalize the patrons of Purdey's."

Cull tapped his mask, saying mildly, "I wasn't planning on going in with you."

Oh...right. She had gotten so used to his mask that she didn't even notice it, although others certainly would. In her mind, she saw him as he was: her potent lover who was no less handsome for his mark of courage.

Curiously, she asked, "Do you ever go out without your mask?"

He shook his head. And when he said nothing more, she didn't want to push.

"I'll be back," she said and exited the carriage.

Darkness had fallen by the time Pippa emerged from the awninged entrance of Purdey's.

As Cull helped her into the carriage, he smothered a smile at her look of pique. She truly was adorable when she was annoyed. Telling her would probably irk her further; he toyed with the idea of doing it, just to get a rise out of her.

It was strange, this lightness he felt in her presence. He'd never felt that with a lover before. Never experienced this heady mix of lust, playfulness, and admiration.

"How did it go?" he asked for the fun of it.

"Dreadfully." As she plopped onto the bench beside him, her

black skirts made a cute poof, as if they, too, were irritated. "I didn't learn anything. I used the story that a servant of mine had found the weapon, and I wanted to return it to its rightful owner, but the clerks refused to disclose any names. Claimed that Purdey's reputation depended upon their discretion. Even my title held no sway. When they suggested I leave the gun with them, I left." She expelled a breath. "I failed in my objective."

"On the contrary, sunshine. You gave a flawless performance."

She wrinkled her nose. "How can you say that when it proved fruitless?"

"Because you kept the clerks so well occupied that they didn't notice when I went in through the back."

She gaped at him. "You did what?"

"I searched through the store receipts and found the file for double-barreled pocket pistols. It was quite a popular model, but the double bands of gold on the walnut handle narrowed it down to one patron. The fellow bought a matching set of such pistols."

He held up the folded piece of paper on which he'd jotted down a name and address.

Pippa narrowed her glorious blue gaze. "Are you saying I was the decoy?"

"A rather excellent one."

She snatched the paper from him. "Next time, *you* play the bait."

"But you're far prettier, sweetheart."

He nearly snickered at her fulminating stare.

With a huff, she unfolded the paper. "Sir John Forsythe-Legg. Never heard of him."

"Me neither." He chucked her beneath the chin. "But we'll soon find out everything we need to know."

A short while later, Pippa returned to her residence...alone. It had taken some willpower as she'd been sorely tempted to invite Cull in for supper. To continue discussing the case and how they should proceed with Sir Forsythe-Legg. And to continue what they'd started in the carriage on the way to Purdey's.

Yet her rational side had intervened. They'd only started their affair, and it wouldn't do to go too fast. To lose herself in the heady feelings that Cull inspired. She'd fallen prey to infatuation once and wouldn't let that happen again. She would control her desires and not the other way around.

Besides, she would see Cull tomorrow night. Since she wanted to visit Ollie, Cull had invited her over to the Nest for supper. She was looking forward to being amid the merry mudlarks...and to spending time with their hot-blooded prince. Her confidence that she had made the right decision tonight was reinforced by her butler Whitby's hushed greeting.

"Mrs. Hunt is waiting for you in the parlor, my lady. She has been here for over an hour." The portly fellow turned red from his chin up to his balding pate. "I tried to dissuade her, but..."

"Mama can be difficult to dissuade," Pippa said with fond exasperation.

Especially for Whitby, who Pippa suspected had a bit of a crush on her mama. Or, rather, on her mother's nom de plume. An unexpected and avid reader of sensation novels, Whitby had nearly swooned when he learned that Pippa's mother, Persephone Hunt, was *the* P. R. Fines, author of his favorite adventure stories. Mama had given Whitby an autographed copy of her latest novel, starring his favorite heroine, and Pippa suspected he slept with it beneath his pillow.

"Please tell Cook there will be two for supper," Pippa said.

As the butler trundled off, Pippa headed for the parlor. She peered through the cracked-open door, and warmth bloomed in her bosom. As a girl, she'd often seen Mama this way: seated at the escritoire, her sunny head bent over a notebook, scribbling madly and muttering to herself.

Pippa cleared her throat to avoid startling her parent. "Mama, I wasn't expecting you."

"Oh, Pippa dear!" Mama blinked as if waking from a dream. An instant later, she hurried over in a swish of figured lavender satin, taking Pippa's hands in a squeeze. "I'm sorry to drop by uninvited. But I didn't wish to give you any excuse to avoid me. Which is why I had to resort to a sneak attack."

Despite her mama's teasing, Pippa felt a stab of guilt. Since the disastrous supper three months ago, she'd been evading her family. Mama was probably worried.

"I'm sorry. I have been busy," Pippa said contritely.

She drew her mama to the blue divan, where they sat side by side.

Mama tilted her head, violets fluttering in her upswept blonde locks. "With what?"

Pippa tried not to squirm beneath the keen maternal gaze. It was like looking into a mirror. She'd inherited her coloring and looks from her mama, and strangers sometimes mistook them for sisters. Yet their personalities were different. As Papa put it, Mama was a "force of nature" who knew what she wanted and went after it. Which was saying something, since Papa also had an iron will. Pippa's brothers, Garrett and Hugh, took after their parents, and there had been no shortage of locking horns in the Hunt household. As the peacemaker of the bunch, Pippa had felt a bit like a strangeling.

Luckily, the only thing stronger than the Hunts' will was their love for one another. Despite the current rift with her family, Pippa never doubted her parents' love. Yet she also felt that they —her father, in particular—did not understand her. Or, at least, her choice to marry Longmere. Being around Papa when he criticized Longmere, even though it was justified, fed Pippa's guilt and inner turmoil until she felt she might burst from her skin.

She didn't want to hurt her family's feelings by avoiding them, but she also feared she might crack like an egg if she didn't.

"I've been doing a lot of work with Lady Fayne's society." It wasn't a lie.

"Hmm." Mama's eyes, a shade brighter than her own, studied her with unnerving acuity. "We could use your help at the academy as well, you know. You were always a favorite with the children."

"I miss them," she said honestly.

She'd loved working with the youngsters. But Edwin hadn't approved of her dedication to the foundlings, and she'd gradually abandoned that work for him. It was another piece of herself that she'd sacrificed for her marriage. That she'd sold off far too cheaply.

Pippa swallowed her shame. "I've found my work with Lady Fayne to be quite rewarding as well."

"It is important that you carve your own path." Straightening her shoulders, Mama said, "Although I would hope it doesn't take you too far away from your family. We miss you, Pippa, and would like to see you more often."

The love and understanding in her mother's eyes heated Pippa's own.

"Papa doesn't mean it, you know," Mama went on. "Well, that's not precisely true. He *does* mean what he says about Longmere, but he doesn't mean to hurt you, my dear. He loves you."

"I know." Pippa's voice trembled; she loved her father too.

"The thought of everything you've gone through drives Papa mad. You waited years for Longmere to come up to scratch. After you wed, you seemed changed. Not like the happy, carefree girl we knew. And knowing how Longmere...how things ended, Papa and I are concerned about you."

Pippa appreciated her mother's tact. Although her parents didn't know the full extent of Edwin's sins, they were aware that he'd died because of his drug use. Her humiliation deepened; not only had she made a terrible choice, but she had also caused her parents to worry.

"I know it's no excuse for Papa's ranting and raving"—Mama cast her eyes heavenward—"but he can't help himself. He feels like he failed to protect you. He is angrier at himself than Longmere, truth be told. But the stubborn man can't let the anger go, even though it has caused a rift between the two of you. Losing you is eating him up inside."

A tear escaped, sliding down Pippa's cheek. "I'm sorry."

"Do stop apologizing, my darling," Mama murmured, passing her a handkerchief. "I just wanted to explain why your papa has been acting the way he has. None of this is your fault—"

"It is," Pippa blurted. "All of it is my fault."

Mama shook her head so vehemently that a violet fell, twirling onto the Aubusson. "You cannot blame yourself for falling in love—"

"I don't know if what I felt for Longmere was love."

The instant the words left her, Pippa felt shock...and stunning relief. While shame slithered in the wake of her confession, the tension that had been gnawing at her for months eased. She'd finally voiced the awful truth: she now doubted her feelings for Edwin. And while she did mourn him, she was also...angry.

Furious, in truth, at her husband's betrayal. The lies he'd told, the secrets he'd kept. And the way he'd treated her...it was a far cry from her experience with Cull. Even though they were having a casual liaison, Cull had shown her what it was like to have a lover who cared about her happiness and well-being. Who fed her sense of self-worth rather than starved it. Cull might keep secrets as part of his job, but he was unflinchingly honest when it came to his feelings and expectations about their relationship.

Beside her, Mama waited in silence. As if she understood Pippa needed space to sort out the tangled skeins of her feelings.

"I thought it was love at first sight," Pippa said haltingly.

She recalled that first time she'd seen Edwin; it had been at a ball, and he'd been surrounded by admirers. Mostly female, all hanging on his every word as he expounded upon his philosophy of art. His desire to capture the true essence of life. Pippa had felt a tingle as she thought of how she, too, tried to convey the wonder of the ordinary with strokes of her paintbrush.

"And now?" her mama asked.

"I think it was just an infatuation." Throat clogging, Pippa confronted the self-deception that had lasted through the years of courtship and marriage. "I was attracted to his artistic sensibility, his passionate way of looking at the world. So much so that I never really let myself see beyond his image. To the man he actually was."

Mama's face hardened. "In your defense, you were only two-and-twenty when you met him. And the one talent I will grant Longmere was his ability to convince others that his high opinion of himself was warranted."

"But you and Papa saw through him. From the start, you did not approve..." Pippa twisted the handkerchief between her fingers, unwilling to let herself off the hook. "I would not listen, however. I insisted that you did not understand him. I defended his bad behavior toward me...toward our family."

In retrospect, that was one of her worst sins: she had not only lost herself, but she'd also abandoned her family. She had allowed Edwin's condescension to drive a wedge between her and the people she loved.

For several heartbeats, Mama said nothing.

"Do you know why I saw through Longmere?" she asked finally.

"Why?"

"Because I was once infatuated with a man just like him."

"No," Pippa breathed.

Knowing how passionately in love her parents were, she couldn't imagine either of them having feelings for anyone else.

"Oh, yes." Mama's smile was rueful. "He was a titled lord and every bit as pompous as Longmere. He fancied himself a poet; the females on my side of the family must be susceptible to artistic sorts."

"But how...you and Papa...?" Pippa couldn't even piece the words together.

"I thought I was in love with this fellow when I met your papa." A twinkle came into Mama's eyes. "Your papa promptly convinced me otherwise."

"You have never mentioned this..."

"You know how Papa gets even now when someone asks me to dance." Mama rolled her eyes. "Trust me, he does not like to be reminded that anyone once held my affections. Not that this other fellow did. It was a silly infatuation, pure and simple. When I met your papa, I realized the difference between that and true love. One day, my dearest girl, you will find the right man as well: someone who makes you realize that you are perfect as you are."

Her mother's words resonated with her experience. Meeting Cull had helped her to recognize all that had been wrong in her marriage. Even if Cull wasn't the "right man" forever—for the future that neither of them was ready to commit to—he was undoubtedly the right lover for now. No matter how long their affair lasted, she would never forget the gift he'd given her.

"Thank you, Mama." Pippa reached for her mother's hands. "I am so glad you came by."

Mama returned her squeeze. "Now, there is another reason for my visit. Papa is throwing a small party in honor of my birthday in a fortnight. The only gift I want is your presence. As it will be an intimate gathering of family and a few close friends, you don't have to worry about being there while you're in mourning."

How could she say no to her mama's request? "I look forward to celebrating with you."

Mama beamed. "It will be splendid for all of us to be together again."

She did miss her family. "How are Garrett and Hugh?"

"Same as always." Although Mama's sigh was long-suffering, affection laced her words. "Besides your papa, they're the most stubborn, hell-raising, and lovable rogues I've ever met."

"Lucky for you one of your children has an easy-going temperament."

To Pippa's surprise, Mama laughed. "Oh, darling, you don't mean *you*, do you?"

"Well, yes. I'm the patient peacemaker of the family, aren't I?"

"And the proudest, most determined one of the bunch." In a conspiratorial tone, Mama said, "I hate to disabuse you of your notions, Pippa dear, but you're even more of a Hunt than your brothers. *Combined*."

Given the discovery at Purdey's, Charlie placed a priority on investigating Sir Forsythe-Legg. Pippa and Fiona, with the assistance of the mudlarks, were assigned that task the following evening. Although Cull could not take part due to other commitments, he'd invited Pippa to the Nest after the mission for a late supper.

Suzette was helping Pippa to prepare for the night ahead. For her job, Pippa had donned a male disguise, but she wanted something pretty to wear afterward for her first meal with Cull. Looking through her wardrobe, she'd decided to forgo her widow's weeds in favor of a simple mauve taffeta gown. She would keep up appearances in public; in private, she felt hypocritical expressing on the outside what she no longer felt within.

As Suzette packed up the evening dress and accessories, a note arrived from Fiona.

Dearest Pippa,

Papa is being an absolute tyrant and insisting that I go to the Brambleton ball. I suspect he wants me to make a match with the Earl of Brambleton's heir—as if I need help securing a husband.

Pippa could imagine the beautiful redhead rolling her eyes.

But Papa is adamant, and I'm afraid you'll have to undertake tonight's mission without me.

Regretfully yours,
   Fi

Pippa felt a stab of empathy for Fi's plight. Both their fathers were powerful, self-made men who had risen from London's underclass. Given the brutality of their pasts, Gavin Hunt and Adam Garrity were ruthless when it came to their enemies...and ruthlessly protective when it came to the ones they loved.

A part of Pippa yearned for the days when she'd been the apple of her papa's eye. When his gaze had held nothing but proud approval. Perhaps Mama was right, and Papa's anger was at himself...but Pippa still felt responsible. In his presence, the shame she felt for her stupid choices made avoiding him seem like the better option.

Silently wishing Fiona better luck with Mr. Garrity, Pippa set off to meet with the mudlarks. The location was a shady-looking tavern in Covent Garden called "The Golden Buck." Her carriage had barely drawn to a halt when the door opened, and Fair Molly clambered in. The mudlark was dressed in her usual male attire, a scruffy cap jammed over her cloud of curls.

Before Pippa could utter a greeting, the adolescent said peremptorily, "You're late."

Pippa consulted her watch. "By two minutes."

"The success o' a mission depends upon timing."

The girl's brusque manner led Pippa to ask, "Have I done something to cause offense?"

Even shaded by the brim of her cap, the girl's amber eyes glowed with hostility. And it wasn't the first time; Molly had been less than friendly during Pippa's visits to the Nest. Pippa had chalked it up to the girl's concern over Ollie...but perhaps that vein of dislike ran deeper.

"We mudlarks don't need outsiders butting in." Fair Molly's chin jutted out. "We 'andle our own business and don't need nobody's 'elp finding Ollie's attacker."

"Ollie wasn't the only one attacked."

"And since nobody's paying us to stick our nose in that lady's business, we ain't got no cause to do so," the girl shot back. "Ollie wouldn't 'ave been 'urt in the first place if 'e 'adn't been sent on that fool's errand."

"That is between you and Cull, is it not?" Pippa said evenly.

Molly's cheeks flushed, and Pippa could see the girl struggle between her loyalty to her leader and her desire to give Pippa a piece of her mind.

"'E ain't thinking straight," Molly muttered. "Not since you came into the picture. You're a distraction 'e can't afford."

There it was: the crux of the animosity. Pippa wondered if Molly might have a bit of a tendre for her fearless leader. Or if it was the strong-as-blood bonds between the mudlarks that made Molly so protective.

Pippa pondered her options. On the one hand, what went on between her and Cull was a private matter. On the other...she liked Fair Molly. She suspected that beneath the adolescent's prickly attitude lay a fiercely devoted nature. Although Pippa didn't take Molly's attacks personally, she wanted to nip them in the bud.

"Cull made the decision to work with my society, and it was a wise choice," she said mildly. "Combining our resources will help us achieve our common goal. As for the personal connection between Cull and me, I will say this once: he and I have an understanding that is no one's affair but our own. Out of respect for your position in the mudlark family, Molly, I will tell you that I have no intention of being a distraction or hurting him."

Molly's gaze widened, her throat bobbing above her collar. She looked surprised as if she hadn't expected her concerns to be addressed directly. Then she squared her thin shoulders.

"Your sort can't 'elp it," she said with disdain.

Pippa was grateful for the patience honed by years of working at the academy. "Can't help what, exactly?"

"Being a 'oneypot." The girl sneered. "With your fancy dresses and come-'ither ways."

The unfair statement edged Pippa's temper toward a simmer. "I think you have me mistaken for someone else."

"Oh, I ain't mistaken. You and 'er...you could be twins." Molly's hands fisted in her lap, emotion seething in her voice. "And when 'e was at 'is lowest, she abandoned 'im. Kicked 'im when 'e was down with 'er fine 'eeled shoe and left 'im bleeding like some mongrel at the side o' the road. The rotted bitch."

It took Pippa a few moments to piece together what the adolescent was saying.

"Are you referring to a previous lover of Cull's?" she asked with a frown.

Molly's look was gloating. "Didn't think you were 'is first, did you?"

Although Cull had obviously had lovers before, the truth was Pippa hadn't thought beyond the present. Or at least, not beyond the twisted thorns of her own past. She'd been so caught up in her own pain that she hadn't considered Cull's romantic history. He'd told her that he had only the moment to offer her and hadn't changed those terms, even after revealing his scars. She'd assumed it was because of his commitment to the mudlarks or his lack of interest in a permanent relationship.

He'd always been so accommodating, so focused on her needs, her pleasure that...

You didn't think to ask. About him. His past.

Heat scalded Pippa's cheeks. As tempted as she was to ask about Cull's mysterious ex-lover, she didn't. Because she shouldn't be hearing about this from Molly. If Pippa had learned anything, it was that she wanted honesty and openness in her relationship... which meant this discussion should be happening with Cull.

"As I've said, what goes on between Cull and me is private. However, you may rest assured that I hold him in high esteem and would never betray him. You have my word."

Was it her imagination, or did respect flicker in Molly's gaze?

"Now, we are not here to discuss your leader behind his back." Pippa made her tone crisp and professional. "Tell me what you and your team know about the target."

"Tom Watkins, age forty-three, valet to Sir Forsythe-Legg for the last two years," Molly said grudgingly. "Got a bone to pick wif 'is employer and apparently starts talking everyone's ear off 'bout the 'cheeseparing slavedriver' once he downs an ale or two. Since 'e was on 'is third pint last I checked, you shouldn't 'ave any problem getting 'im to sing. But if 'e needs encouragement, coin should do the trick."

"Thank you." Pippa reached for the door handle. "I'll be out shortly."

"You'd better," Molly said under her breath. "Or Cull will 'ave my 'ead."

Leaning against a wall in the great hall, Cull watched from a distance as Pippa read Ollie a story. She had changed out of her disguise and looked a treat in her pale purple frock trimmed with bows, her shiny ringlets glinting in the firelight. The colorful voices she gave to the characters in the book coaxed a giggle from

Ollie and the other larks who'd gathered around to listen. Seeing their rapt expressions, Cull felt a pang in his chest.

It was rare for mudlarks to be treated as children, and precious ones at that. Their innocence was often the cost of survival. Case in point: Ollie still had a bandage wrapped around his head and looked like a war survivor. While he was recovering quickly, his memory of the attack hadn't returned. The lost, scared look that would come over him tightened Cull's fists with helpless rage.

Yet Pippa's glowing warmth drew Ollie and the others out of their protective shells. They laughed with her, vied for her tender attention, and Cull could understand why.

Pippa was everything he'd fantasized about...and more.

Not only was she the embodiment of feminine grace, but she also had strength and courage to spare. When she'd arrived an hour ago, she had been giddy with success.

"It took a few coins to joggle his memory, but the valet said Sir John Forsythe-Legg purchased the set of pistols as a gift for a friend. An actor by the name of Vincent Ellis," Pippa had reported. *"Apparently, Sir Forsythe-Legg and his wife were rather ardent admirers of Mr. Ellis, but Mr. Ellis broke off the friendship. That was about six months ago."*

"What do we know about Ellis?" Cull had asked.

"According to the valet, the actor's main talent lies in his looks. He said Mr. Ellis was an uncommonly handsome brown-haired gentleman with silver eyes...which describes the man I saw with Lady Hastings at The Enchanted Rose. The man who went by the name 'Thor.' To be sure, I did a quick sketch of Thor, and the valet confirmed its likeness to Mr. Ellis."

When Cull had congratulated Pippa on her victory, she'd given credit to Fair Molly.

"Fair Molly's reconnaissance made the mission go smoothly." She'd smiled at the mudlark, whose jaw had slackened at the compliment. *"She told me what I needed to know to get the valet to talk. She deserves recognition for her excellent work."*

Cull didn't think he'd seen Fair Molly blush before.

Thanks to Pippa's efforts, they knew that Vincent Ellis was the man Lady Hastings had been with the night before her murder. And they could link Ellis to the likely murder weapon. All they had to do now was find the bastard. When Pippa told him the Angels would take on Ellis, Cull hadn't argued. The mudlarks were getting stretched thin between their work on this case, several others, and the situation with Squibb.

Mrs. Needles emerged from one of the corridors, and Cull nearly groaned when he saw who was with her. From the moment he'd introduced the matron to Fanny Grier, the two had got on like a house on fire. They had many shared interests, their favorite being meddling in Cull's life.

"What are you doing here, Fanny?" he asked warily.

"Can't I visit my dear friend Mrs. Needles?" Smirking, Fanny cast a too-interested glance over at Pippa, who now held a chortling Sally on her lap. "And it looks like I'm just in time to meet a new friend of yours. Well, well, Timothy. It does appear you've developed a taste for finer things."

"Her ladyship has a way with children, doesn't she?" Mrs. Needles said, looking pleased. "Does she have any of her own?"

An image of Pippa rounded with child flashed in Cull's head, and he had to quell a hot, primal pulse of longing.

"No," he said. "She was only married a year before her husband passed."

"Pity that." Mrs. Needles gave him an unsubtle look. "A woman like her ought to have a husband who gives her a nursery of her own."

Cull huffed out a laugh. "Surely you are not suggesting that I apply for the position?"

"Why not?" Fanny demanded.

"She's a countess, to start. No lady with her faculties intact would give up a title and privilege for..." He gestured to the chaos around him. "This."

"You never know until you ask," Fanny averred.

What was the point when he already knew the answer?

"You both know there's never been a Princess of Larks," he said.

"That is just an excuse." Fanny gave a flippant wave. "How will you end that supposed 'curse of solitude' if you don't even try?"

"While you are the Prince of Larks, you are also a healthy and unmarried man." Mrs. Needles picked up the argument. "You need to hang up your mask from time to time and make room in your life for *yourself*."

"Pippa knows what is behind the mask," he muttered.

Fanny arched her brows. "Then why are you wearing it now?"

Cull felt his face heat—good thing he *was* wearing the blasted covering. He'd debated leaving it off; at the last moment before Pippa's arrival, he'd put it back on. She'd seen his scars, true, but that had been in a shadowy carriage. Here in a well-lit room...

Feeling like an idiot, he rubbed the back of his neck. "Why do the two of you want to see me leg-shackled?"

"We want you to be happy," Fanny said. "Your life is spent looking after others; it's time you had someone looking after you. Speaking of which, when was the last time you got a trim? Your hair looks like an overgrown hedge. And why haven't you seen Grier's tailor? You're courting a countess now and had better look the part."

Cull heaved a sigh.

"Never mind his hair and clothes," Mrs. Needles murmured. "He ought to collect his ladyship before the children wear her out. By the by, where are you taking her to sup, Cull?"

"We're dining here."

The women exchanged alarmed looks.

Peering left and right, Mrs. Needles said in an urgent whisper, "Surely you do not intend to serve her ladyship Mrs. Halberd's food—"

"Good God, no. I made other arrangements." He didn't know

whether to be amused or offended that they thought him so lacking in common sense.

"Thank goodness." The matron patted her heart. "For if anything could ruin a romantic evening, it would be that dragon's cooking."

"Where are you taking me?" Pippa asked.

"You'll see." Cull led the way up the narrow winding stairs, his lamp painting the stone walls in light and shadow. "We're almost there."

"You said that thirty steps ago."

"Not tired, are you, my intrepid Angel?"

She made a face at his broad back…and heard him chuckle.

Stupefied, she asked, "Do you have eyes at the back of your head?"

"I'm the Prince of Larks. I've eyes and ears—"

"I know, I know. You see, hear, and know everything."

She rolled her eyes just as he turned, a sensual grin below his mask. She had debated asking him to remove the covering but decided not to push. He would bare himself when he was ready.

"Not everything," he said. "I didn't know about Vincent Ellis until *you* discovered that important fact."

Pleased with her mission's success, Pippa said, "I do have my uses, don't I?"

"Thinking of your uses keeps me up at night. Literally."

She chuckled at his flirtatious banter. Cull could be devilishly wicked and boyishly playful, and she couldn't decide which side of him she preferred the most.

"Mrs. Grier is lovely," she said conversationally.

When she'd been introduced to Fanny Grier, the lady had bluntly disclosed that she owned a bawdy house, appearing to await Pippa's reaction. Pippa wasn't one to judge; her own papa had made his fortune from operating a notorious gaming hell. With a polite smile, she'd asked how Fanny and Cull had met, and from there, the conversation had flowed easily.

"That is because Fanny likes you." Cull's tone was dry. "Trust me, she does not suffer fools."

Amused, Pippa said, "She and Mrs. Needles are quite the pair of meddling mamas."

"Mamas?" Cull shot her a quizzical look. "They're my friends... work associates."

With a tender pang, Pippa realized that while he took care of others, he wasn't used to the idea of having that attention returned. To her, it was obvious that Fanny and Mrs. Needles treated him with maternal pride. And she thought his gruff yet affectionate manner with them was rather adorable.

A wooden door greeted them at the top of the steps.

"Close your eyes," Cull said.

"Must I?" For his benefit, she gave an exaggerated sigh.

He gave her the crooked smile she loved. "Why would anyone give you the moniker of Patient Pippa?"

"That was the old me." With a feeling of liberation, she added, "The new me does as she pleases."

His smile deepened. "Would the new Pippa mind closing her eyes so that I may surprise her with what is on the other side of the door?"

"What is on the other side?"

His laugh bounced off the stone walls. "You would find out sooner if you followed orders and shut your pretty eyes."

When she obeyed, Cull's hand engulfed hers in a warm grip,

and hinges squealed. She felt a blast of warm air, a cacophony of chirps greeting her. It took all her willpower not to open her eyes as he tugged her forward.

"Now open them," he said.

She did...and let out a delighted gasp at the enchanted scene around her. They were in a rooftop conservatory built of glass and steel. Shaped like a hexagon, the room had a soaring ceiling, the glass panels making it seem like its roof was the night sky. Tiny lanterns twinkled like stars overhead.

And the occupants of the greenhouse...there were birds in cages and birds flying free. Some perched on the fronds of potted plants and others on sturdy wooden posts grouped throughout the room to mimic clustered trees. The birds made happy sounds as Cull entered, some swooping playfully close to him, others hopping excitedly in their cages.

Pippa spun around, taking in the beauty. "This place is *magical.*"

His gaze gleamed. "I am glad you like it."

"Where do the birds come from?"

"All over London. They are injured, you see." He led her over to a wire cage. "This starling has a broken wing."

She noted the tiny splint among the lustrous blue-black feathers. "And you tend to them?"

He nodded, his gaze on the bird. He extended a long finger through the wires and held it still. The starling tilted its head, as if considering the proposition. It hopped forward and darted its beak out, giving his finger a friendly peck.

"During my recovery from the fire, Matches—one of the mudlarks—brought in a sparrow that had narrowly escaped being a cat's supper. The bird was in bad shape...worse shape than me, even with my burned face and broken leg. We kept each other company and both survived." He shrugged. "The larks started bringing in injured birds whenever they found them, and it became a hobby of sorts."

Pippa's heart melted. This pastime of Cull's fit everything she knew of him. Protector of the wounded, champion of those that many would not deem worthy of notice, much less saving. He saw treasures in society's discards. Given what she knew of his past, she had an inkling why...and she yearned to know more about him. This powerful prince of the underworld who was gently running his index finger along the side of a starling's head.

"How do you find room to keep all these pets?" she asked.

"They're not pets, and I don't keep them any longer than they need to be here. When they are healed, they go free." The starling hopped to the other side of the cage, and he dropped his hand. "What I offer is a sanctuary, not a prison."

Awareness prickled her. Her heart thumped in a wild, primal rhythm...not unlike that of the wings above her. She couldn't yet give voice to the chaotic thoughts. She only knew that at that moment she experienced some vital truth, the encounter as brief as that between a man and an untamed bird.

Cull cleared his throat. "Are you hungry? I thought we could have a casual supper up here if you don't mind."

"I would love to sup in this beautiful place," she said.

He took her to one of the glass panels, which turned out to be a door. It opened into a second, smaller enclosure; this one was free of birds, filled instead with lush potted plants. Citrus and night-blooming jasmine scented the air. The slanted ceiling gave a breathtaking view of the swirling mix of clouds and fog rising from the river.

A carpet had been rolled out at the center of the room and lanterns set along its perimeter. A blanket, cushions, and an enormous wicker basket sat atop it, along with a bucket of iced champagne. An image flashed in Pippa's head...of a scene she might paint. A pair of lovers stumbling upon a faerie garden and finding an enchanted picnic waiting for them.

"How delightful," she breathed. "But you didn't have to go to the trouble."

"It was no trouble. And this is the only place in the Nest where we are likely to have any privacy." He helped her settle onto one of the charmingly mismatched cushions. As she arranged her skirts, he uncorked the bottle with a pop. "Champagne?"

"Yes, please."

He handed her a flute of the effervescent beverage and filled another for himself. He sat beside her, and they tapped glasses.

"To us," he said. "And our first night together that doesn't involve mayhem."

"Cheers to that." She took a sip, approving of the crisp, dry bubbles. "This is a fine vintage."

"Let's hope the rest of the meal lives up."

He unloaded the basket, and her eyes rounded as he uncovered the elegant dishes. The assortment included jellied *pâté* flecked with truffles, scallops nested in pastry, buttered asparagus, sliced potatoes baked in cream with a crispy crust, and breaded lamb cutlets accompanied by a vegetable-studded sauce. Her stomach rumbled at the tantalizing smells.

"Your chef made all this?" she marveled.

"Hell, no. Mrs. Halberd can't fry an egg without scorching it." Cull served her *pâté*, along with a slice of crusty bread. "This is from the Reform Club."

Pippa lifted her brows. Situated on Pall Mall, the Reform Club was an exclusive gentleman's club and catered mostly to progressive members of Parliament. Their *chef de cuisine* was famous for his innovative kitchen.

"You're a member?" She sampled the paste of liver and spices, savoring its earthy creaminess.

"No." Slathering *pâté* onto a slice of bread, Cull ate it with gusto. "But I'm owed a favor by someone who is."

"You didn't have to go to the trouble—"

"You said that already. And you're worth the effort."

His sincerity made her heart stutter like a debutante's. Flustered, she reached for her champagne and took a sip.

"Besides," he said, "I can't say I mind a respite from Mrs. Halberd's cuisine."

"If she's such a terrible cook, why don't you dismiss her?"

"One doesn't dismiss Mrs. Halberd." Cull glanced around as if he were worried that the cook might materialize out of thin air. "She is older than the hills and has been with the mudlarks since before I joined. Since before I was *alive*."

"And you, the mighty prince, are afraid of her?" The notion amused and charmed Pippa in equal measure.

"I'm not afraid." He served her one of the seafood *vols-au-vent*. "I'm terrified."

Laughing, Pippa sampled the dish and nearly swooned at the delicious flavors. The pairing of the sweet, succulent scallops, flaky pastry, and creamy sauce was exquisite. They ate in companionable silence. Cull polished off two lamb cutlets, mopping up the tangy sauce with more bread. His unabashed enjoyment of his food reminded her of Garrett and Hugh.

Cull quirked an eyebrow. "Why are you smiling?"

"Your appetite reminds me of my brothers," she said candidly.

He grunted, helping himself to a heaping serving of potatoes. "When I met them years ago, they were young and rowdy lads. What are they like now?"

"Older and rowdier," she said fondly.

He was silent for a moment, as if choosing his response with care. "Have you seen them of late? Your brothers and your family?" When she didn't reply, he said, "I don't mean to pry—"

"No, it's fine." She meant it.

Truth be told, it felt good to discuss ordinary things. To have a lover interested in her life and inner workings.

"My mama stopped by last night," she said.

He waited.

"The visit went well," she elaborated. "We talked...in a way we hadn't for a long while. And I realized that you were right."

"Aren't I always?" He grinned at her narrow-eyed look. "What was I right about this time?"

"That night when we first met again, you said that my family loves me, and I've been pushing them away. It's true." She chewed contemplatively on a bite of asparagus. "It wasn't fair to them, and I am going to do better."

"Don't be too hard on yourself. Fairness and family don't always go hand-in-hand. The important thing is that no matter what, you know you can rely on one another."

His voice had a serrated edge. She recalled the pain in his eyes when she'd carelessly thrown Maisie's words at him and accused him of being unreliable.

"Is that true of you and your sister?" she asked cautiously.

"Maisie can count on me," Cull said with brooding intensity. "Whether or not she believes it."

"What happened between the two of you, Cull?"

He set aside his plate. "The story is not mine to tell."

"I understand if you don't want to tell me." Even if she felt a bit hurt by his reticence.

"It's not that." His deep brown gaze was somber and open. "If I were to unburden myself to anyone, it would be to you. But I haven't been a good brother to Maisie. And I don't want to compound my failings by betraying her secrets."

"You don't have to share anything that makes you uncomfortable," Pippa assured him.

"Suffice it to say that I wasn't the brother I ought to have been." Cull dragged a hand through his hair, tousling the thick waves. "You know that I missed occasions. Birthdays, events at the academy. Even her graduation."

Pippa nodded. As a young girl, Maisie had been disappointed; as she'd grown into womanhood, that disappointment had hardened into anger. Knowing Cull as she did now, Pippa couldn't reconcile Maisie's characterization of him as uncaring and unreliable. There had to be a reason for Cull's absences.

"Why weren't you there?" Pippa asked softly.

"Because I was busy with the mudlarks. After what happened with Crooke—after that bastard tried to force the mudlarks into the flesh trade—I knew we couldn't be without a prince. But none of the older boys stepped up, and instead they nominated *me*. Even though I'd been beaten to a bloody pulp by Crooke." He shook his head, as if even now he couldn't believe that the others had seen him as a leader. "I worked my arse off day and night and still didn't know what I was doing. I made mistakes, grave ones... ones that cost lives."

Seeing the shadows spill like ink through his eyes, she pushed aside the dishes and scooted next to him. She touched his coat sleeve and felt his bunched biceps beneath the worn superfine.

"You did your best," she said in gentle tones. "You were willing to take the reins when no one else would. And you were only fifteen—barely more than a boy."

"One grows up fast in the stews. The mudlarks needed someone better, but all they had was me," he said gruffly. "I did my best by them. I just couldn't manage to do that *and* be a good brother to Maisie."

"You were responsible for so many. It was not your fault."

"Maisie doesn't see it that way. And she's right: I did choose the mudlarks over her." Regret and frustration strained his voice. "But I didn't make that decision out of a lack of care."

Pippa understood. "You did it because you *do* care. You brought her to my parents' school, made sure she was safe and looked after."

"She was better off there. Without me. I wanted her to have a different life, a better one than I could offer her. Maisie, she was always the bright one of the family." Pride flared in his eyes. "She caught onto the schooling right quick."

"Maisie was a model student, but she wasn't better off without you. And no matter how angry she was, I know she still looked up to you." Pippa tilted her head. "Have you thought about mending fences with her?"

"She won't forgive me," he said unequivocally. "And I don't blame her."

"But perhaps if you—"

"She's settled now. Happy with her post in Bristol. I won't disturb her peace."

Hearing the finality in his words, Pippa knew better than to argue. It wasn't her place, anyway, to tell him what to do. They were having an affair, not...more. Even though their no-strings-attached relationship felt more intimate than her marriage ever had.

"Relationships are complicated, aren't they?" she reflected aloud.

"Aye, they can be."

"Good thing ours is not." She lightened her tone, smiling at him. "I'm glad that we found each other again, Cull. That we can be friends."

"Is that what we are?"

His question, uttered with a sensual rasp, ruffled her. The truth was their relationship defied conventional categorization.

"I meant that I enjoy our camaraderie," she clarified. "How natural it feels to be with you, whether we are chatting, investigating, or...doing whatever else."

"It feels natural for me as well." He grazed his knuckles along her jaw, down her throat, sending shivers through her. "Especially when we're doing 'whatever else.'"

Cheeks flushing, she heard herself say, "Has it been this way for you with other lovers?"

His lashes swept up. "Why do you ask?"

She bit her lip, uncertain if she ought to reveal what Fair Molly had said about Cull's other lover. Since the mudlark had brought up the topic, Pippa had found herself wondering about this woman—her "twin" who'd apparently abandoned Cull in his time of need. At the same time, she didn't want to land Molly in hot water, especially since she knew the girl's heart was in the right place.

She settled for a compromise. "Before you, there was only my husband, so I'm rather new at this. But I assume this is not your first affair. And I wondered if, well, our relationship is..." She searched for the right word. "Typical. In your experience, that is."

"Are you asking about my past lovers?" Now he sounded amused.

"I suppose I am." She frowned, suddenly questioning how many lovers there had been. How many women had known Cull's lovemaking and enjoyed moonlit picnics on this rooftop? "Have you, um, had many?"

"More than some, less than others."

"Were any of the relationships serious?" she pressed.

"One lasted a year and was serious enough that she met the larks." He hitched his shoulders. "But not serious enough for her to stay after I was injured in the fire."

"Oh, Cull, I'm sorry—"

"Don't be. I'm not. She and I got on well enough, but we weren't a good fit...and there's a reason why there has never been a Princess of Larks," he said prosaically.

Pippa stilled. "That reason being?"

"A woman has to put up with a lot, being tied to a man like me." He gave her a grim look. "Having mudlarks underfoot constantly, dealing with enemy threats, knowing that my attention will always be divided. The life I have to offer ain't exactly one of luxury and ease...which is why all the princes before me ruled in solitude."

Wistfully, she thought that the life he described sounded rather exciting and meaningful.

"But I didn't answer your question. About whether this"—he gestured between the two of them—"is typical for me. The answer is no."

"How is it different?"

"I've never wanted anyone the way I want you."

"Oh." Pleasure unfurled at his unequivocal statement. "Why is that?"

"Because, sunshine, none of them could hold a candle to the girl I kissed in a bell tower fourteen years ago."

23

Cull wasn't ashamed of the fact that he wanted Pippa. More than he wanted anyone.

Then, now, and undoubtedly for the rest of his life.

"But we were apart for so long." She lifted a hand to her bosom, her eyes wide. "Surely you weren't thinking about me…"

"Not every minute. Not always consciously. But you were there," he said gruffly. "A glow at the back of my mind, the memory of the girl who lit up rooms when she entered."

"If that were true, why…why did you leave without saying goodbye?" Her voice was tremulous. "Why didn't you find me sooner?"

"The same reason I wasn't there for Maisie. I wasn't in a place to give you what you needed. What you deserved." He brushed his knuckles against her downy cheek. "You were a lady, and I was little more than an alley rat."

"I never cared—"

"But *I* did. You were so sheltered and sweet; I didn't want to take advantage of your innocence." He exhaled. "As the years passed, my fortunes improved. Sometimes I would think there might be a chance…but my duty to the mudlarks always came first. Then when you met Longmere and had eyes for only him, and I had my accident, I knew."

"Knew what?" Her words were whisper soft.

"That my mam was right. She told me that folk like her and me, we didn't have lucky stars above us. She said that if I wanted to survive, I would have to find my way in the dark."

"As a boy, wasn't that frightening to hear?" Pippa asked with a shiver.

Given the other terrors he'd encountered in the stew's dark alleyways, not really.

He shrugged. "She wasn't wrong. I've found success in the shadows, and the dark is where I belong. But you, sweeting...you belong in the light. When you wed Longmere, I told myself it was for the best."

Even though it had hurt like hell, and he'd drunk himself into a stupor for days afterward.

"It wasn't for the best," she said.

At the sudden lost look in her eyes, steel bands tightened around Cull's chest. What he resented about his fate wasn't his own travails. It was his failure to protect the people he cared about.

"If I had known how he would treat you—the pain he would ultimately cause—I would have stepped in," Cull said in a low voice. "Done something."

"What could you have done?" Pippa blinked at him, her gaze becoming focused and hard. "No one could have stopped me from following what I thought was my heart's desire: not my family, not you. I had to learn the lesson the hard way."

"What lesson?"

"The difference between love and infatuation."

Cull went still, remembering what she'd said about crying for herself, not her husband. He had thought she meant that she was moving through her grief. But had she meant something else?

She drew a breath and carried on. "I'm beginning to see that I was in love with the *image* of Longmere—of the passionate, romantic artist—and not the man he actually was. How foolish is that?"

"Sunshine." Cupping her jaw, Cull felt her trembling tension. "You're not foolish. You were young, and Longmere...let's face it. He was popular with the ladies for a reason."

"He mostly talked about himself." The words left her in a rush. "He wanted everything his way. In our daily life, in...our bedchamber. Whenever I tried to initiate anything, especially of a marital nature, he found it unbecoming. I bent over backward to please him, and it was never enough."

The bleeding popinjay is lucky he's dead.

Yet Cull knew his fury wouldn't help her; she had enough of that aimed at herself already.

"Well," he said after a pause. "Maybe you were a *bit* foolish."

She laughed, just as he hoped she would.

"That is what I like about you, Cull." The beguiling sparkle was back in her eyes. "You listen to me, and you're honest. When I'm with you, I feel like I'm...enough."

God, her vulnerability wrecked him. Made his chest melt and his cock rear to attention. Only Pippa had ever stirred these contradictory needs in him: he wanted to comfort her and screw her senseless at the same time.

"You're more than *enough*," he murmured. "You're everything a man could want."

"Even you?" The corners of her lips tipped up in invitation.

"Especially me." As he leaned in to take what she offered, she brushed her fingertips over his mask.

"I've laid myself bare," she whispered. "Don't you think you ought to do the same?"

Resistance gripped him, and he hated it. Hated his vanity. Hated that facing an army of cutthroats was less intimidating than exposing his ugliness, even though she'd already seen his scars. But that had been in a dark carriage. Here, the lanterns cast a bright glow, and even the heavens seemed to be mocking him: the fog had melted away to a sky of stars, raining their light down through the glass.

Blasted stars would choose now to show up.

"Now who is being foolish?" Her dare was sweetly playful.

Exhaling, he untied the mask and threw it aside. He tried to keep his expression nonchalant even though his chest pounded as if he'd run for miles. He studied her for any sign of disgust...but she only smiled.

"There you are, Timothy Cullen," she said. "I've missed you."

God, she undid him. And since he wasn't actually a fool like her dead husband, he loved being undone by her. Loved her feminine passion...and wanted to unleash all of it.

"Care to show me how much?" he challenged.

Her smile lit up her eyes, her face, until he would swear that she was brighter than the starlight.

"It would be my pleasure," she purred.

With giddy excitement, Pippa took in the sensual male before her. Lounging against the cushions, he was a feast for the senses, and she didn't know what she wanted most: to taste or smell or touch him. But she didn't have to choose, did she?

Since Cull had given her free rein, she could have it *all*.

Having never been in charge before, she wasn't sure where to begin. Letting her instincts guide her, she knelt beside him and traced the straight line of his eyebrows with her fingertip. She stroked the bridge of his nose and around his lips. As if she were sketching him with her touch.

He flicked his tongue out, catching her fingertip. She responded by leaning in and kissing his forehead and the twin dents between his brows. She let her lips follow where she'd touched. As she cupped his strong jaw with both hands, she pressed her lips against his smooth cheek. And heard his breath catch when she did the same to the other side, feeling the rough texture of his scars, part of the tapestry that made up this unique and vital man. Whose beauty was more profound than perfection. Whose every wound and every hurt made him peerless in her eyes.

Her mouth hovering by his, she said, "I want to paint you someday."

He stared at her, as if he didn't believe she was serious. Although she was. Absolutely.

His breath caressed her lips. "One of 'em naked pictures?"

Laughter bubbled from her, and it felt like joy. She grabbed one end of his cravat, unraveling it slowly. "For a nude portrait, I need to do a thorough study ahead of time."

He helped her to remove his coat, waistcoat, and shirt. With his hands planted behind him and veined biceps bulging, his broad chest rippling with muscle, he was a work of art.

"You really are beautiful, you know," she said with a heartfelt sigh.

"Flattery is unnecessary." He directed a meaningful gaze at his groin, where his arousal strained his trousers. "I'm what a betting man would call a certain thing."

"I'm not flattering; I'm giving you a sincere compliment." She grazed her mouth against his, their lips clinging for the sweetest instant. "All you have to say is *thank you*."

"Thank you."

His words came out a bit strangled, perhaps because she was peppering his jaw with kisses. His soap-and-sea scent whetted her appetite, and she searched for more along his corded neck. She nibbled gently on the ridges of sinew, loving his harsh pants. She ran her tongue down a groove, all the way to his collarbone.

She felt hungry and alive. More alive than she'd ever been.

She poked a finger into his chest; although her push didn't have any force behind it, he fell back onto the cushions. He tucked one hand behind his head, gesturing at himself with the other.

"Feel free to proceed with your study," he said with princely grandeur.

She didn't need to be told twice. Her skirts billowed as she made a space for herself between his muscled thighs. She stretched over him, brushing her lips against his, once, twice, the third time running her tongue along his seam. He parted for her, and she shivered at the reversed roles. At the heady power of having this potent male at her command.

She sank her lips onto his, and the kiss turned ravenous. A feast of tongues and lips and teeth. Their hot licking stiffened her nipples and sent a humid pulse of heat to her core. The need to have more of him took over, and she skated her lips down his throat to his chest.

His torso rose and fell with heavy breaths as he watched her, his eyes hotter than molten earth. She ran possessive hands over the blocks of his pectoral muscles, his wiry bronze chest hair a sensual abrasion against her palms. He had scars here as well, and she bent to kiss the healed hurts, his hands stroking her hair lightly as she did so.

Reaching his nipples, she circled them with her thumbs and, seeing his gaze flare, took it one step further. Bending, she kissed the flat brown nub and smiled when he shuddered.

"Do you like being kissed here?" she whispered.

"I like your mouth anywhere on me," he said with guttural emphasis.

Taking him up on his *carte blanche*, she tracked the trail of hair with her mouth. It arrowed downward, bisecting the stacked muscles of his abdomen, and she planted kisses over his taut stomach all the way to his waistband. She paused, a tremor shooting through her as she beheld the long, thick ridge stretching the fabric just below.

Cull caught her chin, turning her gaze to his.

"You're shaking," he said huskily. "We should stop. Do only what you want to."

She realized that he thought she was afraid when that was the furthest thing from the truth. She debated trying to explain what she was truly feeling, then decided it was easier to show him. Shaking with anticipation, she fumbled with his fasteners.

His large hands covered hers. "Pippa, are you sure?"

Seeing his concern, the arousal he kept in check for her, she'd never wanted him more.

"I want you, Cull," she said steadily. "And I want this."

She palmed his manhood, squeezing gently, and his eyes grew smoky and heavy-lidded.

"Then take what you want," he rasped.

He helped her to shove down his trousers, yanking them off with enough haste to make her giggle. Then she was between his naked, muscular thighs, and even though she'd touched him in the darkness of the carriage, her eyes widened at her first unhindered view of his member. The thick column of rosy-brown flesh lay rigid against his muscled stomach, the head stretching toward his navel. Prominent veins girded the shaft, his bollocks hanging heavily in a nest of brown hair.

Heavens, now she *really* wanted to paint him. *Portrait of a Lady's Dream*, she would call it. And she would covetously guard it from all eyes but her own.

Reaching out, she wrapped her hand around Cull's manhood. Shivered when her fingers barely encircled the pulsing girth. His breath hissed as she carefully pried the shaft from his stomach and ran her fist gently along the length, then harder, the way he'd taught her to do it. Dragging the velvety skin over the core of steel, up and down. Down and up.

"How is that?" she whispered.

"Bloody paradise." His gaze scorched her insides. "You frig my cock so well."

As if to punctuate his praise, a drop of seed beaded on the fat tip. Pippa stared at it, remembering how good Cull's mouth had felt. Wondering if she could give him the same bliss. She'd never done it before, never wanted to...but now, with Cull, she did.

With him, she wanted to feel and experience everything.

She leaned over his flared dome, the milky bead quivering with her breath. "What about my lips? Would they feel like heaven as well?"

The feral sound that scraped from his throat was answer enough.

With churning excitement, she kissed the tip of his cock.

Christ Almighty, she was going to kill him.

In his nine-and-twenty years, Cull had never felt anything as arousing as Pippa's mouth. He could tell it was her first time performing fellatio; she didn't exactly know what she was doing. Her brazen enthusiasm more than made up for her lack of experience, however. When she swirled her tongue around his head, bliss sizzled through his veins. He spurted another drop of seed.

Plenty more where that came from.

"Am I doing this right?" Her words teased his moist dome. "Is there more I should do?"

Since she asked... "You could take me deeper, if you want."

"Deeper?" A furrow appeared between her brows. "How much deeper?"

"As deep as you want me inside you," he said huskily.

"Oh." She seemed to ponder his suggestion before making the *sweetest* request. "Show me?"

Weaving his fingers into her silky hair, he guided her head to his cock, groaning as he breached her softness. "Suck on me like I'm a sweet."

She closed her lips around him, the gentle suction tugging all the way to his balls.

Releasing him with a *pop* that made him shudder with lust, she said breathlessly, "Like that?"

"God, yes," he panted. "Relax your jaw and see if you can take more of me."

When she did exactly that, he arched his neck. It was too fine. The feel of her hot little mouth, the sight of those delicate lips stretching around his veined meat. He couldn't stop himself from sliding his fingers against her scalp, urging her to take even more. She bobbed her head, going deeper and deeper, driving him out of his mind. She couldn't fit his entire length, but God's teeth, it was enough. When she hummed with satisfaction, the vibration nearly triggered his release.

"Pippa, you have to stop," he bit out. "I can't hold back—"

He tried to pull her off him, and she *swatted* his hands away.

"It's my turn to taste you." Her eyes shone with sultry resolve. "Sliding down my throat."

Jesus wept. She'd thrown his own words back at him.

He gripped her head as she sucked him. Her cheeks hollowed with her decadent pulls. The stars overhead blurred as white-hot pleasure streaked through him, threatening to burn him alive. Even as his hips bucked into her generous kiss and he spilled himself with a roar, he was aware of the part of him that remained hungry. The frenzied beast Pippa had awakened. And at that moment, he knew.

He would never have enough of this woman. He wanted more. Everything, everything.

Fear reared its ugly head. But desire beat it down, growling that he would have this moment—this one bloody moment—for himself. He dragged her mouth to his, the taste of himself a depraved thrill. She made a sound halfway between a laugh and a moan when he began tearing at her clothes. Between the two of them, they got her naked, and he wasted no time in hoisting her over him, positioning her cunny over his mouth. Clamping his hands on her hips, he guided her to ride his face.

He groaned at her dripping arousal. He licked the length of her juicy slit, from her pearl all the way to her pleated rosebud. She jerked in surprise, then moaned as he swirled his tongue there before going back and thrusting inside her proper entrance. He grunted as her quim clenched, shoving her hips down as he fucked her with his tongue. Her knees trembled against his jaw and she came, chanting his name.

Breathing hard, suffused with the taste of her pleasure, he slid her down his body. With her hair flowing loose over her shoulders, she was a sensual mermaid, her pink-tipped breasts bobbing seductively.

He palmed the flawless apple-sized mounds, grazing his thumbs over the ripe peaks. "I still have to make good on my promise to suckle you here thoroughly."

"All right," she breathed.

In her passion-flushed face, he saw his fantasy come true: she wasn't nearly done. By God, she was perfect—and he had to have her. Now.

"I'll do it while I'm inside you," he decided.

"Oh." Her eyes rounded. "But what about..."

"I have a French letter."

He'd put one in the pocket of his discarded jacket.

She arched her brows. "Confident, were you?"

He grinned at her prim tone. Trust Pippa to sound ladylike while draped naked over him.

"Just optimistic." Reaching down, he brought his cock to her cunny, dragging his crown along her silky-wet petals. Shuddering at how good she felt. "Was I wrong to be so?"

"No," she gasped. "Hurry and—"

Hinges squealed, and Mikey's voice called from the doorway, "You in 'ere, Cull?"

Biting out an oath, Cull rolled over Pippa, shielding her naked body with his own.

"What did I say about privacy?" he barked.

"This is important."

At Mikey's stark tone, Cull stilled. "What is it?"

"An 'our ago, that cove Hastings was shot dead."

24

The next morning, Charlie, Pippa, and the Angels (minus Fiona, who had once again been detained by her family) convened at the Nest. They were accompanied by Mrs. Peabody and Hawker. As Fair Molly led the contingent into the great hall, Mrs. Peabody surveyed the dirty windows, stained furnishings, and cluttered tables.

"Does the Prince of Larks not employ a housekeeper?" she said in an undertone to Pippa.

"Apparently no one wants the job," Pippa whispered back.

"I wonder why." Mrs. Peabody looked at a pair of mudlarks engaged in a gleeful food fight, a shudder going through her slender frame. "Goodness, what is that child doing?"

Ahead of them, a ginger-haired boy was hanging upside down from the chandelier, his knees hooked around the heavy metal ring. Pippa recognized Teddy, the boy who'd fallen the last time.

"Look at me!" Teddy sang. "I'm an acrobat!"

"Have a care—" Pippa began.

But Teddy had already swung too far, his knees losing their grip, his small body plunging toward the ground. Pippa rushed

forward, but Hawker got there first, plucking Teddy out of the air
with a giant fist.

"Watch yourself, lad." The burly man set the boy safely on the
ground.

Teddy tilted his chin up...and up, taking in Hawker with big
eyes. "Are you a pirate?"

"I'm a butler."

"Can I 'ave your eye patch?"

"What do you want it for?"

Teddy angled his head. "I want to look as rough-an'-ready as
you."

Hawker grunted. "It'd take a lot more than an eye patch."

"I 'ave a chipped tooth. See?" The boy pulled back his lips,
showing the missing corner on one of his front teeth.

"Congratulations."

"My name's Teddy."

Apparently unfazed by the non sequiturs, the butler said,
"Hawker."

Digging in his pocket, Teddy pulled out a lint-covered sweet
that looked suspiciously used. "Do you want a treat?"

"You keep it. And the next time you're on that light, hang by
your hands, not your knees," Hawker advised. "Less likely to bash
in your noggin that way."

As Fair Molly ushered their group on, leaving Teddy staring
after Hawker as if the latter walked on water, Mrs. Peabody said
severely, "You should not encourage such behavior, Hawker."

The butler shrugged. "I ain't encouraging it. But no point in
trying to stop the tides, either."

"It is dangerous," the housekeeper insisted.

"Aye, and so is life. Doesn't mean we shouldn't live, does it?"

Mrs. Peabody pinned her lips together and walked ahead, her
skirts swishing with annoyance.

"You oughtn't bait her so," Pippa chided.

Hawker gave her an innocent look—as innocent a look as a

one-eyed giant with a shaved head could muster. "Ain't my fault she has her drawers in a constant twist."

When they arrived at the parlor, Cull was there waiting, once again masked. His gaze sought Pippa out first, and her heart stuttered at the raw longing in his eyes. Memories of last night flooded her: they'd devoured one another and still wanted more. For a few precious hours, they'd found a private Eden. The smile that flickered on Cull's mouth felt like a promise that they would return.

Then his eyes shuttered, and he was once again the Prince of Larks.

"Welcome." He addressed the group. "Please make yourselves comfortable."

The group found their seats around the battered coffee table. Flanking Cull were Long Mikey, Fair Molly, and two other mudlarks Pippa didn't recognize: a boy built like a candlestick with a large head of spiky raven hair, and a man in his twenties who rivaled Hawker in size. A younger pair of larks served tea in chipped cups and offered the guests a plate of ginger biscuits.

Smiling her thanks, Livy took one of the biscuits. She bit in... and her eyes bulged in their sockets. Remembering what Cull had said about his cook, Pippa hurriedly passed her friend a handkerchief. Livy snatched it and brought it to her mouth, discreetly ridding herself of the evidence.

"We are convening today to discuss the latest developments," Cull said.

"You mean Viscount Hastings's murder." Charlie's walking dress of pewter wool matched her steely expression. "Tell us what you know."

"It would be best for you to hear it from the source," Cull said.

Long Mikey stepped forward. "It 'appened like this. I was tailing 'Astings last night with Matches and me brother, Long Joe." He gestured to the spiky-haired boy and large adult lark, respectively; the latter gave a gap-toothed smile.

"I could tell something was off with the toff from the start," Mikey went on.

"What was off about him?" Livy wanted to know.

"'E were as nervy as a virgin on 'er wedding night. Thought it were 'is appetite for the cards and poppy's tears that put 'im on edge and that 'e'd be 'eaded back to Limehouse. Instead, 'e took 'imself off to some shady play'ouse not far from Drury Lane called the New Cytherea. Matches, Long Joe, and I couldn't find 'im once we got inside—too many rooms where the *actresses* ply their trade." Mikey's emphasis on the word, and the way he curled his fingers like quotation marks when he said it, gave a good indication of how the New Cytherea's players made their livings. "Then I 'eard a shot go off, toffs screaming across the street. So I run o'er, and there in the alleyway was our man 'Astings. Dead as a doornail, bullet through the chest."

"Any witnesses?" Charlie asked.

Long Mikey shook his head. "None that stepped forward. It 'appened in the alley, like I said, so good chance no one saw anything. I managed to go through 'Astings's pockets—'ad to be quick, mind you, last thing I needed was to be caught by some peeler—and found this."

He placed the objects on the coffee table. Pippa had already seen the items that her friends were now examining: a miniature portrait of Julianna Hastings and a wrinkled program for a play called *The Grove of Love.*

"Look at the date." Glory tapped her finger on the program. "The play took place at the New Cytherea a year ago. Why would Hastings be carrying an old playbill? And a memento of his wife whom he despised?"

"And who would have cause to kill him?" Livy said in a ruminative manner. "Could it be related to his gambling debts, do you think?"

"I have a list of Hastings's debtors. They're brutes, more apt to maim than kill," Cull replied. "Moneylenders don't profit from dead patrons, and Hastings was making his payments."

"Then who murdered Hastings and why? And is it related to Lady Hastings's death?" Pippa chewed on her lip. "I feel like we're missing something."

"Perhaps the dossiers will help."

Cull nodded to Fair Molly, who brought over a portfolio to Charlie. The latter took out a stack of documents, and Pippa glimpsed addresses, numbers, and neatly organized lists.

"Allow me to summarize." Cull clasped his hands behind his back.

Pippa didn't know what it said about her that she found his pedantic tone stimulating. She felt a quiver in her private parts as her prince did what he did best.

"Starting with Howard Morton. Age thirty, only child of Deirdre and Laurence Morton, the latter being Jonas Turner's cousin twice removed and a childhood friend. As a child, Howard Morton spent summers at the Turners' country estate, and since he and Julianna were of a similar age, they were close. Rumor had it that Jonas Turner hoped his daughter and Morton might make a match of it. But Julianna met Hastings and fell for him instead."

"Do you know if Morton had feelings for Julianna?" Pippa asked.

"On this point, I am uncertain. What I do know is that Morton attended her wedding and apparently got very drunk. And he has never married, nor courted anyone since." Cull paused. "At present, Morton resides near Amwell, Hertfordshire. He makes his living as a schoolmaster and lives a quiet life. This will likely change now that he stands to inherit half of Jonas Turner's fortune."

Pippa tilted her head. "Revenge for being thrown over and greed could be powerful motives for murder. If Morton blamed Hastings for stealing away Julianna, he might have reason to kill husband and wife."

"Agreed," Cull said. "Morton is an important suspect...but so is Louis Wood. As it turns out, there is more to the butler than meets the eye."

"Why am I not surprised?" she muttered. "To think, I believed he was helpful at the funeral."

"I wouldn't take it personally, sunshine." Cull's lips twitched. "It took some digging to unearth Wood's past. He has changed his name, and for good reason: as a young man, he spent several years in Newgate for assault."

"He is a former convict?" Charlie said sharply.

Cull inclined his head. "Wood has seemingly walked the straight and narrow since his employment with the Turners. He has no family of his own. His reputation is that of a loyal retainer dedicated to his work."

"Even so, a butler doesn't usually inherit half his master's fortune," Livy pointed out. "Perhaps Wood was playing some sort of long game."

"That is possible," Cull allowed. "And, if so, the end is in sight for him. I've learned that Turner's solicitor has set an appointment to disburse the funds to Morton and Wood in three weeks."

"The clock is ticking." Charlie drummed her fingers against the documents. "Once the money is distributed, there will be nothing to keep Morton or Wood in London. With vast financial resources, they can go anywhere, do anything. They will be beyond our reach."

"Then we better not waste any time." Glory canted her head. "What is our plan?"

"To begin, we need to check out Morton," Charlie said. "That would mean a team going to Hertfordshire."

"I'll go," Pippa said.

Being a widow, she had more freedom and fewer commitments than her fellow Angels.

"I'll escort you," Cull offered. "I have some pressing business but can leave the day after next, if that suits?"

Aware of the interested gazes in the room, Pippa gave a polite —and what she hoped was professional—nod. On the inside, she was bursting with excitement. She couldn't wait to spend time with Cull, even if they were investigating a murder. In truth, having a shared purpose made her feel even closer to him.

"In the meantime, the Angels will continue looking for Vincent Ellis. And I think a visit to the New Cytherea is in order," Charlie said. "We need to find out what Hastings was doing there on the night he was killed."

25

Pippa, Livy, and Fiona proceeded to the New Cytherea the next afternoon. They'd disguised themselves as trollops in search of employment. A guard ushered them in through the back, and when his hand "accidentally" landed on her bottom, Pippa shoved it away.

"No touchin' the merchandise," she warned.

"Saucy, eh?" He leered at her. "Come find me after, and I'll treat you to a tavern supper."

Fiona, presently a blowsy brunette, hooked her arm through Pippa's. "Me friend's on a slimming plan, so you'll 'ave to sup alone."

The Angels entered the backstage area. The dilapidated room had a few rickety dressing tables set alongside the far wall, and actresses dressed in clingy robes were nudging one another, fighting for space in front of the looking glasses as they primped.

"Watch yer bony elbow," a voluptuous blonde squealed. "You're bruising me tits."

"And those are wot get 'er the nightly encores," a brunette riposted, leading to peals of laughter.

The blonde jiggled said assets, cooing, "Lord Evanston is quite taken with me *talents*."

"Those talents will droop and sag one day, and then where'll you all be?" A newcomer strode through the stage curtains. Thin, dark-haired, and angular, the woman sported male attire and clutched a sheaf of papers in her ink-stained fingers. "Why are you hens preening instead o' practicing your lines?"

"Marg?" Pippa said in surprise.

The woman turned, her eyes widening as she took in the Angels. "Why, as I live and breathe. Wot are you lot doing 'ere?"

"I guess we didn't need the disguises after all," Livy said.

The Angels knew Marg. Marg's companion, the beautiful CeCe, had been Edwin's favorite model and, indeed, the muse for *Portrait of a Lady Dreaming*. Pippa had become friendly with the two women, enjoying their chats at Edwin's studio. The pair had also helped the Angels during the investigation into Edwin's death.

Smiling, Pippa held out a hand to Marg, who took it in a roughly affectionate squeeze.

"Been a while, luv." Marg studied her. "You're looking well. Doing better?"

"Yes," Pippa said. "May we speak to you in private?"

"We'll talk in my office." Turning to the actresses, Marg barked, "As for you lot, I want you to practice the last scene from *The Wings of Cupid*. We'll do a run-through when I return."

"Why bother?" A brassy-haired woman stuck a hand on her hip. "Our audience don't care 'bout Cupid's wings. It's *Cupid's alley* they're 'ere to visit."

The women fell into one another, cackling with laughter. With a frustrated growl, Marg threw the pages she was carrying into the air and stalked out, the Angels at her heels. They followed her down a corridor and into a storage room crammed with costumes and objects used in plays. They all crowded in, and Pippa was squished next to a plaster rendition of Michelangelo's *David*.

Feeling something poke into her back, she looked down...and stifled a giggle at the implausible size of the statue's equipment.

Marg glowered at the protruding appendage, which had to be close to two feet long.

"I curse the day I took this job," she grumbled. "The owner said 'e needed a proper playwright, after the last one developed bats in the belfry. Now I know why: the poor cove was *driven* mad by the talentless hacks that work 'ere. Not one o' the hens out there is willing to lift a finger and *act*; they'd rather lift their blasted skirts."

"How frustrating," Pippa said sympathetically.

"CeCe's afraid I'm going to have a fit o' apoplexy. Speaking of Cece...she misses you." Marg paused. "You haven't visited o' late."

Guilt prickled Pippa. "I'm sorry. I've been busy."

Marg scrutinized her. "Got a follower, do you?"

She flushed. *Do I have a sign hanging around my neck announcing that I have a lover?*

Marg laughed, as if reading her mind. "You got your glow back. And I'm 'appy for you, luv. Life is for the living, eh? Now tell me what I can do for you ladies today."

"We are looking for information about this man." Pippa took out a sketch that she'd done of Hastings. "He was here—"

"That's the nob who was shot across the street the night before last." Marg narrowed her eyes. "It wasn't a robbery?"

"We have reason to believe otherwise," Livy said. "You saw him?"

"Spoke to him after I found him pestering the actresses backstage."

"What did he want?" Fi asked.

"'E 'ad a portrait o' a woman. Brown-haired, plain. Said it was 'is wife." Marg crossed her arms. "'E'd brought an old program and wanted to know if any o' us remembered seeing 'er at that play."

Pippa pursed her lips. "Did any of you?"

Marg shook her head. "That play took place a year ago. I

wasn't working 'ere yet, and neither were most o' the current players. Even if any o' the hens 'ad remembered the cove's wife,
though, they would've kept mum about it."

"Why?" Pippa asked.

"Because he was a brute," Marg said flatly. "And too many o'
the women are 'ere to get away from the brutes in their own lives.
To take control o' their futures 'owever they can. And like thieves,
there is honor among sisters."

"Would you mind if we interviewed the actresses?" Fiona
inquired. "Perhaps they would talk to us if they knew we were
trying to bring whoever killed Hastings's wife to justice?"

"Be my guest." Marg snorted. "It's not as if the hens are doing
anything useful anyway."

That afternoon, Cull arrived early to his appointment at Nightingale's, a coffee house in Covent Garden. The meeting was the
reason why he'd had to postpone the trip to Hertfordshire by a
day. The thought of his upcoming journey with Pippa heated his
blood, but he forced himself to concentrate. He needed his wits
about him for the task ahead.

A pair of guards searched him for weapons before granting
him entrance. A relic of a bygone era, Nightingale's was filled with
the rich aroma of coffee, its long tables filled with chattering
patrons. Years ago, the place had been razed by fire and rebuilt by
Bartholomew Black, a cutthroat so notorious that he'd been
dubbed the King of the Underworld. Despite his infamy, Black
had also used his power for good, establishing a hierarchy in the
underclass that kept bloodshed and chaos to a minimum. He'd
employed Nightingale's as his headquarters and meeting place. As
the Prince of Larks, Cull had been invited to the table on several
occasions to discuss plans of mutual benefit.

Black had retired, passing the mantle to his granddaughter,

Tessa Kent. It was Mrs. Kent with whom Cull would be meeting today. From her that he would request a boon.

The guards led Cull to the private meeting room, a high-ceilinged space with a massive round table which had hosted some of the most intense underworld parleys. The seats ringing the oak slab were empty, save one. In the largest chair—a throne that rivaled the Queen's with its carved giltwood frame and crimson velvet upholstery—sat Tessa Kent.

Many made the mistake of underestimating the sylphlike brunette with jade-colored eyes. Mrs. Kent was in her thirties, dressed in a fashionable crimson gown and pelisse, her skirts neatly arrayed. Despite her charming appearance, anyone who'd dealt with her knew she was cunning and a force to be reckoned with.

Standing by her side was her tall, dark-haired spouse, Harry Kent. A scientist and partner in a prosperous railway company, Kent was known for his intelligence and fierce devotion to his wife. His bespectacled gaze narrowed, as if assessing Cull for any signs of threat. Such vigilance was understandable, given Mrs. Kent's condition. Although Mrs. Kent's pelisse hid her waist, Cull had heard from a source that the lady was expecting again.

"Good afternoon, Prince," Mrs. Kent said pleasantly. "Please, have a seat."

Exchanging a bow with Kent, Cull sat where a silver coffee service awaited him. Partaking of the coffee was a ritual. The offering and accepting of hospitality a sign of mutual respect. Kent took the seat next to his wife; although he did not interfere, his stance made it clear he was ready to act at the slightest provocation.

"Thank you for seeing me," Cull said as he doctored his brew.

Mrs. Kent took a sip from a delicate porcelain cup. "It isn't often you request a meeting."

"I have a favor to ask." With this lady, it was best to come to the point.

She arched her brows. "To ask...or to call in?"

She'd remembered, as he'd known she would. Over a decade ago, she and Kent had asked for assistance rescuing Bartholomew Black from a deadly enemy. Cull had answered their call, and he'd never asked for anything in return. He'd been saving that card, knowing that he would need to play it one day.

Cull took a drink of the rich coffee before answering. "You have a friend, Alfred Doolittle, who owns a slew of pawnshops throughout London. He heads an unofficial guild for his trade, and it is said that all pawnbrokers answer to him."

"And what's it to you?" Mrs. Kent asked.

Cull was not fooled by her mild tone. "In recent weeks, Chester Squibb has tried to kill me twice. He is a nuisance that must be dealt with. Squibb makes his living robbing the houses he's paid to sweep, and I want Doolittle to cut off his lifeblood. To ensure that no pawnbroker in London will take his goods. Squibb's gang is based on greed, not loyalty. When the money stops coming in, his gang will disperse like a dandelion."

"Diabolical." Mrs. Kent turned her cup in its saucer. "Why not just kill Squibb and be done with it? An eye for an eye."

"Because I do not wish to walk through streets littered with eyeballs and running with blood."

Mrs. Kent's lips formed a humorless curve. "A charming image."

A boom suddenly shook the walls, sloshing coffee out of cups. Instinct propelled Cull to his feet. Kent was slower to rise and looked remarkably unconcerned.

He exchanged glances with his wife, who said with a sigh, "Whose turn is it?"

Kent chucked the Duchess of the Underworld beneath her chin. "I believe it is yours, sprite."

"It figures," she grumbled. She stood and said in a voice that carried, "Bartholomew Kent, get in here this instant!"

Footsteps sounded outside the room. A guard let in a boy who was around ten years old, handsome and sturdily built, with a shock of unruly hair that had come from his papa. Currently, tuffs were sticking straight up, ash streaked across his face. He flicked his gaze at Cull, registering the presence of a masked stranger, yet reining in his curiosity to deal with a more immediate peril. He'd inherited his shrewdness from his maternal side, no doubt.

With a confident smile, Bartholomew Kent said, "Hello, Mama and Papa. You called?"

"Don't you *Mama* me, young man," Mrs. Kent returned. "What did we say about setting off Papa's inventions?"

"That I'm not supposed to," the boy said virtuously.

A wise rule, Cull thought, since Kent's rock-blasting explosives had taken down mountains.

Mrs. Kent crossed her arms. "And what were you doing just now?"

"I didn't set off Papa's device," Bartholomew said. "Ask Mr. Parkin."

He pointed to the scholarly-looking fellow who stood trembling in the doorway.

"Come in, Mr. Parkin," Mrs. Kent said imperiously. "Tell us who set off Harry's device."

"Go ahead, Mr. Parkin." The boy's tone matched his mama's. "Tell them."

Parkin edged inside, mopping his brow with a handkerchief, his eyes darting between mother and son. "It was...it was me, ma'am."

Mrs. Kent's brows pinched together. "Explain."

"When I went in to give Master Bartholomew his lesson, I, er, accidentally triggered a system of levers and pulleys. We have been studying the physics of simple machines, you see," the tutor said apologetically. "Anyway, the string on the doorknob was attached to a weight, which lowered onto the lever, which set a ball in motion, which hit a row of books lined up like dominoes, which toppled a lit candle—"

"I get the idea," Mrs. Kent snapped.

Her husband's lips quirked.

"It was an ingenious application of the lesson," the tutor mumbled.

"And an even more ingenious attempt to evade the rules." Scowling, Mrs. Kent turned to her son. "Nonetheless, Bart, you *are* ultimately responsible for the device going off. Papa and I will be discussing your punishment. For now, go with your tutor"—she wagged her finger at him—"and *no more shenanigans*, do you hear me? Or you shall remain in the nursery with your younger siblings, and I shan't let you accompany us to Nightingale's again."

"Yes, Mama," Master Bart said with a beatific smile.

He strode out, the tutor scurrying after him.

Mrs. Kent sighed. "The boy takes after his namesake."

"And his mama." Kent grinned at her. "I seem to recall that you once rigged a similar system."

"I did, didn't I?" Mrs. Kent chuckled.

"If it's any consolation," Cull said, "Master Bart would fit right in at the Nest."

"I don't know how you manage all those mudlarks on your own, Prince." Mrs. Kent's mien turned knowing. "Although from what I understand, you may be in the market for a princess?"

What the devil? Cull's gut knotted. *How does she know about Pippa?*

While Tessa Kent was more friend than foe, he didn't like anyone knowing about him and Pippa. Didn't like exposing Pippa to the dangers of his life.

"You are not the only one with eyes and ears. The lady in question comes from a family with deep roots in our world. Her papa is not a man to cross...but you know that, of course."

Cull acknowledged the advice with a terse nod.

"Good." Mrs. Kent smiled. "As to your request, I will speak to Alfie. Await my word."

Pippa giddily counted the minutes until Cull's carriage arrived at noon the next day. Long Mikey brought the equipage discreetly into the lane behind her cottage, Matches hopping down with surprising grace to let down the steps. Pippa smiled at the mudlarks, trying not to seem overeager as she climbed into the cabin. Cull was waiting for her, and he'd forgone his mask. Seeing him as he was, with a hint of vulnerability in his expressive eyes, she abandoned all pretenses.

"I missed you," she blurted.

His crooked smile made her heart thump faster, and then she was in his arms, his kiss rendering her light-headed. She didn't know the carriage had started moving until they came up for air.

"We'd better stop," Cull murmured, rubbing his thumb along her bottom lip. "Or I'll be tempted to take you here and now."

Daringly, she flicked her tongue at his thumb. "I wouldn't mind."

"Jesus wept, don't tempt a man like that." He looked so pained that she giggled. "Not when we're with two nosy larks who are probably eavesdropping."

Oops. She'd forgotten about Mikey and Matches.

With a regretful sigh, Cull tucked her firmly against his side. He laced their hands together and settled them on his lap. "Distract me, please."

She started by filling him in on the visit to the New Cytherea.

"The night he died, Hastings showed up at the theatre, asking a lot of questions. That was why he had the portrait of his wife: to see if anyone recognized her. When no one did, he demanded to speak with those who'd been working there during the production of *The Grove of Love*. Apparently, he let slip that he'd found the program in his wife's belongings."

Cull lifted his brows. "What was Lady Hastings doing at a place like the New Cytherea?"

"It is becoming clear that she had a private life we knew nothing about." Pippa chewed on her lip. "I happen to be acquainted with Marg, the theatre's playwright; her companion used to model for Longmere. Marg said she would try to get me the addresses of the actresses who had parts in *The Grove of Love*."

"That's progress. Louis Wood, in the meantime, hasn't had a hair out of place. I think he knows he's being watched," Cull said.

"According to the other Angels, Vincent Ellis has more aliases than a cat has lives, but they are working on tracking him down. And perhaps you and I will uncover critical information when we interview Howard Morton. Will we head to his residence straight away?"

"Actually, I thought we could deal with him in the morning. There is something I want to show you tonight. Did you pack an outfit suitable for rambling?"

Yesterday, Cull had sent her a brief note, telling her he'd made all the arrangements for their trip. He'd told her to pack for two nights and bring an outfit suitable for exploring the outdoors. He'd given no further explanation.

Brimming with curiosity, she said, "Yes, but why do I need it? What are we doing?"

"It's a surprise."

"Will you at least give me a clue?"

"It is something I haven't shared with anyone else." He raised her hand, brushing his lips over her knuckles, swirling heat over her skin. "Something I want to share with you."

Drat the man. Now she *really* couldn't wait.

Correctly interpreting her expression, he chuckled. "I can't do it justice with words, anyway. You have to see it for yourself, sunshine, and you will soon enough."

Their destination turned out to be a secluded country estate a few miles from Amwell. Massive oak trees, robed in golden autumn splendor, lined the drive, which led to a charming ivy-covered manor. When Cull helped Pippa alight, she was surprised to see a handful of servants waiting to greet them.

"Who are we staying with?" she whispered.

"No one. The place is mine," Cull said. "Bought it a few years back."

She took in the picturesque property and acres of land that stretched beyond it. "This all belongs to you?"

"I'm not a pauper," he said mildly.

Clearly not. Charlie had mentioned that he was in much demand and commanded a princely sum for his services. Accustomed to his unassuming ways, however, Pippa sometimes forgot that he must be a wealthy man.

"Tillie will take you to your room and help you get changed," he said. "But don't take long. We want to get out there before dusk."

"Get out where?"

But he had already headed off with Long Mikey and Matches.

Equal parts exasperated and intrigued, Pippa followed Tillie, a chatty country girl, into the manor. The interior was as charming as the exterior. The theme of the decorating appeared to be rustic comfort, with overstuffed furnishings and thick Axminster rugs of gold, sage, and maroon. Pippa glimpsed a sitting nook by the window, piled with cushions and perfect for reading or sketching. How long had it been since she'd enjoyed a carefree day with a book or with her drawing pencils?

Tillie led her into a light-filled bedchamber, the walls charmingly stenciled with a vine design. With the maid's help, Pippa refreshed herself and changed into an old blue promenade dress and sturdy half-boots. She donned an Italian straw hat in the Marie Stuart shape, which Suzette had fancifully trimmed with ruched tulle and blue silk flowers.

Checking her reflection, she thought she looked rather well. Her eyes twinkled, and her cheeks were tinted pink with excitement. She hurried back downstairs and found Cull waiting for her in the foyer. He looked brawny and dapper in a brown jacket and checkered waistcoat, his trousers tucked into tall boots.

"Beautiful and punctual," he said. "There's a rare combination."

She blushed. His sincerity made it impossible not to.

"There is only an hour until dusk, so we'd best be on our way," he added.

He hefted up a large, covered basket and took her hand with a spontaneity that swelled her throat. She was rooted on the spot, aware of his callused hold, the way his fingers linked with hers.

He cocked his head. "Is something amiss?"

She didn't know how to tell him that no other man had held her hand in public before. Edwin had offered her his arm, of course, but he hadn't been one for what he termed "vulgar public displays." She hadn't thought holding hands *was* vulgar; growing up, she'd seen her parents do it all the time. But she hadn't shared her logic with Edwin for fear that it would deepen his contempt for her middle-class upbringing.

"No," she said softly. "Everything is fine."

With you, everything feels...right.

Hand in hand, they walked through a quaint maze of over-grown rose-bushes behind the house to the woods beyond. The warmth of the day made it feel more like summer than late autumn. Oaks and silver birches formed a thick grove, mellow sunshine filtering through the branches. A carpet of moss and fallen leaves padded their steps, wildlife rustling and birds chirping in the background. The air smelled of earth, foliage, and a hint of woodsmoke.

"It is so peaceful here," Pippa said in wonder. "A different world from London."

"The estate is my escape," Cull replied. "Although I don't get out here as often as I would like. Autumn is my favorite time."

She took in the beauty around her, her mind translating it into brushstrokes of umber, ochre, and grey. "I should like to paint it one day."

She'd spoken without thinking, and her heart skipped a beat as she realized that she might have overstepped. They were supposed to be having a casual affair, yet she'd brought up the future. Implied that she expected to return here with him. How would he respond?

He squeezed her hand and said easily, "We'll come back. When we don't have a murder investigation hanging over our heads."

Relief flowed through her. "I would like that."

She would, so very much. The truth was it was getting harder to imagine a future without Cull in it. To not develop an attach-ment to this man who held her hand and planned surprises for her, protected children and wounded birds, and treated her like a princess. Yet this was supposed to be a carefree liaison. He'd told her he had nothing to offer but the moment...and wasn't that what she wanted too? Fun, freedom, and pleasure without conse-quences?

Don't make the same mistakes, she told herself. *Enjoy the moment.*

It wasn't difficult to lose herself in the joy of being with Cull, ambling through the woods with him hand-in-hand. They came upon a clearing, where a small building—a gamekeeper's cottage, perhaps—stood near the edge of a pond. Reeds, rushes, and sedge grew thickly at the water's edge. The sun was beginning to sink toward the horizon, rendering the sky in vivid strokes of purple, pink, and orange.

It was another scene that made her itch to paint.

"Cull, this is beautiful," she murmured. "What a lovely surprise."

"This isn't the surprise," he said.

He set down the basket on a grassy spot by the cottage. Opening the lid, he removed a blanket and spread it on the ground. He helped her to sit, settling next to her.

She gave him a quizzical smile. "If this isn't the surprise, then what is?"

The answer came not from him, but from a burst of energy and movement that made her gasp. Out of nowhere, thousands of starlings—nay, tens of thousands of them—shot into the sky. They flew in perfect synchrony, their tiny bodies merging to form an ever-changing array of shapes. Dipping and soaring, the birds moved as one unbreakable whole, their flapping wings as loud as ocean waves crashing against a shore.

Awe pounded in Pippa's chest. She couldn't find the words to express what she was feeling. The majesty and magic of what she was witnessing and how alive it made her feel.

"It's the most magnificent thing I've ever seen," she said, her voice cracking.

"Yes, it is."

Tearing her gaze from the aerial display, she saw that Cull wasn't watching the starlings. He was looking at her. His gaze warm, he reached out and thumbed away a tear that she hadn't realized had escaped. She wanted to say something, to tell him what it meant to her to be sitting here with him, but she was too overcome.

He slung an arm around her shoulders, tucking her close.

"You don't want to miss the rest," he murmured.

Together, they watched the sky. The feathered dance shifted across the heavens, morphing into helices, pyramids, and countless other breathtaking shapes. The birds twirled and dipped, their feathers flashing iridescent ruby and gold in the last rays of the sun. The show was beautiful and wild and mysterious; just as quickly as it began, it was over. The sky went still again, shades of mauve bleeding into the violet horizon.

"Show's done for the evening," Cull said. "What did you think?"

Her pulse raced at his expression. The brutality of his scars made the joy in his eyes that much rarer. All that Cull had endured had not dimmed his appreciation for life or beauty. For the things that mattered. And he had shared this extraordinary spectacle with her: reminded her of all the reasons life was worth living.

And it was. Like an eruption of wings, a part of her that remained caged by the past broke free. It shattered the bars of self-doubt, regret, and anger into glittering dust. What was left was her: the strong, beating, vital essence of herself.

"I think," she said steadily, "that I want you. Now."

Reaching up, she pulled Cull's mouth to hers.

27

Watching Pippa observe the starlings, Cull had known he was right to bring her here. The wonder lighting up her eyes had chased away the shadows. She'd lost herself in the wild pulse that connected living things, and he knew how that felt. He'd first heard of the flight of the starlings a few months after his injury. Weary in body and spirit, he'd come here, hoping for a diversion from his damnable self-pity. He'd left renewed in spirit and faith.

No matter how arduous the journey, a life that held beauty like this was worth living for.

As Pippa pressed her mouth against his, he felt that beauty pour into him like liquid sunlight. She heated his blood, stirred his heart and cock in equal measure. He threaded his fingers into her silken ringlets, knocking off her bonnet as he took everything she offered. The sweet and sensual succor that only she could give...that had fueled his dreams for years.

He dragged his mouth to her ear, and she mewled like a kitten.

"We should go inside," he murmured.

"I don't want to wait," she panted. "I want you *now*."

Jesus wept. How could he resist her command? It was an unseasonably warm day, after all...and even if it wasn't, he would find ways to heat them up.

With a growl, he tore at her buttons and laces. She laughed breathlessly at his haste, but that didn't stop her from doing the same to him. Never had he wanted a woman so badly; never had he felt this wanted in return. When their clothes lay strewn around them, he pressed her down on the blanket and caressed her breasts, savoring their firm yet supple heft.

"Finally," he said. "I've been wanting to suckle these pretty nipples for ages."

Bending his head, he circled her areola with his tongue before drawing the taut peak into his mouth. She moaned and speared her fingers into his hair as he sucked and licked. He took his time, going back and forth between her heaving mounds, adoring how sensitive she was here. Glancing down, he saw a smear of wetness on her thighs, and the needy way she clenched them together injected steel into his cock.

I wonder if I could make her spend from sucking her tits.

A man who enjoyed challenges, he redoubled his efforts, taking one nipple deep into his mouth while he played with the other, rolling the damp tip between finger and thumb. Her whimpering grew desperate, her squirming even more so. That was before he grazed her with his teeth. Her back bowed, and she let out a shocked cry.

He looked into her dazed eyes, steeped in the sultry violet of dusk.

"Did you come?" he asked.

Her nod was bashful and bloody arousing.

"Splendid. Keep playing with those lovely tits while I avail myself of your other delights."

She stared at him. "Um...play with them?"

"Touch yourself. Don't be shy," he said huskily. "It arouses me to watch you. To see your pleasure."

After a heartbeat, she brought her hands to her breasts, her slim fingers brushing the plump undersides. When she brushed her fingertips over the peaks, she trembled with pleasure. Hell, so did he. Biting her lip, she rolled an engorged bud between her thumb and index finger, tugging delicately.

He kissed his way down the gentle valley of her belly while enjoying the view of her naughty, ladylike hands. "Pretend those are my hands touching you. Squeezing your breasts. Teasing those stiff little nipples. How does it feel?"

"So good." Her voice was slurred with pleasure.

"And this?" He spread her thighs and bent his head, swiping his tongue up her slit.

"*Cull.*"

Her cry was as sweet as the nectar coating his tongue. Fucking hell, she was delicious. He buried his face in her cunny, eating her with savage hunger. Feasting on her womanly bounty. When he tickled her pearl with his tongue, her sleek thighs tightened. He spread her wider, laving her nub and sucking it into his mouth. He thrust two fingers inside her, groaning at the lush constriction, imagining that snugness around his prick.

She came again, this time with his name on her lips, and the sound enthralled him.

Blood pounding, he raised his head, licking her cream from his lips. Her eyes were heavy-lidded as she raked a hungry gaze down his chest to his heavy, rearing cock.

In a throaty voice, she said, "I want to feel you...inside."

Christ, yes.

Gripping his prick, he rubbed the head along her satiny folds. Her abundant dew bathed him, made his stones throb in anticipation.

"Hurry," she whimpered.

He reached for his discarded jacket, taking out the French letter. Her avid gaze as he sheathed his erection made the sheep gut feel tighter than normal. He crawled atop her, keeping his weight on one arm, using the other to guide his cock to her entrance.

Staring into her eyes, he thrust himself home. She was tight—God was she ever—but she was also soft and wet from her climaxes, blossoming around him. Pleasure poured over him in a hot wave as he hilted himself and held.

"How is that, love?" he said hoarsely.

"Oh, Cull." Her expression was awestruck. "I never knew."

Pride expanded his chest that he had been the one to show her.

I'm the luckiest bastard alive.

He pushed a tress off her damp cheek. "Ready for more, sunshine?"

"Yes, I want more," she breathed. "Everything."

Groaning, he claimed her mouth and began to move.

Pippa hadn't known that coupling could be like this. This raw and full of need. As Cull pushed inside her, she gulped at the feeling of fullness. At his size and heat and thickness driving into the heart of her. He went deeper and deeper, touching places that had never been touched. Setting off sparks of bliss.

He made her mad with wanting. Moaning, she wrapped her legs around his hips, feeling the hard flexing of his buttocks against her heels as he drove into her. *This* was what she'd always longed for—what she'd always craved. A passion that consumed her thoughts and senses so that she wasn't Patient Pippa or the perfect countess or even a lady...she just *was*.

With Cull, she was just herself. And it was enough. Everything.

"More," she pleaded. "Please, Cull."

An animal gleam came into his eyes. "Want it harder, love? Like this?"

The rough shove of his hips lifted her spine off the blanket, and she moaned her approval. He was so big, so vital, his presence expanding her capacity for sensation. Then he *really* began to move, making her realize that he'd been holding back. He drove into her with thrilling aggression, and she held onto his shoulders, feeling the powerful shifting of muscles beneath his taut skin. Losing herself in the wildness of their mating dance.

Soon their passion began to overwhelm her. Need filled her, pushed at her insides, pulsed under her skin until she couldn't stand it any longer. She *craved* release.

"Cull," she begged.

In answer, he withdrew. At her mewl of protest, he gave her a sensual grin and grabbed her legs one by one, hooking her knees over his shoulders. Then he pushed inside her again, the angle even deeper than before. He pounded into her, grunting with pleasure, the cords of his neck standing out in brute relief. Staring up into his glittering gaze, she felt a tautening at her center, and an instant later, ecstasy burst.

The slow, grinding lunges of his hips kept her adrift in pleasure.

"Christ, I love the way it feels when you come around my cock," he rasped, his eyes heavy-lidded. "So tight and hot and wet. You're going to take me with you."

"Come with me." She framed his face, her palms curving around smoothness and scars. "I want to feel you, Cull."

With a growl, he thrust harder, faster, so virile that, even in her spent state, she felt her blood quickening. Then he pulled out, tearing off the sheath. Kneeling between her legs, he gripped his cock, and her breath snagged at his magnificence. At the rippling animal power of him as he jerked his enormous shaft. He roared as he reached his finish, as he lashed her belly with his hot essence. He sprayed her skin with silky trails until he was wrung dry.

Panting, he collapsed atop her and kissed her, slow and deep.

She would have been content to lie there forever, blanketed by his musky warmth, floating in the twilight.

"My arse is getting cold," he muttered.

Laughing, she said, "I can think of ways to keep it warm."

"I'm going to hold you to that, sunshine." He rose and scooped her up effortlessly, striding toward the cottage. "All night long, as a matter of fact."

Pippa awoke, her cheek pressed against something warm and scratchy. Her lips curved as she took in the delicious expanse of Cull's chest, the hard-paved muscle with its covering of wiry hair. They were in the bed of the gamekeeper's cottage, and she was cuddled up against him, his arm around her, her leg over his. She had never woken up tangled with a lover before. Wistfully, she thought she could get used to it.

Memories of the night returned, suffusing her with heat. After making love to her outside, Cull had carried her into this rustic one-room cabin. Before the wood fire, they'd feasted on the simple repast of bread, cheese, and ham he'd packed in the basket, but their real appetite had been for one another. The food had just been the fuel to keep their energies up.

After eating, they'd made a meal of each other—at the same time. She blushed, recalling the wicked position Cull had introduced her to and how much she'd loved it. He'd taken her twice more until she was too exhausted to move. Fully sated, she'd fallen asleep in his arms, and the only thing better than that was waking there too.

She leaned her head back to look at him. Asleep, Cull looked boyish, his features relaxed, his long lashes resting against his cheeks. Bronze scruff glinted on his strong jaw and unblemished cheek. In the light of the new day, his scars seemed diminished. He was so attractive that she felt a stirring of lust...but she had other bodily needs to attend to first. Taking care not to wake him, she extricated herself and went to use the necessary.

When she returned, he'd rolled onto his side, his back to her. His backside was an artist's dream, a network of ridges and hollows, shifting shadows and light. The sheets were draped just below the vee of muscle that girded his lean hips, revealing a hint of his delectable derriere. She didn't know what she wanted more: to paint him or have her way with him.

Then she noticed the markings. Since it had been dark last night—and she'd spent most of it beneath him—she hadn't seen the small triangle of dots nestled between his shoulder blades. Slipping into bed, she took a closer look at the tattoo and saw that each dot was an inverted "W." A pair of wings...like the drawing a child might make of a bird in the sky. There were six birds in all, one on the top row, two on the next, and three on the bottom.

She gently touched the top of the triangle, wondering what the markings meant. When his muscles bunched beneath her fingertip, she pulled away.

"I didn't mean to wake you," she whispered.

Cull was rolling over. They lay on their sides, facing one another. Her chest warmed at the boyish appeal of his sleep-tousled hair and drowsy eyes.

"That one is for Toby," he said in a sleep-roughened voice.

She blinked, not understanding.

"The lark at the top of my tattoo," he clarified. "His name was Toby, and he was twelve when he died. A rival gang captured him, wanting information that he'd gathered for one of our clients. His body was found in the Thames a few days later."

Horror swept through Pippa. Now she realized what the tattoo was: a memorial for fallen mudlarks. Her heart squeezed at the burden that Cull literally carried on his back.

"He was just a child," she said with helpless sorrow.

Cull nodded, his gaze stark. "So were the others who died under my watch. Except for Patrick."

"Patrick?" she asked softly.

"He was my best chum. We came up the ranks together. The fire that caused my injury took Patrick's life." Cull's voice was gritty with emotion. "He died getting others out because that was the kind of fellow he was."

"I'm so sorry." She didn't know what else to say.

"Death—whether from enemies, disaster, or disease—is no stranger to the mudlarks. The only thing we can do is weather it together." Shadows lurked in his eyes. "Do you know why the starlings fly together the way they did last night?"

She shook her head.

"According to birdwatchers, it is how the starlings thwart their predators. I've seen it myself. A falcon trying to hunt was confused by the constant movement and shifting of the group. It swooped in and out, trying to capture a single bird, but it left without a meal because of the coordination and cohesion of the flock."

And the bonds between the members of Cull's gang were just as strong. Pippa recalled how worried the larks had been after Ollie's injury. How protective Fair Molly was of Cull. And how Cull took responsibility for them all.

"The former prince had a saying: *Alone, we are easy to defeat. Together, we are invincible.* I've tried to make the mudlarks invincible, but I've failed...six times too many."

She touched Cull's jaw, felt the harsh tension in that muscle. "It is not your fault. You're a wonderful leader, but even you can't control everything."

"When it comes to you, that terrifies me."

His blunt admission took her aback. She hadn't thought that Cull was a man afraid of anything.

"A part of me wonders if I have been selfish starting things with you," he said with burning intensity. "That's why I stayed away all those years. I knew the life I led wasn't right for you."

"I told you before. I don't need a life of luxury and ease—"

"But *I* need you to be safe." Exhaling, he rolled onto his back, staring up at the slatted ceiling. "I have a history of failing to protect the people I care about the most. My mam, Maisie, Patrick...the list goes on. And I can't—*won't*—let that happen with you."

Pippa's heart was hammering. Not because of his asinine notion that she needed protection.

"You care about me?" she said in an aching whisper.

He turned his head, his expression incredulous. Pulling her into the crook of his shoulder, he looked into her eyes. "Jesus wept, Pippa. Did you think I didn't?"

"I guess I knew you, um, liked me." She fumbled for the right words, hating how unsure she sounded. Hating her lingering self-doubt. "But this is an affair. Without strings. And you told me from the start that you could only offer me the pleasure of the moment."

"Is that what you want?" His gaze probed hers. "For this to be a casual liaison?"

Responses swarmed her mind. *Keep it casual and safe. This was just supposed to be a fun diversion. Don't get attached too quickly.*

Yet this wasn't just any lover; this was Cull. A man who had survived the cruelest of environments and still saw beauty in the everyday. A man who cared so deeply that he inked his penance onto his skin. A man who was kind, passionate, and trustworthy... and worth the risk of heartbreak.

"I want more," she whispered.

I want the dream that started in the bell tower. What fourteen years didn't erase. I want you, Cull...please don't hurt me.

"Thank Christ," he said gruffly. "Because I'm falling in love with you, Pippa."

Her breath stuttered. "You are?"

This good, noble, powerful man was falling for *her*?

He gave her a lopsided grin. "Don't know why you're surprised, sunshine. I started falling for you fourteen years ago."

"You didn't know me then," she countered. "Not really."

"True. But you were the prettiest lass I'd ever laid eyes on. Gave me the best kiss I'd ever had." He leaned in, the hot and tender claim of his mouth curling her toes into the sheets. "And fourteen years later, you're still giving me that...and more," he murmured against her lips. "You're even more perfect than my fantasies."

"I'm not perfect, Cull. Far from."

Unease twinged as Pippa remembered other times he'd alluded to her flawlessness. At first, it had been flattering; she supposed she'd needed the boost to her self-confidence. Yet being with Cull was helping her to get over her past, and she didn't need the reassurance any longer. Or rather, she needed honesty *more*.

"You're perfect for *me*," he amended.

She sat up, drawing the sheet over her breasts. "Don't idealize me, Cull," she said quietly. "I made that mistake with Longmere— saw who I wanted him to be instead of who he truly was. I don't want you to be disappointed like I was when I finally opened my eyes."

"You could never disappoint me." Cull got up beside her, his mien serious. "While you are a lady in the truest sense of the word, I know you are also more than that. You're strong and capable and can handle yourself. That is why I'm going to take a chance on this...on us. But I have enemies, Pippa, and if you are exposed to harm because of me, if I fail to protect you"—his pupils dilated, darkness edging out the warmth of his irises—"I couldn't stand it."

"And I couldn't stand it if you shut me out. If you kept secrets from me."

"I'm nothing like your husband," Cull said, his tone curt.

"I know that. Which is why I am willing to trust my heart."

She touched his arm, feeling the taut bulge of his biceps. "I think...I think I'm falling for you too, Cull."

"You are?" he said hoarsely.

The wonder in his voice cinched her throat. Maybe they were more alike than she realized. Maybe they were both afraid to trust themselves...to risk getting hurt again.

Yet wasn't love worth the risk?

She drew a breath for courage. "I am. But I need to know that we will share our lives, support one another, and be true partners. I want to be a part of your world and for you to be a part of mine. I won't countenance walls between us. If you can promise me that, I can promise you that I will do my utmost to make you happy."

"Christ Almighty, you make me happy just by breathing." He cupped her face with a reverence that made her eyes sting. "I want you in my life, Pippa. To share things with you that I've never shared with anyone else."

"I want that too," she said tremulously.

"And you are certain you want to take on a man like me? A man not from your world, who cannot offer you the privileges to which you are accustomed?"

The vulnerability in Cull's searching gaze astonished her. How could this prince of a fellow doubt his worth when he had so much to offer?

"True nobility is not about titles," she said in a steadfast tone. "You, Timothy Cullen, are a real gentleman. And I would be honored to have you in my life."

Relief flashed in his eyes. "Then it's settled," he declared. "We're falling in love."

Smiling at his decisiveness, she tipped her mouth up, and they sealed their new promise with a kiss.

28

C ull scaled the rear fence of Howard Morton's property, moving stealthily toward the small two-story house. In a few minutes, Pippa would be knocking on Morton's door. When she did, Mikey and Matches, who were discreetly keeping watch, would sound the signal. While Pippa distracted Morton, Cull would enter through the back and search the man's house for clues.

Pippa had one of the mudlark whistles with her; if she used it, Cull, Mikey, and Matches would rush to her aid. Or she could take care of the problem herself, Cull thought wryly, using the pistol tucked in the pocket of her skirts.

An Angel always comes prepared, she'd told him primly.

It was the damnedest thing: trusting Pippa didn't lessen his protectiveness. He felt *more* possessive now that he had some-thing to lose, and he wasn't used to the feeling. Wasn't used to life giving him anything, let alone his heart's desire. Truth be told, allowing himself to love Pippa, to be happy and contemplate a future with her, felt almost selfish.

Years ago, he'd left Maisie at the Hunt Academy because he thought that was the safest place for her. At the time, it had been the most painful decision of his life, letting his sister go and knowing he'd hurt her. Yet he'd believed he was doing the right thing...until she'd come to him, soon after graduating from the school, and told him she was with child.

The father was her employer, a married nob with a family.

Recalling the shame in Maisie's eyes still felt like a blow to the gut. For the first time, Cull had wanted to commit murder. But Maisie had stopped him. Told him that if he did anything to the father of her child, she would never forgive him. She'd made him swear on their mam's grave that he would stay away from the blackguard and keep her secret.

Cull had given her his word. He'd also taken her to Fanny, who ran a place called the Nursery House, which helped women in Maisie's predicament. Fanny had taken care of Maisie. After the babe was born, Maisie had turned down Cull's financial support, instead finding another position, this time in Bristol. She was still there, employed as a housekeeper to a spinster.

Cull's letters to Maisie went unanswered. She wanted nothing to do with him, the brother who'd failed her, and he didn't blame her. He'd learned from his mistakes, however, and kept a better eye on her, though she never knew it. Over the years, he'd even had glimpses of his nephew, now a robust young boy. Cull wished that he could make things right with Maisie. But he didn't know how. Didn't know if it was possible.

Having Pippa in his life made him acutely aware of his failings. Of all that could go wrong, even if you cared about someone, even if you thought you were doing the right thing. He wanted to confide in Pippa about Maisie, but he'd given his sister his promise. And he knew the last thing Maisie wanted was for her friends at the Hunt Academy, who'd thought of her as a success, to find out her secret disgrace.

Hearing Mikey and Matches's signal, a subtle whistle that sounded like a bird call, Cull shook off the past. Pippa was inside. Time to get to work.

He used a trellis to scale the back wall, going through a window into Morton's bedchamber. Having sent mudlarks to do surveillance last week, he'd planned his visit to coincide with the cook's weekly shopping trip to the village and the maid's day off. There was no one to disturb him as he rifled through Morton's room.

Finding nothing of consequence in the man's personal effects, he continued to the adjoining chamber, which appeared to function as a study. The décor featured crammed bookshelves and teetering stacks of newspapers and suited a bachelor schoolmaster. Spotting a globe on a stand next to the cluttered desk, Cull felt the upward jerk of his eye muscles. Why the gentry believed that a globe with a "secret" compartment would fool any thief was beyond him. The silly contraption stuck out like a sore thumb and practically shouted, "Search me."

It was the work of a moment to find the mechanism that unlocked the globe. Flipping open the top half, Cull was greeted by the scent of floral perfume, which came from the stack of letters nestled in the bottom half. Cull picked up the letter on top. The cream-colored stationery was thick, the handwriting neat and feminine.

"What do we have here?" he said under his breath.

In the ten minutes that Pippa had been in Morton's company, she'd come to two conclusions: he was a mild-mannered fellow, and he was hiding something.

The schoolmaster seemed pleasant enough, offering her tea, which they took at a table in the front parlor. They were sitting at one end as the other was piled with books. Morton was handsome in an unassuming way, with wavy blond hair, moss-green eyes, and a slender build. His clothing was simple and somber as befitted his profession. Yet Charlie had taught the Angels to recognize the tell-tale signs of deception, and Morton exhibited quite a few of them.

He was fidgety, his hair disheveled from the times he'd run his fingers through it. When Pippa had explained that she was a friend of Julianna's who'd come here in hopes of finding justice for the murdered lady, his gaze had shifted like that of cornered prey. And now, as he spoke, his voice had a slightly raised pitch that suggested nerves.

"I don't know why you think I can help, Lady Longmere," Morton said.

"I was given to believe that you and Lady Hastings were quite close."

Morton's cup rattled in the saucer as he set it down. "How do you mean?"

"Did you not spend time together as children?"

"Oh...that. I mean, we did." Morton ran his hand through his hair again. "Her father and mine were cronies, and I spent several summers at Mr. Turner's estate. I was saddened at his passing—and Julianna's too, of course," he added hastily. "No one should die in such a horrible fashion."

To Pippa, his words sounded trite...practiced. *What is he concealing?*

She leaned forward. "I agree. That is why I am here. Lady Hastings confided in me that she was afraid of her husband. But now he, too, is dead. And I believe the murders might be somehow related."

"Surely that is a matter for the police."

"The police have concluded that both were victims of random crime. They're washing their hands of the case."

"They are the experts. I am sure they arrived at their conclusion after careful consideration." Morton moistened his lips. "Julianna is dead. Mucking about in her business will only stir up a scandal. If you are her friend as you claim, you should let her rest in peace."

"How can she be at peace when her murderer is on the loose?"

"Why won't you let it go?" Desperation colored the schoolmaster's tone.

Pippa decided to switch tactics. "Perhaps you want me to let it go because her death made you a wealthy man? I know about Mr. Turner's codicil, sir, and that you now stand to inherit half of his fortune."

She had wanted to see Morton's reaction and was rewarded by the angry flash in his eyes.

So, the schoolmaster is not as placid as he seems.

"I don't care about the money," he said tightly.

"You don't care about two hundred thousand pounds?"

He straightened in his chair. "I would not hurt anyone for any sum. For any reason."

Deliberately, she looked around the modest room. "With such an inheritance, you could dispense with the drudgery of work and enjoy a life of leisure. You would have the freedom to do whatever you wish."

"I take pride in my profession, and I *am* doing what I enjoy. Indeed, I plan to use the money to establish schools for children of the working class." Morton rose, his shoulders rigid. "If you'll excuse me, my lady, I have lessons to prepare. I will see you out."

Cull handed Pippa up into the carriage, following behind her. As the conveyance bumped down the country lane, she blurted, "They were having an affair."

He blinked; he'd said the exact words at the same time.

Chuckling, she said, "Is it a sign of our growing intimacy that we're now having the same thoughts?"

"Soon we'll be finishing each other's sentences," he said with a grin. "Ladies first. How did you arrive at your conclusion?"

She described her interview with Morton. "He was clearly

nervous talking about Julianna and didn't want me looking into her death. Which made me think something was going on between them. Yet he was also rather convincing when he said he wouldn't hurt anyone for money."

"Morton was having an affair with someone. I found a stack of letters from his lover—unsigned, unfortunately, but the notes are likely from Lady Hastings. Here is one of them." As Cull removed the perfumed paper from his jacket pocket, its cloying scent filled the cabin. "If Lady Fayne has a sample of Lady Hastings's hand-writing, we can match it."

"The writer was Lady Hastings," Pippa said with conviction.

"How do you know? You haven't even opened it."

"That particular blend of violet, musk, and ambergris was Lady Hastings's signature scent," she explained. "The room always smelled of it after she left."

Unfolding the letter, Pippa read the lines aloud.

My dearest love,

How I regret the last words we exchanged. And how I wish I could undo my life's biggest mistake, for never have the shackles of matrimony weighed so heavily. But as Father so often said, if wishes were horses...

Please do not lose faith, my love, for I know my solution will work. Wait for me.

I count the moments until we meet again.

"What solution do you think she was referring to?" Pippa asked.

"I cannot say. There was no mention of it in the other letters," Cull said meditatively. "But my guess is that she was either going to leave her husband...or make him leave her. How else would she undo her 'biggest mistake'?"

"Hastings would never agree to leave her. Not with Turner's fortune within reach."

"Precisely. To get rid of him, she would probably have to kill him."

Pippa gaped at him. "You don't think Lady Hastings would plan to..."

"One never knows. Love and hate are sides of the same coin, and both can drive people to unimaginable behavior," Cull said broodingly. "Whatever the case, Lady Hastings wound up dead before her husband, so if she did have such a plan, it did not come to fruition."

"Which leads us back to Morton or Wood as the most likely suspects," Pippa said. "They stand to gain the most with Lady Hastings gone."

"You're right. Morton is likely spooked by your visit. I'll leave Mikey and Matches to monitor him, see what he does in the next few days."

"A splendid plan." Pippa slid him a glance. "I suppose we should head back to London straight away?"

"I'm afraid so." He paused. "In addition to the case, I have other pressing business."

"Oh?"

He hesitated. This business of being intimate was new to him. Before Pippa, Nan had been the closest he'd had to a sweetheart, and she hadn't been all that interested in him beyond the bedchamber. Frankly, he'd felt the same way. Even so, Nan had resented sharing his attention with the larks, and they'd fought over it constantly. Christ, that tug-o'-war between her and his duty had been exhausting.

Looking into Pippa's curious blue eyes, he saw the pitfalls. Yet he'd promised to share himself with her and thus had to try. He outlined the situation with Squibb.

"I won't be able to see you for a few days while I deal with the bastard," he said. "I need my wits about me and don't want you getting hurt in any crossfire."

"Will you be safe?" Pippa said in a rush. "Could I help?"

"You'll help best by staying at a distance, love. As for Squibb, I've handled far more dangerous men than him. I've everything in hand."

He braced himself for an argument.

Pippa blew out a breath and said, "All right."

He stared at her. "Is it?"

"Well, yes. I am worried, of course, about your safety, and hope you would tell me if I could be of assistance. But you are a man capable of handling his own affairs." She gave him a rueful smile. "As you've told me more than once, you're not the Prince of Larks for nothing."

His shock must have shown for she frowned and added, "Is something amiss?"

"The opposite." Baldly, he said, "I thought you might be angry at me."

Dents formed between her brows. "Why would I be angry?"

"Because I'm putting my duty to the mudlarks first." When she continued to give him a perplexed look, he muttered, "The relationship I mentioned...the one that lasted a year. The demands of my work were a cause of contention."

"I see." After a moment, Pippa said, "I am not like your past lover, Cull."

"Trust me, I know—"

"And it seems you and I both have pasts to overcome." When she took his hand, he held on. "While I want us to share every-thing, it does not mean we need to live in each other's pockets. You will have your work; I will have mine. And I do not resent your dedication to the larks any more than you resent mine to the Angels. In truth, your commitment makes you even more attrac-tive in my eyes."

Although it was the middle of the day, he felt fortune's stars blazing upon him. Unable to help himself, he snatched her onto his lap. Cupped her smooth cheek.

"Do you know how long I've waited for you?" he said hoarsely. "For this?"

Her smile lit up her eyes. "I feel the same way. And I hope you know that I never want to come between you and the larks. On the contrary, I want to be a part of your world...and for you to be a part of mine."

"We are going to have that," he vowed. "Just as soon as I deal with Squibb."

She fiddled with his lapel. "Be quick about it, will you? I shall miss you dreadfully."

"Don't miss me yet," he said. "There's still the journey back."

"However shall we pass the time?" she inquired coquettishly.

"I have a few ideas."

He put them into play, and she moaned her approval.

29

The following afternoon, Pippa met up with Livy, Glory, and Fi at Mrs. Quinton's. The dressmaker's Bond Street shop was a premiere destination in London; rumor had it that the waiting time to get onto her exclusive clientele list was over a year. Luckily, Mrs. Q, as she was known to intimates, was a friend of Charlie's, and not only did she dress the Angels in her exquisite fashions, but she also designed some special items for their line of work.

An assistant led the Angels through the front of the shop, which resembled a sunlit forest with its gleaming rosewood counters, emerald velvet upholstery, and gilt-framed looking glasses. They passed through a curtain into a back corridor lined with dressing rooms. At the end of the corridor was a heavy door, which the assistant unlocked with a key. The workroom contained long tables piled with colorful bolts of fabric and tools of the trade. Dressmaker's forms stood like soldiers along one wall. Against the adjacent wall was a massive ornate wardrobe.

With a wink, the assistant said, "You know the way, my ladies. Mrs. Q is finishing up with a patron and will be with you shortly."

After the door closed, Pippa and her friends made a beeline

for the wardrobe. Opening the carved doors, Pippa parted the hanging clothes to expose the wooden back. Feeling along the side of the panel, she activated the hidden mechanism.

The back of the wardrobe swung open like a door, revealing steps that led downward. The Angels took the path down to the basement, which occupied the same footage as the shop above. The space was brightly lit by wall sconces. Dressmaker forms with garments in various stages of completion shared the area with several worktables.

The tables held objects not commonly found in a dress shop. There were weapons of all kinds, from pistols to daggers to cudgels. Metal components were organized in trays next to assorted frippery, including fans and bonnets. Glass bottles containing liquids in a rainbow of hues occupied a nearby surface. One bottle held a pitch-like substance and was labeled, "Caution: Explosive."

"I wonder what is inside that bottle," Glory mused.

Perched on her shoulder, her ferret tilted its head in shared curiosity.

As she reached for the bottle, the rest of them lunged forward. Fiona got there first and swatted Glory's hand aside.

"Lud, Glory," Fi exclaimed. "The label is supposed to *deter* you from opening it."

Glory looked perplexed. "Then why make the label so intriguing?"

Fi's gaze veered heavenward. "Just refrain from touching things. Recall what happened here the last time."

"How was I supposed to know that the canon was loaded?" Glory grumbled.

Nonetheless, she left the bottle alone, the rest of them exhaling with relief.

"While we're waiting," Livy said, "tell us what you discovered in Hertfordshire, Pippa."

Pippa summarized the findings with Morton.

"This morning, I showed Charlie the letter Cull found. She confirmed the handwriting matched that of the notes she had from Lady Hastings," Pippa finished. "So now we know Morton and Lady Hastings were having an affair. While Morton didn't act like a homicidal villain—"

"Which would make him an excellent homicidal villain," Fi noted.

"Indeed. That is why Cull has mudlarks monitoring him. If Morton does anything suspicious, we'll know."

"The two of you certainly made progress," Livy said.

In more ways than one, Pippa thought with secret delight.

Only a day had passed, and she already missed Cull. Couldn't wait until he completed his business and they could be together again. Yet she wouldn't mope about it; she was busy too.

"Any luck with Ellis?" she asked the other Angels.

"Ellis is as slippery as a greased pig," Glory replied. "Thus far, we've discovered he uses a variety of pseudonyms and has left a trail of wealthy lovers in his wake. Currently, we've followed that trail to a Lady Effingworth; from what we've gathered, she and her husband are currently at their country seat in Lancashire."

"If both the Effingworths are there, then it's unlikely that Ellis is there as well..." Pippa trailed off, seeing her friends exchange glances. "Isn't it?"

Fiona cleared her throat delicately. "From what we've gathered, Vincent Ellis has been a companion to several, ahem, couples."

Pippa blinked. "Oh."

Her cheeks rosy, Glory added, "Charlie has sent Mrs. Peabody to Lancashire to investigate."

Just then, steps sounded, and Mrs. Q descended the stairs. Dressed in a black frock that showcased the simple elegance for which she was known, the modiste came toward them with a smile. She was a handsome and curvaceous woman in her thirties, with light-brown skin and keen, tawny eyes.

She exchanged air kisses with each of them. "Sorry to keep you waiting, my dears."

"We don't mind, Mrs. Q," Pippa said. "We were discussing our current case."

"Ah, yes. Lady Charlie told me about it. *Two* murders, no less." Mrs. Q shuddered. "It is no wonder she requested that I outfit you with some new designs."

"May we see them?" Livy's eyes sparkled with the excitement all the Angels felt.

Shopping at Mrs. Q's was a guaranteed adventure.

"Indeed. Come this way."

The modiste led them over to a dressmaker's form, which displayed a white linen corset shaped like a vest. Embellished with lace and pink ribbon, the undergarment was pretty but unremarkable. Mrs. Q picked a knife up from a table, its sharp blade glinting.

Handing it to Pippa, she instructed, "Stab the corset as hard as you can."

Pippa grasped the handle and plunged the blade into the corset, tearing the delicate fabric.

"Again, if you please," Mrs. Q said.

After Pippa stabbed the corset several more times, the modiste halted her and unlaced the garment. Pulling the corset free, Mrs. Q gestured to the wooden dummy.

"What do you see, Angels?"

Gasps of disbelief went up. The smooth, polished surface of the dummy didn't bear a single nick, scratch, or dint from the blade.

Pippa drew her brows together. "How can that be...?"

"Chainmail." Holding up the corset, Mrs. Q widened the tears in the linen, exposing the layer of delicate metal links beneath. "I took an ancient idea and adapted it for modern use. Mr. Q helped, of course."

Mr. Q, the dressmaker's adoring husband, was a master black-smith who collaborated on many of his wife's projects.

"How utterly *brilliant*," Pippa breathed.

Mrs. Q accepted her due with a nod. "We experimented with various metals to see which would provide the strongest protection with the lightest weight. This corset is no heavier than its whalebone counterpart. Not to mention, it gives an excellent shape to the figure. But, come, I have more to show you."

The Angels spent the next half-hour marveling over Mrs. Q's innovations. Garter belts that doubled as explosive devices, fans with razor-sharp edges, and reticules with hidden compartments numbered among the inventor's creations. Then they came to more dressmaker's forms, these ones wearing some of the most beautiful evening gowns Pippa had ever seen. Cut in the latest silhouette with fitted, elongated torsos and full skirts, each of the dresses was unique and spectacular.

"How lovely." Sighing, Fiona stroked a sapphire blue ballgown with an overlay of glittery silver netting. "What are these dresses designed to do?"

"These are the most important weapons of your arsenal. They are for catching husbands," Mrs. Q said with a wink. "Or, if you already have one, enticing him."

The Angels laughed. Fi, Glory, and Livy dashed behind the nearby dressing screens to try on the sublime creations. Pippa lingered behind, wistfully studying a gown that was the color of the last hour of sunlight. She had once loved painting subjects bathed in that rich, golden hue.

"That dress is made of shot-silk from China and suits you perfectly," Mrs. Q said. "Why don't you try it on, my lady?"

"But I am in mourning," Pippa said in surprise.

She'd worn her widow's weeds today. It was one thing to abandon mourning clothes in private, another to do so in public. And trying on such an extravagant dress, even in front of friends...she felt an odd prickle of panic, as if she were tempting fate by flaunting her newfound happiness.

"You look improved since I last saw you." Like any modiste who'd reached her level of success, Mrs. Q had an unerring instinct for reading her clients. "The light is back in your eyes. And if I am not mistaken, the spark of love as well?"

Pippa's cheeks warmed. So much for hiding her affair.

"I...I have met someone, Mrs. Q," she confessed. "Is that terribly scandalous?"

"You are part of a covert female society that investigates murders"—Mrs. Q arched her brows—"and you worry that being in *love* is scandalous?"

"You have a point," Pippa said, chuckling.

"Life is short, my dear. Do not waste it worrying about what others might think. I have always admired you Angels for going after your hearts' desires."

Pippa looked at the golden gown. Imagined Cull's reaction to seeing her in it.

"Thank you for the advice, Mrs. Q," she said. "And I would love to try on the dress."

"I want a word wif you, Cullen!" Squibb bellowed as he stood in front of the Nest. "Get your arse out 'ere!"

Looking down from the glasshouse, Cull thought, *Right on time*.

He'd been expecting Squibb. Mrs. Kent had been true to her word: her friend Alfie had seen to it that Squibb's goods were no good anywhere in London. The sweep had tried pawnshops one after another, to no avail. Apparently, Squibb wasn't as dim-witted as Cull believed; it had only taken the bastard three days to figure out who was responsible.

"Are you really goin' out there, Cull?" Fair Molly asked.

"I am. Time to finish this business."

As the birds squawked around him, Cull walked the perimeter of the aviary, counting off the enemies in the deepening dusk. Squibb had only brought five men...which Cull took as a sign of the sweep's dwindling power. True loyalty couldn't be bought with money. The moment Squibb's funds were cut off, he was done.

Exactly as Cull had planned.

"How many men do you see?" he asked.

"Two wif Squib, three in the surrounding alleyways," Molly said promptly.

"Good eyes. Now, remember the plan?"

"Station larks at the windows and entrances. We fire first if any o' the bastards make a move," Molly recited. "Most importantly, we 'ave each other's backs and fight as a team."

"Excellent." Cull checked his pistol, shoved a pair of blades in his boots. Then he placed a hand on Molly's shoulder. "If anything happens to me, you're in charge until Long Mikey gets back."

Worry flickered in Molly's amber eyes. "Nothing's goin' to 'appen to you, is it?"

"No," he said firmly. "Now assemble the larks."

Fair Molly dashed off to organize the troops. Cull returned to the front of the glasshouse; from his bird's-eye view, Squibb was the size of a gnat, and it was time to get rid of the annoyance. After that, the larks would be safe...and Cull could see Pippa again.

Christ, he missed her. After the intimacy of their trip, three days apart felt like an eternity. He still couldn't believe that she had accepted his duties as prince. She hadn't made a fuss or given him an ultimatum; instead, she'd offered him an incentive.

"After you're done with Squibb, let's celebrate with a quiet supper at my house," she'd said. *"I want you to stay the night. And I want to wake up in your arms."*

She exceeded his wildest fantasies with her strength and passion. Her willingness to accept him as he was. Even though he would never be a toff, he would work to be a partner worthy of Pippa. Someone who she would consider a real future with. Who she might even...marry.

First things first, however. Time to dispense with Squibb.

Cull descended the stairs. In the great hall, the larks were armed and ready. They gave him brave nods, and he nodded back. As their leader, he didn't believe in hiding the threats against them. They had to know what they were up against in the world. They also had to know that, no matter what, mudlarks stood together. Faced their enemies and shared their triumphs as one.

At the threshold, he turned and looked at them all. "We don't go looking for trouble, but we don't run away from it either. What is our motto?"

"A wrong against me you'll regret, but a favor to me I'll ne'er forget," the larks chanted.

"We fight together and fight strong," Cull declared. "Let's show our enemies what happens when they challenge the mudlarks."

Cheering shook the rafters. Cull went to the door, saying to Molly, "Lock this behind me."

The street was quiet, but Cull felt the eyes on him and Squibb from behind shuttered windows. The Devil's Acre was watching. Waiting. Wagering on the outcome.

Stocky and bow-legged, Squibb had eyes like cloves pressed into the doughy folds of his face. He wore a tall velvet hat and a wine-colored frock coat that didn't have a speck of soot on it...no surprise there. The sweep had others do his dirty work. Case in point: the two lumbering brutes behind him. One had hair, the other didn't, and they had a full set of teeth and a single brain between them. They sneered, cracking their knuckles.

"What do you want, Squibb?" Cull said.

"You know why I'm 'ere," Squibb spat. "Because o' you, my merchandise ain't good anywhere. All the pawnshops are refusing my goods!"

"What makes you think I am behind this?" Cull asked mildly.

"Because it's your bloody way o' retaliating—" Squibb cut himself off. While the sweep had bacon for brains, even he must have realized that admitting to hiring a cutthroat to kill Cull wouldn't support his stance as the injured party.

"Go on," Cull said. "What am I retaliating for?"

"I ain't got time to argue wif you like a bleeding barrister," Squibb snarled. "You destroyed the livelihood o' me and my gang, and I demand payment."

"You'll get nothing from me but what you deserve," Cull said with lethal precision. "If you're wise, you will take your motley crew and leave—and never set foot on mudlark territory again."

"I tried to reason wif you, everyone 'eard me." Vicious intent glinted in the sweep's beady eyes. "You left me no choice. Get 'im, boys!"

The brutes came at him, but Cull was quicker. He evaded the bald one and plowed his fist into the other's gut. The man groaned, doubling over. Baldy came at Cull again, swinging his ham-sized fists. Ducking, Cull went on the offensive, tackling the other to the ground. He gained the upper hand, pounding his opponent's face into the dirt.

He heard a shot go off, then another. Cries of pain erupted from the alleyways. His larks had taken care of the hidden assailants—had come through as he'd known they would.

Cull's nape tingled, and he rolled off his unconscious opponent in the nick of time. The other brute's blade cut through the air where he'd been a moment earlier. Cull unsheathed his own blades, he and his foe circling one another. He had an eye on Squibb too, knowing the blighter was weighing the wisdom of trying to shoot Cull while dozens of guns were aimed at him from the Nest.

The brute charged, his knife flashing high. Cull went low, the other's blade whispering by him while he swept his own steel in a sideways arc. He felt his blade sink into flesh, felt the spurting warmth as his enemy let out an agonized cry. The man fell to his knees, clutching the wound on his side.

Knife dripping, Cull stood over him. The man looked up, fear and pain carved on his features.

"You won't die if you get help now," Cull said.

The man's eyes widened. Then he surged to his feet, groaning as he stumbled away.

Cull heard a click and spun around. Squibb had a flintlock aimed straight at him. An instant later, a shot exploded, and Squibb screamed as the bullet hit his hand, sending his weapon skittering across the dirt.

Cull spared a quick glance at the Nest, where Molly gave him a jaunty salute from a window.

Then Cull advanced toward Squibb, who backed away, clutching his shattered hand.

"I d-don't want no trouble," the sweep stammered.

"I told you that you would get what you deserve," Cull said softly. "Yet you stayed."

Squibb stumbled backward. "I-I'll leave now. I swear, I won't bother you again."

"Will you send cutthroats to murder me?" Cull held up his bloodied knife, seeing it gleam in Squibb's terrified eyes. "Try to take over *my* gang?"

"Never again, I swear it. I-I'm sorry." The coward fell on his knees, blubbering. "'Ave mercy, Prince. I'm begging you."

When Cull raised the knife, Squibb whimpered, the stink of his piss filling the air. Cull brought the blade down...into the sweep's tall hat. Squibb's gaze rolled upward, and he gave a moan, crumpling onto the ground.

The lily-livered bastard had fainted, although Cull hadn't even nicked him.

Shaking his head, Cull retrieved his blade, unskewered Squibb's hat, and tossed it aside. He assessed Squibb's remaining men, who were wounded but alive. They were looking at their leader, swooned in his own urine, their faces reflecting the disgust that Cull felt. He knew that gossip was spreading like wildfire behind the shuttered windows and closed doors.

By morning, everyone would know of Squibb's spinelessness and defeat. The sweep was done in the underworld. Cull had achieved his goal, and he'd done it with minimal casualties.

"Mudlarks never forget a wrong." He let his voice carry through the streets. "Next time, we'll show no mercy."

Cheers and whoops erupted from the Nest, the doors opening for their prince's return.

❧ 30 ☙

As Pippa ushered Cull into her cottage, he halted abruptly. Grabbing his chest in an exaggerated manner, he declared, "God's teeth, woman. Your beauty could stop a man's heart."

Cull's playful appreciation set off happy ripples in Pippa. She had hoped that he would like her new dress. She hadn't worn anything this beautiful in a long time and had fretted that the golden gown might be a bit much for an intimate night at home. Yet tonight felt like an occasion: the celebration of a new chapter in her relationship with Cull.

Perhaps Cull shared that sentiment, for he'd taken obvious pains with his appearance as well. He removed his stylish new hat, revealing that his chestnut-brown hair had been trimmed and combed into gleaming waves. He wore a Prussian blue frock coat and mustard-yellow brocade waistcoat expertly tailored to his strapping form. A matching stripe of yellow ran down the sides of his dark trousers, which skimmed his muscular legs. Even his cravat was perfection, tied in an elegant *De Joinville*.

Best of all, he hadn't bothered with his mask.

"Thank you, sir." Smiling, she curtsied. "You look exceedingly handsome yourself."

Color rose on Cull's broad cheekbones, deepening the chocolate brown of his eyes. He rubbed the back of his neck, muttering, "Fanny has been nagging me to visit her husband's tailor. I obliged her."

"I shall have to thank Mrs. Grier when I see her next."

Cull looked around the small antechamber. "Where are the servants?"

"I dismissed them for the eve. I thought privacy would be nice—"

Her words faded into a gasp as Cull pulled her into his arms and kissed her senseless.

"Now that is a proper hello," she said breathlessly when they parted.

"Been thinking about kissing you for days." He brushed his knuckles along her jaw before taking her hand. "Now show me your home, sunshine."

Pippa gave him a tour of her cottage. Although she didn't think her residence was all that interesting, Cull studied her belongings as if they were objects on display in a museum. He seemed fascinated by the most ordinary things: the cabinet filled with her collection of ceramic figurines, the ormolu clock and other bric-a-brac on the mantel, her painting implements which had been collecting dust on a shelf.

They ended up in her sitting room, where she'd had a small table set up for supper. Pippa's heart skipped a beat when he went over to *Portrait of a Lady Dreaming*, which sat in a corner facing the wall. Crouching, he flipped it around.

He rose and asked, "Wasn't this the picture at that fancy exhibition?"

Even now, the sight of the painting tightened Pippa's chest. She saw her hand moving across the canvas, creating the oppressive damask-lined walls and that one bright pane of glass. And the lady herself, with her red-gold hair and longing eyes, staring out the window, dreaming of the love that would set her free.

Looking at the portrait, Pippa saw her loss and guilt immortalized in swirls of paint.

"Yes," she said tautly. "The Royal Academy selected the piece for its exhibition."

"Then what's it doing on the floor?"

She wanted to tell him. The truth she'd buried so long. Yet the old vise of guilt clamped around her throat.

"I am just careless, I guess. Anyway, I don't want supper to get cold. Let's eat, shall we?"

Her pulse hammered as he studied her, his head angled.

Then he came over. "Whatever you want, sunshine. As it happens, I'm famished."

Relieved, she said, "That's good, because I asked Cook to prepare a special supper."

His eyes crinkled at the corners. "I suppose I'm hungry for food, too."

They went to the round table by the fire, which Whitby had set cozily for two. The butler's romantic soul showed in the crisp white table linens, beeswax tapers, and epergne arranged with fragrant hothouse roses. He'd laid out the best china and silverware, and a cart stood next to the table, the tiers filled with cloche-covered dishes. A frosted bottle of champagne waited in a silver bucket.

Cull held out a chair for her. Then he lifted the champagne bottle, opening it with an expert pop. He filled her glass, then his own.

Sitting, he raised his flute. "To you, sunshine."

She tapped her glass to his. "To us."

Cull took a gulp. "Delicious. I wonder what else your cook has in store for us."

"I was instructed that we are to start at the top of the cart and work our way down."

Cull removed the covers from the top dishes, serving the *hors d'oeuvres*, which consisted of *oysters au naturel,* chilled and served in their shells with lemon and dill. Pippa smiled as Cull consumed his appetizer with gusto.

"You really are hungry," she commented.

"Spent the day cleaning up after the Squibb mess." He reached for the basket of bread, slathering butter on the crusty roll. "Didn't have time to eat."

"In your note, you said the Squibb matter was handled?"

"The bastard has branded himself a coward," Cull said matter-of-factly. "No one in the stews will work for him again. And anyone thinking about taking over the mudlarks will think twice."

"No one was hurt?" she asked worriedly.

"I nicked one bastard in a knife fight, and Fair Molly shot Squibb's hand when he tried to shoot me in the back." Cull's brawny shoulders moved up and down. "The blighters will survive."

The thought of how close Cull had come to being hurt chilled Pippa to the marrow. Shivering, she made a mental note to thank Molly.

But what if something had happened? I should have been there.

Cull had uncovered the soup tureen, releasing a spicy aroma.

"Mulligatawny is my favorite," he said with satisfaction.

"If there's trouble again, I want to help," Pippa said in a rush.

He looked up at her, his surprise evident. "It's just mudlark business, sweeting—"

"Mudlark business *is* your life, and I want to be part of it. I didn't want to interfere this time because you obviously had everything in motion. But in the future, I want to know what is going on and assist however I can."

"You want to be involved with the larks?"

She didn't know what to make of his sudden stillness. He stared at her, his features taut, his eyes dark and watchful. With sudden wrenching anxiety, she wondered if she'd overstepped.

Although they'd talked about sharing each other's lives, maybe he'd only meant certain aspects. Maybe he only wanted companionship...and sex. Most men kept their public and domestic spheres separate, after all.

She remembered how Edwin had hidden his financial problems and use of drugs from her. How he'd berated her whenever she'd asked about money or his strange and secretive behavior.

"A man doesn't like a woman who meddles," he would say in tones of frigid displeasure.

"Pippa?"

She started. "Sorry. What did you say?"

"Where did you go just now?" Cull's tone was quiet.

"Nowhere." Angry at herself for letting the past dig its claws into her once more, she fumbled for a response. "I...I was thinking about your question. And I don't want to intrude where I'm not wanted."

Hearing herself, she cringed. She sounded so meek and pathetic. Where was her spine, her fire? She focused on her soup, stirring the thick golden liquid as she tried to calm her raging emotions.

"You're wanted."

Her gaze flew up. Cull was watching her with a burning intensity, as if she were the only thing that existed for him. Her heart thrashed against her ribs.

"I want you, Pippa. Not just in my bed, but in my life," he went on. "I know we talked about sharing things, but I wasn't sure how far the sharing went. I've never done this before. Never wanted to do this with anyone but you. And if you are saying that you want to help me with the mudlarks, that you want to be part of that life...I cannot tell you what that means to me."

I want everything with you, her heart cried. What came out was, "Longmere didn't paint *Portrait of a Lady Dreaming.* I did."

Panic besieged her. *Why did I blurt that?*

Cull cocked his head. "I know."

She stared at him. "How could you possibly know?"

"I arranged for a private viewing of the exhibition. When I saw the painting, I knew it was your work," he said steadily. "I'm no art expert, but Longmere wasn't capable of capturing such... such feeling."

"The critics hailed it as evidence of Longmere's buried genius. They praised his technique. Said that if only he'd lived longer, he might have been one of the greatest painters of his generation."

"They're idiots."

"They're experts," she countered.

"Experts can be idiots." Cull reached over and covered her hand where it lay on the table. His strong, callused grip warmed her chilled skin. "I don't know technique from a toenail, but I do know this: Longmere was not capable of understanding that woman's feelings, never mind rendering it in paint. A cove like him would never know what it was like to love someone with his whole heart, to be willing to give himself up for that person...only to find that he'd been alone in his dream. Nor would he understand the sadness, yearning, and hope of a dreamer's heart."

Cull's insight pierced her to the quick.

A tear sliding down her cheek, she confessed, "That painting killed my husband. It is my fault he's dead."

Unable to stand her pain, Cull pulled Pippa into his arms and carried her over to the turquoise settee. He sat her on his lap and said gently, "Explain."

"Longmere was obsessed with his art. With showing the world his genius. It was all he cared about, and I wanted him to have his dream." Tears streamed down her cheeks. "One night, I found him passed out in his studio, with this painting half-finished. I thought he'd been drinking...I didn't know he'd been taking a new drug called Devil's Bliss, which was more potent than even opium.

Because of the upcoming exhibition, he'd put so much pressure on himself, had worked day and night. Yet when I saw this piece, I knew that it wouldn't gain him the recognition he craved." Her breath hitched. "So I...I fixed it."

It was as Cull had suspected. The emotion of the portrait—the luminous longing and pain—was pure Pippa. It was her eyes in the model's face, her heart that lit up the paint.

"Go on," he said.

"When Longmere came to, he thought he'd created his masterpiece. I was overjoyed that I'd finally given him what he wanted. I thought we would be happy at last."

The crack in her voice made Cull want to slam his fist into something. That bacon-brained bastard Longmere had had *every-thing*...and he'd thrown it away for his pride. For his insatiable need for glory.

"Longmere never suspected your hand in the painting?" Cull asked.

She shook her head. "Before we were married, he would say he found my artistic endeavors charming. But after we were married...I had the sense that he didn't like our shared interest." She bit her lip. "He would make comments about my 'dabbling' and how I was wasting time on a hobby instead of properly attending to my role as a countess. I didn't want to displease him, so I painted less and less."

Cull struggled to throttle his anger. He stroked her back, soothing himself as well as her.

"Anyway, Longmere attributed his new success to the Devil's Bliss," she said in hollow tones. "Unbeknownst to me, he was taking more and more of it in hopes of replicating what he'd done with *Portrait of a Lady Dreaming*. He got himself entangled with the villains who'd introduced him to the drug and ended up being a part of their nefarious operations. Eventually, Longmere was murdered by one of his depraved cronies."

When you make your nest with vipers, Cull thought dourly, *chances are you were going to get bit.*

"I fail to see how that makes you responsible for Longmere's death," he said.

Sniffling, she said, "If I hadn't tampered with his work, maybe he wouldn't have taken more of the drug. Maybe he wouldn't have gotten involved with those villains. Maybe he would still be alive today."

"That reasoning is shit, and you know it," Cull said.

Her gaze flared, and he was glad for it. Glad to see that golden fire back in her eyes.

"It is not shit—"

"It's as daft as a brush. You didn't kill Longmere—his bastard of a crony did."

"I hastened him down that dark path," she said stubbornly.

"He took his own bloody self on that trip. With his arrogance and conceit."

"I was his wife. I should have known..."

"A countess *and* a mind reader, are you? Never mind that he was deliberately keeping you in the dark about his nasty habits."

Pippa pinched her brows. "You're doing this on purpose, aren't you?"

"Doing what?"

"Arguing with me so I won't feel as guilty."

"And what, exactly, are you guilty of, Pippa?" he challenged. "What is it that you truly cannot forgive yourself for?"

He saw the answer blaze in her eyes.

"I let him do it," she said hoarsely. "I let him make me feel small and insignificant. Let him cut me off from the people and things I love best. I let him take away who I *am*." Rivulets ran down her cheeks. "God, I'm such an idiot."

"Even if you are a bit daft," he said gently, "I love you."

She made a sound halfway between a sob and a laugh. He

tucked her head against his shoulder, holding her as the poison drained out. He fished out a handkerchief, wiping at her tears.

When the storm passed, he asked, "Better?"

She took his handkerchief and blew her nose. "Yes. But I've ruined your nice cravat."

"It was too tight anyway."

She let out a watery laugh. "Why do I always end up in tears around you?"

"Must be my charming personality."

"Being charming isn't your forte—"

"I know," he said dryly.

"But you are honest, noble, and kind." She touched his jaw. "And I'm so lucky that you're my lover."

"I'm the lucky one," he said and meant it.

Her fingers trailed lower, tangling in his damp neckcloth. His breath quickened when she tugged it free. The glow of her smile lit his world.

"Then let's show each other how lucky we are," she whispered.

Pippa gradually awakened. Without opening her eyes, she smiled.

She rubbed her cheek against Cull's warm, naked chest, his clean musk filling her nose. Their limbs were entwined, his burly arm holding her close, her top leg intimately wedged between his. This was the *best* way to wake up.

And what they'd done before was the best way to fall asleep.

Dreamily, she took in her lover's boyish yet rugged appeal. The tousled sweep of hair over his brow and the sensual curve of his bottom lip. She ran her gaze over his prime form, from the carved planes of his chest to the delicious trail of hair that disappeared beneath the sheet. She was intimately acquainted with where that hair ended, had worshipped that destination with her hands, mouth, and pussy last night. Cull had let her do whatever she wished.

And he'd made a few requests in return.

Taking her hand, he'd guided it down her stomach...all the way to her sex.

"Touch yourself," he'd said.

She'd laughed nervously. *"Why? You're here."*

"I like to watch."

His wicked desire had sent a hot spark dancing along her spine. She'd done what he asked, and he hadn't lied: his member had grown long and hard as he watched her. Seeing her effect on him and hearing his sensual encouragement had brought her right to the edge.

"Frig your sweet pearl for me," he'd ordered. *"Do it harder. I want your fingers glistening with your pleasure."*

When she climaxed, he stretched atop her, thrusting deep inside. Her spasms were so lush and decadent that she didn't know if he was prolonging her bliss or making her come again. Snagging her hand, he'd brought it to his mouth, sucking her fingers as he drilled into her.

"Christ's blood, you're delicious, Pippa," he'd growled.

In between the lusty bouts, he'd cuddled her close. His whispered words of love were a balm to her spirit. With that last sliver of the past dislodged, she felt herself finally healing. Forgiving herself for her mistakes allowed her to see the future more clearly. To see what she wanted...and whom she wanted it with.

I love you. Cull had given her that gift as he had so many things, without strings or expectations. While the answering response had thumped in her chest, she hadn't felt quite ready to give voice to it yet. When she gave her heart to Cull, she wanted it to be fully healed and whole. She wanted to be a woman who was secure in herself and her desires...because Cull deserved no less. A man like him deserved everything.

In time, she was certain she would be the woman to give him that.

Meanwhile, what she could give him was...breakfast. They'd been so busy devouring one another that they'd never gotten back to supper. He would be famished when he woke up, and she wanted to have a nice meal waiting for him.

Extricating herself, she donned a wrapper and slippers and went downstairs. The house was quiet; she'd given the staff the day off to have as much privacy with Cull as possible. Although she had work to do—Marg had sent her a note yesterday, with a list of actresses who'd performed in *The Grove of Love*—she could at least share a lazy breakfast in bed with Cull before they went their separate ways.

In the kitchen, Pippa hummed as she rummaged through the larder for eggs, butter, and bacon. Her grandmama had taught her the culinary basics, insisting that a lady ought to know how to cook, even if she didn't do it herself. While Mama didn't have any interest in domestic matters, Pippa had enjoyed the hours in her grandmama's kitchen. She put the skills she'd learned to use, frying the bacon and using the rendered fat to cook the eggs.

She inhaled the delicious smells, listened to the sizzle and pop of the eggs. The yolks were a bright yellow against the creamy whites, the edges a lacy golden brown, a beautiful contrast to the ruby-hued bacon and black iron pan. And it was then that she noticed it.

How alive she felt. Her love of the ordinary had returned. She had a sudden desire to dust off her brushes and paint again.

Smiling, she turned to get the bread for toasting—and let out a startled shriek when two figures blocked her path.

Pippa's scream jolted Cull out of bed. He yanked on his trousers, grabbed his knife, and barreled out of her room. He took the stairs three at a time, smelling bacon... Pippa had dismissed the servants, so she must be cooking. He rushed down to the kitchen, his blood raging at the sound of a booming male voice.

Gripping his knife, Cull charged into the room.

And stopped short.

Pippa stared at him with panic in her eyes. His field of attention expanded to include the man and woman flanking her... Her *parents?*

Bloody. Fucking. Hell.

In the electrified silence, Cull saw that Gavin Hunt hadn't changed much over the years, except for some grey mixed into his tawny hair. He was still burly and larger-than-life, the knife scar on his right cheek a memento of his underworld roots. He slitted his gaze at Cull, a muscle ticking on his jaw. Beside him, Mrs. Hunt, a pretty blonde with merry blue eyes, looked like she was trying not to laugh.

Aware that he was half-naked in the presence of his lover's parents, Cull felt his face burn.

"It's been a while, Cullen." Hunt's deep tones dripped with menace. "Put down the bloody knife. I want a word with you."

"Papa won't do anything rash, will he?" Pippa fretted.

"Stop pacing, my darling," Mama said. "Come sit with me."

Pippa went to join her mother, who handed her a cup of tea.

"Drink this. It will calm your nerves," Mama advised.

"How can I be calm when Papa and Cull have been locked in the parlor for *half an hour?*" Pippa wailed.

After the disastrous encounter in the kitchen, Pippa and Cull had rushed off to change. Then Papa and Cull had gone into the parlor to "talk man-to-man" while Pippa and Mama waited in the kitchen.

"If they were coming to blows, we would have heard it by now," Mama said blithely. "I wouldn't worry about it."

"Not *worry?* But you know how Papa is! He is overprotective—"

"Which is why he will exercise restraint when it comes to your...ahem, gentleman. Give Papa some credit, dear. He won't hurt anyone he knows is important to you." Mama paused. "And I gather Mr. Cullen is important?"

Pippa bit her lip. "He is."

"And you are happy?"

"Yes. Very," she admitted.

"Then all will be well."

"How can you be so certain?"

"Because *I* fell in love with a rough-and-ready fellow rather like your young man"—Mama's eyes twinkled—"and look how splendidly that turned out."

Pippa couldn't help but laugh. "You are a hopeless romantic, Mama."

"Love made me that way. And it is my hope, my dearest girl, that it will do the same for you." Mama patted her hand. "Now tell me how you and Mr. Cullen met up again."

Pippa hesitated. While she wanted to confide in her mother, she couldn't betray the vow of secrecy she'd made when joining the Angels. It was a balancing act that all the Angels had to manage.

"I found myself in a spot of trouble, and he assisted me," she said truthfully.

"What sort of trouble?" Mama's forehead creased. "If you need help, Pippa—"

"No, I'm fine. I was helping...a friend. Through Lady Fayne's charity."

"Oh." Looking relieved, Mama said, "Well, I am glad you've found a positive outlet for your energies. You are far too young to be moping about."

"I've been in mourning, not moping," she said wryly.

"As far as I am concerned, Longmere has taken up enough of your time," her mother declared. "Even if you cannot re-enter Society yet, it's time you rejoined the family. That is why Papa and I came today: to remind you that my birthday party is in three days. Since it will be an intimate affair, you may bring Mr. Cullen."

Pippa wondered if Cull was ready for a night with her family. "I don't know, Mama..."

"Would Mr. Cullen prefer not to socialize with us?"

Hearing her mother's tone cool, Pippa felt a guilty twinge. Edwin's snobbery toward her family had been inexcusable. She'd vowed not to get involved with someone who didn't respect the people she loved—and, by extension, *her*—again.

"It is not that," she said. "But Cull and I are just getting to know one another—"

"You had obviously spent the night together when Papa and I arrived. How much better acquainted must the two of you be before he meets the family?" Mama inquired. "His intentions are honorable, are they not?"

Pippa's face flamed. "Well, um, yes. I think."

"You *think*?" Mama frowned.

"We haven't gotten around to discussing the specifics. I'm still in mourning, after all—"

"What goes on in public is one thing, in private another. I consider myself a modern woman, Pippa, and I respect your freedom as a widow. But I must know that Mr. Cullen treats you with respect."

"He does," she said hurriedly.

"Then it is decided. He will come to my birthday celebration," her mother said in a tone that showed why she held her own in the Hunt household.

Just then, Papa strode into the kitchen with Cull. Pippa was relieved to see them both looking unscathed. When she widened her eyes at Cull, his response was a twitching of his lips.

"Would either of you gentlemen like tea?" Mama reached for the teapot.

"No thank you, buttercup. Cullen and I had something stronger," Papa said.

Mama arched her brows. "But it is not yet ten o'clock in the morning."

"Couldn't be helped, given what we had to discuss."

Papa looked at Pippa, and she tried not to quaver. Even though she was a grown woman and a widow, she still felt like a

girl in her father's presence. Still felt the weight of his disappointment. Nonetheless, while her father had been right about Longmere, it wasn't about right or wrong, was it? She'd made a mistake
and borne the consequences. What she wanted now was for her
papa to trust her judgment...especially when it came to her choice
for a new mate.

She prayed that Papa would not take a dislike to Cull the way
he had to Edwin.

"What were you discussing, Papa?" she managed.

"Mama's birthday party," Papa replied. "Cullen, here, will grace
us with his presence."

To Pippa's astonishment, Papa clapped Cull on the shoulder.
Granted, it was with enough force to knock most men off their
feet, but Cull didn't budge. Papa's gaze glinted with approval.

"Can't afford to tarry, buttercup," Papa said to Mama. "We
have that event at the academy."

"What event?" Mama's eyes rounded. "Oh, right. *That* event."

She rose, taking the arm Papa gallantly offered her.

"We'll see ourselves out," Mama said brightly. "Lovely to see
you again, Mr. Cullen."

Cull bowed. "The pleasure was mine, Mrs. Hunt."

Papa halted beside Cull. He offered Cull his hand, then leaned
in to say something in a low tone Pippa couldn't hear. Whatever
the message was, Cull gave an affirming nod.

After her parents left, Pippa burst out, "What happened with
Papa in the parlor?"

"Not much." Cull shrugged. "We drank whisky. He asked
about the mudlarks, and I answered. Then he invited me to your
mother's birthday party."

"Did he force you into accepting the invitation?" she asked
suspiciously.

"Why would he have to do that?" Cull gave her a quizzical
look. "I want to go and meet your kin. Unless..." He drew his
brows together. "Would you rather I not go?"

"Of course I want you there. But only if you *want* to be there."

His shoulders relaxed. "Then it's settled. I'm going."

"My family can be a handful," she warned.

He raised his brows. "More of a handful than mine?"

He had a point.

"Papa has never approved of any of my suitors," she said, bemused. "But he seems to actually like you."

"What's not to like?"

When she rolled her eyes, Cull grinned and curled a finger beneath her chin. "Your father isn't hard to win over, sunshine. He just wants the best for you."

"And I suppose you're the best?"

"Have you had better?"

Blushing at his wicked, knowing smile, she asked, "What did Papa say to you on the way out?"

"It was nothing."

She angled her head. "He said *something*."

"It was just man-to-man talk. Your father wanted to make sure I understand the situation." Cull's smile was bland. "And I do."

"What did he say?" she repeated.

"I don't recall the exact words. But it was something to the effect of, '*Hurt my daughter and even your larks won't find the pieces of you in the Thames.*'"

To Pippa's surprise and delight, Cull offered to accompany her to talk to the actresses.

"Don't you have business to attend to?" she asked.

They'd decided to eat breakfast in the kitchen. Even though the bacon and eggs had gone cold, Cull wolfed down the meal as if it was the best he'd had.

"As a matter of fact, I do." His eyes gleamed. "Very important business."

She squealed when he hauled her into his arms and carried her back to her bedchamber for a quick but lusty romp, during which she moaned her satisfaction into a pillow...twice. Heavens, the man was passionate in the morning. Afterward, they dressed and started working their way through the list of addresses Marg had sent.

Progress was slow. By midday, Pippa and Cull had interrupted the sleep of several grumpy ladies and narrowly dodged the contents of a chamber pot thrown their way. Now they were at the eastern end of the Strand, knocking on the door of a shabby flat.

"Let's hope we have better luck with this one," Cull muttered.

The bloodshot eye that blinked at them from the door's peephole did not bode well.

"Who're you and what do you want?" The female voice had an impatient growl.

Pippa kept her tone pleasant. "Good afternoon. We're here to speak with Miss, ahem, Penny Cunnyngham."

"You're speakin' to 'er. State your business."

"Would you mind opening the door? We would like your assistance identifying a portrait," Pippa said politely.

"What's in it for me?"

Cull held a coin purse to the peephole and jingled its contents. "Yours if you open the door and talk to us."

After a moment, the door creaked open.

Cull went in first, keeping Pippa behind him. She peered over his shoulder, taking in the single-room abode that made the Nest look as neat as a pin in comparison. Clothing, empty gin bottles, and assorted sundry were scattered about. The place reeked of cheap perfume and an earthy musk.

Miss Cunnyngham was a pretty, plump-cheeked woman with brassy curls. Her voluptuous figure was covered—barely—by a robe of gaudy apple-green sateen.

She held out a palm. "Payment first."

Cull dropped the bag in her hand.

She counted the sum, then tossed it onto a table piled with wigs. She yanked on the belt of her robe, the panels parting like curtains. At the sight of the woman's generous breasts and bushy sex, heat scalded Pippa's cheeks.

She couldn't help but peek at Cull. With a tug of possessiveness, she wondered what his reaction would be. Not that she could fault him for looking at another woman; Edwin often had. The one time she'd brought it up, Edwin had said dismissively, *"You can't blame a man for looking, my dear. And as an artist, it is my job to look."*

Moreover, Cull had told her more than once that he liked to...

watch. At present, however, his expression was dour, without a spark of interest.

"One at a time or both at once?" Miss Cunnyngham drawled.

"For Christ's sake, cover yourself," Cull snapped. "We're not here for that."

Her forehead creasing, Miss Cunnyngham fastened her robe. "What're you 'ere for then?"

Pippa took out the portrait of Julianna Hastings. "As I mentioned, we're trying to identify the woman in this portrait."

"Oh, you want 'elp with an *actual* portrait." Miss Cunnyngham looked bemused.

"What did you think I meant?" Pippa asked, puzzled.

"Thought you were using slang, luvie. For the position where the woman is sitting upright, supported by a gent beneath 'er and another female—"

"Can you identify the painting?" Cull cut Miss Cunnyngham off. "We believe the lady attended a performance of *The Grove of Love*, which we're told you had a part in."

"I 'ad the starring role." Miss Cunnyngham preened. "Played Rosalinda, the fair virgin who was sacrificed on the altar o' Pan. The part left me sore for days. The actor who played Pan 'ad the biggest—"

"Just look at the portrait." Cull scowled. "Do you know the lady or not?"

Peering at the portrait, the actress let out a snort. "Oh, *her.* I know that tart all right."

Pippa's pulse sped up. "How did you meet Lady Hastings?"

"I don't know no Lady 'Astings," Miss Cunnyngham said. "But I know the woman in the picture. 'Er name is Mary Brown, and she was one 'oity-toity bitch."

Lady Fayne sat up in her chair. "Julianna Hastings has a *look-alike?*"

Even the indomitable lady appeared astonished.

After the interview with Miss Cunnyngham, Cull and Pippa had wanted to share the discovery straight away. It put everything they knew in a different light, and Cull's mind spun with possibilities.

Had Lady Hastings been conspiring with Mary Brown? Was this part of the "solution" she'd referred to in her letter to Morton? What had the two women been up to? And perhaps the most disquieting question of all: whose body was buried in Lady Hastings's casket?

"Both of you saw who we believed to be Julianna Hastings after her death." Lady Fayne was obviously aboard the same train of reasoning. "Mr. Cullen, you discovered the body, and Pippa, you saw her remains at the funeral. Is there any chance that the dead woman was, in actuality, Mary Brown?"

"It is hard to say," Cull said pensively. "At the time, there wasn't a question in my mind that the woman was Julianna Hastings. Earlier that day, the larks had followed her from her residence. As Ollie has no memory of that night, however, we don't know what happened in the hours leading up to her murder."

Pippa spoke up. "When we interviewed Mrs. Loverly, she told us that the woman at her brothel that night was named 'Mary Brown.' I had assumed Lady Hastings was using an alias. But now I am not as sure. The woman I saw looked a lot like Julianna Hastings, but she was wearing a mask and could have been Mary Brown. If so, the two women are virtually indistinguishable."

"Good God," Lady Fayne murmured. "We may need to have another look at the body."

"Digging up the grave may not help us. It's been over two weeks since the victim died." Cull cleared his throat. "Even though burial may have slowed the process, the body will still have undergone significant decomposition."

Pippa looked slightly queasy.

"You have a point." Lady Fayne tapped a pen against her blotter. "Even when the body was fresh, no one suspected that it belonged to anyone other than Julianna Hastings. Which may prove to be the truth, but we can no longer ignore the other possibility."

"What is our next step, then?" Pippa asked.

A brisk knock sounded on the door. It was Lady Fayne's housekeeper.

"Excellent timing," Lady Fayne said. "Mrs. Peabody, here, has been on the trail of Vincent Ellis. She followed him and his paramours, Lord and Lady Effingworth, to their estate in Lancashire. Hopefully, she brings us news."

"It was a wild-goose chase," Mrs. Peabody stated. "When I arrived in Lancashire, I discovered the trio had returned to London."

"They're in Town?" Lady Fayne said alertly.

"Yes, my lady. According to the whispers of the servants in Lancashire, the Effingworths and Ellis came back to stay with their friends, Baron and Baroness de Tremblay, in Hampstead." Mrs. Peabody's mouth flattened into a disapproving line. "Apparently, the de Tremblays are holding a private bacchanal in their honor tomorrow night."

❧ 33 ❦

As the unmarked carriage neared its destination, Pippa's heart thumped with anticipation. The de Tremblays' manor was situated on the northern edge of Hampstead Heath, bordered by grassy knolls and woodland. In the indigo twilight, the place felt wild and isolated.

A place where anything could happen.

"I don't like this," Cull muttered beside her.

It had been his refrain since she and Charlie had hatched the present plan.

Through her contacts, Charlie had secured Pippa and Cull entry as "performers" for the event. As part of the hired help, Pippa was unlikely to be recognized by any acquaintances who might be in attendance. The theme of the bacchanal was "Gods Walking the Earth," and performers were required to follow a specific dress code.

Cull was going as Hephaestus, the blacksmith god. Pippa hoped it was his sardonic sense of humor rather than any true sense of self that had led him to dress as the deformed Olympian. Whatever his intention, he radiated male sensuality in his black domino, mask, and tight black breeches. He was shirtless beneath the cape, the glimpses of hair-dusted muscle making Pippa's insides flutter. The god's huge hammer, made of lightweight *papier-mâché*, rested on the carriage floor.

Pippa, herself, was disguised as Hephaestus's wife. She'd modeled her Aphrodite after Botticelli's *The Birth of Venus*, choosing a wig of long, red-gold curls that cascaded past her waist. Beneath her woolen cloak, she wore a sleeveless white robe with a crisscrossed bodice and tasseled gold belt knotted at the waist. The dress had high side slits that reached mid-thigh; per the instructions given to the performers, she wore nothing beneath it.

She felt altogether scandalous...and liberated. She wondered if women might move differently in the world without corsets and petticoats to impede them. She wasn't even wearing stockings; her footwear consisted of thin golden sandals with laces that climbed like vines up to her knee.

Elation thrummed in her. It was as if she'd shed a part of herself along with her unmentionables. Patient Pippa, with her inhibitions and insecurities, was nowhere to be found. Tonight, Pippa felt like a true Angel: strong, confident, and determined to solve the case.

"This is a bad idea," Cull more or less repeated.

With an exasperated twinge, she said, "I heard you the first dozen times."

"We can turn back."

"We are not turning back." She frowned at him. "Why are you being a wet blanket?"

Cull glowered back. "I'm not being a wet blanket; I'm being sensible. You have no business going to a sodding orgy."

"No business? I am an *agent* on a mission." She huffed out an annoyed breath. "I thought we'd moved past your overbearing tendencies."

"I know you're an agent, but you're also a lady," he said obstinately. "I don't like the idea of you being exposed to this depravity."

Her simmering temper reached a boil. How dare he?

"Whether or not you like it is irrelevant; I make my own decisions, Timothy Cullen. Why are you acting this way? This isn't my first visit to a den of iniquity—remember The Enchanted Rose?"

"No matter how hard I try to forget it," he ground out. "But you weren't mine then. Now you are and..."

"And what?"

"I don't want other men to get an eyeful of what belongs to me."

Seeing his clenched jaw and balled hands, she suddenly realized the truth.

"You're jealous?" she said in disbelief.

"What if I am?" He jutted his chin out. "I reckon I have a right to be. Fourteen years I've waited for you, Pippa, and I'm not a man who shares. Especially not the woman I love."

His possessiveness ought to have irked her, but for some reason it had the opposite effect. Her annoyance subsided. Perhaps it was his honesty and the vulnerability he was exposing. She was struck by a keen awareness: she had the power to hurt him...and vice versa. After all, hadn't she felt the bite of possessiveness when Miss Cunnyngham had exposed herself to Cull?

The present spat reminded Pippa that a relationship was seldom all smooth sailing. Truth be told, Cull had been tirelessly supportive...more than she could imagine most men being. If she wanted space, he gave it. If she wished for help with the case, he provided that too. If she had a humiliating emotional outburst, he took care of her and told her she was perfect.

He was almost *too* accommodating. He focused on her needs and asked for little in return. As if he felt he wasn't worthy of more...

Perhaps this fight was a good sign. A sign that he trusted her enough to be honest and not hold back his feelings. A sign that they could disagree, get angry, and still be blissfully happy together. Her own parents had locked horns over the years, and she couldn't think of two people more passionately in love.

Strangely enough, the fight gave Pippa the courage to voice what she'd held back.

"This is a ruse, and I'm only playing a part for the case," she said. "My heart belongs to you and you only. I love you, Cull."

"Pippa." Bright longing flashed in his eyes. "Do you...do you mean that?"

"Yes. And I want to share my life with you." She held his gaze. "But I won't make myself smaller to fit your expectations. I've gone down that road, and it only leads to misery. Being an Angel is important to me. I would never betray you, and I need you to trust me."

"I do trust you. And I love you exactly as you are." He cupped her jaw in his hand. "My perfect Pippa."

"I'm not perfect..." she began to protest.

His hot kiss claimed her breath. She debated arguing. Yet he overwhelmed her senses, and sighing, she surrendered herself to the joy of being in love.

Cull's sense of foreboding came back full force upon their arrival at the de Tremblay manor. Set within a dark woodland, the secluded Palladian mansion looked exactly like the sort of place where bluebloods purged their ennui with decadence and debauchery. The torches that lit the drive added to the paganistic ambiance. Statues of the Greek gods loomed over the guests at the colonnaded entrance, as if welcoming them to Olympus on Earth. The elegant windows were curtained to conceal the lewd revelry taking place within.

Cull and Pippa were directed to the servants' entrance at the back of the manor. A footman divested them of their outerwear and led them to the servants' dining hall, where other performers were already lined up. Everyone was wearing masks and Grecian-style costumes. Noticing the men ogling Pippa, Cull stayed close to her and issued warning glares.

He trusted her. But he didn't trust *them*. The bastards who coveted what was his.

"Now that is a glower worthy of Hephaestus." A slender male with winged sandals that marked him as Hermes came up beside Cull, chuckling. "First time, eh?"

Cull narrowed his eyes, gripping the handle of his hammer.

Before he could reply, Pippa chirped, "Yes. And we don't know what to expect."

"I'm a repeat performer, and it's simple, really." Hermes's mouth formed a smirk beneath his golden mask. "We're here to stoke the flames by giving the guests a show. You can choose your own partner...or partners." He waggled his brows. "Are you looking for a third? The guests love that sort of thing, and the gratuities are excellent."

Pippa's eyes grew wide, her cheeks cherry-red against her snowy mask.

A growl erupted from Cull's throat.

"I'll take that as a no. Pity, though. Given the size of your... hammer, I think we could've brought down the house." Hermes's shrug was good-natured. "Off to try my luck elsewhere."

As the bastard sauntered off, Pippa whispered in a rush, "We're not going to have to give them a show, are we?"

She sounded concerned. About bloody time.

"Worried, my reckless Angel?" Cull inquired. "And here I thought you were up for anything."

"Not *that*." She chewed on her bottom lip. "Once we're up in the public rooms, we'll search for Ellis. Hopefully, we can find him quickly and get him somewhere private to interrogate him about Mary Brown."

"As I mentioned when you and Lady Fayne cooked up this plan, I see no pitfalls whatsoever."

"Sarcasm doesn't suit you," she said crossly.

He was saved from replying by the butler, who began herding them up the stairs to the party.

Reaching the main floor, Cull set aside the idiotic hammer and took Pippa's hand, leading a methodical search. He noted that footmen stood guard outside each room, controlling the flow of guests in and out. He and Pippa went into the drawing room first. The lamps, topped with crimson shades, cast a lascivious glow over the guests, who were crowded around an Aubusson.

Upon the rug, two couples were giving a show.

Two naked women wearing identical blonde wigs were on their hands and knees, facing one another. They let out simultaneous moans as their male partners entered them from behind. Titillated murmurs rose from the audience as the men's thrusting pushed the women's lips together in a frenzied kiss.

Cull slid a glance at Pippa. She was staring at the scene, transfixed. Her throat bobbed above the vee of her robe. The depravity affected her senses, which was only natural. Watching his sweet Pippa get stirred from all the wickedness was also damned arousing. When she swiped her tongue over her lips, his trousers grew distractingly tight.

"Do you see Ellis?" he murmured.

Swallowing, she tore her gaze from the performers who were now tangled together, the women sandwiched head to tail, the men switching partners and resuming their vigorous screwing. Pippa ran her gaze over the guests, many of whom were inspired by the performance to engage in debauchery of their own. Clothes rustled to the ground, accompanied by moans and grunts.

"I don't see him." She sounded breathless. "Let's move on."

The music room featured similar entertainment. Lying on her stomach on a piano bench, a brunette Athena received the attention of two men, one at each end. The fellow behind her was

Hermes, who winked at Cull and Pippa as he dutifully pounded away.

Mischief sparkled in Pippa's eyes. "I guess he found what he was looking for."

"Keep moving," Cull ordered.

They searched the library, billiards room, and dining room with no luck. The latter had erupted into a free-for-all, with a chain of naked guests writhing along the length of the table, no orifice left unfilled. No sign of Ellis there either.

They followed a long corridor to the back of the house, where a pair of burly footmen were posted outside the doors to a conservatory. One was dark-haired, the other fair.

"Here to try your luck?" the dark-haired one asked. "Word of advice: put your best foot—and other body parts—forward."

"The master and mistress are entertaining discerning guests," the fair footman added. "They've tossed two sets of performers out on their arses. Said the show wasn't 'authentic' enough."

Cull shot Pippa a look of warning.

She ignored it. "We'll take our chances," she said.

The footmen opened the doors, releasing a blast of warm, humid air scented with citrus. Cull led the way and saw that the conservatory resembled his glasshouse. There were even birds, but they were kept in gilded cages. Potted orange and lime trees lined the steel-and-glass walls, oil lamps providing a muted glow. At the center of the room, wicker seating formed a ring around a mattress heaped with pillows. He counted two couples and a trio occupying the chairs.

"That's Ellis," Pippa said in a hush. "On the chaise lounge with the couple."

Cull saw that Pippa's sketch had captured the fellow to a tee, from the dark-brown hair worn dramatically to his shoulders to the sculpted bone structure that his silver mask didn't hide. His gaze was the same cold shade as his mask. He was lounging on the chaise, his head in the lap of a voluptuous brunette, who had to be Lady Effingworth. Lord Effingworth was on her other side, his arm draped around her shoulders.

The host and hostess, Baron and Baroness de Tremblay, were sitting on cushioned wicker loveseats...although not together. The baron had a naked redhead draped over him while his wife had a muscular blond fellow sitting on the ground in front of her. He wore what amounted to a loincloth, his head resting against her knee.

"Well, well," Effingworth drawled. "Looks like more entertainment has arrived."

Lady Effingworth raked a gaze over Cull. "They seem more promising than the last group. I was starting to think we would have to entertain ourselves."

"That comes later, my love," Lord Effingworth drawled. "If we can get inspired."

"I do apologize for the earlier performances. Nothing is more tedious than obviousness." Baroness de Tremblay had an affected lisp. "Good help is so hard to find these days."

"Get on with it, then." The baron's voice was imperious as he gestured to the mattress at the center of the circle. "Entertain us."

Dash it all. Pippa glanced at the mattress. Like the arena of the famed Roman Coliseum, it was surrounded by a ravenous audience who wanted to see their sport. She and Cull could make an excuse and leave, but they had finally closed in on Vincent Ellis. Their target...who held the key to their investigation.

I'm an Angel. I can handle this. Think.

Taking a breath, she willed the moment of panic to pass. She ran through the options. If she and Cull spooked Ellis now, they would have a difficult time getting him alone for the interrogation. They couldn't physically detain him, not with all the footmen around. They could leave and try to keep an eye on him, but what if he got away? He'd proved to be as slippery as a lamprey.

She came to a swift conclusion: the best option was...to play along.

Cull stood behind her, aggression pouring off him in waves. He was braced to fight, yet that wouldn't help them achieve their goal of getting Ellis alone. The situation required finesse. Her mind made up, praying that Cull would play along, she leaned back against him. The contact with his sinewy length sparked a sudden flame at her core.

He was aroused. Hard as a rock. From all the depravity they'd been witnessing, no doubt.

I like to watch, he'd told her more than once, and heaven help her, she was beginning to understand why. The lack of inhibition had lit a primal fire inside her. Made her aware of her desire for Cull, the pulsing, impolite enormity of it. She realized that she had to expend energy to keep her passion in check until the private moments when she could set it free.

She was tired of restriction. Of caging her wants and desires and keeping herself small. In this moment, she did not want to deny herself what she wanted.

Cull's erect member pressed into the small of her back as she reached up her arm, cupping the back of his head. Twisting her neck, she looked into his smoldering brown eyes.

Trust me. She willed him to understand her thoughts. *We can do this together.*

His nostrils flared. Then he bent his head, taking her mouth. Her entire being shivered at the slow, deliberate kiss. He took his time, his tongue tracing her lips before plunging in between. She opened for him, taking what he gave her. She moaned when he drew her bottom lip between his teeth, tugging gently.

"Well, this is promising." Lady Effingworth's voice pierced the sensual spell.

Pippa had nearly lost track of the audience.

Ellis, who was sitting up now, spoke for the first time. "Come closer. I want a better look."

Cull's voice scalded her ear. "Are you sure?"

Breathlessly, she nodded. In the next instant, he swept her into his arms. He carried her to the circle, but he didn't take her to the mattress. Instead, he chose an unoccupied loveseat, sitting and positioning her on his lap, her back to his chest.

Clever man, keeping both their gazes free to monitor Ellis, who was directly across the circle from them. He was watching them avidly while Lady Effingworth stroked his hair like he was a prized pet.

Pippa leaned her head to one side, exposing her neck to Cull. He took the invitation, dragging his mouth down the sensitive column and then back up. She grabbed onto his thighs, feeling the corded muscle as she squirmed on him with helpless delight. Without her petticoats, she felt every inch of his turgid cock. He licked the shell of her ear, flicking her plump lobe before drawing it into his mouth. His hot sucking pulled her nipples into visible points against her bodice, a gush of dew dampening her thighs.

She fought to keep her attention on her audience. To remember this was for show. The two other couples were kissing, as were the Effingworths. Ellis, however, had his gaze trained on her and Cull.

She drew Cull's head to hers, whispering, "He's watching. Keep going."

Cull drew down the strap of her robe, exposing the rounded top of her breast but keeping her nipple covered. The possessive fire in his eyes blazed through her, his message clear. He would go along with her plan but on his terms. He would control what the others saw of her. And he wouldn't let anything happen to her.

Love swelled in her. Cull was everything she'd fantasized about when she'd painted *Portrait of a Lady Dreaming*. The lover the lady with the red-gold hair had been looking out the window for; a man whose love expanded, rather than reduced, her world.

A partner who allowed her to explore, and explored with her...and who always, always kept her safe.

Relaxing into Cull's embrace, Pippa sighed as his mouth brushed along her shoulder. The hot kisses and tender nips raised goose-pimples on her skin. He cupped her breast, trapping the stiff tip between finger and thumb, making it jut out rudely against the thin fabric. Her head fell back against his shoulder, and she saw that he was looking straight at their audience as he fondled her.

His arrogant expression spoke louder than words. *She's mine. You can look, but you'll never touch.*

His possessiveness pushed a moan from her lips. Their audience echoed the sound, clothes swishing to the ground. Pippa's blood rushed beneath her skin as Cull ran a possessive hand down her front and into the high slit of her dress. When he cupped her bare sex, she whimpered with need.

"What a wicked girl you are," he rasped in her ear. "Getting wet from being watched."

"That's not why," she gasped.

"Why then?" He stroked her slick folds, the sight of his hand moving beneath the fabric a study in eroticism. The suggestion of what he was doing was somehow more titillating than if the act were exposed. Their audience clearly agreed, for the sounds of coupling filled the room.

"Why is your cunny drenched, then?" Cull demanded in a harsh growl.

"Because of you." He rewarded her honesty with a swirling touch just where she needed it, making her sigh, "Always you."

"Remember that the next time you decide to play games."

His reprimand made her wetter. Then he gave her mound a sharp slap.

Despite the thrilling tingles, she narrowed her eyes at him, and he gave a dark chuckle the instant before he plunged his fingers inside. Pleasure cascaded through her as he pumped his long, thick digits into her aching sheath. With his other hand, he played with her breasts, pinching and rubbing the tips through her bodice, her pearl throbbing in unison.

She felt how hard he was, his shaft an iron pole pressed against the crevice of her bottom. Leaning back against him, she lost track of the mission, the room, of anything but being in Cull's arms. She stared up at the blazing stars, and the barrier of glass melted away.

Nothing held her back from her desires. Nothing.

In a dark, regal tone, Cull commanded, "Come for me now."

Bliss exploded, and she soared into the night sky.

When she returned to earth, she was still in Cull's arms. He held her securely while he kept watch over the room. As she gazed at his profile, her heart overflowed.

I love him so much.

"Get ready," Cull said under his breath.

She swung her head to see Ellis approaching.

Lust glittering in his silver eyes, he said, "While my friends are otherwise engaged"—he gestured to the Effingworths, who were buried beneath a tangle of limbs on the mattress—"what would you say to a private *tête-à-tête?*"

🕊 34 🕊

Grabbing Ellis by the collar, Cull slammed him into the wall of the bedchamber.

"Easy there, big fellow!" Ellis yelped. "I like it rough, but there are limits, you know."

"Tell us about Mary Brown," Cull demanded.

Ellis's gaze grew wide. "W-what? How do you know Mary?"

Pippa said, "Tell us about her, or my friend here will make you."

"Friend?" Cull quirked an eyebrow at her. Is that what she called the man who'd made her come in front of an audience? Watching Pippa let go of her inhibitions had made him hotter than hell, and he meant to get his due as soon as they were done here.

She cast her gaze heavenward. "Figure of speech."

Mollified, Cull tightened his grip on Ellis's neck. "Tell us about the scheme you, Mary Brown, and Lady Julianna Hastings concocted."

Gasping, Ellis said, "What? I wasn't part of any scheme. I don't know what you're talking about."

Cull squeezed harder.

"All r-right. I'll t-tell you whatever you want to know about my sister."

"Sister?" Pippa demanded.

Cull released Ellis with a shove.

The bastard bent over, wheezing. "Mary's my sister...well, half-sister. We have the same mother. Her real name is Mary Ann O'Connell, but she went by Mary Brown."

"Where is Mary now?" Pippa asked.

"I don't know." He glanced at Cull, holding his hands up. "It's the truth. The last time I saw her was nearly three weeks ago. She came to see me while I was working."

"At The Enchanted Rose," Pippa stated.

Ellis looked surprised. "How did you know?"

"We're asking the questions," Cull growled.

"Right-o, no need to get nasty." Warily, Ellis went on, "When I saw Mary that night, she was acting rather strange."

"Explain," Cull said.

"First of all, it's not exactly the done thing to hunt one's brother down at an establishment like The Enchanted Rose," Ellis said wryly. "But Mary's always been bull-headed. Not her fault, though." Affection crept into his voice. "She wouldn't have survived an upbringing like ours otherwise. That night, she was agitated and said she needed a favor. She knew I had a set of pocket pistols, and she wanted one of them. When I asked her why, she said she needed it for protection. So I gave it to her.

"The truth is, I've been worried about Mary. It's been nearly three weeks since I've heard from her...and I think she was mixed up in some shady business."

Cull exchanged a grim look with Pippa. The timing of Mary's disappearance coincided with the death of Julianna Hastings. What were the two women mixed up in together?

"Why do you say that?" Pippa asked.

"In the last year, Mary was always flush in the pocket. My sister's a talented actress, but she wasn't making that blunt treading the boards. I assumed she'd found a rich protector." Ellis shrugged. "When I asked her about it, she laughed and said, *'Better than that. I've found myself a rich husband.'*"

Pippa's shoulders stiffened, and Cull knew they shared similar thoughts. Had Julianna Hastings hired Mary Brown to take her place so that she could escape the husband she loathed? And then, when she was ready to leave her marriage permanently, had she used Mary Brown to do it?

"I assumed she was joking. Mary had an odd sense of humor." Ellis glanced at Pippa, then Cull, his expression growing suspicious. "You don't mean Mary harm, do you?"

"No," Pippa assured him. "We are investigators. We're trying to discover what happened to one of our clients, who may have involved Mary in a dangerous scheme."

Paling, Ellis said, "You don't think something...happened to my sister, do you?"

"Does Mary have any birthmarks or distinguishing physical characteristics that could be used to identify her?" Cull asked.

Ellis shook his head. "Something has happened to her, then?"

"We don't know for certain." Pippa gentled her voice. "But there is a chance, yes."

A spasm crossed Ellis's features, and Cull knew then that the man had been telling the truth. Because he knew that look of pain. It stemmed from the knowledge that one had failed one's sibling, and it was too late to right the wrong.

In Ellis's case, it was almost a certainty.

Cull's chest knotted. For him, it wasn't quite too late. Not yet.

"Could you give us your sister's address?" Pippa asked.

Nodding, Ellis drew a slow breath. "If you...if you find out anything about my sister, will you let me know?"

"We will," Pippa promised.

The next morning, Pippa woke up alone in her bed. She wasn't surprised; Cull had stayed the night but told her he had to leave early. Rolling over, she buried her face in his pillow, inhaling his delicious scent as memories of last night assailed her.

A part of her couldn't believe what she'd done with Cull in a room full of strangers. At the time, it had felt right...arousing. Yet on the journey home, Cull had been brooding and taciturn, and her thoughts had grown increasingly anxious.

How could you have made such an exhibition of yourself? What were you thinking? Can you blame Cull for being disgusted with your shameful behavior?

Her tension had mounted until she couldn't stop herself from blurting out an apology. She'd hated how small she sounded. At the same time, she couldn't deny that she *had* been reckless. Had Cull not played his part so brilliantly, the outcome could have been disastrous. She realized that, in her efforts to assert her independence, she might have gone a bit too far.

In her marriage, she'd always been the follower, never the leader. Her relationship with Cull was an intricate dance that went back and forth; she loved having him for a partner, but she felt as if she were just learning the steps. Sometimes she stumbled; sometimes she stepped on his toes. Yet she trusted him not to let her fall...and wasn't that the most important thing?

All of this had come out in a confused babble. Halfway through, Cull had silenced her...with his mouth. Then with his hands and cock. His possession had been savage, his vigorous plowing thumping her back against the carriage wall. She'd climaxed repeatedly. After her fourth or fifth time—she'd lost count—he'd pulled out with a roar, jerking himself to a hot finish upon her bared breasts.

Afterward, he gathered her close, saying quietly, "Don't ever apologize for your desires, Pippa. I'm not your dead husband. To me, you'll always be perfect as you are."

She'd been too relieved and sated to quibble over her so-called perfection.

Now Cull was gone, and she already missed him. He'd told her he would be busy today, but he planned to meet her tomorrow night. At her parents' house. Sending up a silent prayer, she decided to cross that bridge when she got there. That is, if the family affair did not cause her to throw herself over said bridge.

There's no use fretting about it now, she told herself. *You've work to do.*

Getting out of bed, she rang for Suzette to help her get ready.

When she arrived at Charlie's, all the Angels were present in the drawing room...save one.

"Fi's stuck with the Brambletons again." Glory's expression was rueful. "She is *not* happy about it."

"Poor Fiona," Pippa murmured.

"Pippa, please fill us in on the de Tremblay affair," Charlie said briskly.

Trying not to blush, Pippa described the pertinent facts, glossing over the intimate details.

Livy canted her head, her looped braids swinging against her cheek. "And you believe Ellis's story about Mary?"

"Both Cull and I thought he was genuinely worried about his sister," Pippa replied. "The details he gave us match what we know thus far and help us to establish a theory of the crime. According to Ellis, Mary's financial situation improved around a year ago. That coincides with the date of the playbill found in Lady Hastings's possession. She could have met Mary at the New Cytherea and hired Mary to impersonate her."

"A rather diabolical plan on Lady Hastings's part." Glory pursed her lips. "Did she do it to get away from her husband?"

"Ellis mentioned that Mary said she'd found a '*rich husband*,' which meant she was probably fulfilling some, ahem, unwanted duties for Lady Hastings." Pippa grimaced. "And Lady Hastings had another reason to get away."

"Howard Morton," Livy said with her usual acuity. "Any news on him?"

Pippa shook her head. "According to Cull's larks, Morton goes to work and comes home. No extracurricular activities of any kind."

"Maybe he knows he's being watched," Glory put in. "Your visit probably put the fear of God in him. If Julianna Hastings is still alive, he's likely involved in some way. By faking her own death, she would guarantee his inheritance—"

"Then they could be together *and* have her father's money. To her mind, that might seem like a fitting ending. A part of me understands her desperation," Pippa admitted. "Yet nothing would justify her killing Mary Brown and hurting Ollie."

"Or killing her husband...if she was indeed the one behind Hastings's murder." Livy tapped a finger against her chin. "I wonder why she didn't just kill him in the first place. It would have achieved her goal with half the trouble."

"Perhaps she was afraid she would get caught?" Glory suggested. "As it stands, no one can accuse a dead woman of murdering her husband."

"Splendid reasoning, Angels." Approval gleamed in Charlie's grey eyes. "Your deductive skills have improved tremendously. But there are still loose ends."

"Louis Wood," Livy said promptly. "Is he somehow involved?"

"According to Cull's surveillance, Wood was let go from his position last week when Hastings's distant relation took over the townhouse," Pippa said. "Wood has taken up rooms in a lodging house in Chelsea. At night, the larks have trailed him to various gin palaces and theatres, but he's done nothing incriminating."

"Wood *is* a former criminal," Livy pointed out. "What if he is in cahoots with Lady Hastings? He gains a fortune out of this, after all."

"Wood's involvement makes sense," Pippa agreed. "While Lady Hastings might have been able to fool her indifferent husband with a double, Wood has known her since she was a girl. He would have noticed something amiss...unless he had a reason to turn a blind eye."

"Wood is shaping up to be a prime suspect," Charlie said with a nod. "In the meantime, let's have a look at Mary Brown's residence."

They waited until dark to go to Mary Brown's flat, located above a butcher shop in Cheapside. Livy and Glory kept watch while Charlie and Pippa took the back stairs up to the flat. Using a pair of hairpins, Pippa unlocked the door. The sweep of their lamps showed that the modest two-room flat was unoccupied.

Charlie swiped a finger along a table, leaving a trail in the dust. "It appears no one has been here in a while."

"I'll take a closer look at the bedchamber," Pippa said.

The room had an eerie quality. A collection of wigs hung on hooks, looking like a creepy wall of scalps. When Pippa opened the scratched wardrobe, its colorful innards burst out. The array of costumes included that of an Egyptian queen and a faerie's wispy dress.

"You were good at disguising yourself, weren't you, Mary?" Pippa murmured.

Pippa sat in the wobbly chair in front of the dressing table, which was cluttered with assorted jars and containers. She uncapped one the perfume bottles; Lady Hastings's signature scent wafted out. The table had three drawers, two filled with grooming implements. Opening the third, Pippa found a collection of handwritten notes...recipes for cosmetics. For everything from rouge to lip stain to hair tonics.

She leafed through the recipes, stopping at one.

1. *1 pint common wine*

2. *2 drams common salt*
3. *2 drams green copperas*
4. *2 drams oxide of copper*
5. *4 drams bark of walnut*

Boil no.'s 1, 2, and 3. Add 4, boil 2 minutes. Take from fire, add 5. Rub into the hair using a warmed cloth. Rinse with water. Repeat weekly.

Heart pounding, Pippa fumbled to open the drawer with the grooming implements. She took them out one by one until she found what she was looking for.

"Heavens," she breathed.

"Did you find something?" Charlie's voice came from behind her.

Pippa spun in her chair, holding a hairbrush.

"Mary Brown was a *blonde*," she blurted. "At The Enchanted Rose, she was a brunette, and I just assumed that was her natural hair color. Her brother, Ellis, also has dark hair. But I found a recipe for hair dye containing green copperas and walnut bark, both used to create dark pigments in paint, and I realized..."

She held up the pale-blonde strands she'd plucked from the hairbrush.

"Excellent work, Pippa. We now have a means of distinguishing the two women. Which means—"

"We have a grave to dig up," Pippa said resolutely.

35

Cull paused in the antechamber of the Griers' house in Belgravia.

"Thank you for supper," Cull said.

Fanny sent Grier a look.

The grizzled Scot cleared his throat. "You are welcome any time, lad. Now I must, er, see to a matter. Excuse me."

He strode off. No doubt to give Cull and Fanny privacy.

"I'll walk you to your carriage," Fanny said. "I need a breath of air."

Outside, the tree-lined street was quiet. The fog obscured the stars tonight, and the only light came from the windows of the stately white houses.

"It's a different world from the one you and I came from." The night breeze rustled the plum taffeta of Fanny's skirts, and she looked like she belonged here, on the portico of her grand home. "Never thought I'd be living in a place like this. Some days I can't believe it."

"You've earned your life." Cull meant it. "You deserve fine things, Fanny."

"So do you, Timothy." She paused. "You did the right thing,

writing your sister. Knowing Maisie, she'll be glad to hear from you."

This morning, Cull had sat down and penned a letter. It had been the most difficult letter he'd ever written. Asking not only for forgiveness, which he'd done plenty of times before, but for another chance. To be her brother and an uncle to her son. He'd even told her about Pippa. About how, for the first time in his life, he felt deserving of happiness.

After he sent it off, he had experienced instant regret, anxiety gnawing at his gut. His first instinct had been to seek out Pippa... but he couldn't explain the situation without betraying his promise to Maisie. The only one he could talk to was Fanny. She knew what had happened to his sister. Had helped Maisie through the birth and recovery. Although Maisie had wanted nothing to do with Cull, she'd accepted Fanny's assistance. Fanny cared about both Maisie and him and could be trusted to give sound advice.

"I hope you're right," he said with feeling.

"When am I wrong?" Fanny snorted. "If you're wise, you'll take my advice on another matter too: marry that sweetheart of yours."

Cull felt his lips twitch. "You do like her, don't you?"

"More importantly, *you* do. You take after me in that way. We both have excellent taste when it comes to spouses."

Grinning, Cull said, "Grier's ears must be burning."

"The Scot knows how I feel about him." Fanny gave him a pointed look. "Does your lady know how you feel?"

"She does. And she returns my feelings." He heard the wonder in his voice; a part of him still couldn't believe that Pippa loved him back. "She doesn't care that she is a countess and I'm, well, me. Not only does she accept my duty to the mudlarks, but she also offered to help me with my role."

"Did she now?"

Fanny sounded as impressed as Cull had felt while discussing mudlark business with Pippa. She turned out to be an excellent listener who gave thoughtful opinions. He had told her about the venture he'd started to improve the futures of his charges. The problem had always been that mudlarks preferred freedom and excitement over respectable drudgery, making them ill-suited for most occupations. What they needed was a job that was exhilarating, made use of their information-gathering abilities, and offered first-rate renumeration.

The idea had struck Cull: why not teach mudlarks to invest in the 'Change?

It might seem outlandish, but he'd seen plenty of men make fortunes from investments...and just as many lose their shirts. The trick, Cull thought, lay in the accurate collection of information and evaluation of risk. The larks had a leg up on the former, but they needed to work on the latter. Thus far, they were managing to break even with the stake Cull had provided. At least they found the work fascinating.

Pippa had come up with a suggestion: Cull should hire experts to train the larks. Given the snobbery Cull had encountered, however, he wasn't sure anyone would apply for the position. No one he would trust, at any rate. Pippa had advised him to talk to her father, who'd had great success investing on the 'Change. She'd been confident that Hunt would be happy to share his counsel and winning strategies.

"Pippa has the strength of will and heart to be part of the larks," Cull mused aloud. "And you saw how wonderful she was with the children."

It was a miracle, but he could picture Pippa living at the Nest with him. Being happy with him. Larks, mayhem, and all.

"Your sweetheart is a rare one. You had better snatch her up before someone else does."

"That is my plan. But I have a gauntlet to run first." He rubbed the back of his neck. "I'm having supper with her family tomorrow night."

Fanny's face split into a rare smile. "Meeting the in-laws, are you? No wonder you got a haircut and a set of dapper new clothes."

"Actually, I've already met Pippa's parents. They showed up at her cottage unexpectedly one morning while I was, er, still there."

Fanny's eyes bulged. "Gavin Hunt didn't tear you from limb to limb?"

"He gave me a warning," Cull said ruefully. "Not that I needed it. I *want* to treat Pippa right...to make a life with her. I just didn't think it was possible for a man like me."

"You're a good man, Timothy Cullen." Fanny braced her hands on her waist. "Why wouldn't it be possible?"

He looked up at the sky, black as the mythical River Styx, no stars in sight. He drew his gaze back to Fanny, was about to share his mam's words about fate and fortune, the way a man might a funny story...when a movement caught his attention.

Across the street, a shadow separated from a dark tree. The hairs rose on Cull's nape, instinct driving his hand to his pistol. He whipped it out, twin shots booming in the night.

The assailant let out a groan, crumpling to the ground.

Heart thudding, Cull turned. For an instant, shock paralyzed him. "Fanny?" *No, no, no...*

He fell onto his knees beside her. Ripping off his neckcloth, he pressed it to the gaping taffeta at her side. Her blood ran over his hands as he shouted for help.

36

H er heart fluttering beneath the bodice of her new silver-grey gown, Pippa arrived at her parents' house. She had come early, hoping to talk to her brothers before the guests arrived. Cull was making his way separately; strangely, she hadn't heard from him all day...but he was likely just busy. She'd been as well, helping Charlie to formulate the plan for unearthing Julianna Hastings's remains.

She and Charlie had spent the day surveilling the funeral grounds and making note of the obstacles. The place had a regular patrol to deter graverobbers. Moreover, digging up the grave would be a demanding physical task. To get the job done efficiently, the Angels would need Hawker's help, but he wasn't due back from an assignment for several days.

Pippa told herself to worry about the case tomorrow. Tonight, she had other concerns. She found Garrett and Hugh drinking whisky in the drawing room.

"I want your promise that you'll be nice to Mr. Cullen," she said.

Her brothers looked at one another.

Garrett, a tall blond Adonis who took after their mama,

quirked a brow. "Our dear sister must be talking to you, Hugh. Since I don't do *nice*."

"Neither do I. Nice is for namby-pambies." Hugh's charismatic personality and looks came from their papa. Crossing his muscular arms, he said, "If this Timothy Cullen wants to get on my good side, he will have to earn it. Maybe I'll test him out in Papa's boxing ring. See if he can keep up."

Pippa rolled her eyes. "There will be no sparring at Mama's birthday party."

Even though Garrett and Hugh were in their twenties, they still acted like boys. Everything was a match to prove one's manhood. Neither had met a competition that they didn't like.

"You cannot blame us, Pippa," Garrett said. "As your brothers, it is our job to make sure the fellow is good enough for you this time."

This time. Her chest tightened as she sensed the seriousness behind her brothers' joking. Like Papa, her brothers thought they'd somehow failed to protect her from the mistake of her marriage. When it had never been their responsibility. For all their neck-or-nothing ways, Garrett and Hugh were good boys...good men.

"We just want you to be happy," Hugh added.

"I promise you that, this time, I truly am." On impulse, she got on tiptoe and kissed each of them on the cheek. "Thank you for your concern."

"Have a care, Pippa. It took my valet hours to perfect my cravat," Garrett groused.

But his cheeks were ruddy. As were Hugh's. The boys would take any comers, Pippa thought with amusement, but at the mere hint of sentiment, they wanted to bolt.

Taking pity on them, she changed the subject. "Where are Mama and Papa? Shouldn't they be down by now? The guests will be here soon."

"Mama was down here earlier. She had on a new dress," Hugh

muttered, "and you know how Papa gets. Garrett walked in on them..."

"For the love of God," Garrett burst out. "I already had to wash my eyes out with soap. Must I be forced to relive that scene in my head which, I might add, cannot be scrubbed clean?"

Pippa felt her lips quiver. Their parents had a habit of being affectionate with one another, and Garrett, for some reason, had a propensity for walking in on them during inopportune times. He liked to joke that he was scarred for life.

Yet Pippa's experience had taught her that passion and love were naught to be ashamed of.

"True happiness is rare. We should be glad for Mama and Papa," she said softly.

"I am glad, in theory," Garrett retorted. "I just don't want to see their happiness *in action*."

Hugh burst into laughter, and Pippa joined in.

"What has our lovely children so amused, I wonder?"

Mama floated into the room, a vision in a gown of azure silk. Diamonds sparkled at her neck and ears, but what made her truly shine was the glowing love in her eyes as she gazed at Papa. He had an arm around her waist and a look of satisfaction on his face that...well, Garrett was right. It was best not to think too keenly on the cause of it.

"We're just happy to be together," Pippa said sincerely. "And to celebrate your birthday with you, Mama."

Mama came over, hugging them each in turn while the boys groaned.

"You are the best presents any mama could wish for," she told them.

"Papa, will you save us from these sentimental women?" Hugh groaned.

"The stronger a man, the gentler he can afford to be." Papa cuffed Hugh on the shoulder. "But, as it happens, I want a private word with your sister. Would you accompany me to the study, Pippa?"

Pippa felt the flutter of nerves. For months, she'd avoided private talks with her father because she already knew how he felt about her life choices. And she'd been angry enough at herself that she didn't need him to add fuel to the fire. Yet her talks with Cull had helped her to make peace with the past. What remained was mending the relationships with the people she loved.

She took her father's offered arm. "Of course, Papa."

As they headed out, Mama gave her an encouraging smile.

Entering the study, Pippa was assailed by memories of her childhood. Of the hours she and her brothers had spent playing here. While Papa had a larger-than-life presence, with his family he'd always shown a gentler side. For her, the scent of leather, cigars, and her papa's sandalwood cologne were associated with security and happiness. Both of which she had willfully abandoned.

"I'm sorry." The words rushed from her.

Papa quirked a brow. "I thought that was my line."

"I made a bad choice, Papa." She gripped the back of a chair. "And I know you're disappointed in me, but I promise I've learned from my error. Mr. Cullen isn't like Longmere—"

"We'll get to Cullen. After I say what I want to say." Papa's broad chest heaved. "I was never disappointed in you, Pippa. Only in myself, that I had allowed such unhappiness to befall you. You're my only girl, my poppet, and the way that self-important popinjay treated you..." His hands fisted at his sides, and he clearly struggled to rein in his temper. "No one treats my daughter that way."

"I brought him into our lives...saddled you all with his conde-scension and snobbery." Her eyes burning, she remembered all the times Edwin had refused to attend her family gatherings, all the excuses she'd had to make for his absence. "I let him get between me and everyone I love."

"Nothing can get between us Hunts," Papa declared.

She realized those were the words she needed to hear. That some part of her had feared she would never hear again. Then Papa was there, his arms enfolding her in a hug, and with flooding relief, she hugged him back. And she knew that everything would be all right.

When the embrace ended, she sniffled, "I'm sorry it took me so long to talk to you, Papa."

He passed her his handkerchief. "You've always been an obstinate thing," he said complacently. "You take after your mama."

"Am I the only one who thought I was easy-going and patient?" she pondered aloud.

Papa barked out a laugh. "Well, you are easy-going when you get what you want. And patient when you're biding your time to get it. In those ways, you take after *me*." His tawny eyes grew serious. "Now, poppet, you're certain Timothy Cullen is what you want?"

"Yes," she said definitively. "Cull is a good man, Papa. I know he seems a bit rough around the edges, but he has a noble heart... you should see him with the mudlarks. In truth, the Nest is run quite similarly to the Hunt Academy."

"I know all about the Prince of Larks. What I want to know is how the man treats *you*, Pippa. Is he deserving of my girl...or do I need to pound him to a fare-thee-well?"

"Cull loves me." She didn't hide the wonder she felt. "He treats me like a princess."

"He had better." Papa's words held a warning edge. "I sat on my laurels once, and I'll not do it again. Anyone who makes you unhappy—who disrespects you in any way—will answer to me."

One by one, the guests arrived.

It was a small party consisting of family and her parents'

closest friends. Mama's brother, Uncle Paul and his wife, Aunt Charity, were the first to show up. Pippa was happy to catch up with them and hear how her cousins were faring. Then came Mr. and Mrs. Ambrose Kent, who'd traveled from their country estate to wish Mama many happy returns. Finally, the Marquess and Marchioness of Harteford arrived. Pippa knew them as Uncle Nick and Aunt Helena, the former being Mama's brother in spirit if not in blood.

Aunt Helena, a beautiful curvy brunette, drew Pippa aside.

"How are you, my dear?" Aunt Helena studied her with concerned hazel eyes.

"I'm better, Aunt Helena," Pippa said truthfully.

"Mourning takes a toll," Aunt Helena continued with a sigh. "It is unfair that someone as young as you had to go through it. I felt the same way about Thomas."

Thomas, the Earl of Hawksmoor, was Aunt Helena's eldest and a widower.

"How is Hawksmoor?" Pippa asked.

"Oh, the same. Not that one would know," Aunt Helena said dryly. "He gets his stoicism from his papa. Still, I worry about him and wish he would move on..." She caught herself, saying with a smile, "Here I am rambling on when I want to hear about you, Pippa dear. I'm told you have a...friend coming this eve?"

Seeing as Mama and Aunt Helena were as thick as thieves, the latter likely knew all about Cull.

"Yes," Pippa said. "I hope you like him."

"If he makes you happy, then I will," Aunt Helena said warmly. "I cannot wait to meet him."

Pippa pushed aside a pang of unease. Cull had not yet arrived, and it wasn't like him to show up late. But maybe he'd just been detained by business.

Another half-hour came and went. As the guests chatted over preprandial drinks, Pippa participated half-heartedly. Where was Cull? Had something happened to him? Seeing her papa's darkening countenance and her brothers' scowls, her worry grew. Her family had been burnt before. If Cull didn't arrive soon and have a good explanation for his lateness, they would hold it against him.

When the door to the drawing room opened, she exhaled. *Finally.* Yet her relief proved short-lived: it was only the butler.

"What is it, Jeffries?" Mama asked.

"A note arrived, ma'am. For Lady Longmere."

Pippa went over, taking the note from the silver salver. Her hands trembled as she unfolded it and read the words.

Please convey my apologies. I won't be coming tonight. I will be in touch when I can. -Cullen

She read the note again. It didn't take long. Three lines...that was all he thought she merited?

Her disbelief morphed into rage.

Mama came up to her, murmuring, "Is everything all right, my darling?"

Aware of the eyes on her, Pippa tamped down her fury. She fixed a smile on her face and said the words she'd been forced to say so many times before.

"Perfectly, Mama," she said. "My guest sends his regrets, so we mustn't wait on him. Let us go in for supper."

37

Cull was not surprised when one of the larks informed him of Pippa's arrival. He'd had her followed for her protection. Yet he had not expected her to come here straight from her mama's party. After his rudeness to her family, he hadn't known if she would want to see him...and the truth was, he didn't want her here. He wasn't fit for company. Wasn't fit...for anything.

Pain twisted his gut. He could still feel Fanny's blood on his hands. Still see the anguish in Grier's eyes. Even though the physician had said that Fanny would survive, she'd had a hole punched through her because of Cull. Because of his arrogance and stupidity. Because he'd thought he could play with fire and not get burned.

He should have anticipated that Squibb would seek revenge. That the bastard would do it in the most cowardly of ways, a sneak attack in the dark. Now Squibb was dead. Cull had killed him, which was what he should have done from the start. But he hadn't, and now Fanny was fighting for her life—after she'd fought so bloody long and hard already—because of his failure.

Another failure to add to the tally. Another person he loved and failed to protect.

The marks between his shoulder blades burned; the starless night pressed down on him.

He couldn't—wouldn't—let his darkness touch Pippa. He'd rip his heart out before he let that happen. She belonged in the light...and because he loved her, he had to let her go.

The door to the glasshouse opened, and Pippa swept in, looking like a princess in a silvery gown. Her expression was stormy, but her beauty shone through. He'd never met her equal and never would. And he refused to be the one to snuff out her brightness.

"You owe me an explanation," she said into the stillness.

The glasshouse was quiet because he'd let the birds go. It had been time.

It *was* time.

"Something came up." He flashed to Fanny lying in a pool of blood; Patrick, lifeless beneath the smoking rubble; all the mudlarks lost during Cull's watch. Maisie's blood on the sheets and tears of shame in her eyes.

His throat tight, he said, "It's the nature of my life, Pippa. Something will *always* come up."

"What happened, Cull?" Pippa stared at him. "Why are you acting this way?"

"I am not putting on an act. That is what I'm telling you. This *is* me: I'm the Prince of Larks." He clenched his jaw. "It's when I am with you that I'm not myself. When I forget my duties, the responsibilities that come with the job."

That wasn't a lie. Being with her distracted him, although he didn't blame her for it. He blamed himself: if he'd been paying closer attention to Squibb, Fanny wouldn't have been shot. And what if Pippa had been there beside him? What if he had to ink *her* onto his back? God, he would rather take a knife there instead.

Time and again, he'd fought to balance his duties with his personal wants and desires...and each time he failed, hurting someone important in the process. He couldn't be the Prince of Larks *and* a brother, friend, or lover. Couldn't escape the curse of solitude. That much was written in the stars.

When am I going to learn? he raged at himself.

"*You* are angry at *me?*" Wrath blazed in Pippa's eyes. "After you showed my family utter disrespect—after you humiliated me in front of them and their closest friends?"

"It would have been worse if I had shown up. I don't belong in that world, Pippa. Any more than you belong in mine," he said flatly.

Several heartbeats passed.

"So that's it?" Her words were cold, free of inflection. "The talk of sharing our lives, accepting one another as we are, love... was just that. Talk. Meaningless words?"

Cull balled his hands. Wanting so desperately to hold her. Knowing he couldn't.

"I can't hurt you, Pippa. My world is full of danger, and if something happened to you because of me..."

I would go out of my mind. I wouldn't survive. I could take anything...but that.

"It won't," he said with finality. "Because I will not allow it."

"Why is it your choice? What about what *I* want?" Her voice trembled. "I don't care about the danger. I can take care of myself...or better yet, we can look out for each other, Cull. That's what we've been doing, isn't it? And it's working...at least for me. I'm happy and feel like I'm finally becoming the woman I am meant to be. Aren't you...aren't you happy too?"

Christ, I'm the happiest I've ever been. And because of that, Fanny got hurt.

He shoved aside his despair. Ruthlessly chose his next words.

"It was fun while it lasted," he said with calculated indifference. "*You* were fun. But I ought to have stuck to my original rules: nothing beyond the moment. And the moment is over."

"You arrogant blighter," she choked out. "You are no different from Longmere."

He couldn't stop himself from scowling. "I am nothing like that bastard."

"Aren't you?" Her smile was bitter. "Both of you want a fantasy version of me. Longmere wanted the perfect countess at his beck and call. You only want the lady who will never leave her pedestal of perfection."

"I *never* put you on a bloody pedestal. The Enchanted Rose? The sodding orgy?" He glowered at her. "I want you to be free to experience life as you wish."

"But only when it comes to pleasure. Under the cover of masks. What about the rest of life, Cull?"

Her pleading tone shredded his insides.

"I want everything with you," she said. "For better or worse."

"I...I can't, Pippa," he said hoarsely. "The life I have to offer—it's not good enough. You deserve better."

"I deserve a man who loves me." Her voice cracked but did not break. "Who is willing to fight for our love heart, body, and soul. Clearly, you are not that man."

Shoulders high, she turned and left.

Just as his mam had predicted, he was left alone beneath the starless sky. His eyes and scars burned. As he watched Pippa exit onto the street below, he knew that she would not return, and anguish smothered his last flicker of hope.

❦ 38 ❦

Pippa had had her heart broken before.

But never smashed to smithereens. Never reduced to grit and dust.

With Edwin, she had mourned a fantasy she'd created. With Cull, she had experienced something better than any relationship she could dream up in her head. The passion and friendship, the laughter, tears, and even the fighting—at long last, she'd discovered what real love felt like.

Until Cull took it all away.

Pippa spent the day after licking her wounds. When Mama and Papa stopped by early that morning, she wept in the former's arms and begged the latter not to interfere. It had taken visible effort, but Papa reined in his temper.

"It is for the best, poppet," he said gruffly. "Better to find out the kind of man he is now than when it's too late."

Pippa didn't have the heart to tell him that it *was* too late. She'd fallen in love with a man who didn't want her. Who would rather keep her in a cage of perfection than let her fly by his side.

After her parents left, she sent Charlie a note to explain why she wasn't up for working today. She was plagued by restlessness...

and a sudden unstoppable urge. She went to her sitting room and dragged out her paints. Propping a canvas onto the easel, she didn't bother to sketch or plan; she just grabbed a brush and let herself go.

As tears streamed down her face, she lost herself in color, in the movement of her brush, the play of darkness and light and life filling the canvas. When Suzette came to inquire about luncheon, Pippa waved her away. She wanted nothing but the solace of her art: the fire that burned inside her, that Cull had revived. That not even a broken heart could douse again. She painted freely and fiercely and fearlessly even as her world went up in flames.

When a knock sounded on the door, Pippa said absently, "Not now. I'm busy."

The door opened anyway, and Livy, Fi, and Glory traipsed in.

"Charlie told us what happened," Livy said. "We wanted to see how you were."

Setting down her brush, Pippa ran a hand through her tangled hair. She rubbed her eyes, which were puffy from weeping. Looking down at her robe, she saw splatters of paint.

"I am surviving. I think," she said ruefully.

Fiona held up a box tied with ribbon. "I brought cakes from Gunter's."

Heartbreak had dulled Pippa's appetite. But these were Gunter's cakes.

"Did you bring the almond ones with custard and raspberry jam?" she asked.

"Given the situation," Fiona said, "I brought two dozen."

It was wonderful to have friends who understood. Fortified by tea and cake, Pippa haltingly told the Angels about what happened with Cull. All of them evinced surprise.

"That seems out of character for Mr. Cullen," Livy said. "Thus far, he's been steadfast and a man of his word."

"The times I've seen the pair of you together, he was absolutely smitten with you," Fi declared. "I can always tell with men."

"Perhaps something happened?" Glory suggested. "To make him change his mind?"

"I asked him about that. And his only answer was that he is the Prince of Larks. As if I wasn't aware of the fact." Her chest ached with bewildered pain. "I have never, not once, asked him to be anyone but who he is. I don't care that he has responsibilities; on the contrary, I wanted to be his partner and helpmate. To build a life together. I adore the mudlarks and thought I'd found my place..." Her throat swelled, and she was suddenly close to tears again. "I was wrong."

"I think there is something he's not telling you." Livy ate a forkful of cake. "A man in love doesn't just change his mind overnight."

"You're probably right. But why wouldn't he talk to me? I deserve better."

Anger momentarily blocked out Pippa's despair. With a sense of irony, she realized that her time with Cull had renewed her self-confidence in time for her to be utterly livid at his treatment of her. While she was heartbroken, she also knew she deserved an explanation—deserved *better* from him.

"Of course you do. It is Mr. Cullen's loss," Glory said loyally.

"Thank you." Pippa gave her friends a watery smile. "Talking about it makes me feel less sorry for myself."

"Actually, we have an even better distraction to offer, if you're up for it." Excitement sparkled in Livy's eyes. "We're taking a trip to Kensal Green tonight."

"To dig up Lady Hastings's grave?" Pippa said in surprise. "But I thought we were waiting for Hawker to return?"

"Since time is of the essence, I convinced Hadleigh to help," Livy said. "He's bringing his friend Mr. Chen as well."

Pippa had met Mr. Chen, who'd helped the Angels before. Chen operated a clinic in the East End that specialized in treating opium habits, and Livy had confided that he'd been pivotal in Hadleigh's recovery years ago. Not only was Chen a skilled healer, but he was also a master of the fighting arts, which made him a valuable addition to any mission.

"We've come up with a plan to deal with the guards," Glory added.

"And I, for once, am Brambleton-free this eve." Fiona raised her auburn brows. "So, dear Pippa, are you in?"

"She woke up earlier," Grier said quietly. "She was in pain, so I gave 'er the tincture the physician left. She's going to be fine."

With a tight nod, Cull said, "That is a relief."

Fanny had been asleep when he'd arrived and had looked improved, thank Christ. Grier had invited him into the study, and now they were in the wingchairs by the crackling hearth. Grier took a swallow of whisky as he stared into the flames, deep lines creasing his face. Cull wished the Scot would yell at him, punch him, do *something* to him for the pain he'd caused. But Grier didn't. And that made Cull hate himself even more.

He set down his untouched whisky. "Grier, I...I cannot tell you how sorry I am."

Paltry, pathetic words. Yet they were all he had to give.

Grier met Cull's gaze. "You ain't got anything to be sorry for, lad."

"It's my fault Fanny was shot. If I'd just listened to you and taken care of Squibb—"

"You listen to me now." Grier slammed his glass down onto the side table, startling Cull into silence. "My wife is lying in our bedchamber with a bullet wound in 'er side. She's going to live, but the recovery ain't going to be a stroll through Hyde Park."

Cull's gut twisted. "I know."

"And when she came to and was aware of everything that 'ad 'appened, do you know what she said to me?"

"No."

"Don't let that fool lad think this is his fault."

Cull's eyes heated.

"Now you know Fanny, she's not one for regrets. But I know that if 'er life 'ad taken a different direction, she would've wanted a son like you. Even if you're not 'er blood, she looks at you with a mother's pride. And do you know why?"

Dragging his sleeve across his eyes, Cull shook his head.

"Because you grew up like she did, like I did, and you didn't let that destroy your decency." Grier nodded. "In fact, you remind Fanny and me of our friend, the former owner of our club."

Cull knew of Andrew Corbett, of course. He was a legend in the rookery. A former prostitute turned successful businessman, he'd used his wealth to champion charitable causes. He'd founded Nursery House with Fanny, and his good deeds numbered so many that he'd been knighted by the Queen.

"I don't see why," Cull said wryly. "No one is addressing me as *Sir*."

"Corbett was made a knight *because* he's a gentleman. Not vice versa. And that's 'ow you're like 'im. The way you treat others, protect those little birds...not many would take that on. So even if you fail from time to time, lad, you *try*—which puts you 'ead and shoulders above most men."

Cull hunched his shoulders. "When I fail, people get hurt—"

"It wasn't you who shot Fanny but that bastard Squibb. You may be the Prince o' Larks, but you're still a man, which means you cannot know everything and protect everyone. As a leader, you'll suffer losses no matter what you do. Do you try to minimize them? Yes. Do you learn from your mistakes? Absolutely. Do you sit 'ere and blame yourself for every bad thing that 'appens? No, you do not—because that is not what a leader does."

Grappling with his friend's counsel, Cull said, "The truth is I... I never wanted to be a leader."

"That's too bloody bad. Because you're a damned fine one who 'as stepped up time and again when no one else would. Why do you think those mudlarks look up to you, eh? Why do you think my lass who, let's face it, ain't no soft touch, acts like a meddling mama where you're concerned? They know your worth, Cullen. And they choose to be around you.

"Who else are you carrying on your back? Your sister, your mam?" Grier's gaze was unrelenting. "This is what you have to learn: *people make their own choices.* It ain't only foolish o' you to take responsibility: it's bloody arrogant."

Pippa had called him arrogant too. And, Cull realized with a jolt of clarity, he had deserved it. She and Grier were right. It wasn't his responsibility to decide what was best for others. And it certainly wasn't his place to tell her where she belonged. Jesus wept. He had a strong, loyal, and beautiful woman who wanted to be part of his world and to stick by him, through thick and thin... and he'd shut her out, telling her all he'd wanted was a bit of fun?

"I'm an *idiot*," he said, stunned.

"'Appens to the best o' us, Cullen."

"I pushed away the woman I love." He dragged both hands through his hair, planting his elbows on his knees. "And I told her it was for her own good."

Grier winced. "Ach. I don't envy you the groveling that's in your future, lad."

Cull's gut clenched as he recalled the hurt in Pippa's eyes. How she'd compared him to her sod of a former husband...and she hadn't been wrong. Remorse percolated through Cull as he recognized that he *had* locked her up, even if the cage was a pedestal. By idealizing her, he hadn't allowed himself to see the dazzling complexity of who she was: a lady, yes, but also a bold and capable partner, a sensual wanton...and his true companion.

His princess, who belonged in his bed and by his side.

He shot to his feet. "I have to talk to her, beg her forgiveness—"

"Cullen! I know you're in there." A deep voice boomed

through the house. "Come out, you lily-livered bastard, and face me like a man."

Grier sprang to his feet. "Who in blazes is that?"

Already headed for the door, Cull turned and said with a grimace, "God willing, my future father-in-law."

After nightfall, the Angels and their team arrived at the General Cemetery for All Souls in Kensal Green. Their carriages dropped them outside the gates; they couldn't risk the sound of the conveyances alerting the guards to their presence. The public cemetery ran east to west and occupied over fifty acres. Pippa had visited during the day to pay respects to Longmere, but at night the place lost its tranquil, garden-like ambiance. Moonlight filtered through the drifting clouds, illuminating an eerie landscape of swaying trees, looming mausoleums, and jutting gravestones.

Earlier surveillance had identified two separate patrols of guards to dissuade any would-be body snatchers. One group started at the eastern side of the cemetery, the other at the western edge, and they met in the middle, where the Anglican chapel and catacombs were located. Julianna's plot was located closer to the east end, which meant a diversion was needed for the eastern patrol. Glory and Fiona had volunteered for the task.

That left the remaining group—Pippa, Charlie, Livy, Hadleigh, and Hadleigh's friend Mr. Chen—to dig up Julianna's grave. Even with many hands, the task would take time, especially since they needed to leave the plot looking undisturbed. Glory and Fiona's decoy would only buy them so much time; if the eastern patrol failed to show up at the Anglican chapel, their western counterparts would surely come looking for them.

Charlie gathered them into a circle.

"Is everyone clear on the plan?" she whispered.

Like Pippa, she'd tied a dark scarf over her hair and was dressed head to toe in black. All the ladies wore trousers, their outfits designed by Mrs. Q to meet the demands of the mission.

The Duke of Hadleigh held up the pair of shovels he was carrying. "Dig up the grave. Don't get caught. Am I missing anything?"

"Do not anger the spirits." This came from Mr. Chen, an austerely handsome fellow with thick black hair and a lean, wiry build. "It is best to disturb the dead as little as possible."

Glory shuddered; perched on her shoulder, her ferret mimicked her.

"Can we *please* not speak of ghosts before we enter a graveyard?" she requested.

Chen gave her an amused look.

Charlie said, "Glory and Fi, keep the guards occupied as long as you can. We'll meet back here in two hours. All right, everyone, let's go."

The men scaled over the high wrought-iron gate first, Chen doing so with a lightness of movement that made Pippa blink.

"How does he do that?" Glory said in hushed tones.

"Perhaps by not consuming two dozen of Gunter's cakes?" Pippa replied wryly.

The Angels made it over easily enough. Glory and Fi went east to deal with the guards, and Pippa and Charlie led the way toward Lady Hastings's grave. They didn't risk lighting their lamps, relying on the moonlight. As Pippa traversed the pebbled walk lined with stone mausoleums and sarcophagi, her senses were on high alert, her muscles tensing at the scurrying of animals through the underbrush.

"Julianna's site is in the next grove," Charlie whispered.

As they neared the thick cluster of trees, Pippa drew to a halt. Voices were coming from within the grove. Heart thudding, she saw that Charlie was already drawing out a pistol; she did likewise. She strained to hear what was being said.

She heard two voices, male and female. The conversation was muffled.

Suddenly, the woman's voice rang out. "You couldn't leave well enough alone. Do it, Clive."

A shot blasted through the night.

Pippa charged ahead, Charlie at her heels. They dashed along a leafy path, which widened into a circle of trees. Here, moonlight fell like a silver web over the gravestones. And caught in the gossamer strands of light was...Louis Wood? He lay on a pile of fresh earth, and he was gasping, clutching the dark bloom spreading over his chest.

Chen rushed over to examine the wound. "I can temporarily stanch the bleeding. But I need to get him someplace with the proper equipment to remove the bullet. Otherwise, he will not survive."

Pippa crouched on the man's other side. "Mr. Wood, who did this to you?"

"Stop her, can't let her get away with...Julianna..." Wood's gaze was glassy. "Has a brute with her..."

"Which way did they go?" Livy pointed to the three paths leading out from the grove.

Wood's face slackened; he'd lost consciousness.

"Chen and Hadleigh will have to carry Wood out of here," Charlie said. "The rest of us will each take a path. One of them should lead to Julianna."

"It isn't safe to split up," Hadleigh cut in. "That woman already shot a man."

"Now, darling—" Livy began.

"Don't darling me," Hadleigh said in stern tones. "I'm not letting my wife, the love of my life and mother of my child, go after a murderess *on her own*. And before you argue, it's not about your sex. Would you want *me* to take such a risk?"

Pippa had to admit he had a point.

Footsteps came from the entrance of the grove. Pippa spun around, aiming her pistol at the intruders who burst into the clearing.

"Cull?" she said in shock. "What are you doing here?"

Jesus wept, he'd missed Pippa. Yet now wasn't the time to get into all that he had to say to her. He'd heard a gunshot come from this grove, and Wood was on the ground, bleeding out.

Soon, Cull promised himself. *Soon and, God willing, for the rest of our lives.*

"I had larks on Wood," he said. "They followed him here and alerted me."

Pippa's gaze widened. "Why do you have that shiner?"

Back at Grier's, Hunt had greeted Cull with a fist to the face. Cull hadn't fought back. He'd taken his due for being a fool.

"Hunt paid me a visit," he told her.

"Papa *hit* you? Your poor face..." She reached toward his cheek, then snatched her hand away. Remembering his despicable treatment of her, no doubt.

"I deserved it," he said hoarsely. "For pushing you away when that is the last thing I want to do. I love you, Pippa. I want you by my side and for the rest of our lives. I was afraid that I couldn't protect you, that the darkness of my life would cause you harm. But whether you are willing to take me on isn't my decision to make, is it? It is yours. And if you'll still have me...if you still love me..."

His heart lodged in his throat. Because he couldn't bear it if she said no.

"Oh, Cull," she whispered. "You're such a dolt."

"I know. But I'm still your dolt...aren't I?"

A smile tucked into her cheeks, and when she nodded, his chest expanded with relief.

"Pardon the interruption." Lady Fayne's voice was dry. "But we do have a murderer to catch."

"The mudlarks have the cemetery surrounded." Cull kept his gaze on Pippa, riveted by the glowing love in her eyes. "Julianna Hastings won't get out."

"Then let's go find her." Pippa held out a hand.

He grabbed onto her and knew he would never let go again.

The group split off into teams to comb the grounds for Julianna and her accomplice. Pippa and Cull had started off westward when they heard a mudlark whistle go off up ahead. They sprinted toward the sound, which led them to a group of larks.

Sally was among them. "We saw them go in there." She pointed at the Anglican chapel, a building with a porticoed entrance flanked by colonnades. "It were a lady and a great 'ulking cove. Teddy wanted to follow, but I told 'im you said to stay put and sound the alarm," she said virtuously.

"Tattletale," Teddy muttered.

"Good work," Cull said. "Now go and inform the others where we are."

The larks scampered off, and Pippa and Cull ventured forward to the chapel. The light of their lamps slid across the Doric columns as they passed under the pediment. The doors were ajar. They slipped inside, pistols held at the ready as they went through the shadowed pews row by row.

No sign of Julianna or her brute. Pippa cocked her head at a thumping sound...footsteps?

"Do you hear that?" she whispered. "It's coming from beneath us."

"The catacombs." Cull raced ahead toward an open door, nearly hidden by a column. His light showed steep steps winding down into the dark vault.

"Watch your step," he whispered.

Heart hammering, she followed him into the gloom. A dank smell curled in her nostrils. The air grew humid, pressing upon her lungs as they descended into the catacombs. Passing through an arched doorway, they were greeted by a grid of narrow brick passageways lit by flickering wall sconces. They set aside their lamps to free their hands.

"Be ready." Cull cocked his pistol. "They could be anywhere."

Pippa kept close to the wall, her eyes sharp as she and Cull passed intersecting tunnels. Built into the walls themselves and guarded by iron grates were the loculi, niches which held stacked coffins. There must be hundreds of them in the crypt. Pippa tried not to think about what lay within, the remains trapped here in the suffocating darkness. She and Cull turned a corner and found themselves staring down another corridor lined with grated niches.

Movement flashed at the far end: a slender figure disappearing around the corner.

"There she is," Pippa breathed.

Cull took off down a parallel passageway. He was faster than Pippa, several paces ahead when a grate flung open into his path. He slammed into it, bouncing backward, his weapon skittering into the shadows. The brute who'd been hiding in the alcove attacked. He and Cull grappled, trading punches.

Pippa gripped her pistol, afraid to shoot for fear of hitting Cull. The bullet could ricochet off the walls and do unpredictable damage. Luckily, although the brute was large, Cull was stronger, smarter, outmaneuvering the other and gaining the advantage.

"I'm fine," Cull shouted. "Go after her."

Trusting that he had everything in hand, Pippa raced off down a tunnel parallel to the one Julianna had taken. She shifted her gaze between her path and Julianna's trajectory, tried to listen for the other's footsteps but could hear nothing beyond her own pounding heart. As she glanced ahead, panting, she saw the glint of a muzzle poking around the next corner. She reacted, throwing herself backward the instant before the shot rang out. The bullet whizzed by, stirring the air by her cheek.

A heartbeat later, she was back on her feet, sprinting forward.

She rounded the corner, aiming her pistol at the brunette, who was trying to reload.

"Drop it," Pippa said.

The woman slowly let go of her pistol. Her eyes suddenly filled with tears, her expression pleading...and that was when Pippa knew.

"You understand why I had to do it, don't you? You, of all people, understand," the woman said in a tremulous voice. "Life is unfair to women like us. Hastings looked down upon me, used me, treated me like dirt. I had to escape my husband—*I had no choice.*"

"As unfair as life may be, you had a choice," Pippa said levelly. "And you made it when you murdered Julianna Hastings."

"I don't know what you mean..."

The woman feigned confusion. Pippa had to admit that the resemblance between Julianna Hastings and her impersonator was uncanny.

"The jig is up, Mary," Pippa said. "I've had my suspicions that it was you, not Julianna, who was behind this plot. But I knew for sure when you tried to get rid of Louis Wood tonight. Julianna Hastings was a desperate woman, driven to desperate measures...

but she was no killer. If she was, she would have simply murdered her husband and been done with it."

And Pippa finally saw the depth of Mary Brown's talent: the other's expression morphed with terrifying ease. One instant, she was a wronged wife. The next, she was a calculating murderess, capable of anything.

"You're cleverer than I gave you credit for," Mary said. "Unlike that nitwit Lady Hastings."

Pippa held the gun steady. "Why did you kill her?"

"Because she used me." Mary's gaze was colder than the surrounding crypt. "She hired me to take her place, and at first, she was grateful and kind. Treating me like we were friends, taking me into her confidence. I got to know everything about her and convinced everyone I *was* her, even her arse of a husband. Bastard didn't even know who I was when he was rutting inside me."

Pippa pushed aside the twinge of empathy. "But Lady Hastings tired of the ruse."

"The bitch got greedy. Decided that stealing away to meet with her lover on occasion wasn't enough. She wanted her freedom. I told her there was an easy way to do it...but she was horrified. Refused to contemplate doing away with Hastings, even though the bastard had it coming.

"Instead, she came up with an asinine plan to fake her own death. She knew about her father's will, you see. Plotted to get Morton his share of the money so that he and she could run off together. She hired you to throw everyone off her scent. She knew you would point to Hastings as the guilty party and wanted the focus on him until she and Morton could get away, even though she knew the codicil would surface and her husband would eventually go free. What a bleeding coward she was," Mary said in disdain. "Playing all those ballroom games, yet afraid to dirty her lily-white hands getting rid of the real problem."

"So you took the situation into your own hands," Pippa said evenly.

"She left me no choice. When she made up her mind to fake her own death, she no longer had any use for me. Now *I* was a problem. When she set up that final meeting with me, I knew that she intended to end our arrangement. To cut off the payments which were my livelihood and which I had bloody earned!" Rage contorted Mary's features. "I'd played her simpering self for a year and lain beneath her pig of a husband. After what I'd sacrificed, I wasn't going to let her take it all away."

"You killed her. And hurt Ollie," Pippa bit out.

"Ollie? Oh, the urchin." Mary shrugged. "He should've minded his own business."

"He's an innocent child." Anger sizzled through Pippa. "Did you kill Hastings too?"

"He'd started figuring out Julianna's original plan, and I couldn't let him unravel all my hard work. I had my associate take care of him."

"And Wood?"

"That trained cur?" Mary snorted. "He would do anything for Julianna. He knew about me and supported her plan to fake her death—there was plenty in it for him—but when she died in truth, his sentimentality got the better of him. Instead of accepting his windfall, he tried to find out what happened to her. He came looking for me, and I arranged the meeting tonight. It was supposed to look like a butler's suicide over his beloved mistress's grave. After all, I couldn't have him ruining my ultimate goal."

"Morton," Pippa said with sudden understanding. "He thinks you are Julianna?"

Mary's smile was feline. "He's not very bright, but he is very much in love. He bought my cock-and-bull story that Julianna's body was a corpse I'd bought to be my double. After he gets his money, we're going to elope. A tragic accident on our honeymoon will leave me as the grieving Mrs. Howard Morton, and I'll get what I'm owed at last."

Mary moved in a flash, throwing her empty pistol at Pippa. Pippa dodged, and Mary sprang on her, knocking her to the ground. Pippa's pistol flew out of her grasp. The other pressed on her throat, cutting off her air. Pippa swung her left arm against the exposed side of Mary's neck and used her legs to kick Mary off. She scrambled to her feet, facing Mary, who now held a gleaming blade.

Before Pippa could reach for her own knife, Mary came at her. Pippa dodged the other's blade once, twice, staying on the defensive. The woman was strong, quick, and desperate...a lethal combination.

Patience is your friend. Let your foe win the battle while you win the war.

Pippa danced around, tiring her enemy out. Then she deliberately left her defenses open. Triumph glittered in Mary's eyes as she came in and struck the blade at Pippa's heart.

"No!" Cull's roar shook the walls.

Glimpsing Mary's shocked expression when the knife failed to penetrate, Pippa went on the offensive. She grabbed Mary's weapon arm, twisting it; with a pained scream, Mary lost hold of the blade, which clattered onto the stones. Pippa issued a series of strikes that drove the other into the side of the tunnel. She finished with a right kick that made Mary double over, then brought her right arm in a backhanded strike that snapped Mary's head against the brick.

With a moan, Mary slumped down the wall and didn't move.

In the next heartbeat, Cull was there, running shaking hands over Pippa.

"I saw her stab you," he said roughly. "You're...you're not hurt?"

Pippa widened the tear that Mary's blade had made. The knife had pierced through her waistcoat and shirt all the way to her corset, exposing the gleaming chainmail.

God bless Mrs. Q.

"That is some corset." Cull huffed out a laugh. "I should have known you would be prepared."

Pippa smiled demurely. "An Angel always is."

※ 40 ※

S lowly awakening, Pippa smiled before she even opened her eyes. She snuggled closer to Cull, rubbing her cheek against his bare chest, and his arms tightened around her. Surrounded by his warmth and scent, she would have been content to lay there forever.

"I've never known you to be a sleepyhead." His amused voice rumbled beneath her ear.

"That is because we haven't had a moment of peace since we met." Yawning, she tipped her head back to see his smiling face. "What time is it?"

"Past noon. But we can stay in bed if you like. After last night, we deserve a day off," he said with feeling.

They'd been up past dawn, wrapping up the case. Charlie had delivered Mary and her accomplice to her contact within the police. Hadleigh had dealt with the cemetery guards, greasing their palms to ensure their discretion. Afterward, the entire group had debriefed at Charlie's. Pippa had filled everyone in on Mary's confession.

Livy had furrowed her brow. "So Wood and Morton are innocent?"

"Of actual crimes, it appears so," Pippa had responded. "Both did, however, withhold information. Morton played along with Julianna's fake death, thinking that she was alive and they would eventually elope. And Wood knew she was dead, but he didn't tell anyone who he suspected the killer of being. Likely out of loyalty since doing so would also expose Julianna's scandalous scheme and ruin her reputation forever."

"If only Julianna had trusted us, instead of using us as pawns, perhaps we could have helped her," Fiona had mused.

"What could we have done?" Charlie's voice had been hard and brittle. "When it comes to a woman's right over her future, society stacks the deck against us. Julianna saw only one way out. While I do not condone her choices, I am also not surprised that her situation ended badly."

Cull had needed to settle the mudlarks back at the Nest, and Pippa had gone with him. She'd helped tuck in the youngest ones, who'd protested they couldn't sleep after the night's excitement, then dozed off as soon as their heads met their pillows. Then she and Cull had gone to his bedchamber, a big comfy space that had instantly felt like home. After a quick bath, they, too, had hit the mattress...which brought them to now.

"I don't want to leave this bed all day," she declared.

"Sweeter words I've yet to hear." Cull shifted onto his side, facing her. Tucking a tress behind her ear, he said, "There are things I need to tell you, Pippa. To explain why I acted the way I did."

"I'm listening," she said intently.

When he told her what had happened to Fanny, she bolted upright. "Heavens, why didn't you tell me sooner? Is there anything I can do—"

"Fanny's fine." Sitting up against the headboard, Cull curled a finger under her chin, his eyes tender. "We'll visit her later today, if you wish."

Pippa nodded. "Yes, please."

"I'm telling you about Fanny, not as an excuse but to explain why I acted the way I did. Seeing Fanny get hurt because of me...I was terrified."

"Squibb is to blame, not you," Pippa said hotly. "You were trying to do the right thing."

"That is what Grier said. And he set me straight on something else, too." Cull took her hand, lacing his fingers with hers as he gazed into her eyes. "I'm yours, Pippa. Scars and all. I've already made my choice, and that is to love you. To do everything in my power to make you happy and that includes supporting your work with the Angels, your painting, and whatever else you desire. That is what I have to offer." He dragged in a breath. "In return, if you're willing to take me on, mudlarks, mayhem, and all, then that is *your* choice to make. And I hope to Christ that you'll say yes."

Pippa's eyes grew misty. "Yes, Cull. A thousand times *yes*."

He kissed her with a tender ardor that set her heart aflame. Other parts of her, too. When he hauled her atop him, she felt the strength of his arousal. She rubbed sinuously against him, painting his thick length with her dew, grinding her pearl against his steely flesh. Growling with approval, he gripped her bottom and urged her on. They teased one another with no hurry or rush, no end in mind save the pleasure of being together.

Gazing down into her lover's smoldering eyes, she said, "Do you know what the woman in *Portrait of a Lady Dreaming* desires more than anything?"

"If you say what we're doing now, I'll get hard every time I look at the blasted thing."

"That's part of it," she said with a grin. "But what she wants— what she's yearned for her whole life—is a love that makes her world bigger instead of smaller. That tears down any walls that try to confine her and makes her feel safe to fly. Because no matter what, she knows that love will always catch her."

He cupped her cheek, his touch reverent, his gaze reflecting the wonder she felt.

"You are meant to soar," he said huskily.

"We both are, and we do it better together. You told me once that what you offered your birds was a sanctuary and not a prison," she said tremulously. "And that is what our love is."

"Now and forever," he said.

They sealed their pledge, first with the meeting of their lips, then with their bodies. He surged inside her, and she took him deep, her back bowing with bliss. He guided her hips as she found her cadence, as she filled herself with his love and gave him all of herself in return.

The ride soon grew frantic. When he slid his hands up her spine, urging her to lean forward as he thrust up, she gasped his name. Grunting, he continued shafting her, stroking her pearl with each plunge of his cock. The sparks inside her gathered and exploded into a flame that incinerated her earthly tethers. She soared into rapture, and he followed with a harsh groan, pulling out and drenching her bottom with his hot fulfillment.

They lay together, floating and boneless. Her heart pounded in unison with his, and there was no need for words. Only for kisses and soft touches, until it was time to love again.

Two months later

As Cull entered the Nest, he removed his mask and took in the changes with a feeling of awe. The sparkling windows and tidy sitting areas. The larks dutifully setting the clean tables with crockery. The delicious smells wafting from the platters waiting on the newly polished sideboards. Some days it felt like he had wandered into some fantasy, but this was his reality now.

And he owed it all to Pippa. His beloved...and his betrothed.

He spotted Pippa chatting with Fanny and Mrs. Needles by the fire. Fanny, now fully recovered, was holding Pippa's left hand, exclaiming over the engagement ring Cull had recently given her.

At first, Pippa had wanted to wait out the rest of her mourning period before getting engaged. Wanting to protect her reputation, Cull had agreed.

A few days ago, however, Pippa had entertained her mama-in-law. Cull knew that she dreaded the visits but felt obligated to look after the old harridan. One look at Pippa's tense features afterward had told Cull that things hadn't gone well. He'd pulled her into his arms.

"I told the dowager that I had met someone...and she called me a wicked slut." Pippa's shaky voice had made Cull want to punch something. "She said that she would never forgive me. That she would not tolerate being in my ungrateful presence unless I recanted my sins."

"I'm sorry, love," Cull had murmured.

"I'm not." To his surprise, the shakiness in Pippa's voice turned out to be laughter. She tilted her head back, her eyes glowing with mirth. "Now I never have to see the termagant again."

As a parting gift, she had given the dowager *Portrait of a Lady Dreaming*.

"Let her hold onto her fantasy," Pippa had declared. "I have a life to get on with."

In the end, Cull had the dowager to thank for moving his nuptial plans along. Pippa had realized that, no matter how long she waited, Society was going to judge her marriage to Cull as scandalous. And she cared not a whit.

Hearing that, Cull had wasted no time in getting down on a bended knee and offering her the ring that he'd carried around in his pocket for weeks. He had already asked for her father's permission. These days, Cull got on well with Hunt, the two spending long hours discussing the intricacies of the 'Change. As Pippa had predicted, her father was more than willing to impart his business knowledge to the mudlarks.

"Cull, you're back early," Pippa exclaimed. "We weren't expecting you for luncheon."

She was taking a brief hiatus from the Angels to prepare for their wedding. She spent a lot of time at the Nest, and Cull adored having her here. As did the larks. Ollie, who'd fully regained his memory to everyone's relief, followed her around like a puppy.

"I wanted to see what my favorite ladies were up to." He bowed to the women before settling next to Pippa, slinging an arm around her shoulders. "Also, I heard *coq au vin* was on the menu."

In another miraculous feat, Pippa had convinced Mrs. Halberd to retire on a handsome pension. She'd hired a new cook whose talents rivaled that of the chef at the Griers' club.

"Here I was thinking it was my charms that lured you from work," Pippa said with a flirty grin. "Turns out, it was just your stomach."

Cull murmured in her ear, "I thought I showed you my appetite for your charms this morning."

Pippa turned bright pink. And well she should. He'd licked her awake and eaten his favorite meal for breakfast.

"Timothy, stop harassing the poor girl," Fanny chided. "You don't want her to change her mind before the wedding."

"You're making dear Pippa blush," Mrs. Needles agreed.

Cull sighed as Pippa smothered a laugh. She and her soon-to-be "mamas-in-law" got on like a house on fire, and she found it endlessly entertaining when the matrons ganged up on him. He picked up her hand, enjoying the sparkle of his claim. He'd commissioned the ring from Rundell, Bridge, & Co., selecting a three-carat yellow diamond for the center stone and smaller white diamonds to surround it.

The sun and the stars: the light that Pippa brought into his life.

"Pippa is not going to change her mind," he said confidently.

She beamed at him. "I cannot wait to be Mrs. Cullen."

No woman in her right mind would relinquish a countess's title to be his wife...except the perfect woman for him. Moreover, Pippa had shown him that he was perfect for her, too. She made him realize that he had more to offer than his protection and care (although both were hers until his last breath). With her, he felt worthy of love...just by being himself.

Pippa had broken his curse of solitude. He could not wait to officially claim her as his extraordinary Princess of Larks. As he leaned in to kiss her, a ruckus interrupted them.

"Cull," Fair Molly yelled from the entrance. "There's someone 'ere to see you!"

Frowning, Cull rose. He wasn't expecting visitors.

"Excuse me," he said to Pippa and the others. "I'll be right back."

As he headed to the door, he checked for his knife. The defeat of Squibb had dissuaded others from challenging the mudlarks, but better safe than sorry. Fair Molly opened the door...and Cull froze at the sight of the brunette standing on the front step.

She was still too thin, her nose dusted with freckles. She wore a servant's simple frock. Beneath the brim of her bonnet, her brown eyes were wide and unsure in her lovely face.

"Maisie?" he said hoarsely.

"Hello, Tim," his sister said.

She hadn't responded to his letters. He thought he might never hear from her, despite Pippa's encouragement to keep trying. Now that his sister was here, he didn't know what to say. How to express all that flooded his heart.

So he opened his arms.

With a small sob, Maisie ran into them.

"Are we there yet?" Pippa asked.

She was blindfolded and wearing a flannel wrapper, her husband of ten hours leading her carefully up the stairs to the glasshouse for her "surprise." As an Angel, she knew exactly how many steps were left—sixteen—but she liked playing along. When Cull had knocked on their bedchamber door, her lady's maid had been putting the final touches on her wedding night ensemble. She had her own surprise for Cull.

"Almost there, impatient minx."

Cull's deep amused tones sent a tingle up Pippa's spine. Their wedding had been a jubilant affair. The ceremony had taken place in the flower-festooned great room of the Nest, attended by their family and friends. The Angels had acted as Pippa's bridesmaids; Grier, Long Mikey, and Ollie had stood with Cull. Maisie's adorable young son had been the ringbearer.

Walking toward Cull in her pale-blue wedding dress, the frothy skirts trimmed with lace, Pippa had felt like a princess going to her prince. Cull had certainly looked the part in his immaculate smoke-grey tailcoat and trousers, a diamond pin glittering in his cravat. The joy on his face had made the rest of the world vanish. They had exchanged their vows gazing into each other's eyes. Their kiss had made her every bit as light-headed and giddy as their very first in the bell tower.

After a lavish wedding luncheon, they had spent the rest of the day celebrating. Pippa's heart had brimmed over to see their family and friends mingling with natural ease. Papa had been deep in conversation with several adult larks who'd tripled their earnings last month using his investment strategies. Her brothers had badgered Cull into showing them the Nest's sparring room.

Mama, Fanny, and Mrs. Needles had pulled Maisie into their protective circle. Pippa adored Maisie and knew how much it meant to Cull to have his sister and nephew back in his life. She had also introduced Maisie to the Angels, noticing Maisie's rapt conversation with Charlie.

The party had ended an hour ago. Feeling the waft of lush, humid air as Cull opened the door at the top of the steps, Pippa shivered with anticipation. The private celebration was about to begin.

"Watch your step, love," Cull said.

He led her by the hand into the quiet space. Of late, there had been a lull in the arrival of injured birds...which was just as well since she and Cull were leaving for their wedding trip tomorrow. They planned to spend a cozy fortnight at his property in Hertfordshire.

"Ready for your surprise?"

Cull stood behind her, his breath tickling her ear and raising goose-pimples over her skin.

"Yes," she managed.

He removed the blindfold.

She blinked. "Is that...a swing?"

Her blood rushed as she recalled the one at The Enchanted Rose. This one was similar, a small hammock composed of black leather straps. It was attached by ropes to four wooden posts that had served as bird perches.

"I thought you might enjoy a ride," Cull murmured.

He reached in front of her and gave the swing a push. The carnal possibilities of that back-and-forth movement made her intimate muscles clench.

She spun to face him, breathing, "I would adore a ride."

He was a vision of sensuality with his lazy smile, his bulging form encased in a sleek black dressing gown. "There is one condition, sunshine."

She tilted her head. "What is it?"

"You take this ride the way I posed for your portrait."

It had taken a bit of coaxing, but she had convinced Cull to pose nude for her. She'd painted him scars and all, every inch of him beautiful and princely. When he viewed the finished version of *Portrait of a Lady's Dream*, his chest had puffed out at the way she'd depicted his virile proportions. She had only captured the truth. The sittings had been charged with erotic tension; more than once, she'd ended up beneath Cull, moaning his name.

With those steamy memories heating her brain, she reached for the belt of her wrapper. Shedding it, she heard Cull's fervent oath and smiled.

"Surprise," she said saucily.

She wore a scandalous negligee of yellow silk so fine it was nearly transparent. The garment clung to her figure, plunging in a deep vee between her breasts and ending just above her knee.

"That is quite a nightgown, Mrs. Cullen," Cull said in a guttural tone. "Give us a turn."

Knowing how he liked to watch, she made a show of slowly pivoting and presenting him with her back.

"You're like a bleeding present," he rasped.

As the negligee was held together by the three satin bows along her spine, he wasn't wrong.

She gave him a coy look over her shoulder. "Would you care to unwrap me, Mr. Cullen?"

He tugged on the bows one by one, and the silk slid off her

shoulders, pooling at her feet. She sighed as he came up behind her, grazing his callused palms over the aching tips of her breasts, her ribs, and her trembling belly. When he cupped her between her legs, she whimpered.

"My present is nice and wet for me." He teased her pearl with his fingertip, drawing forth more dew. "I think you're ready for that ride now."

Her heart thumping, she allowed him to help her into the swing. She gasped as she wobbled a little, almost tipping over.

"Hold onto the ropes for balance," he said.

As she lay back against the web of leather, her hands wrapped around the cords, she experienced a disorienting weightlessness. She looked up through the ceiling and felt like she was floating in the starlit sky. Cull knelt beside her, taking her mouth in a long, dreamy kiss that enhanced the heavenly feeling.

Then he grew wicked, and she discovered another aspect of the swing: it made her utterly helpless to his desires. Suspended as she was, holding the ropes for balance, she could only lay back and receive his attentions. And she loved it. She moaned as he devoured her breasts, his mouth hot and demanding. Pleasure spread from her nipples to her core. She felt his forceful sucking in her pussy, which throbbed unbearably.

Her hands tightened on the ropes. "Please, Cull. I need..."

He lifted his head, his gaze smoldering. "You want to come, sweetheart?"

"Yes."

"On my tongue or on my cock?"

Faced with an impossible decision, she furrowed her brow.

He laughed. "Never mind, my greedy wife. You can have it all."

As always, he was good to his word. His oral loving brought her to an instant climax, but he didn't stop there. Grabbing hold of the leather straps, he moved the swing back and forth, working her sex on his tongue. She moaned as he penetrated her, licking deep inside as he rubbed her pulsing love-knot. Bliss gushed from her, earning his growl of approval.

Rising, Cull stripped off his robe.

Sated as she was, her pulse leapt at his hard-carved virility. The brawny, hair-dusted muscles and flexing grooves. He was her prince, her husband...all hers.

Fisting his rampant cock, he brought it to her lips. "Suck me, sunshine. Make me wet for your tight little quim."

His husky command chased a thrill through her. She parted her lips, welcoming his thick incursion. She loved taking him this way, seeing his eyes flare with lust as he fed her his cock. With her fingers clenching the ropes, she could only take what he gave her. She moaned around his girth as he sank his fingers into her hair, holding her steady for his plunges.

Wanting more, she breathed through her nose and loosened her jaw as much as she could. He panted harshly as he went deeper and deeper. His delicious essence coated her tongue, whetting her feverish appetite. When she licked his blunt tip to search out more, his hips jerked, his member butting against a silken limit. Her throat muscles clenched in reflex.

"*Christ.*" He pulled out, his eyes glazed and chest heaving. "Sorry, sunshine."

In answer, she licked her lips and said sultrily, "I want you, Cull."

He wasted no time. Positioning himself between her thighs, he entered her in a commanding thrust. She cried out as his huge shaft vanquished the emptiness and opened her to sensation. His determined drives set off tremors of bliss...and that was before he started using the swing. Grabbing the leather straps, he yanked her into him as he slammed his hips forward. The momentum jolted a moan from her.

"So damned perfect, Pippa. Every time," he growled over the rhythmic slapping of their flesh. "I will never get enough of you.

You are worth every second that I waited for you—longed for you, heart, body, and soul."

"Oh, Cull," she panted. "My love."

"I'm going to spend so hard inside you, sunshine. Do you want that? Want to feel my seed deep in your cunny for the first time?"

She yearned for it. "Yes, *yes*."

His gaze burning into hers, he fingered her pearl as he plowed her. The added stimulation threw her over the edge, and she soared into bliss, staring into her husband's eyes. He clenched his jaw, the tension spreading to his neck and shoulders, the tendons there standing out as he threw his head back and roared. Her breath caught at his magnificence as he exploded, flooding her again and again with his copious heat.

Afterward, they lay on the hammock together. There was just enough room with her cuddled atop him. They swung gently in the starlit darkness, passion cooling on their skin.

"Are you sure the swing can hold both of us?" Pippa murmured drowsily.

"No. But if worse comes to worst, we only have a few feet to fall." Cull's relaxed voice rumbled beneath her ear. "My arse can handle it."

"I don't want anything happening to your arse."

"Taken a fancy to it, have you?"

"I've taken a fancy to *you*." Raising her head, she looked into his soulful, smiling eyes. "I love you, Timothy Cullen. You were worth the wait and more."

AUTHOR'S NOTE

For those of you who have been following the books, I've been waiting for Timothy Cullen to tell me his story, and the inspiration for *Pippa and the Prince of Secrets* came in an unexpected way. In the midst of the pandemic, when we were in a lockdown in my area and it was literally the darkest time of the year, something magical happened. Thousands—maybe millions—of starlings gathered at a town close to mine, and at dusk they flocked together in murmurations, performing aerial displays that were so awe-inspiring that they seemed not of this world. Or maybe they were simply the best of this world: beauty, togetherness, and wonder.

The starlings reminded me of the sacred in the everyday. Of how lucky I was to be alive in that moment, even when things were terrifying and dark. And so I shared that moment with Pippa and Cull, two wounded souls who deserved to find their joy with each other.

Speaking of joy, in the story Pippa quotes the first lines from Book I of John Keats's, "Endymion," a narrative poem published in 1818. While this poem was "famously savaged by critics"[1] at the time of its publication, it nonetheless displays Keats's technical genius and is a powerful meditation on the transcendent impact of beauty and how our encounters with it, no matter how fleeting, can change us for the better. For me personally, there is nothing more beautiful than love...which made writing Pippa and Cull's story a gift. I hope you enjoyed it.

NOTES

AUTHOR'S NOTE

1. Voigt, B. "John Keats 101." Poetry Foundation, 14 June, 2018. https://www.poetryfoundation.org/articles/147110/john-keats-101.

ACKNOWLEDGMENTS

First and foremost, thank you to my readers. You make what I do possible, and I could not be more grateful. Special thanks to the amazing bookstragrammers and advance readers who have helped to spread the word about my books: I am humbled and touched by your incredible support.

Thank you to my editing team: Ronnie Nelson, Faith Williams, Alyssa Nazzaro, and Judy Rosen. You make my books shine.

To my writer besties Barbara and Anne: you inspire and sustain me and make the business of writing fun. I couldn't have finished this book without our weekly chats.

And to my family, who teaches me about love every day.

ABOUT THE AUTHOR

USA Today & International Bestselling Author Grace Callaway writes hot and heart-melting historical romance filled with mystery and adventure. Her debut novel was a Romance Writers of America Golden Heart® Finalist and a #1 National Regency Bestseller, and her subsequent novels have topped national and international bestselling lists. She has won the Daphne du Maurier Award for Excellence in Mystery and Suspense, the Maggie Award for Excellence, the Golden Leaf, and the Passionate Plume Award, and her books have been shortlisted for numerous other honors. She holds a doctorate in clinical psychology from the University of Michigan and lives with her family in a valley by the ocean. When she's not writing, she enjoys dancing, dining in hole-in-the-wall restaurants, and going on adapted adventures with her special son.

Keep up with Grace's latest news!

Newsletter: gracecallaway.com/newsletter

facebook.com/GraceCallawayBooks

bookbub.com/authors/grace-callaway

instagram.com/gracecallawaybooks

amazon.com/author/gracecallaway

Made in the USA
Middletown, DE
23 January 2022